KISSING THE HIGHLANDER

MacKerrick gave a mighty tug on the cloak and Evelyn was jerked against his chest. In a blink, he had dropped his mouth to hers in a hard kiss, wrapping one long arm around her shoulders and pulling her to him.

Evelyn was so shocked that she froze, her very toes tingling from the sensation of MacKerrick's warm, dry lips against hers. The scruff on his upper lip chafed at hers with a delicious prickle. He eased his head back and softened his mouth, kissing first her upper lip and then her lower, then sliding his tongue along the seam. He kissed her again gently, wetly, and Evelyn felt her knees go watery, her eyes close, her fingers uncurl.

MacKerrick's solid chest twisted for an instant, and then his other arm was around Evelyn, pulling her even closer. His skin smelled of fresh winter air and his own masculinity and Evelyn let her hands creep up over his chest, let her mouth soften and her head tilt. It was achingly brilliant, his kissing, his strength all around her, and she felt protected from the harsh season, from the grays, from her haunting past . . .

Books by Heather Grothaus

THE WARRIOR

THE CHAMPION

THE HIGHLANDER

Published by Kensington Publishing Corporation

The
HIGHLANDER

Heather Grothaus

ZEBRA BOOKS
Kensington Publishing Corp.
www.kensingtonbooks.com

ZEBRA BOOKS are published by

Kensington Publishing Corp.
850 Third Avenue
New York, NY 10022

All Kensington titles, imprints, and distributed lines are available at special quantity discounts for bulk purchases for sales promotion, premiums, fund-raising, educational, or institutional use.

Special book excerpts or customized printings can also be created to fit specific needs. For details, write or phone the office of the Kensington Special Sales Manager: Attn. Special Sales Department. Kensington Publishing Corp., 850 Third Avenue, New York, NY 10022. Phone: 1-800-221-2647.

Zebra and the Z logo Reg. U.S. Pat. & TM Off.

ISBN-13: 978-1-4201-0242-0
ISBN-10: 1-4201-0242-7

First Printing: September 2008
10 9 8 7 6 5 4 3 2 1

Printed in the United States of America

Prologue

*November 1077, the Scottish Highlands,
near Loch Lomond*

"I'm dying, Eve."

The words washed over Evelyn colder than the icy sleet pelting her back through her cloak, causing her to stumble over a tree root in the night-soaked forest. She yanked on the bridle in her hand, halting the mare that carried Minerva, and tried to blink away the frigid rain running into her eyes. Thunder, low and threatening and foreign to this cold November storm, drowned out the old healer's rasping breaths.

Evelyn swallowed, her own throat thick and raw in the brutal wind. "Now?" she croaked. At Minerva's nod, barely a twitch of rough, black wool, Evelyn released the exhausted mare and reached patting, grasping hands up the old woman's bony thigh. "Give me your hand. I'll—"

But to Evelyn's horror, the frail woman teetered to the far side of her mount and slipped from the horse's back, landing in the wet darkness without a cry, but with a sound that mimicked dropping a bundle of dry sticks. As Minerva hit the ground, a delicate thread of lightning struck deeper in the forest and the mount reared in fright, bolting away before Evelyn could regain hold of the beast. In a blink, the mare—and the women's few remaining supplies—was absorbed into the dense wood.

Evelyn stood in the sleet, as rooted to the ground as any of the thousands of trees crowding around her, stealing her breath with their evil, eager closeness. The stinging rain seemed to sizzle on her fevered cheeks and brow, and her chest tightened even further, painful wheezes her only sustenance as she stared down at the still jumble of ragged clothing that was Minerva.

So this is how it is to end, she thought apathetically, and for a brief moment, she let all the fragments of her life swirl around her like dead leaves in the stormy gale, nicking her cold, thin skin with painful memories. The horror of her own birth; her father's vicious murder; the hellish priory she had escaped. Only weeks ago, Evelyn had felt there was nothing and no one left for her in England, and so had impulsively accepted the invitation to accompany this dying witch on the month-long journey to the land of the old woman's birth—the wild, inhospitable terrain of the Scottish Highlands.

Evelyn had thought to make a fresh beginning. A new life.

Instead, it looked as if her life would end, lost in the malicious depths of this Caledonian forest, her body too ill and weak to carry on alone now that the ancient healer was dead. No mount. No food. Not even a flint and blade.

Mayhap the monks were right, her fevered brain

reasoned. *I am evil, unnatural. This is God's punishment for my wickedness.*

So be it, then, she rallied. *I am weary—let Him judge me.*

Evelyn sank to her knees on the wet, rocky ground. What little faith she still retained would not allow her to seek death outright, but she would no longer try to evade it. Let Him take her in His time. She would but wait.

Then the bundle of dry sticks that was the old healer rattled and stirred and rose up in a lumpy mound.

Evelyn could only blink as the ancient one crept across the frozen forest floor, a strange, breathy moaning coming from her with each spindly limb she dragged forward.

"*Haah. Haah*," Minerva wheezed, inching relentlessly onward.

Evelyn felt tired, helpless tears well in her eyes at the pathetic sight, but she had no strength left, no will.

Until she heard Minerva's next rasping whisper.

"*Haah. Ronan.* I'm coming, Ronan. At last, at last . . ."

Evelyn's eyes narrowed. Was it a man's name Minerva had spoken? Mayhap they were nearer the old witch's clan than Evelyn knew.

Mayhap there was hope for them yet.

Evelyn scraped together the last crumbs of energy she possessed—she'd not eaten in four days—and drew herself forward onto numb hands to crawl after the old woman.

"Minerva," Evelyn called, the voice coming from her blistered throat as little more than a creak. "Wait."

"*Ronan*," was Minerva's only answer as she pulled

herself up a low drift of jagged rocks piled at the base of a tree so wide and tall that Evelyn could not glimpse its ends in the winter night's gale.

Evelyn followed Minerva up the rocks, then crouched over the woman now propped against the massive oak. Evelyn snaked an arm behind Minerva's thin shoulders and drew her close. Overhead, the invisible branches of the tree clicked and scraped and crashed together in maniacal glee, wicked applause for the women's arrival. Evelyn began to shake.

"Ronan," Minerva sighed again.

"Minerva," Evelyn croaked, "who is Ronan? Where is he? Are we at last on Buchanan lands?"

The old woman's head lolled back on Evelyn's shoulder, and she rolled her watery, black eyes over Evelyn's face. "Buchanan lands? Nay, lass—we left Buchanan lands days ago. Days and days and days . . ."

Evelyn's heart froze in her chest. "What?"

The old woman gave a skeletal grin. "We're on MacKerrick lands. *Ronan's lands.* Where my journey ends"—she drew a shallow, hitching breath and Evelyn felt the reverberations of it like a chilling sizzle in her spine—"and yours truly begins."

It was then that Evelyn noticed that the sleet had stopped, the wind quieted. Impossibly fat snowdrops, the size of the tip of Evelyn's thumb, now floated down, luminescent in the blankets of glowing lightning that rolled within low clouds. The forest seemed to hold its breath.

"Minerva," Evelyn pressed, desperate to make the old witch understand. "The mare has fled, and our last provisions with her. In which direction do I seek this Ronan to aid us? No more riddles— I beg you."

The old woman's eyes closed, her mouth gaped open, and her frail frame quivered.

Minerva was laughing.

Then the black eyes opened and a gentler smile further creased the lined face as lightning flashed again. "He's already here, lass." She let a knobby arm fall to the rocks beneath her and she patted them fondly, the sound like wet parchments sliding together. "I've returned to him at last."

Evelyn let her fledgling hope melt away like the snowflakes on her flaming cheeks. The old healer was obviously delusional in these last, horrible moments of her life. Evelyn could harbor no ill will toward Minerva, even though the woman had led the pair of them blindly past the certain aid of the Buchanan clan to die in this cold, vast wood.

Because there was naught else to do, Evelyn laid her cheek atop Minerva's rough hood with a sigh and wondered if she herself would go to Heaven when it was all over with, and if she would at last meet her mother there. If she did, Evelyn knew the first thing she would ask Fiona is: Was I worth it? Was I worth your own life?

It seemed such a waste.

"Ye'll nae die," Minerva whispered, startling Evelyn from her morbid fantasy. The old witch raised her trembling hand from the rocks and swiped her thumb across Evelyn's lower lip. "Nae for many a year."

For an instant, Evelyn thought she felt the stones beneath her seat shudder. She realized she must have been biting her lip, for when she swiped her parched tongue across it, she tasted rich, warm blood.

Evelyn drew a searing breath, choosing to ignore

the old woman's cryptic prediction. "Shall I say a prayer for you?"

Minerva gave a silent chuckle. "Nae, lass—none of yer fancy prayers." Her eyes locked onto Evelyn's gaze, and when she spoke again, the old woman's voice held a pleading note Evelyn had never heard in all the weeks she'd known Minerva.

"But we all should leave this world with love, do ye nae think?"

Evelyn swallowed past the slicing blades in her throat, the taste of blood still sweet in her mouth. "I do." She leaned down and pressed her tingling lips to each of the old woman's cool cheeks, in turn. "Go in peace, Minerva Buchanan," Evelyn whispered. "You were indeed loved by many. Including me."

Evelyn drew away and looked down into the ancient healer's face, glowing pale in the dark, wet night, like a withered moon. Her black eyes were faraway and happy, her thin lips curved into a satisfied smile.

But the old woman made no reply.

Minerva Buchanan was, at last, dead.

Her own startled cry woke Evelyn from her slumber and she squinted, heart pounding, against the watery, gray sunlight filtering through the frigid fog of the wood.

Her throat felt as if it had been turned inside out and left out to dry, but the painful tightness in her chest had lessened by half. Her fever must have broken as well, for she felt frozen to her very bones.

Evelyn looked down at the dead healer, still cradled in her arms. Minerva's face was covered by a crystalline layer of blue frost, her eyes open and staring at

Evelyn, but now silvered and full of nothing. A gnarled hand still clutched the front of Evelyn's cloak and she worked quickly to pull the garment from the rigid grasp, a sudden superstitious desire to be unlocked from the corpse causing her to pant and whine. Once the talons of death were empty, held frozen in the air, Evelyn saw the thin gash in the pad of the old woman's thumb.

Evelyn scrambled from the pile of rocks with a whimper and tumbled to the frozen forest floor, her hand going instinctively to her lips. She scrubbed at her mouth with her fingertips—no tenderness—then drew her hand away to look down at it.

No blood, either.

Evelyn stared warily at the old witch for what seemed like hours, as if expecting Minerva to rouse from her icy sleep and descend the rock drift. When the corpse remained quiet, Evelyn rose gingerly to her knees and clasped her hands before her breasts. Closing her gummy-feeling eyes, she raised her face to the low sky.

But no prayer came. Try as she might, Evelyn could not beg the most simple, memorized verse from her mind. After months of prayerful life at the priory, her faith felt used up, tired, and impotent.

She'd once sought haven in religion but had encountered only death and debauchery, greed and hypocrisy. God had not heard her confused pleas then, and now she had forgotten how or why to ask for mercy. It mattered not. From the moment Evelyn had decided never to return to the priory, she felt she had damned herself. God would have no mercy for a strange young woman, once of noble station, who had deserted her calling out of fear and cynicism. A woman who would rather spend her time with animals than people, who understood them better than anyone had ever understood Evelyn. Her gift with beasts was an evil penchant, she'd been told many times by the monks. Sinful. Blasphemous. And evil, sinful blasphemies were aught in which the brethren were well practiced.

Her dark thoughts were interrupted by the screams of a horse, and Evelyn's eyes snapped open. Had she, in her desperation, imagined the cry? Or had God not completely forsaken her, after all? As if in answer, the animal shrieked again, and Evelyn thought the horse sounded near.

Her heart pounded sharply—a hammer on cold stone. "Amen," she breathed, although no true prayer had left her lips, and then scrambled to her feet.

She stumbled around the wide skirt of rocks that was Minerva's pyre and farther into the wood, swerving drunkenly through the trees, ears straining for the horse's whinny. It must be Minerva's mare. *It must be.*

"Where are you, lovely?" Evelyn whispered. "I need that saddle bag." Her life depended on it. Although it contained no food, the soft leather satchel tied to the mare's saddle held two flint stones and Evelyn's own dagger—items crucial to her survival. The other prizes in the bag were but outrageous luxuries at this point.

She paused, one chapped palm braced against the scarred skin of a straggling beech, and listened.

There! To her right, a rustling sounded, and a cracking like the snap of a fallen branch. Evelyn pushed away from the tree and tried to walk calmly in the direction of the sounds, despite the hysterical voice in her head screaming at her to run, run as fast as her watery legs would carry her. 'Twould do no good to spook the beast and send her deeper into the wood.

It began to snow again. Small, delicate flakes floating like goose down turned the world of the forest into contrasts of black and white, light and shadow, dusk and dawn at once.

From within a copse of pine just ahead, a plume of dry snow fanned out, once, twice. She heard a low snuffling, a snort, a ragged breath.

Evelyn stopped again and clicked her tongue. The snuffling ceased and all was quiet, save for the timpani of Evelyn's own heart.

"Here, girl," she called to the horse. She moved forward a step, whistled low. "'Tis all right—I'm here now." She crept around the edge of pine, stiff, brushy needles snagging her cloak and then springing free, sending fresh, powdery white down upon her. The green scent was so thick here, Evelyn's empty stomach churned.

A flash of black through the boughs caught her eye and then danced away behind the needles. She penetrated the heart of the copse.

The blood would have been enough to stop Evelyn in her tracks. Red, steaming snow, melted into black mud. Fresh crimson starbursts exploded and splattered away from the crater where a short but deadly battle had been waged.

Evelyn had indeed found Minerva's mare. Lying dead on its side, its mouth slack around square, bloodied teeth, as if in surprise. Its throat was torn away.

But beyond the mare's barreled chest lay an even greater horror, and it now growled at Evelyn— a low, wet sound full of fresh death.

A black wolf crouched on its haunches, its blood-slicked muzzle still clamped around shiny entrails ripped from the horse's belly like satiny ribbons. The animal was enormous—big-boned and wide of chest beneath matted, shaggy fur.

"Oh my God," Evelyn croaked as wild yellow eyes locked onto her. The wolf's sides heaved in and out with exertion and alarm, and even from this distance, Evelyn could see skeletal ribs and the lump of thick hipbone jutting through the beast's matted fur. The animal was nearly starved.

It growled again, this time more insistently.

Stay away. Mine.

Evelyn swallowed, her eyes flicking to the saddle-bag still tethered to the dead horse. "I'll not hurt you," she said in a low, quavering voice. Her mind raced, and she decided quickly that the best course of action was to back a fair distance away and leave the wolf to its meal. The horse was of little use to her any matter, now. When the wolf had eaten its fill, Evelyn would return and retrieve the satchel.

She began to back away.

The wolf sprang to its feet, dropping the entrails with a spray of bloody saliva as it lunged forward, barking, and skidded to a halt in the snow not ten feet from where Evelyn stood.

Had she any water in her bladder, she would have lost it in that moment.

"All right! All right," she rushed. "I'll not move."

The wolf growled and backed up slowly until it was returned to the horse's torn underbelly. Its eyes never left Evelyn's, even as it began to feed once more.

After what seemed like an hour of watching the wolf gorge, Evelyn's numb feet and legs would no longer support her and she slowly sank down to her bottom in the accumulating snow. The beast tensed at her movement.

"Just taking a rest," she whispered.

It resumed its meal.

Evelyn ate a handful of snow.

She was covered in a blanket of powder and frozen to her core it seemed when, at last, the wolf stood. It stared at Evelyn, licking its muzzle noisily.

Evelyn swallowed. "Well. What are we to do now?" she asked lightly. The wolf cocked its head and Evelyn flicked her eyes to the saddle, blinking away the snowflakes clumped on her eyelashes.

The wolf shifted its weight and then sat down in the snow.

Evelyn drew a steadying breath. "I must have it, you understand."

The beast stared at her a long moment and then stood once more and circled away from the carcass. It walked stiffly to the far edge of the copse and lay down with a grunt. It looked at Evelyn and yawned.

"All right, then." Evelyn took another deep breath. "Just the satchel, I swear it."

The wolf did not move.

She rolled to her feet so slowly it took her nearly a full minute before she stood upright. Creeping, she slid her feet through the snow, inching toward the horse, barely feeling the fiery cold burning the exposed skin above her worn leather slippers. Her heart felt swollen with ice and shuddered as if it would explode when she reached the mare and crouched down slowly. The smell of blood caused her to gag and her mouth to water, the fresh carcass still radiating a glowing heat.

The wolf lowered its head to its paws.

Evelyn slid a hand beneath the satchel's ice-stiffened flap and grasped blindly until she felt the hilt of her blade, as cold as her own skin. She withdrew it from the bag slowly, slowly.

"'Tis not for you, lovely," Evelyn crooned when the wolf's ears pricked, praying the beast would not charge her before she had removed the satchel. She sawed clumsily through the strap holding the bag to the horse and dragged it to her, clutching the dagger to her bosom.

"There—that's it. That's all." Evelyn stood, wanting to sob. Her salvation was in her own hands now. "The rest is yours, as I promised." She began to back away.

The wolf raised its head with a low growl and Evelyn froze in place. But the animal was looking past her, deeper into the copse of pine.

Then Evelyn heard the soft crunch of snow behind her. She spun around.

No fewer than five more of the beasts ringed the copse—all gray in color and smaller than the black behind her, but still large and deadly. They watched her greedily, long tongues lolling out of their mouths and running with saliva.

Live meat. Fresh. Warm. Hungry, hungry . . .

Evelyn's throat closed as images of her body being ripped open like the mare's filled her mind. Fear unlike any she had ever known paralyzed her so that she could not have commanded her legs to move had she a place to flee.

She was trapped in the thick stand of trees.

The boldest of the newcomers hedged toward her in a swift, side-to-side motion and then stopped, as if taunting her. And this wolf had a different air about him—an awareness like a sinister fog that seemed to slither over the snow and swirl about Evelyn's ankles. An old, old beast, grizzled and scarred, his bloody intent clear in his soulless eyes.

Run? Will you run?

The animals behind the leader began to whine and Evelyn heard her own wild squeal of fear squeeze past her throat. *Oh, God,* she prayed, at last able to address her maker now that she was mesmerized by the long fangs, the curled, quivering lips. *Please make it quick.*

The wolf leader pounced with a snarl and Evelyn closed her eyes.

She was knocked sideways with a cry, and the sounds of hellish screams filled her ears. But when no teeth sank into her flesh, her eyes snapped open.

The black wolf was entangled with the gray, their forelegs locked around each other in a writhing, blurry mass of teeth and fur.

Another gray leapt onto the black's back, fangs bared, eliciting a bone-shuddering squeal from the larger animal.

Evelyn knew it would only be a matter of seconds before she, too, was attacked. She scrambled backward, her knuckles still clenched around her dagger and the satchel dragging through the snow, and then she was somehow off the ground and running—*flying*—through the forest away from the frenzy behind her, mumbled sobs bubbling at her lips as her breath roared in and out of her nose. Running, running for her life.

The life the black wolf had spared her. But why? Why? Yellow eyes glowed in her mind.

Evelyn ran for what seemed like hours before she saw the slope ahead—rounded, snow-covered ground that swelled away into a view of distant trees at midtrunk. How far was the drop? Two feet? A score? And what lay below? A forgiving bog? A frozen river, punctuated with jagged boulders?

Evelyn did not know, nor could she stop. She barreled toward the brink and prepared to leap.

She was still two yards from the precipice when she fell through the very earth itself, and the darkness swallowed her scream.

Chapter One

December 1077

Conall MacKerrick trudged through the shin-deep snow of the wood, his eyes scanning the white powder for animal tracks, his heart heavy and weary in his chest.

Hopeless.

He glanced only briefly at the pronged indentations of a small deer track—the hoof mark was soft at the edges and half filled with fresh snow—that animal had passed hours ago. Pursuit would be pointless.

Conall slogged onward.

A howling wind whipped around the trees and seared his skin through his thin léine, prompting Conall to shrug his length of plaid tighter across his chest and tuck it more firmly beneath his belt and the straps of his pack. He hitched his bow and quiver higher onto his shoulder and then jerked at the tether pulling the small sheep behind him. The animal bleated and skittered to catch up.

Conall felt numb, and not entirely from the bitter

cold blanketing his highland home. Here he was, the MacKerrick, chief of his clan, abandoning his town and the people he was to protect. And 'twas only for their own good.

Conall was glad his father was not alive to witness his son's failure.

Conall's wife, his newborn bairn, were dead. Was it only one turn of the moon since they had passed? Mother and daughter, both too small and weak to harbor life in this mean tract of Scotland.

It had been his brother, Duncan, who had grimly announced the birth, ducking out of Conall's own house, his thin face gray and pained.

"'Twas a wee gel," he'd whispered after a blink of mournful eyes. "Conall, they . . . Nonna didna—"

But Conall had not paused to hear the rest of his twin's declaration. He had charged toward his low-roofed sod house and shoved open the door, going instinctively to the box bed at the far end. He chose to ignore the fecund smell of blood that caused the hairs on the back of his neck to bristle ominously. Perhaps it had not been too early; he'd heard no babe cry, but perhaps God would have mercy on him, just this once.

"Nonna," he'd called gently. "Nonna."

A plaid-wrapped bundle was snuggled against his wife's side and even as Conall heard Duncan enter the house behind him, as he heard the wails of the townswomen gathered beyond his door—even as Conall reached out a trembling hand to lay it upon Nonna's still bosom, he'd known.

They were both dead.

"I'm sorry, Conall," Duncan had whispered.

God had no mercy for Conall MacKerrick.

The wind gusted again and the sheep bleated

pitifully behind him, bringing Conall back to the present. He sniffed and swiped at his nose.

He'd left before dawn's first weak rays crawled over the MacKerrick town this morn, despite Duncan's and his mother's protests. Nonna was gone. His child was gone. Conall would not burden an already sick and hungry people with their chief's care throughout the remainder of the harshest winter he'd ever witnessed. If naught else, the MacKerrick was a skilled hunter. He would winter alone and seek out game in the deepest part of the wood. Should he prevail, he would return to the town.

Should he fail, he would starve.

In the meanwhile, he would use his self-enforced exile to mourn in private, and to decide once and for all what to do about the curse that plagued his town, the decades-old damnation set upon his clan name by a woman long ago passed from these lands. A curse that had grown more malevolent with each passing season. Their crops failed. They suffered drought, or flooding rains. Illness was a constant caller on the town.

And now Nonna and the bairn were gone.

Conall knew he would likely be forced to at last beg quarter from the clan to the south, as his father had refused to do, or watch his entire town die, person by person.

He knew each black word by heart, passed down to Conall with bitterness by his father, Dáire MacKerrick: *Famine and illness are my gifts to you, you MacKerrick beasts, who have ripped my very heart from my bosom and fed it to the crows. So let those winged harbingers be aught that fills your bellies and let it be only their song that fills your ears until my return. For I will return. Only heartache and toil shall you reap*

until a Buchanan bairn is born to rule the MacKerrick
clan. And when you are on bended knee, I will have
my revenge.

By spring's first thaw, should Conall still live, he
would beg forgiveness from Angus Buchanan, for a
wrong committed against the clan chief's sister while
Conall and Duncan still nursed in their mother's
arms. Although his people cried out against it as
bowing to the Buchanan's witchery, Conall knew
'twas likely their only chance for survival.

He traversed a narrow bog, tugging the sheep
after him, and scanned the upper bank for the
jumble of rocks that marked the path leading to
Ronan's old hut. He had not traveled this far to the
edge of MacKerrick lands in months—mayhap
more than a year—and he hoped that the long-
abandoned hut in the vale was still habitable.

'Twas peace and solitude Conall so desperately
needed, and he was certain to find it in his uncle's
hunting cottage, just beyond this bank . . .

He saw the weak column of filmy smoke from
the roof before he smelled the smoldering peat.

And meat. He smelled meat cooking. Conall's
stomach growled.

With two more strides, the ancient sod house
came into view, snuggled into the earth like a toad-
stool, its short wooden door standing slightly ajar.

Conall's face darkened. He slid his bow and
quiver and his pack from his shoulders and dropped
the sheep's tether, and reached for his sword.

Evelyn plucked the blackened strip of meat from
the spit with forefinger and thumb, blew on it, shook
it, then tossed it to Alinor, who snatched it from the

air with an expert chomp. Two swift bites and the piece was gone. Alinor swiped a long, pink tongue over her pointed canines with obvious relish.

"Oh, I agree," Evelyn said, retrieving another strip of meat. "Quite good." She bit into the tough, half-burnt chunk, trying to rip off a piece small enough to chew. "A tad dry, though," she amended around the mouthful of meat. She tossed the remaining hunk to the wolf lying nearby.

Alinor made quick work of the morsel and then set to licking the fur in front of the makeshift bandage wound around her middle.

"Itching, is it?" Evelyn asked, and then sucked her fingers clean before rising from the fire and limping the width of the hut to the ragged lengths of cloth dangling from the ceiling. She gripped several in her hands, testing their dryness, before choosing two and tugging them free.

She picked up the shallow bowl filled with melted snow and floating chunks of moss and returned to the wolf's side, sinking to her bottom with a hiss. Her ankle, knee, and hip were improving each day, the swelling nearly gone, but each joint in her right leg was still painted with deep black and purple and green bruises.

Alinor flopped completely onto her side with a great sigh and stretched out her legs to either side of Evelyn. The wolf closed her eyes.

"You like this, do you?" Evelyn grinned, reaching for the knot and picking it loose. She slipped the bandage from beneath the animal and set it aside to be washed later, then reached for the gummy clump of moss pressed to Alinor's ribs. She flung the soiled mass onto the fire.

The wound beneath had improved significantly.

Although crusty, the skin around the long, ragged edges was no longer blazing red and emitted no foul odor. Evelyn could even see tiny black stubble in Alinor's startlingly white skin where the fur was beginning to grow back.

Satisfied, Evelyn wadded up one of the clean strips of cloth and dunked it in the bowl, wringing the water from it before dabbing gently at Alinor's wound. The wolf flinched slightly at first, but then relaxed again.

Thank you, God, Evelyn said silently as she tended the animal. She'd probably spoken the phrase a thousand times in the last—how long? Three weeks? Four? Evelyn was not certain how much time had passed since discovering Minerva's dead mare, but in truth, it no longer mattered. She felt she could never be grateful enough for the divine intervention that had brought Alinor into her life.

Evelyn had thought she'd fallen into the very depths of the coldest, darkest hell after fleeing the gray wolves those many weeks ago. She'd landed hard on her right leg and hip and her breath had left her, as had her consciousness. When she had awoken, it was to a world of grainy darkness, a smell of rot and mildew, and to a screaming pain in her leg. She could feel cold, dry dirt and stone beneath her cheek and she wondered if she was dead, although she could not imagine who would have been about to bury her.

But there had been no soil pressing down on her, and so after mustering the courage to move her battered body, she'd dragged herself blindly along the packed dirt until she'd reached a cold, crumbly barrier. Evelyn had pulled herself up into a seated position when the watery-sounding whine first reached her ears. Her body went rigid, her mind still gripped by images of gnashing fangs and blood arcing through snowy air.

Her eyes traveled upward instinctively to find a ragged hole in the black above her, where foggy light filtered down. Was she trapped once again, this time in some sort of cave?

The whining sounded again and Evelyn shivered, even as the tone of the cry pierced her heart.

Hurts.

She listened to the animal for what seemed like an eternity, until tears ran down her cheeks and she sobbed into her elbow. Her fear waged battle on her soul. Yellow eyes and a twisting, fighting, black body filled her mind, and Evelyn knew 'twas the black wolf who cried.

Hurts. Hurts.

Evelyn began to drag herself along the dirt again, feeling the moist barrier with her fingers.

She touched rough wood and her palms skimmed up and down, testing its dimensions.

A door?

Her fingers caught on a rough L shape and Evelyn grasped it, pulled. Wood creaked.

She could hear the wolf still beyond the door and she wondered if she was not opening the gateway to her own death.

Hurts.

She pulled harder, and a weak sliver of gray light sliced across her face—fading daylight.

Evelyn grunted as she strained at the door and it dragged open at last.

The giant black wolf slumped not three yards from Evelyn in the growing, dense dusk. The animal's head bobbed and swayed on its thick neck, its muzzle pointed at the ground. One paw was held delicately in the air, and a wide path of crimson snow led to the animal's hindquarters.

Blood. The wolf's blood.

The beast raised its yellow eyes to Evelyn, as if just realizing it was being watched. It whined again, faintly, and tried to scoot backward in the snow, away from Evelyn.

Hurts. Afraid.

But the wolf's injured paw combined with its obvious blood loss conspired against the animal and it fell sideways with a frightened yelp. It struggled to rise again for a moment, but then gave up, its sides rising shallowly, the bloom of blood widening.

This animal had saved her life, of that Evelyn was certain. Although it might now mean her death, she could not watch it suffer. Would not.

Afraid.

Evelyn dragged herself through the doorway toward the wolf, her arms sinking nearly to her elbows in the snow, but she no longer felt the cold.

"Please do not kill me. Please do not kill me," she breathed over and over as she neared the fallen animal.

Afraid. Afraid—afraid—afraid . . .

A sob caught in Evelyn's chest. "I know, lovely. I am afraid, as well," she whispered as she closed the gap.

Evelyn was finally close enough to the animal that she could have touched it. But she did not have the opportunity as the wolf abruptly kicked and yelped and tried to gain its feet.

Evelyn screamed and instinctively threw up an arm, but the wolf crumpled to the ground once more, its little remaining energy spent. Its ragged breaths squealed in its wide chest.

Hurts.

Evelyn drew a deep breath and moved closer to the enormous beast. Her leg throbbed and her heart pounded so that she fancied she could hear her ribs rattling together.

She saw the deep gouges in the wolf's back and neck, the still-trickling stickiness on its muzzle and wide, black nose. But the ragged gash in the animal's flank was the most dire—gaping, torn flesh revealing stringy muscle and a white chip of rib. Here, the blood flowed onto the snow.

How had it escaped when so outnumbered?

"Have a bit of a scrape there, did you, lovely?" she asked in a shaky whisper.

The wolf whined deep in its throat.

Evelyn looked back the way she'd come for the first time since crawling from her accidental shelter, and was so shocked at what she saw that, for an instant, she forgot her injuries and her fear.

It was . . . a cottage.

Of sorts.

Low, sod walls and a thatch roof poked out from beneath the snow on the bank behind it, and Evelyn realized she must have fallen through the smoke hole.

A cottage. Abandoned, obviously.

The wolf whined again in a series of short, breathy bursts and then Evelyn heard the chorus of howls from the wood beyond.

Her eyes sought the path of blood leading from the forest and she knew the gray beasts had likely torn what was left of Minerva's mare to shreds and were now on the trail of the fallen black. Should they find the animal—and Evelyn, as well—injured and exposed as they were, Evelyn knew both their lives were forfeit.

She looked to the cottage door and then back at the black. To the door again, then the considerable mass of the wolf, trying to gauge the distance against her own meager strength.

The animal whined pitifully.

Afraid.

Evelyn closed her eyes. *God, give me strength.* Then she opened her eyes and without hesitation, laid a palm firmly on the black's hip.

It flinched, whined again, but did not turn on her.

Deep in the forest, but closer now, gaining, the grays howled again.

Closing her mind to the fact that she was readying to take into her hands a deadly, wild, injured animal nearly equal to her own size, Evelyn slid through the snow closer to the black's back, her hand never breaking contact with the animal.

She tried to steady her voice. "I'll not hurt you. I'll not let *them* hurt you," she promised.

The wolf's ears twitched, but it did not move.

So, before she could think better of it, Evelyn snaked an arm around the black, leaned into it, and pulled up.

The animal gave a weak struggle and an even weaker growl, but Evelyn did not loose it. Instead, she quickly fished her other arm beneath the wolf and lifted it to her chest, crying out in pain as she did so. Her back now toward the cottage door, she dug in the snow with her uninjured leg until her slipper found purchase with the frozen ground beneath and she pushed with all her strength.

They moved perhaps an inch.

She hitched the animal higher onto her torso,

clasped her hands together in a tight fist beneath
its chest, conscious of the warm blood soaking
through her thin cloak and into her kirtle. The
black suddenly went limp against her and Evelyn thought her arms would rip from their
sockets.

She kicked again, pushed at the ground. And
again. Over and over she crooked and then straightened her leg. Her muscles screamed, burned. She
began to weep.

After what seemed an eternity, the doorway was at
last at her back, a red path of blood spread cleanly
over the crushed and rutted snow before her.

And the gray wolves burst from the woods.

With a final, scrambling shove, Evelyn slid into
the cottage. She kicked the springy door closed
and held her foot against it even as it shuddered,
jarring her leg to her spine. She screamed in both
pain and surprise.

One of the grays had thrown himself at the door
with a furious snarl.

The black in her arms stirred and Evelyn let it
slide to the ground. "'Tis all right, lovely—we're
safe," she breathed. "We're safe now."

She spied a length of rough-planed wood leaning against the wall in the dim light of the hut, as
well as the crude brackets embedded in both the
door and the sod walls to either side. Without removing her bracing foot, she reached for the plank
and stretched up to mate it with the brackets.

The door shuddered again and Evelyn skittered
backward in the dirt. She felt a warm wetness on
the back of her palm and snatched her hand to her
bosom with a cry before looking down.

The black stared up at her through glassy, clouded eyes.

It had licked her hand.

Now, Evelyn hummed as she laid a fresh piece of damp moss against Alinor's side and held the spongy mass in place as she slid the other wide length of rose-colored cloth—remnants of her ruined kirtle—under and around Alinor's midsection. She fastened the rather fine linen bandage in a stiff knot and then, on impulse, tucked the ends into a pretty bow.

"Fetching," Evelyn said, leaning back to inspect her handiwork.

Alinor's thick tail thumped the dirt floor twice.

Evelyn ruffled the wolf's fur and then rose stiffly, gathering up the used strips of cloth and then dropping them in a bucket near the door. While she set to laying more peat on the fire, Alinor, too, gained her feet and crossed the hut to enter one of the cottage's odd indoor pens. The black lay down on the fresh pine boughs Evelyn had piled within and promptly closed her eyes.

The fire smoking in earnest now, Evelyn pulled the remainder of the cooked meat from the spit and laid it next to her dagger—its tip now broken and jagged—on the narrow plank set into the rear wall. The afternoon light was fading into an early evening and she made mental note not to forget the snow bucket when she and Alinor went out to seek their final relief. After that, they would barricade themselves in for the night.

The two already had some semblance of a routine to their days in the primitive shelter, one of gathering snow for drinking and washing, fallen branches to supplement the dwindling pile of ancient peat, and of harvesting meat. Evelyn would tend the wolf's wound, and as the animal and Evelyn regained their strength, they took to walking in ever-widening circles around the cottage, looking for forage. Most days they returned empty-handed. Sometimes they would stumble upon a few nuts, only half rotted. Once, Alinor nearly caught a rabbit.

But they only explored when the sun was near its pinnacle, for the grays owned the forest from dusk till dawn, and even now they still stalked the hut and its occupants. Each night, after the door was closed and braced firmly, Alinor would lay in the rickety, narrow box bed at Evelyn's side shaking, her ears pricking at the minutest sound, hackles raising when the grays called from the woods, taunting them. The beasts had nearly killed Alinor once, and they still wanted her. Hungered for her. Evelyn herself could still clearly see the grizzled gray leader in her mind—how he had looked into her eyes as if he'd known her, had been waiting for her to venture into that part of the wood . . .

Thoughts of the gray devils made Evelyn skittish, and so she jumped when Alinor gave a low growl. Alarm raised the hairs on the backs of Evelyn's arms as she turned toward the door.

Surely 'twas too early in the day for—

Alinor shot to her feet with a bark, staring at the half open door, her hackles raised in a prickly ridge above her bandage.

Evelyn frowned. Blasted beasts! If it was the grays, there would be no snow gathering, and no way to relieve themselves for the whole of the night, save the crude bucket. She stalked across the floor with a frustrated sigh, ready to close and bar the door.

But before she had reached even the fire pit, the door slammed against the wall, the frame instantly stuffed with a large, wide—

Man!

Alinor lunged with a snarl.

Chapter Two

Conall thought for an instant that he had gone mad.

One moment, he was charging through the hut's door, sword drawn, ready to oust an ambitious squatter, then in a blink, he was on his back on the hard dirt floor, the largest, blackest, most ferocious-looking wolf he'd ever laid eyes upon pinning him to the ground.

The wolf's pearly, pointed teeth were bared, the short, bristly hairs of its lips brushing Conall's. The beast's head was nearly as large as Conall's own, and hot spittle misted his face with the wolf's every growling breath.

The first thought that entered Conall's mind was: How could a wolf start a peat fire?

And when he saw the ivory angel's wary face peer down at him from over the wolf's head, Conall was certain he'd gone completely over the brink.

"Who are you?" the angel demanded. "And what do you want, barging into our house?"

Conall was stunned into silence for a moment. *Our* house? *Our?*

Then he realized the angel had spoken English.

"Are you mute?" the English woman asked with a frown. She scrunched her mouth to form Gaelic words with halting difficulty. "What is your name?"

Conall gritted his teeth and answered her in her own tongue. "Call yer hell-beast off me and mayhap I'll tell you."

The woman's eyes narrowed for a moment and then she reached out a slim, pale hand and actually *touched* the monster. "Come, Alinor—let the rude man up."

The wolf—*Alinor?*—growled a final, menacing warning before backing slowly down Conall's length, the woman's hand still on the beast's thick neck. The pair retreated to the hut's rear wall.

Conall gained his feet slowly, his eyes never leaving the wolf. He spoke to the woman, his sword once more at the ready. "Stand aside, woman—I'll nae share my home with a bloodthirsty killer."

"I beg your pardon," the woman said, stepping neatly in front of the wolf. "You'll put that weapon away immediately, is what you *will* do, sir. Alinor could have already supped upon your scrawny frame had she the desire, and should you come one step closer to either of us, I will most certainly let her have you!"

Conall blinked, shook his head to clear it. The woman continued.

"Furthermore, this is *our* home, and I'll thank you to adopt a more respectful demeanor while you are our guest." She sniffed, looked Conall up and down. "Now, tell us your name."

Conall frowned and then looked to his right hand—aye, his sword, glinting and deadly, was still in his grip, and still pointed at the odd pair before him.

And yet the daft woman—English, at that—dared to order him about? On his own lands?

"You're a long ways from London, English," Conall growled. "Trespassing on MacKerrick lands—*my* house. With one swing I could end your life."

The woman arched a slender brow. "A poor house-keeper you are then, sir. This cottage was quite abandoned when I found it, I assure you. Had I not come along, 'twould most likely lay completely in ruin by now." She cocked her head, sending her long, auburn hair swishing about her waist. "You should thank me instead of threaten me. But if you insist on this villainy"—she withdrew her hand from behind her back and Conall saw the small, damaged dagger in her fist—"come on with you, then. We are not afraid, are we, Alinor?"

The wolf growled and stepped from behind the woman, and 'twas then that Conall noticed the wide, pink belt about the animal, complete with a jaunty bow.

Before he could stop himself, he laughed and blurted, "Is that beast wearing a *sash*?"

The woman flushed scarlet beneath the dusting of freckles on her cheeks, and the wolf's growl deepened.

"Get out," she said, flicking her blade toward the doorway behind Conall. "Get out, and do not come back or I'll—"

"You'll what?" Conall challenged, a chuckle still in his voice. "Tie me hair up in ribbons?"

The woman's chest heaved and Conall could not help but notice its fullness beneath the gray kirtle that practically hung on her otherwise slender frame.

"Get out," she sputtered again. "And stop staring at my breasts."

Conall felt his face heat at being caught in his appraisal of her body. Any matter, the time for sport had come to an end. Conall's patience was run out.

"The only one of us who'll be leaving this cottage is you," he said, stepping forward. The wolf's hackles raised. "Now, gather your beast and—"

A chorus of howls echoed from beyond the hut, cutting short Conall's directive. He heard his sheep—forgotten until now—bleat pitifully from the dooryard.

The woman's demeanor—and that of the wolf as well—instantly changed.

"Is that your animal calling, sir?" she demanded. The wolf whined and circled behind the woman once more, obviously distressed by its brethren's howls.

"Aye—my sheep," Conall said. "Why? Is that the rest of your well-dressed pack calling to sup?"

"'Tis the grays, you fool," she said. "And if you value the animal's life, you'll bring her inside before they descend upon her and rip her to pieces, as they nearly did Alinor."

The black wolf whined again.

Outside, Conall's sheep bleated insistantly, and the pack from beyond howled in evil, discordant harmony.

"They're wolves," Conall said calmly. "Besides this one, obviously"—his eyes flicked to the shivering black—"they'll keep to the wood."

The woman looked him up and down, blatantly taking his full measure. "Are you hungry, sir?" she asked after a moment.

Conall frowned. Of course he was hungry. Everyone was hungry this winter. But what business was it of this uppity English woman's that there was not enough food to be had?

She gave him no opportunity to answer. "Because *they* are." She turned to lay a hand along the black's muzzle. "Stay here, lovely. I'll return in a thrice." Her eyes flicked to Conall briefly. "You may take his fat head off should he attempt to harm you."

Then she stormed past Conall, shoving into him rudely as she fled the cottage, her dagger still in hand. He let her pass, too stunned and bewildered by her strange actions to put up any real resistance.

"Is she daft?" Conall asked the black.

The wolf called Alinor turned from him and skittered into one of the hut's animal pens meant to house the breed of small Scottish cattle throughout long, harsh winters such as this. But, of course, the MacKerrick clan had no cattle this year. The wolf lay down and whined and shook, the vicious beast of earlier nowhere to be seen.

The wolfsong from the forest sounded closer.

Conall turned with a grimace and a shake of his head and followed the woman from the hut.

Evelyn's heart pounded as she ran into the dooryard, eyes scanning the close clearing for the sheep.

Was he daft? Or deaf? Could he not hear the gray's mad, bloodthirsty taunts?

Hungry, hungry . . .

There! The brown and white shaggy animal ran in frantic circles, its short tether tangling around its forelegs in the dirtied, trampled snow. Evelyn tucked her dagger into the ragged rope belt around her waist and walked toward the sheep calmly, making soft shushing noises. "Easy, lovely. 'Tis all right." She reached down and unwound the tether from the panting animal's legs, then tugged it toward the hut. "Come, now. Come along."

The large interloper emerged from the dwelling, a frown creasing his strong features. In another time—another life—Evelyn would have been terrified of the giant highlander. He was slender, yea, but his big-boned frame suggested that mayhap he had carried more meat on him at one time. His legs were long under his odd, shin-length tunic and tall leather boots, and his belt and sheath hung low across slender hips. His plaid drape strained across the breadth of his shoulders and chest, and his brown hair looked streaked by the very sun, hanging silky and chopped down his back, a thin, leather-twisted braid adorning one side.

He was beautiful, in a hungry, desperate way, and Evelyn sensed he carried a heavy sorrow about him. And a resentment larger than the Caledonian forest surrounding them both.

Yea, this was a thoroughly dangerous man.

He blocked the doorway with his width and Evelyn was forced to stop some lengths away from him, glancing over her shoulder. The grays would emerge at any moment.

"I would think," he said with a nasty smirk, "that a lass as brazen and foolish as yourself, who squats in another's home and keeps such close company with wild beasts, wouldna be so fearful of a few stray wolves. Surely you could charm them as you have the black."

"Verily?" Evelyn challenged. She could allow herself no fear of this man. Not now, when she had fought so hard for her life, for Alinor's life, in this treacherous land. She had come too far, survived too much, and she would let no one—*no one*—take it from her. "If all it requires is brazenness and foolishness . . ."

She walked up to the man, grabbed his thick, bony wrist and slapped the sheep's tether into his palm. Then she looked up into his eyes—golden, sparked with green and brown—and smiled fiercely.

"You should fare quite well."

Evelyn darted around him into the cottage and slammed the door, dropping the board in place before his first fist-falls pounded the old wood.

"*Woman!*" he roared from beyond the door.

After a short scrabbling of claw on stone, Evelyn felt Alinor nuzzle her hand and she pulled the wolf's neck against her hip. "Well, we made short work of him, did we not, lovely?"

The pounding continued. "Open this door!"

"I think not," Evelyn called. "This home is mine and Alinor's now. And *you* are a very rude man."

She heard the man growl, then let loose a string of vicious Gaelic. The few words Evelyn could understand made the tips of her ears burn.

"If I must, I'll chop this hut to bits and drag you *and* your animal out," he warned. "You'll nae stay here and that's the whole of it!"

"We shall see," Evelyn called.

She knew the instant the grays emerged from the wood by the highlander's hoarse shout of surprise. She crouched down near the floor to peer through a small knothole in the door. Alinor pressed her wide head to Evelyn's ear, as if also trying to see.

Evelyn spied the backs of the man's boots. He was facing the forest now, and had dropped the sheep's tether. The poor animal bleated in fright.

"Hah!" the highlander shouted, taking a step away from the cottage. "Get from here, you hell-beasts!"

Evelyn kept her eye steady on the view through the knothole and slowly, carefully, silently, reached both arms above her head to remove the bar from the door.

The man took another step toward the edge of the forest and Evelyn saw a flicker of steel swing in a wide arc. "Hah! Get back!"

Evelyn jostled Alinor to the side with an elbow and eased the door open just wide enough to squeeze her hand and forearm through. Her fingers dug in the snow until she felt the sheep's rough tether. She opened the door a bit wider and pulled hard on the rope.

The sheep bleated and popped through the narrow opening.

The highlander turned with a surprised shout.

Evelyn slammed the door once more and dropped the bar back in place. Behind her, Alinor growled.

Evelyn turned on her heels and rose to see the giant black wolf with her jaws around the back of the small sheep's neck. The brown and white animal's eyes rolled in fright and it screamed as its forelegs rose off the floor.

"Alinor!" Evelyn chastised. "Naughty!"

The wolf turned sorrowful, yellow eyes up to Evelyn but did not release the sheep.

"Let her go, immediately."

Slowly, reluctantly, Alinor opened her mouth and the sheep fell out. Alinor sat on her haunches and licked her muzzle three, four times in rapid succession.

"Naughty," Evelyn scolded the wolf again as she

grabbed for the now slobbery, panicked sheep, who once more ran in frantic circles. She pulled the sheep to one of the pens and shut it safely behind the gate.

The door to the hut thudded again. "Woman, you had better—*aaghhh*!"

The highlander's shout was drowned out by a ferocious snarl and Evelyn cringed, trying not to imagine long fangs sinking into the man's thick neck. Then she heard a shuddering squeal and the snarling was abruptly silenced.

Evelyn rushed to the door again and pressed her ear to it—she couldn't bear to look through the knothole at the carnage that lay inevitably beyond.

"Sir?" she called. "Sir, are you injured?"

A beat of silence and then a loud groan.

"Oh God, forgive me," Evelyn breathed. She looked to Alinor. "We've killed him!"

The wolf whined.

"I know, he did ask for it, but—" Her conscience kicked at her. "Sir!" Evelyn shouted at the door once again. "Sir, answer me!"

"Och, lass," the highlander moaned. "They got me, they did. Oh, the pain!"

Alinor lay down near Evelyn's feet and covered her muzzle with one paw.

A strangled cry of dismay burst from Evelyn's throat. She drew her dagger from her belt and then grabbed for the bar. "Hold on! I'm opening the door!"

No sooner had the rough length of wood scraped clear of the brackets than the door flew open, knocking Evelyn to the dirt on her backside, her dagger skittering across the floor. The highlander

ducked inside quite ably, his face dark with rage. He
slammed the door shut and replaced the bar.

He turned back to Evelyn, murderous fury sparking to life in his amber eyes. He bore not one scratch
on his person, although the length of his sword was
bloodied.

Alinor scrambled to her feet and fled to the
other pen.

"You . . . you *lied* to me!" Evelyn stuttered.

"I'll do worse than that," he growled, seizing her
arm and jerking her to her feet. He swung her toward
the door and his brogue was thick as peat smoke with
his next words. "I'll have nae sneaking, backstabbing,
sheep-stealing, English filth in me house."

The highlander kept tight hold of Evelyn as he
slid his sword into the sheath on his belt and then
reached for the bar on the door, and Evelyn knew
he intended to toss her to the grays.

"You can't! You can't!" she screamed, flailing at
him as he struggled to lift the bar and retain hold
of her. She could fight neither the man nor the
beasts beyond the door physically. Her mind raced
and she latched on to the one excuse that filtered
to the top of her panicked thoughts. "I'm . . . I'm
not English—I'm Scots!"

The man paused, looked down at her with one
wry eyebrow raised. "Och, aye—blind I must be,
and deaf as well, to nae have noticed yer gentle
brogue and fine highland costume before now."
He shook her. *"Liar."*

"Nay, listen!" Evelyn insisted, assembling the details of the lie so quickly they began to flow out of
her mouth like water. "Listen, I"—she swallowed—
"I was born and raised in England, yea. But my

mother . . . my *mother* was Scots. She was born near Loch Lomond."

"Well, what are you doing on MacKerrick lands, then? And where is your kin, hmm? You're nae claiming to have MacKerrick blood in your veins now, are you?"

"Of course not." Evelyn tried to laugh. "That's ridiculous. I . . . I was accompanying a member of my family—*my kin*—back to her beloved highland home to die." Evelyn cleared her throat. "Ah, my great-aunt. 'Twas her dying wish, you see. I can take you to her body, should you require proof."

The highlander smirked. "Unlikely, English. But I'll humor you through one more falsehood before I toss you out on your skinny arse. Give me the name of your kin, then. You can do that, can you not?"

Evelyn nodded frantically. "Of course."

"*Well?*" the man fairly shouted.

"'Tis . . . Buchanan," Evelyn squeaked. "My great-aunt was Minerva Buchanan."

The highlander's face went the color of the snow piled outside the hut and he dropped Evelyn's arm as if it were afire. He staggered backward.

"*Minerva Buchanan?*" he repeated in a croaking voice.

Evelyn was unsure if her answer spelled good or ill for her immediate future, but felt she had no choice now but to press on. "Yea. Sister to Angus Buchanan." She licked her lips, winced. "Did you know her?"

The highlander shook his head faintly and stared at Evelyn as though she were one of the grays from the forest. "Nae. But my uncle did, before he died. Ronan MacKerrick." His eyes flicked about the hut. "This was his cottage."

Evelyn instantly recalled the moments before the old healer's death, and the moan of the man's name on her lips.

"Of course," Evelyn said, breathing a huge, silent sigh of relief. "She spoke of Ronan. I—I'm sorry to hear that he's passed."

The highlander's eyes narrowed. "Have you . . . have you seen your Uncle Angus, gel?" he asked. "Does the Buchanan know you're here, on Mac-Kerrick lands?"

"Ah . . . nay," Evelyn stammered. "I fear Minerva led us quite astray before she passed, and I have no idea in which direction the Buchanan village lies— I've never been there, you see. Is . . . is it far?" she asked, praying that it was. Too far, any matter, for this man to take her there immediately and out her lie.

"'Tis a town, nae a village," he said absently. "And 'tis verra far, indeed, for winter travel." The highlander spoke almost gently now, and Evelyn's heart was buoyed with desperate relief. He placed one of his large, bony palms upon his chest. "I am Conall MacKerrick. Ronan's own nephew."

"And I am Evelyn . . . *Buchanan* Godewin." *God forgive my lying tongue.*

For the first time, a genuine, if bewildered, smile cracked the highlander's face. His eyes were alight with amber fire and their sparkle nearly took Evelyn's breath.

"Welcome home, Eve."

Chapter Three

"Well." The willowy woman looked quite taken aback, in Conall's opinion. She opened her lips as if she was about to speak again but then pressed them back together and twisted one hand in the folds of her skirt. She was quite fetching, Conall had to admit, discomfited as she was, and thinking hard about something.

"Well, indeed," Conall said. His own head was still spinning with the realization of their predicament. He needed time to sort it out, to make sense of it all.

"Well," Evelyn said again. She seemed to stand taller in her threadbare gown, which at one time had likely been quite fine. "Thank you very much for the welcome." Her eyes met his briefly and then danced away to the floor, the pens, the ceiling. "Er . . . good day, then."

Conall shook his head with a grin and then strode back to the hut's low door, pressing the side of his face to it. "I'm nae going anywhere, lass."

"Oh, of course not this *instant*," Conall heard her

say from behind him, a nervous laugh in her voice. "I do not expect you to—"

"Shh!" Conall held up a palm. "Quiet!"

"—to go while the wolves are still about," she continued in a loud whisper. "Do you hear anything?"

He raised up from the door and sent her an exasperated look.

She winced. "Quiet. Yea, of course."

Conall shook his head and then turned back to the door, taking hold of the bar that spanned it. Behind him, Alinor gave a low growl. "Take your beast in hand, Eve," he said over his shoulder. He began to ease the bar from its brackets.

"Why? What are you doing? I thought you said you weren't leaving?" she demanded in a prissy, anxious tone, although Conall knew she obeyed him by the way her voice now carried from the opposite side of the hut. "Come, lovely," she crooned to the wolf. "To me, Alinor."

Conall rolled his eyes at the rough-planed wood in front of his face. "I left me pack beyond the clearing. There're supplies to be had if the wolves havena ripped it to bits." He leaned the bar against the wall and then braced his shoulder and hip into the door, taking hold of the pull.

"Oh." Her voice sounded next to him and he glanced at her. Her arms were folded stingily against her bosom and the black wolf stared at the door, head down, ears back. "Of what sort are the supplies?"

"Nae sense in telling you until I see they're still there. But we shall be in sore need of them if we are to survive the season," he answered. Could the gel speak in naught but questions? "And I said to take *hold* of the animal, lest you wish her to bolt from the house."

"I can assure you that Alinor has no more desire to be in the company of those savages than I do, sir. She'll not bolt if they're still about."

Conall shrugged and eased open the door but a hand's breadth, bracing it against his body lest one of the grays lay in wait. He scanned the dooryard beyond.

Empty, except for the body of the slain gray.

Conall slid his foot back half a step, opened the door a bit wider, and poked his head out. It was eerily quiet.

Conall ducked back inside quickly and collided with the woman and her animal, who had both eased closer to him during his perusal.

She squeaked at being jostled and threw him an offended frown when Alinor whined and pulled a paw from beneath Conall's booted foot.

"A bit of a warning next time, sir, if you don't mind! Alinor is still recovering and is not yet as nimble as she once was," she snipped.

"I didna know the pair of you would try to climb me when I turned my back," Conall growled, and then drew his long sword from his sheath. "I'll have a look 'round, then fetch the pack if 'tis safe. Stay here."

The woman nodded eagerly and clasped her hands at her waist.

A bit *too* eagerly, Conall thought as he made to step through the portal. He turned abruptly, causing another scuffle as the woman retreated farther back into the cottage once more.

"And I'm warnin' you, Eve," Conall said sternly. "Should you think to bar the door after me again,

I'll set fire to this hut, you ken? By all that is holy, I'll burn it to the verra ground."

Her eyes narrowed, as if debating the sincerity of his threat.

"*The verra ground*," he promised, and then stepped though the doorway into the clearing.

Evelyn's knees were shaking so badly that she sank to her bottom next to Alinor once the door closed after the highlander. Her heart thudded in her chest and she realized she was covered in a thin layer of icy perspiration, although the hut was still quite cold inside.

Her lie about her lineage might very well have saved her and Alinor's lives—she was no more Buchanan than was the king of England. Thanks be to God Evelyn had known just enough about Minerva's kin to satisfy the highlander's inquisition and stay him from throwing them both to the grays.

For now, any matter.

Evelyn knew that either she and Alinor or the highlander would have to go. 'Twas too dangerous by far to risk being found out. Obviously, Conall Mac-Kerrick was on familiar terms with the Buchanan clan by the quick manner in which he'd known Minerva and Angus by name.

And he was Ronan MacKerrick's very nephew, no less. The man Minerva had called for in the last moments of her life. This was *Ronan's hut*.

For all Evelyn knew, the MacKerricks and the Buchanans were great allies, and Angus might appear in the clearing one day, come for a fortnight of hunting sport with his neighbor, Conall.

Evelyn shivered at the imagined repercussions.

Every fiber in her being screamed at her to get up and bar the door to the hut, but Evelyn was not at all certain the highlander would not do as he promised and burn the cottage "to the verra ground," with her and Alinor inside. After all, he would have already sacrificed them to the grays had she not come up with the blatant falsehood to save her own life.

The beast.

Should she and Alinor be found out now, MacKerrick would evict them from their cozy little home—likely without even their few paltry belongings—making them easy prey for the wolves. Nay, if ever they must abandon the hut, 'twas far better they do it of their own accord, with time to prepare.

Alinor sat down beside Evelyn with a breathy whine, the bow of her rose-colored bandage brushing Evelyn's face. The forgotten sheep bleated from its pen as if in answer and Alinor turned longing yellow eyes to the rear of the hut.

Evelyn patted the wolf absently. "I think not, lovely."

'Twould be nobler for Conall MacKerrick to take his own leave, although Evelyn doubted by the man's heretofore incessant rudeness that he had any notion of the word's meaning. Evelyn's leg was healing, true, but too slowly to undertake a journey of any length. And her energy seemed to wane only moments after waking in the mornings, likely from lack of adequate food. Alinor was still recuperating from the attack and there was no other shelter for either of them in this deepest part of winter. The towering Scot had to have come from a village of some sort, and he could very well return to it posthaste. Surely, barbarian though he was, he did not expect to cohabitate with an unmarried lady in such intimate quarters.

Evelyn's eyes instinctively flew to the narrow box bed at the end of the hut and she felt her face warm at the lurid possibilities the piece of furniture now evoked in her imagination. Smiling amber eyes and flashing white teeth caused her to shiver once more.

"Sinful," she whispered aloud, and then crossed herself—an exercise she hadn't performed in months—as if she'd come face-to-face with the devil himself.

And then she was decided. One way or another, Evelyn had to get away from Conall MacKerrick.

Conall could not let Evelyn get away.

He stepped over the dead wolf with care and crept across the narrow clearing, turning in slow circles with his sword at the ready, his eyes scanning the wall of trees that surrounded the hut like a stockade. His breath hung in steamy clouds 'round his head and he tried to stay focused on the task at hand, lest he be ambushed and killed before he had chance to work out his scheme properly.

Find the pack. Get the supplies . . .

But there was a Buchanan woman—a young, shapely, smart-mouthed, sneaky, uppity Buchanan woman—in his own *house*! It was a bloody miracle. Perhaps—

A sound like the snapping of a twig underfoot startled Conall so that he jumped and gave a strangled cry. He swung his sword around in a wide arc and fell into a crouch, but the clearing was still empty. Sweat ran down his back in a slushy river.

Concentrate, damn you!

Conall sidestepped to the gentle bank on the edge of the clearing and let his eyes flick over the sloped shoulder. He saw the curve of his bow poking from a drift, and his pack lay where he'd dropped it; both appeared undisturbed save for the rutted paths of tracks circling them. It looked to Conall as if the wolves had indeed sniffed his belongings and perhaps turned them over on the packed snow, but the animals had not destroyed the precious items as Conall had feared.

He crouched down on the cusp of the bank for several moments, listening intently for any sound that might indicate that the bloodthirsty beasts were near. When all remained still, Conall dropped over the rise and scrambled through the snow to his pack.

He vowed to kill every last gray wolf in Scotland when he looked down upon the satchel and saw the dark puddle run off one bottom corner into a well of yellow snow.

Conall jerked the pack up by its strap and held it away from him, looking at it distastefully and biting off whispered curses.

"Nasty beasts," he muttered, setting the pack back down in a clean patch of snow. He sheathed his sword and dropped to his haunches over the bag, quickly undoing the ties and peering inside. Satisfied that the contents still seemed wrapped securely in the pieces of oilcloth he'd packed them in, he allowed himself to pause with his thoughts.

Evelyn Godewin Buchanan—Angus Buchanan's own . . . niece? *Granddaughter*? Conall felt a wave of dizziness come over him so that the snow on the bank seemed to advance and retreat in quick turn. Sweet God in Heaven—'twas rumored that Angus Buchanan's daughter had fled to England those

many years ago with Minerva Buchanan and had
born a girl child. Could Evelyn be her? Now alone
with Conall in the deepest, most dangerous thickness of the forest in high winter, and the Buchanan
had no knowledge of it?

Conall wanted to shout, to laugh, to vomit on his
boots from the nervous excitement that threatened to shake his bones from his flesh.

*Only heartache and toil shall you reap, until a Buc-
hanan bairn is born to rule the MacKerrick clan . . .*

Conall thought of his crippled and dying town,
his people sick and starving from the black curse
that had smothered them these nearly two score
years. He thought of the seasons of empty animal
shelters and the smell of diseased cattle flesh being
consumed on the charnel fires; of grain stalks
moldering in flooded fields; of the dry, baked
riverbeds in summer, where no fish swam to spawn.

He thought of the haggard faces and thin bodies
of the people in his care, a people who had looked
faithfully to him for longer than loyalty should
have bidden them. He thought of Nonna and the
wee girl bairn.

The weight of it all was crushing.

And now, the hag who had once damned them
all had carried back with her the very cure for this
evil fever and delivered it directly into Conall's
trembling hands.

One of those trembling hands went to the stiff
leather knot tied 'round his neck. He gently rolled
the small lump against the knuckle of his forefinger
with his thumb.

Conall had lain with no other woman save
Nonna the whole of his life, and he'd not lain with
even his wife since the night she'd taken his seed

which had bravely become their child. He closed
his eyes against the pain that welled up inside him,
the shame.

Conall pinched the bridge of his nose and drew
a deep, shuddering breath before rising. He slung
his bow, quiver, and pack over one shoulder and
drew his sword once more. Gaining the crest of the
bank in five great strides, he then paused to look at
his uncle's hunting cottage, thinking of the possibilities that rested with the woman beyond its sod walls.

Evelyn Godewin Buchanan. *Eve.*

Conall began the short walk across the trampled
clearing, his mouth set.

The slain gray was gone.

Conall halted and stared at the shallow depression
where the dead wolf had lain only moments ago.
There was not a drop of blood to be seen against the
flattened snow, although Conall had plunged his
sword into the beast's chest and the red flow had
painted the ground. He looked down at his blade:
clean and gleaming in the fading daylight.

No drag marks leading to the forest. Not even a
single wiry gray hair.

A gusting wind barreled through the clearing
and the night seemed to lean over the wood suddenly. Conall shivered, and although he was no
coward, an awesome feeling of lonely longing
wrapped arms about him on the frigid breeze and
licked his icy cheek obscenely. Conall had the immediate urge to run to the hut and bolt himself
and Eve inside.

He forced himself to walk calmly, though, backward and facing the rippling darkness of the forest.
He felt behind him for the door and was grateful
when it pushed open easily.

Conall stepped inside and quickly shut out the single, mournful, high-pitched howl, calling to him through the twilight.

The highlander stumbled backward into the hut and slammed the door shut, slinging a bow and a large pack to the floor and leaning against the door while he scrambled to drop the brace in the brackets. When he turned to face her, Evelyn noticed the paleness of his lips, his furrowed brow.

"Have the grays returned?" she asked, praying silently that they had not—even one night alone in the small hut with this man would be too many. Evelyn felt she should advise him to be on his way quickly. For his own safety, of course.

And possibly her own, from the haunted look in his eyes.

He shook his head as if coming out of a daydream. "Nae." MacKerrick scooped up the pack and walked past Evelyn and Alinor to sit upon the low stool. It piqued Evelyn how the man so quickly made himself at ease in her home. He set the bag between his boots and did not look up at her as he began to rifle through its contents. "Even the one I took is gone."

"Gone?" Evelyn frowned as Alinor slid from beneath her hand and ambled cautiously nearer the highlander, circling his stool and sniffing the floor around him.

"Aye. Gone." He pulled a small jug from the pack and attacked the cork with his back teeth. He spit the dislodged stopper into one palm and lifted the jug to his mouth, drinking deeply. While he was occupied, Alinor sidled closer and began sniffing the bottom of his pack in earnest.

"What do you mean, 'gone'?" Evelyn demanded. "Alinor, to me."

MacKerrick lowered the jug and rested it on his knee. "I mean, the gray wolf . . . I just killed . . . is . . . *gone.*" He looked at her curiously and then at the jug on his leg. He held it out to her abruptly. "Mead?"

Evelyn nearly refused it. But the opportunity to drink something other than melted snow—anything but melted snow—was too tempting.

She reached for the jug with both hands. "Thank you." She paused before drinking, although the sweet, mellow scent coming from the mouth of the vessel was enough to flood her mouth with saliva.

Alinor was now rudely scratching at the man's pack.

"*Alinor!* To me!" she commanded.

The highlander glanced down at the wolf, then waved a careless hand at Evelyn. "Drink your mead, Eve. She canna harm it."

Evelyn was not at all certain she appreciated being told how to handle her animal, but she raised the jug to her lips and let the mead flood her mouth—explosions of rich, tangy honey— while the highlander addressed the wolf directly in his low brogue.

"But if you *do* harm it, wolf piss or nae wolf piss, I'll have your hide for a new one."

The delicious mead in Evelyn's throat backed up into her nose and she choked. "Sir," she gasped, coughing and wiping at her mouth. "Language, if you please!"

"What?" The man looked at her mildly. "One of the bloody beasts pissed on me pack. I doona wish

for yours to take out hard feelings against my per-
sonal belongings."

Evelyn could not stop her chirp of laughter, but
she quickly covered her mouth, shocked at her
own crudeness, and handed the jug back to its
owner with no little regret.

The highlander grinned at her. "I'd be thankful
to trade a taste of the meat I smelled you cooking
for the swallow of mead you've enjoyed, Eve."

Evelyn's gaze flew to the shelf on the wall and she
winced. She and Alinor could hardly afford to
share what little food they possessed with a man
who would soon be leaving them, but the sweetness
of the mead still lingering on her tongue roused
her conscience.

"I'm not certain 'twould suit you, sir—'tis rather . . .
dry." She hesitated. "A bit burnt, as well." She tried to
laugh. "I'm afraid as a cook I'm no prize."

The man looked at her as though she was daft.
"I'm hungry, lass. Would you deny me food because you doona wish me to criticize your cooking
skills? Vain woman—I wouldna care a fig were it
horsemeat and you served it raw."

Must he find a way to insult her with every breath?

"Very well." Evelyn let her lips curve in a small
smile as she crossed the floor to the shelf. She
picked up a scrawny strip at first, but then replaced
it in favor of a longer chunk—thick in the middle
and guaranteed to be a bit . . . *chewy.*

She faced the highlander once more and he
took the piece eagerly. "Here you are, then. Enjoy."

MacKerrick bit into the strip and chewed and
chewed . . . and then looked at Eve, his mouth
slack around the half-masticated wad of meat.

"Iss hors-meet, innit?"

Chapter Four

Evelyn did not wish to open her eyes. She could tell by the numbness on the tip of her nose that the peat fire was exhausted and the hut was cave-cold, but in the little box bed under the woolen horse blanket and snuggled with Alinor, 'twas toasty. She felt as if she'd not gone to bed at all, was weary to her bones still, even after a night of unusually peaceful sleep. Evelyn wanted only to drift away once more, where 'twas always warm and quiet and no wolves howled. Fire be damned.

If she opened her eyes, she would also have to deal with Conall MacKerrick once more, and she blamed her unusually large deficit of energy on the highlander's arrogant presence.

Evelyn had allowed him the shelter for the night, only because she could not in good conscience demand he expose himself to the threat of the grays on a night journey. Although "allowed" might have been too generous to her pride—the highlander had not asked her permission to stay in the hut, only nonchalantly made a pallet out of Alinor's pen with pine boughs and his long length of plaid. He'd then simply lain down upon it with a mumbled, "G'night, Eve" and was asleep.

So 'twas a choice of "Eve" sleeping out of doors or climbing into the box bed with Alinor, which Evelyn did after several moments spent staring confusedly toward the pens. At least she was not fearful of her virtue with the wolf at her side, and Alinor ensured a cozy companion to huddle with. Evelyn had fallen asleep instantly, it seemed.

"Good girl," Evelyn whispered and snaked a hand from beneath the blanket to tangle her fingers in the wolf's thick ruff. She encountered bony rump instead, and smoothed her palm up Alinor's haunch, letting her lips curve in a contented, exhausted smile.

The smile fell from her lips when her palm moved onto rough, warm linen, radiating heat from the hard flesh beneath. Evelyn's eyes snapped open.

"Good morn to you, Eve," the highlander said, his face inches from her own, Evelyn's fingers resting on his shoulder.

Evelyn was so shocked that she could not speak. She took quick, mental inventory of her person: belly, warm; thighs, warm; feet and legs, warm and weighted down. She was facing the highlander fully on her side and she raised her head to peer down the length of her body.

Alinor was curled across the end of the bed, atop the woolen blanket, the highlander's plaid, and both Evelyn's legs.

The traitoress.

Her eyes flicked back to Conall MacKerrick's. "What are you doing in my bed, sir?" she asked in a low, calm voice.

"Gettin' warm," he trilled in his equally low brogue and gave her a sleepy smile.

Those two words—their meaning deeper than his simple answer—combined with the man's big body to cause Evelyn's stomach to lurch uncomfortably. And so she did the first thing that came to mind.

She slowly, languorously, gently, placed both hands on the man's thick, muscled chest, returned his smile, and shoved.

The highlander disappeared over the side of the bed with a strangled cry and a grunt. Alinor lifted her head to peer down onto the floor and then flopped back across Evelyn's legs with a great sigh.

"Why, good morn to *you*, as well, Conall," came the highlander's disembodied voice. "Did you sleep well? Oh, that's *grand*! My thanks to you for keeping me warm through the night, and I do apologize for snorin' in your ear like a bull elk. Terrible rude o' me."

Evelyn rose up on one elbow to look down at the man on the cold, hard floor. "Collect your things, sir, and be gone. You've taken enough liberties with my person and I'll not tolerate it a moment longer." She started to lie back down but paused. "And I do not snore—'twas Alinor."

MacKerrick snorted and sat up with a groan. "I've a hard time believing a great black wolf could make a sound like a duck being strangled, but as you wish, Eve."

Evelyn frowned crossly and turned over on the thin ticking to face the wall. Already she could feel the hut's chill creeping beneath the covers. She just wanted to go back to sleep. God help her, she had never been so tired.

The sheep bleated from her pen and Evelyn cried out indignantly as Alinor trampled her to turn 'round and bound from the bed. *Both* her legs ached this morn, an unwelcome change.

"Och, back . . . *back*, you beast!" MacKerrick chastised from somewhere over Evelyn's shoulder. The sheep bleated again and then Evelyn heard the scrape of wood and felt a rude rush of frigid air before the hut door closed and all was blessedly still.

She closed her eyes, only barely acknowledging once more how unusually poor she felt. She really ought to rise—'twas scandalous to lie about, drowsy as she was, while a strange man came and went as he pleased. She ought to get up and see him on his way, and that he didn't abscond with the rest of the meat—'twas all she and Alinor had to eat. In truth, 'twas all they'd had for weeks.

But she didn't care at that moment. She had no energy. Her hip and leg pained her more than they had in days. She was cold and tired and wanted only to sleep . . .

Conall watched the great black wolf bound off into the forest and he followed in her tracks at a more leisurely pace, tugging the sheep along on her tether. He relieved himself on the edge of the wood, letting the shaggy little sheep nose around in the dry undercanopy of a wide pine.

Dawn had come, but Conall didn't bother looking for the bright rays of morning sun in the east. The sky was low, thick, and the color of the gray tree trunks surrounding him. Weather coming. A slight breeze caused the branches overhead to sway, sending echoing crackles ricocheting though the wood, the sound of ice everywhere.

Finished with his business, Conall led the sheep back toward the hut. The small enclosure to the left of the house was covered over with snow and so Conall was forced to spend the better part of an hour digging it out. He sent the sheep inside with a swat to her rear and kicked over the small, half-rotten trough to empty it of yet more white stuff. He'd have to melt water for her in a bit. For now, the animal was content to explore beneath the snow with her soft brown muzzle.

Conall secured the pen and stood looking at the hut. No smoke came from the roof yet and Conall was mildly surprised and a little perturbed. The long, sloping room had been cold enough when he'd left Eve abed—'twould be like ice since he'd opened the door, for certain.

Mayhap she was waiting for Conall to start the fire. He thought about that for a moment. He'd wanted to do that very thing when she'd tossed him out of bed, but by her prickly behavior, Conall had thought it best to let her be and get accustomed to the fact that he was still at the hut. Obviously, he'd been mistaken, but he would be more than pleased to build a fire for Eve Buchanan, aye.

In fact, he'd do it right now.

Alinor came trotting out of the wood, sparkling with snow, and met Conall at the door. The wolf looked up at him expectantly.

"You're a *wolf*," Conall whispered. "Do you nae wish to be out in the wild?" He swept an arm around to indicate the clearing. "'Tis nice, is it nae?"

Alinor raised a paw and scratched once at the door, then looked at Conall again.

Conall sighed and shoved the door open, admitting the beast reluctantly. He followed her inside and left the door ajar in preparation for laying the fire.

Conall frowned when he saw that Eve was still abed—Alinor had swiftly rejoined her with a graceful leap. He told himself that she might not have drifted off to sleep quickly last night, a strange man being about. He stacked some rotting peat on a loose pile of kindling, and smoke soon curled toward the ceiling.

That chore done, he stood near the bed, looking down at Eve's still, slight form. He didn't wish to wake her, but he could not locate the hut's fine, large crock and he had need to water the sheep. Eve's back was to the room and Alinor had her wide head resting on the curve of Eve's hip.

"Eve?" Conall called softly and reached out a hand to place it on her shoulder. In a flash, Alinor growled and snapped her powerful jaws but a hairsbreadth from Conall's smallest finger.

"You bitch," Conall hissed, snatching his hand back and glaring at the animal.

Alinor's lips quivered with a final, breathy growl before she laid her head down again.

"Eve," Conall called more loudly, keeping a wary eye on the wolf.

The form under the covers twitched. "Go away." She sounded more than half asleep.

"I've need to get the sheep water and us some food—where's the pot you cook in, lass?"

She didn't reply for several moments, so that Conall was readying to turn her over himself—and wrestle the wolf to do so, more likely than nae. He was growing concerned at the woman's lethargy.

From their meeting last night, he hadn't gotten the impression that Eve Buchanan was a layabout.

But then she did speak. "I don't cook in the pot. Cook on the spit. Meat over there." She raised an arm from beneath the blanket to point past Conall and when she did, her loose sleeve slid up past her elbow. "On the shelf."

Conall's head drew back—the woman's spindly right arm was mottled with purple and green bruises.

She drew the covers back over her shoulder, hiding her arm from view. "Now, do go 'way."

"What happened to your arm, lass?" Conall asked carefully. "Did you fall?"

He saw her head move slightly, a jerky nod. "Through the smoke hole. When I found the hut."

Conall felt his worry ease, although with bruises like that, the lass was lucky she hadn't broken anything. He crossed the floor to the shelf and surveyed the pitiful supply of dry-cooked horsemeat. "When was that, Eve?" he asked conversationally over his shoulder. "How long have you been at Ronan's hut?"

A long pause, then, "I know not—a month? Mayhap . . . longer."

Conall froze. The bruises should have long since faded. He thought of her sudden lethargy.

Not wishing to have his arm removed, Conall moved quickly to the door once more and opened it wide.

"Come on, you bea—*Alinor*," he amended, gesturing through the portal. He had to get rid of the wolf in order to confirm his dire suspicion.

The wolf looked at him disinterestedly.

Conall stepped through the doorway. "Come on,

then." He slapped his hands on his thighs, feeling the ultimate fool. "To me, Alinor. Lovely, to me."

The wolf unfolded herself slowly, stretched leisurely, and at last stepped from the bed. Crossing the floor with an inky swagger, she stood before Conall, still inside the hut. She looked as though she knew exactly what the man was about and had no intention whatsoever of exiting the house.

But fate chose to smile upon Conall for once, and sent a rabbit to bumble into the clearing at just that moment.

Alinor was through the doorway and across the narrow clearing in a black blur.

Conall ducked back inside and closed the door. After pausing for only an instant, narrow-eyed, he dropped the bar in place—just in case. Then he quickly crossed to the bed, taking hold of Eve's shoulder and pulling her gently onto her back.

"What are you doing, sir?" she demanded groggily, and Conall noticed then the deep purple circles beneath her eyes. "Unhand me at once."

"Shh . . . Eve, I must look inside your mouth, lass." He reached his fingertips to either side of her face.

"What? You'll do no such thing." She tried to turn her head away weakly.

But Conall easily pushed her lips away from her teeth with his thumbs and what he saw in that brief moment confirmed his fear.

Eve began to struggle in earnest and Conall released her, sitting down on the edge of the bed. "Eve, listen to me, lass—you are verra ill. You've had naught but horsemeat to eat since you've come?"

Eve's eyes narrowed over flushed cheeks. "What

else is there to eat, I'd like to know. I'm not ill,
MacKerrick, only tired."

Conall nodded, not wanting to further upset her.
"Where's the pot, lass?"

"Buried."

Conall blinked. "Buried?"

"I cooked all the meat I could, put it in the pot,
and buried it. But there's not much left to be had,"
Eve answered wearily. She sighed as if in defeat.
"Under the large, flat rock, straightaway from the
door. Mayhap twenty paces."

Conall was stunned for a moment by the woman's
ingenuity. He'd had no idea until now how dire
Evelyn Buchanan's situation had been when she'd
found Ronan's hut. 'Twas little wonder she was terri-
torial over the small sod house.

"Well done, lass." He smiled at her. "You just take
your rest and I'll return in a bit." Conall kept the
smile on his face even when Eve only frowned and
rolled away to face the wall once more.

He had to hurry.

It seemed to Evelyn that no sooner had Mac-
Kerrick left her be at last, he was immediately returned to the hut, making a cacophony of racket.
She dozed during this time, frowning to herself at
the aching in her joints. Once, Alinor rudely shoved
her cold, wet nose into the warm crook of Evelyn's
neck, but quickly retreated after MacKerrick chastised the wolf with a string of Gaelic spoken too
quickly for Evelyn to decipher. She drifted away
once more.

Then he was pulling at her shoulder again, coaxing

her to roll over, his hand like a branding iron through her thin sleeve.

"Eve," he called, his palm skimming down her arm to her hand. He molded her fingers around a warm, smooth object. "Take hold of it now, and drink."

Evelyn opened her heavy eyelids to look first into Conall MacKerrick's face and then at the object he'd placed in her hand. 'Twas an earthen mug, steam rising deliciously off the reddish liquid within and releasing a scent that was familiar to Eve, but one that she could not put name to.

"What is it?" she asked, drawing herself up on one elbow. She noted with a queer hitch in her stomach the way the highlander had snaked one long arm behind her shoulders expertly to bolster her—his muscled bicep felt like a stone against her back.

"Tea."

Evelyn cast him a suspicious glance and sniffed the steam from the mug. "It smells . . . odd. What sort of tea?"

"'Tis good. You need it. Drink it."

"Tell me what it is," she demanded.

MacKerrick drew his head back. "You doona trust me?"

"Well, why will you not tell me—"

"It's nae *horsemeat*," he cut her off pointedly, and Evelyn felt properly chastised. She noticed that, up close, the highlander's amber eyes were ringed with dark green, and his lips were full and oddly soft-looking for one of such savage appearance. His mouth fascinated her, and she wanted to study it while falling back asleep . . .

"*Eve*," MacKerrick insisted.

She blinked, realized she had nearly dozed off while sitting up and frowned into MacKerrick's wide, concerned face.

"What's wrong with me?"

He brought the cup in her hand—his fingers guiding them—to her mouth. "Drink," was his only answer.

Evelyn did as she was told and sipped. The liquid was warm and thin and . . . absolutely the most intoxicatingly delicious tea she'd ever drunk. The beverage was still quite warm but, after her first hesitant swallow, it was as if she could not help but gulp down the entire mug.

She lowered the mug with a gasp to catch her breath and looked at MacKerrick.

He was smiling. "I told you 'twas good. More?"

"There's more?" Evelyn asked in disbelief. "More" was a concept she'd put completely from her mind since leaving England.

MacKerrick took the cup with a chuckle and refilled it from a tall clay urn, set near the fire pit. "A whole wood full of it, lass." He returned to the side of the bed and handed her the mug.

Evelyn raised it to her lips and gulped and immediately regretted it as her mouth, tongue and throat were washed in the boiling hot liquid.

"Easy," the highlander chastised. "It hasna had time to cool."

Evelyn's eyes watered from her scalded mouth but she only blew on the surface of the tea.

"Pine," MacKerrick said.

Evelyn glanced at him, saw he was watching her mouth when she pursed her lips to blow. "Pardon?"

"The tea—pine needles. With a splash of mead for sweetness," he added with a grin. "You've had nae greens—nae fruits—for weeks, lass." He gestured to her arm. "Those bruises, the sleepiness . . . you've need of fortification."

She raised an eyebrow. "And this simple tea will cure all that?"

Conall nodded. "Most of it. Along with what's in yonder fine pot."

Evelyn looked to the fire again, still blowing on the delicious brew, and saw the large pottery crock in which she'd buried the horsemeat. Its lid was barely tilted and the tiniest wisps of steam were only just escaping.

MacKerrick rose from the bed and drew a short blade from his belt. Crouching down on his haunches, he wrapped his hand in the hem of his long, tuniclike shirt and moved the lid of the crock away. Evelyn caught a glimpse of rich, brown liquid and mayhap—could it be?—a speck of green, as the highlander stirred the concoction with his dagger.

He replaced the lid and looked up at Evelyn, wiping his blade on a rag before sheathing it. "Stew," he offered.

Evelyn's throat tightened with a welling of emotion that stemmed from both relief and desire. She sipped at the tea and noticed the tremors in both hands and arms. *Stew. My God.* A wave of unexpected—and very unwelcome—nausea misted her face, chest, and back with perspiration.

"You'll be fine in a day or so," MacKerrick was saying to her now, approaching the box bed. The angles of his hawklike face were softer than she had seen them since meeting the highlander. He truly was a handsome man.

"Thank you," Evelyn managed to croak in a low voice. She was grateful for the care this large stranger had shown her, but his generosity also laid a heavy burden on her. How could she continue to demand that MacKerrick depart the hut when he had quite possibly saved her life? But if 'twas she who must go, to where would she and Alinor hie? They would most certainly starve on their own. 'Twas worse than ironic.

There was a time when Evelyn would have been terrified of the dilemma she now faced. She was an only child reared by her father, a lord, and her every need had been met, often before she recognized she had a need. She had been surrounded by friends and rarely quarreled with anyone. Betrothed to her fondest childhood companion, she was slated for a life of endless privilege. But she had thrown it all away to join the hellish priory, where no one was her friend. Where she was condemned verbally and punished in terrible physical ways for simply being who and what she was. It was no religious haven to escape the frightening unknown of marriage and motherhood as she'd hoped—indeed, Evelyn's fear was made worse by the young women the priory took in, unwed and with child. Evelyn herself was forced to assist countless births, and the outcomes of the majority of them were not good.

Life became a practice of fear for her, and her every thought was consumed with planning her escape. That bright dream was smashed to pieces, though, when her father had been killed and she was summoned to the home of the man she'd scorned. Her only chance had been to take up with the old witch she'd met there and run.

And she had survived it. Survived it all till now, on her own. And so she was not afraid to drag this impasse before the large highlander, now feeding Alinor bits of horsemeat from his fingertips. Mayhap regretful, but not afraid.

"Sir," she began.

The highlander glanced up. "Aye, lass? Are you needing more tea?"

"Nay, thank you." Evelyn noted with chagrin that the man seemed recovered of his manners since their initial meeting. "We cannot continue in this fashion. Surely you understand that."

MacKerrick raised his eyebrows. "I'm sorry to say that I doona."

"We . . . I mean to say—" Evelyn hesitated. "We cannot both keep residence in this cottage. Together," she emphasized.

"And why is that, now?" he asked easily, wiping his hands on his shirt and moving to where a wooden bowl and dipper rested near the bubbling crock of stew.

"'Tis entirely improper, that's why." Evelyn watched him remove the lid from the crock once more. "Before traveling to Scotland with Min—*my aunt,* Minerva, I was dedicated to a priory. Before that, I was a lady in my father's home. I cannot hope to maintain my dignity whilst living in such small quarters with a man I know naught of."

"I see," the highlander said thoughtfully. He ladled stew into the bowl, but said no more.

Evelyn sipped from her mug, cleared her throat. "Well . . . what do you propose we do?"

MacKerrick rose with the bowl and brought it to the bedside. He took the mug from Evelyn's hands and replaced it with the bowl of steaming, fragrant stew.

"I *propose* we do naught," he said.

"But—" Evelyn began.

MacKerrick held up a palm. "I am *the MacKerrick*, Eve—chief of my clan. My honor is as steadfast as any English laird. *Especially* to Buchanan kin," he said. "I canna allow you to leave for . . . for fear of your safety. And I came to the hut to hunt—a thing I do well. My townsfolk are starving, Eve. I canna fail them."

For some reason, his speech sent chills spiraling around Evelyn's spine. But he was not done. The stew in her hand was untouched, forgotten, as his voice continued to mesmerize her.

"There is weather coming—a fierce storm, do I read the signs correctly. Neither of us would survive a journey of more than a half day." He bent to pour more tea into the mug, sipped thoughtfully from it himself, then looked at her.

"It may be a long, long winter, Eve, and I canna tell you that there is chance we will soon part company. But on my word, you'll be safe here with me."

Evelyn did not know what to say. Her gaze fell onto the wooden bowl in her hands and so she raised it to her lips and sipped from its rim, her eyes catching the colorful bits of peas and carrots and flecks of barley caught in the rich gravy. God in Heaven, it was divine! She closed her eyes, held the soup in her mouth for a long moment, savoring it, before swallowing it.

"The stew is delicious," she told him quietly. "Thank you."

"You're welcome to it, Eve," he said solemnly. "'Twas you who provided the meat, saving me from setting out on a hunt straight away. I'm in your debt."

Evelyn could not believe she felt a flush creeping

over her face at the simple compliment and so she attributed it to the wonderfully warm stew.

"What say you then, Eve?" MacKerrick asked, stoking the fire with Eve's pointed stick and no longer looking at her. "Do we stand together?"

A thought occurred to Evelyn then, one that was oddly disturbing. "Are you married, sir?"

The highlander paused in his movements for only a blink of time. "I was," he said mildly. "She's dead."

"Oh." Evelyn sipped from the bowl again, sucking a chunk of carrot into her mouth and chewing to give her time to cover her out-of-place relief that the large man did not have a wife eagerly awaiting his return. "I'm sorry."

The highlander only nodded curtly and did not meet her eyes.

'Tis still painful for him, Evelyn thought to herself and the realization of it swayed her just enough. A man in mourning, hunting to feed his villagers. Mayhap he was nobler than Evelyn had once thought him to be.

"Well, you most certainly cannot sleep in the bed with me again," she said, a bit loudly for their heretofore quiet conversation.

The highlander nodded again, his attention still focused on the fire pit. "Agreed."

"And no one can be aware of my presence," Evelyn said suddenly, as earlier worries of a Buchanan happening along sprang into her mind once more. "I'll . . . I'll not have my reputation ruined."

"'Tis unlikely we'll be takin' company, Eve," he said with a wry lift of an eyebrow. "But I'll nae tell anyone, if you so wish it."

Evelyn pressed her lips together. "All right, then. Agreed."

Then he did look up at her. "I have a condition of my own, if you would."

Evelyn swallowed. "Yea?"

"That you call me Conall. Or MacKerrick, at the very least." He grinned. "'Sir this' and 'sir that' has me lookin' over my shoulder for an English bloke."

Evelyn felt a small smile lift the corners of her mouth. "Very well. MacKerrick it is."

MacKerrick grinned wider, winked cheekily, and then drank from the mug.

Evelyn's heart pounded and she ate her stew.

Chapter Five

Conall's prediction regarding the storm was correct. By early afternoon, the flakes had begun to fall, and by the time evening traded the steely sky for a darker blanket of nightfall, a fresh layer of white covered the clearing, with fat, wet flakes falling as fast and hard as rain and showing no sign of slowing. The temperature had fallen almost as fast as the snow, setting an icy crust about everything beyond the hut's rickety wooden door. The wind called to them in whistling whispers through the cracks and crevices, as if coaxing them to venture out of doors into the midst of the wicked storm. Even the grays were silent.

Inside Ronan's hut, though, 'twas peaceful and warm. The peat fire smoldered happily and a small oil lamp produced from Conall's pack lent a mellow glow to the primitive walls and shaggy ceiling. The great black wolf—Conall was almost accustomed to the beast having a proper name—had taken up position lying in front of the sheep's small pen in the lower part of the house, her long, sleek back pressed against the slats. Conall's sheep mirrored the wolf's pose beyond the gate, the two animals back to back.

'Twas one of the queerest things Conall had ever witnessed.

Conall himself sat on the low stool near the fire, twisting thin, springy branches into a trap. The stew he'd made earlier would last the hut's occupants a full day, mayhap two, but he would need to be about catching fresh meat straightaway after the storm lifted.

In the box bed to his right, Eve slept on. Looking at her lying so peacefully caused an uncomfortable sensation in Conall's gut—'twas reminiscent of caring for Nonna those last months of her life, when she was so weak—and so he tried to keep his mind on the task at hand: bending twigs, twisting twine. 'Twas repetitive, meditative work. He needed a smaller blade to twist a particularly short section of twine and knotted whip together and remembered Eve's sorry, broken dagger.

Setting the nearly finished trap on the floor, he rose from the stool quietly and moved to the shelf. He found the blade lying where she'd left it, but his fingers stopped short of the handle as Conall noticed the rough saddle bag hanging limp beneath the shelf. Conall would have thought it empty save for the pointy corner pushing out the rough material below the flap.

He glanced over his shoulder toward the bed— Eve still slept, with her back to the room.

He lifted the pack from the peg and returned to the stool. Reaching inside, he found a smooth leather surface, square, and of a thickness of his palms stacked together. He pulled the object out carefully.

'Twas indeed a square of richly prepared leather, a thin thong holding the two edges together, an intricate tangle of grapevines burnt into the tanned skin. Conall undid the tie and the fine skin opened easily, revealing its content of bound pages of thick vellum. Conall's eyebrows rose at the costly piece and his gaze caressed the fanciful squiggles and colorful decoration of the topmost sheet. He turned the page and was rewarded with more illustration—the entire page was covered over with beautiful swirls and tight, black writing. Conall was fascinated. He let his fingertips skim over the page.

"'Tis quite rude to go through a person's belongings without their leave."

Eve's quiet voice startled Conall so that he jumped and the weighty package of vellum and leather slipped from his hands.

The woman gasped and stretched out an arm as if to catch the piece before it hit the floor, but of course she was too far away.

"Sir!" Eve chastised. "Would that you take greater care with that manuscript! 'Tis costly, not to mention holy."

Conall felt his face heat as he carefully retrieved the . . . manuscript, was it?

"I thought you were sleeping," he barked, embarrassed at being caught admiring the item, and of dropping it.

"Obviously."

"What is it?" Conall asked, turning the manuscript over in his hands.

"A book of the Bible." She paused. "Do you know what the Bible is?"

Conall rolled his eyes. "O' course I know what

the Bible is, woman. We have a priest come to our town once a year, regular. We're nae savages."

"Oh." Eve sat up in bed. "I beg your pardon, then." She sounded much better to Conall. "If you don't mind, please put it back in the satchel. 'Tis most delicate."

Conall made no move to replace the manuscript. He pulled the covers apart once more and continued to study it. "Where did you get it?"

"The priory where I was interred," Eve said brusquely. "'Twas the work of the monks to produce the books for the priests."

"'Tis the Gospel?" Conall ran his fingertips over a page again, enchanted.

"The Song of Solomon. Now, please—"

"The monks *gave* this to you?"

Eve did not reply right away and so Conall turned his head to look at her. Eve's mouth was pressed into a thin line and her cheeks were pink.

"Well, not actually. I, er . . ."

"You *stole* it!" Conall grinned. "Tsk-tsk, Sister Eve."

"Do not call me that," Eve snapped. "I was . . . *studying it* when I received word that my father was dying. It accompanied me on my journey quite accidentally. I simply never returned to the priory after my father's death, so . . ." She shrugged and looked away. "I didn't *steal* it."

"Ah. Of course nae." Conall knew his grin remained. "Can you read it?"

Eve nodded. "Certainly."

Conall rose from the stool and approached the bed. Eve frowned when he sat on the edge of the ticking, but he ignored it and handed the packet of pages to her.

"What?" She took the manuscript carefully into her hands.

"Read me a piece of it."

Eve pinkened again. "I . . . another time, mayhap, MacKerrick. In truth, I am still weary. My eyes—"

"Just a bit," Conall pressed. He leaned over and flipped the cover back. "I would hear this Solomon's Song."

Eve sighed. "Very well." She cleared her throat. "'The Song of Songs, which is Solomon's. Let him kiss me with the kisses of his mouth, for thy love is better than wine. Because of the savor of thy good ointments, thy name is as ointment poured forth, therefore do the virgins love thee.'" She paused.

"Go on," Conall urged.

"'Draw me, we will run after thee: the king hath brought men into his chambers: we will be glad and rejoice in thee, we will remember thy love more than wine—'" Eve suddenly closed the book. "I think that's enough."

Conall's heart pounded in his chest and his hands took a tremor where they rested on his thighs. The effect of Eve's soft voice speaking such beautiful words—sensual words—stunned him.

He wanted more.

"Nae." He reached for the book. "Continue . . ."

Eve snatched the manuscript out of his reach. "I tire, MacKerrick."

Conall wanted to shout at her, to demand she reveal more of the mystery of the strangely erotic passage, but he caught his impatience by the scruff of its neck.

"On the morrow?" He tried to temper his anxious tone. "Mayhap you could read a piece each day. 'Twould be a fine way to pass the time."

"Mayhap," Eve said evasively and would not meet his eyes. "For now, I would like to get up and have a cup of tea if there is any made."

Conall rose from the mattress immediately. "I'll fetch it for you."

Evelyn threw the horse blanket back and the cool air of the hut washed over her bare ankles. She scooted to the edge of the bed, her cheeks still tingling from the verses she'd read, and carefully fastened the cover of the manuscript. The silence of the cottage seemed weighty.

What had she been thinking, reading to the Mac-Kerrick from the most provocative book of the Bible? But the large highlander gave no outward sign that the piece had discomfited him in any way—he only squatted by the fire, pouring steaming pine tea into the mug for her.

Alinor ambled over to the bed from the far side of the hut and sat down against Evelyn's legs, the once-jaunty pink bow around her middle now undone, dirtied and dragging the ground. Left alone in her pen, the sheep bleated pitifully. The wolf raised a rear leg and scratched in earnest at her side.

"I know, lovely," Evelyn said regretfully, patting Alinor's wide head. "I will see to you in a moment."

MacKerrick was standing near them now, holding forth the fresh mug of tea. Evelyn took it with a murmured thanks, and tried not to pull away too quickly when their fingertips touched.

"What is she needing?" MacKerrick asked.

Evelyn sipped tentatively and then cleared her throat. She was surprised at how much better she felt. "Her wound wants cleaning and her bandage changed. It looked nearly healed yesterday. Mayhap she'll not need a bandage at all, now." Evelyn was relieved the Song of Solomon was no longer the topic of conversation. She slid her feet into her shoes.

MacKerrick grunted. "I'll have a look at it."

"Nay." Evelyn stood, the mug in one hand and the manuscript in the other. She fought back a little twist of dizziness. "I doubt she'd allow you. Any matter, she is my animal, and I would care for her myself."

A frown darkened his features as his eyes swept her body from crown to slippers and back again. Evelyn felt oddly exposed by his close scrutiny.

"I doona think you've the strength yet, Eve, to be—"

Evelyn cut him off as she brushed past him to the stool. "You are not my keeper, MacKerrick." She set the mug on the low seat and took hold of her abandoned saddle bag, straightening with caution lest she topple over into the fire pit and prove him right.

She shook open the pack and slid the priceless book inside, a pang of guilt at her snappishness tempering her next words. "I owe you a great deal for your kindness, but I will not be dictated to. I left that life behind when I made the decision not to return to the priory." She met his eyes for only a moment. "You may be chief of the MacKerrick clan, but you are not my lord."

She turned from him to replace the bag on its hook below the shelf, fully expecting a belligerent reply from the Scot.

"Very well, Eve. But you must tell me if you come

over weary. I'll assist you if you have a need. There's nae shame in it."

Evelyn paused, her back to MacKerrick. She had not been prepared for that response at all. She reached for her dagger and the bowl of moss from the shelf before her. Hearing slurping noises, she turned.

MacKerrick was once more crouched at the fire, this time over the crock which held the stew, and he was holding forth the long wooden spoon to Alinor, who licked it greedily.

The highlander glanced up at Evelyn. "She's takin' a fancy to me, though, I vow." The sharp planes of his face softened into a boyish grin.

Evelyn couldn't help the twitch of her own lips as she reached overhead to pull two lengths of cloth from the ceiling. "She fancies your stew is all."

"Mayhap." MacKerrick shrugged good-naturedly and returned the spoon to the crock to stir it. Alinor hedged closer to his side, sniffing longingly at the rich aroma. "I am a fine cook, so I canna fault her. We must begin somewhere."

He replaced the lid on the crock and rested the spoon across it. "That's all you get, beastie," he said to Alinor and the wolf lay down meekly near him. MacKerrick looked up at Eve and she could see the remains of his smile in his sparkling eyes. "I reckon if I feed her, care for her long enough, perhaps she may become fond of me, as well."

Evelyn looked at him for a long moment, trying to divine if MacKerrick's neat speech did not have a double meaning. But a voice from somewhere in her mind warned her against dwelling upon such things and so Evelyn broke gaze with the highlander to sit upon the floor with her supplies.

"To me, Alinor."

Conall wasted no time in dragging the low stool closer to where Eve sat before the great black wolf. He held her abandoned mug in both palms, his elbows on his knees, and sipped at the cooling brew. From his vantage point, to her side and slightly behind her, he could easily see Eve's pale, graceful hands as they flitted over Alinor's lumpy side, as well as the long curve of Eve's neck, the bones and delicate cording in sharp relief when she turned her head a bit this way and that.

His last remarks had given her pause, and Conall cautioned himself to move slowly. But he'd never had need to woo a woman before. Nonna had been promised to him since her birth, and he now felt at a great disadvantage at having to learn the ways of seduction as he stumbled along.

The thought of his own romantic inexperience gave him an idea.

"Were you never married, Eve?"

Her fingers paused only for a moment as she considered his question. "Nay. Never married." She continued her nursing of the wolf.

"I canna hardly believe that," Conall said when she did not elaborate.

Eve dabbed at Alinor's wound with a moistened rag. "Why not?"

"A titled lady, comely and learned—I would think some laird to have claimed you early on."

The tips of her ears pinkened. *Slowly, Conall,* he reminded himself. *Slowly . . .*

"I . . . was betrothed." She glanced over her shoulder, showing Conall a bit more of her flushed profile. "The wound looks much improved to me. Moss or nay?"

Conall was pleased that she had asked his opinion, and he leaned forward and looked at Alinor's side thoughtfully.

"Why, it appears all but healed to me, lass. A fine job you've done." He gave her a wide smile.

Eve frowned and her eyes narrowed a bit, so Conall dropped the grin from his face to replace it with what he hoped was a more suitably serious expression.

"Nae moss, I think," he said. "But mayhap it should remain bandaged for a day or so, to be certain."

Evelyn nodded curtly, the suspicion gone from her face. "I agree." She reached for a long rag and folded it lengthwise.

"Did your betrothed die?"

"Nay. I—" She paused while she tied the bandage in a stiff knot around Alinor's middle. "I joined the order before we were wed."

Conall raised his eyebrows as a twinge plucked at his guts. "Most men wouldna take kindly to his intended running out on him before they are to take their vows."

"He was . . . upset, yea." Eve gathered her materials and rose from the floor with a soft hiss. "But he married another not long after I left. They are very happy."

"Fickle man," Conall remarked lightly. *Idiot, more likely*, he said to himself.

"A good man," Eve argued. "We would have never suited each other. I simply discovered it before he did."

"Why's that?" Conall asked, waiting for a lady's speech of love and honor and courtly manners.

"Because I don't want children."

The bottom dropped out of Conall's stomach and he was so stunned that he said the first thing that came to his mind.

"Surely you doona mean that, Eve."

"I most surely do," she said briskly, crossing the floor and taking the mug from him. She drank the whole of it and then moved to the urn to pour more. "'Tis why I joined the order—I knew I could remain childless."

Conall's hastily constructed plan began to creak and sway. The very thing he needed most from this woman was the one thing she was not willing to give.

"But . . . why, lass?"

"Why? Why, indeed. Not every woman wishes to have children, MacKerrick," she snapped. She seemed to pause and collect herself. "Childbirth is a terrible wager. I saw it end not in joy, but tragedy, more oft than not during my time at the priory. My own mother died while giving birth to me. I would not wish that on a child of my own blood."

Conall did not know what to say as thoughts of Nonna and their bairn sprang into his mind. He knew all too well the tragedy that could result from a birthing. But he had never thought about it from a child's point of view. 'Twas a heavy burden for a young heart to carry—knowing your birth caused the death of your mother. And he wondered if his daughter would have come to feel the same guilt had she survived and Nonna perished.

He pushed the vision of a dark-haired little girl—playing, laughing, *alive*—from his mind.

But at least Conall now suspected 'twas merely fear

that persuaded Eve in her choice, not an aversion to mothering. He watched her ladle a bowl of stew for herself and noted how she smiled gently at the great black wolf lying nearby. Alinor's tail thumped the dirt happily, and Conall marveled at the ways of this strange Buchanan woman who could tame the wildest of creatures.

She will make a fine mother, Conall thought.

Chapter Six

The storm relented the next morning, leaving the clearing around the hut in the vale and the wood beyond encased in a shroud of fresh white. Evelyn felt vastly improved upon waking—alone, this time, thankfully—although she noticed with ornery temper that she was much colder without the highlander's solid form lying next to her.

Sinful girl.

MacKerrick was already up and about, digging out the small corral for the sheep before moving the animal to it, setting Alinor loose to her morning constitution, and gathering up the two new traps he'd constructed. He left the hut only after Evelyn too had ventured out into the frigid morning, and after a polite inquiry to her health and a respectful request that she remain in the hut until his return.

Evelyn took the time alone to wash her face and hands, rinse out her mouth, and straighten the few items on the hut's stingy shelf. That done, she picked up discarded bits of nothing from the flagstones in the uppermost part of the hut, then threw out the top layer of soiled pine boughs from the pens.

She looked around the empty cottage. Straightened a corner of the wool blanket on the bed.

She combed and plaited her hair.

She made a fresh urn of tea.

She waited for MacKerrick to return.

It put her in somewhat of a foul humor to realize that, after only a pair of days with another's company, she now rather disliked being alone in the small house. It wasn't as if she and MacKerrick had become fast companions, but 'twas comforting to have someone *not* to talk to, if she so desired.

She heard Alinor's high-pitched yelps from outside and, grateful for any task, Evelyn crossed the hut and opened the door to peek outside.

The wolf was running in crazed half-circles around the little pen where MacKerrick's sheep was interred, kicking up plumes of snow and then flopping down and panting for only a moment before running the circuit again, yelping and jumping. The sheep mirrored the wolf's antics, trotting the length of the enclosure, turning gracefully, and waiting for Alinor to continue.

"Having a bit of sport, are you?" Evelyn called to them. Alinor looked up at the sound of Evelyn's voice and gave a single, sharp bark. The sheep also stopped to look at her expectantly.

"Oh, I think not," Evelyn chuckled.

Alinor took a few running lopes toward her, barked again, and bowed low over her forelegs, her rump swaying eagerly.

Play.

The sheep bleated a mimic of the command.

Evelyn's grin widened and she stepped from the

doorway and crouched down to scoop up a handful of snow. Packing it firmly, she lofted it at Alinor, who caught it expertly and shook it back to powder. The wolf's muzzle sparkled around her panting mouth and she barked gamely again.

Play! Play!

Evelyn threw snowballs at the wolf while the sheep bleated in merriment until her hands were numb and throbbing and the hem of her kirtle was soaked, flapping wet and cold around her ankles.

"That's quite enough, Alinor," she laughed, panting a bit herself. Alinor threw herself onto her side and rolled around in the snow, and Evelyn was pleased she had made the wolf happy.

"Let's give you a name also, girl," Evelyn said, pushing sweaty, curling tendrils of hair from her eyes and looking at the little brown sheep waiting patiently in the pen. "Hmm . . . how do you fancy Bonnie? A fine name for a pretty highland lass," she said in a mimic of MacKerrick's brogue.

The sheep bleated in happy agreement.

Evelyn smiled at the animals a final time and had turned to go back into the hut when Alinor sprang onto her feet, facing the wood, the fur on her back raised. A low growl rolled out of her. Evelyn looked to the wall of trees but saw nothing.

Alinor growled again, this time more insistently.

Intruder.

Stranger.

A chill raced over Evelyn's already cold skin and her thoughts jostled each other for order. If a stranger was coming and MacKerrick was still gone—What . . . Who . . . They might try to take the sheep. They might hurt Alinor. They might . . .

Evelyn struggled in her wet skirts to run in awkward, high-stepping strides though the deep snow to the pen while Alinor kept watch, her growls not ceasing. She jerked open the rickety gate and tangled a hand in the sheep's long wool, dragging her out of the corral.

"Alinor! Alinor, to me!" Evelyn commanded as loudly as she dared as she pulled Bonnie toward the hut, her heart pounding, galloping. "Alinor, to me!"

The wolf finally turned and raced to the hut just as Evelyn pushed open the door. She herded both animals inside and dropped the bar into place. "Good girl," she panted.

The sheep went directly to her pen and Alinor followed, standing guard before the opening. Evelyn dropped to her knees to look through the knothole.

Her eyes scanned the clearing slowly, right to left, left to right. And then she saw the figure step from the treeline as if he'd been one with the silent gray trunks.

'Twas a man.

And 'twas not MacKerrick.

Conall slogged through the crusted snow with no little effort after carefully setting both traps with dried bits of carrot and leaving them nestled in locations likely for small game to roam. At the least, he expected to catch a bird, although he pinned his hopes on a hungry highland hare.

'Twas bitter cold and Conall quickened his pace, eager to return to the cozy hut-turned-snow cave and the enigmatic lass it housed. She was a riddle, for certain, with her proper English manner of speaking, her troubled past, and her secret fear. Conall wished to solve her. He was intrigued al-

ready with how her mind worked and her odd kinship with the great black wolf. It seemed he'd not
in the whole of his life had so many questions he
wished to ask another living person, but he knew
for the sake of his clan that he must bide his time
and not press her. Eve had been tempered by her
long and dangerous journey to Ronan's hut, and
Conall suspected her newfound strength would
only push him back.

And she was Buchanan—a stubborn, vengeful
lot if ever one existed.

There would be time aplenty to learn all of Eve's
secrets once she was his wife. All Conall had to do
now was figure out how to make that happen.

He was nearing the edge of the wood when he
froze and dropped like an anvil to the snow, his
heart hammering so loudly that he fancied it could
be heard in England. He shimmied soundlessly on
his belly through a drift to conceal himself behind
a large tree.

There, on the fringe of the clearing, stood a
figure staring at the hut, his back to Conall and the
wood. Conall squinted through the bright glare of
the snow for sign of Eve but thankfully saw none.
He knew he must lure the stranger back into the
wood and discover his identity before the man decided to try the shelter.

Conall clucked like a chicken, just once and low.

It was the first thing that came to his mind, but he
was rather proud of the idea. Who expects to hear
a common chicken in the wood in high winter?

The stranger immediately spun around, but
Conall could not discern the man's features, bundled head to toe against the icy cold and misshapen

by the large pack he carried. The interloper peered through the trees.

Conall gave another cluck.

It had the desired effect. The unknown traveler turned back into the wood, stepping cautiously, his covered head swiveling, searching for sign of the nonexistent fowl.

Closer, Conall said to himself. *Just a bit closer . . .*

When the stranger moved within reach, Conall sprang. He launched himself horizontally, arms outstretched, and tackled the man about his knees with a roar. The stranger screamed as both he and Conall were plunged into yet another deep drift, and Conall scrambled up the man, drawing his dagger as he went, until he was face-to-face with the still-screaming visitor. Conall pushed the dagger point beneath the man's chin.

'Twas his brother.

"Och, for the love of—Duncan! *Duncan!*" Conall shouted to be heard over his brother's shrill yells. Conall slapped Duncan's gray cheeks. "Shut up! 'Tis only I!"

Duncan's teeth clicked shut and he focused wide, wild green eyes on Conall.

"Conall?" Then he began to flail. "You arsehole bastard pig, son of a whore from England, dung-eatin'—"

Conall stood and pulled the still-cursing Duncan from the drift.

"—bugger! You nearly scared the life from me, you mangy warthog!" Duncan shook himself and spat snow from his mouth. "And me bravin' this weather to bring you supplies out of the kindness of me own heart, you sneakin' rat's cock."

Conall couldn't help but chuckle. "You've nae

called me a sneakin' rat's cock before—good on you, Dunc."

"To hell with you," Duncan grumbled. Conall's scrawny brother threw his pack higher onto his back. "Why'd you attack me like that? Glory, Conall, who else'd be teched enough to wander about these woods in the corpse-cold?"

"I—" Conall cut himself off. He had promised Eve he would not reveal her presence and so he would keep his word. Besides, Duncan was not the exact definition of discretion; if Conall told him he was making house with a young Buchanan lass, the whole of the MacKerrick town would know it by sunset.

Conall had his own reasons for keeping Evelyn Buchanan's existence a secret from his clan.

"Well?" Duncan demanded. "Doona stand there starin' at me like a knot on a log—I'm near to freezin' me bollocks off." Duncan made to stalk past Conall, but Conall reached out an arm and dragged Duncan back, nearly taking the smaller man off his feet once more.

Duncan shook free with a hoarse cry and put his face near Conall's, a slender, bony finger pointing at Conall's nose.

"Grab at me once more, brother . . ." he warned.

"You canna go to the hut, Dunc. I'm sorry."

"And why is that, you stingy bastard?"

Conall couldn't help but glance over his shoulder. "I canna tell you the why of it just now. You must trust me."

Duncan's green eyes narrowed. "Who's there?"

"No one." Conall felt himself flush.

"Liar! I *knew* I heard a voice. And"—he put himself nose to chin with Conall once more—"it sounded like a *woman!*"

Conall shook his head adamantly.

"Who is she, Conall?"

"I canna say."

"Ha!" Duncan fairly jumped into the air. "It *is* a woman!"

'Twas moments such as this when Conall wondered if he had any brains in his head at all.

Conall made a grab for Duncan's pack to cover his discomfiture. "What did you bring?"

But Duncan stepped nimbly aside. "Ah-ah," he taunted. "Nae until you tell me what mischief you've run upon." His eyes narrowed with concern and he looked Conall up and down. "You've nae been taken in by the fae, have you?"

"Of course nae."

"Then tell me, or I'm leavin'—*with* me pack."

Conall closed his eyes for a moment and sighed. "Duncan, you are my brother, me very twin. If I could tell anyone, 'twould be you."

"But—"

"Listen," Conall implored. "There is someone at the hut, aye. And I will have leave to tell you exactly who, I hope, soon. But until then, you must trust me. And you canna stay."

"But—"

"Nae buts. Trust me, Dunc. I need time to work it all out properly."

Duncan frowned crossly, but Conall could sense he was starting to relent. "What am I to tell the townsfolk? Mam?" he challenged. "They expect me to stay on a few days."

"Tell them . . ." Conall paused. Then he met Duncan's gaze directly. "Tell them all is well. Tell them to hold on—the MacKerrick has a plan to

reclaim our town's good fortune. A wondrous plan.
You'll lead them in my stead, of course."

Duncan looked doubtful.

"A wondrous plan, Dunc," Conall repeated.
"You'd nae believe it if I told you now, any matter.
Now, what have you brought me?"

Evelyn could not help but shriek when a giant
thud shook the door as if someone was trying to
shove it open. The subsequent pounding startled
her from her seat next to Alinor and the sheep.
But Alinor was no longer alarmed. Indeed, the
wolf was already bounding toward the door with a
happy-sounding yelp when MacKerrick called from
outside the hut.

"Open up, Eve—'tis I."

Evelyn blew out a heavy breath and went straight
for the door's brace. God in Heaven, he'd been
gone for *hours*, it seemed. Evelyn had been terrified the highlander had met up with the stranger
she'd seen, with horrific consequences. She flung
open the door.

"Where have you been, sir?" she demanded before
the door was open fully. "There was a man—"

"I know." MacKerrick stepped inside with his plaid
tied in a lumpy bundle and Evelyn shut the door
behind him. "'Twas only me brother, Duncan."

"Oh." Evelyn felt somewhat deflated at Mac-
Kerrick's easy reply, although her heart still pounded.
Then another fearful thought struck her. "You did
not tell him of me, did you?"

"Nae." The highlander sat his plaid bundle near
the fire pit and crouched down. "Although he knows
someone else is indeed at the hut."

"What? How?" Evelyn walked past MacKerrick to return her dagger to the shelf.

Amber eyes found hers and she saw disappointment there. "He heard you."

She frowned confusedly for an instant and then understood. "Alinor was making a fuss. I went out to see what she was about and—"

"'Tis well, Eve," MacKerrick said lightly, turning his attention back to untying his bundle. "I would not have you a prisoner to the hut—my request was only to be sure you were not still feeling poorly should the grays return. Obviously, you're feeling more of yourself."

"I am much improved, yea." Evelyn was a bit flummoxed at MacKerrick's reasoning. His request had been for her own welfare, and he did not seem upset in the least that she had deliberately disobeyed him, although in truth, his caution had been warranted.

"I'm sorry I went out when you asked me not to, MacKerrick. I'll try to be more mindful in the future."

Conall shrugged, as if what she did made absolutely no difference to him one way or the other. "'Twas nearly your own undoing, lass. Had Duncan come to the hut, you'd have been found out, for certain." He reached into the bundle and began removing items and setting them on the floor near his feet. Alinor appeared at MacKerrick's side, sniffing at each object. The sheep clattered over as well, causing Evelyn to realize she'd not closed the animal's pen.

"What in the bloody hell—?" MacKerrick mumbled as the sheep butted his arm playfully. But he had a smile on his face when he pushed the animal's head aside. "Get back, you mangy rug."

Alinor trotted around MacKerrick and buffeted

the small sheep beyond the fire pit. The sheep bleated in weak protest.

"I hope you don't mind," Evelyn said hesitantly, "but, er . . . Alinor and I have christened your sheep."

MacKerrick glanced up, one eyebrow cocked above an amused expression. He seemed to be waiting.

"Bonnie," Evelyn elaborated. "It suits her, does it not?"

Conall chuckled and went back to unpacking his bundle. "It's fine, lass. Although you may be more unwilling to eat a 'Bonnie' than you would a nameless sheep."

Evelyn gasped. "*Eat* her?"

MacKerrick looked up again. "It's nae pet, Eve."

"We most certainly will not be eating *her*, sir," Evelyn proclaimed. "Alinor loves *her*!"

"And Alinor will love *her* roasted, with a bit o' sage."

Evelyn shrieked and crossed to the sheep. Dropping to her knees, she wrapped her arms around Bonnie's short neck. "Shh, don't listen, lovely. I'll not let him eat you," she said, glaring at MacKerrick.

"You will, if the food we have runs out."

"I *won't*, so you'd better well be as skilled a hunter as you claim, sir."

Alinor whined.

To Evelyn's surprise, MacKerrick actually laughed out loud, and the deep sound of his voice raised in mirth sent gooseflesh over her clammy skin. "We shall see, Eve. We shall see."

The highlander's moods seemed to change like the flicker of a flame.

Seeing no point in arguing with the maddening

man over an issue Evelyn felt had been resolved, she let her eyes tick curiously across the line of objects MacKerrick had removed from the pack.

"Why was your brother about?" she asked, releasing Bonnie when the sheep strained toward Alinor. "Is there trouble at your village?"

"*Town*," MacKerrick corrected. "Nae trouble, save nae enough food, as it was when I left. Duncan was bringing me more supplies."

"He thinks you incapable of caring for yourself?"

MacKerrick shook his head and set the bundled plaid—not quite empty, Evelyn noted—slightly behind him. "I departed suddenly and, in truth, without much thought for what I'd need. Duncan thought I might be in want of some company by now, so he raided the house for anything I had lying about."

"Why did you leave suddenly?"

MacKerrick eyed her in exasperation. "You're full o' questions, are you nae?"

"I answered yours last night," Evelyn parried, undaunted. "Were you running away?"

"O' course nae."

"Were you banished?"

"You canna banish a clan chief from his own town, Eve." He frowned then, as if the idea made him thoughtful.

"What then?" Evelyn's curiosity goaded her on. It made no sense to her that a man such as MacKerrick would suddenly abandon his home in high winter, with inadequate supplies to maintain himself.

MacKerrick was silent for a long time before he sighed. "As I told you, my wife . . . died." He rose, taking hold of a small sack of mysterious content, and crossed to the shelf. "I didna tell you, though, that 'twas quite recent."

"Oh," Evelyn said quietly, rebuking herself now for her refusal to drop the subject. For some reason, she was unsure she wanted reminding that MacKerrick had once been a married man. And now Evelyn knew that his wife had not faded comfortably into the highlander's distant past, as Evelyn had been content to think.

"You're in mourning, then." It was not a question.

"Aye. I mourn," MacKerrick answered in a low voice, fiddling with the sack.

"I'm sorry, MacKerrick," Evelyn said, and realized it was the second time that day she'd felt the need to apologize to the man.

"You didna know," he replied, his back still to her. "I—*aaghh!*"

Evelyn bolted to her feet at the highlander's shout of surprise and his jump backward. "My God, what is it?"

Then he was chuckling and drawing his dagger from his belt. "Naught but a wee mouse, likely closed up with the barley when Duncan packed it. I'll get rid of it."

"Nay!" Evelyn cried and rushed forward, grabbing MacKerrick's arm when he readied his dagger.

"Turn me loose, lass, else it'll escape and be into our supplies." The highlander tried to shake her off, but Evelyn clung to him like seaweed.

"Don't kill it," she pleaded, eyes immediately finding the tiny gray rodent with shiny black eyes, frozen and cowering between the sack of grain and the hut's rear wall. It was so helpless and frightened. "I'll catch it," she promised, trying to pull

MacKerrick away from the shelf, but it was as effective as attempting to move a mountain. "Please?"

To her relief, the highlander gave an exasperated sigh and stepped away. Evelyn released his arm and he tucked his blade back in his belt. "Fine," he grumbled. "But doona lose it."

Evelyn moved to the shelf slowly, looking into the mouse's glistening eyes above its trembling whiskers.

"Hallow, lovely," she whispered, ignoring the highlander's snort behind her. "Don't be frightened— I'll not harm you."

The mouse remained motionless. Evelyn stepped closer and tapped her tongue lightly behind her upper teeth. She cupped her palms and slowly moved them toward the animal.

"Come to me, lovely," she whispered, then tapped her tongue again. "'Tis safe." Her fingertips bumped the tiny mouse and it quite suddenly bumbled into her hands and froze again.

Evelyn smiled and cupped her palms completely around the small, warm body. "That was very brave of you," she praised.

"I can see why the priory didna suit you, Eve," MacKerrick said from behind her.

Evelyn's heart rose to her throat and she turned, ready for the mockery of her gift. "And why is that, sir?"

MacKerrick was busied with sorting the rest of the supplies, but he nodded toward Evelyn's cupped hands.

"They likely didn't keep enough rodents."

Evelyn let her breath out slowly. But the highlander was not finished.

"'Tis obvious you're a Buchanan," he said, more

crossly now. "Witches, the whole lot of them. Likely as nae, you'd bewitch the thing and set it upon me in me sleep."

Evelyn could not help the smile that spread across her face.

Witch, indeed.

Because she dared not disappoint his opinion of the Buchanans' reputation, and also because she knew 'twould irritate the highlander, Evelyn let her eyes scan the hut for any suitable vessel.

"A fine idea, MacKerrick," she said brightly. "I shall call him Whiskers."

Chapter Seven

"Whiskers," Conall muttered to himself and shook his head in disbelief as he set off from the hut again later in the day, his quiver and bow slung over one shoulder. She'd named a field mouse and was keeping the rodent in an old, wide wooden bowl she'd found discarded for a long crack in its bottom. Conall had tried to reason with the lass—'twould be but a matter of hours before the little blighter chewed through the piece of hole-punched leather Eve had fastened over the bowl, and then the mouse would be loose in the hut, befouling the barley once more and gnawing at the ticking.

But she wouldna listen. Nae, "Whiskers" was a wee, gray angel, sent from God for Eve to protect.

Conall rolled his eyes and crunched through the snow, nearing the spot where he'd left the first trap that morning, hoping in the back of his mind that a long, lean rabbit awaited him there.

Eve was proving a trial to Conall's patience, but oddly, he didn't mind so much. He needed the Buchanan lass to ensure his clan's survival and he would put up with near any of her foolishness to endear himself to her.

Anything for his clan.

He tried not to think of the way her face softened when she spoke to one of the—now *three*—animals housed with them in the hut, or the way her long plait brushed over the curve of her hip, or the shy lilt of her voice when she had read to him from the Song of Solomon. He'd ask her to read more of the manuscript later that night, hopefully over a meal of rich rabbit stew. Surely a gentlewoman such as she would find the activity properly romantic. Perhaps she would even be moved to sit near Conall's side. Perhaps their shoulders would brush together as she read . . .

Conall shook himself. He'd obviously been too long without a woman to be fantasizing about a half-English Buchanan lass who held queer ideas about the keeping of livestock.

He saw the bent gray twigs of the trap snuggled down between two pines and quickened his pace in anticipation.

Empty. And the bait was gone.

Conall cursed and crouched down before the trap. He reached into his pouch for another precious chunk of dried carrot and fastened it to the now-frayed twine dangling within the trap, the cold making his fingertips clumsy. The wind buffeted him as he rose and moved west toward the other trap.

That one was empty, as well. Conall rebaited the trap and made to circle back to the hut, angry as his foolish fantasy of sensual verses read over a hearty meal melted away.

He scrambled up a snowy ravine and looked at

his surroundings. If Conall wasn't mistaken, the great oak where Ronan was buried was ahead to his right.

Conall looked to the sky. There was just enough daylight left.

He passed through a tiny clearing surrounded by pines and saw the lumpy, snow-covered bones of Eve's horse. He stood there a long moment, staring at what was left of the carcass, and had a sudden pang of sympathy as he thought of how difficult harvesting the meat must have been for Eve. Injured and alone, save for Alinor, and both of them being hunted by the grays. He could not imagine her angst at having to saw frozen flesh from an animal she had cared for all the way from England—she'd likely named the beast.

Conall moved on from the copse of pine and saw Ronan's tree ahead—the tallest, widest gnarled oak in this part of the forest, ringed by a tapering skirt of rocks. He stopped, still some distance away, and stared at the tree where his uncle was buried, facing the distant, hated Buchanan town. A punishment even in death.

He betrayed us. Conall could almost hear his father's voice speaking the words he'd heard so many times, slurred with drink and perhaps regret. *He would have given the Buchanan our lands, brought them into our very town and welcomed them to all we had. For* her. *He would rather pay homage to Angus Buchanan before his own clan, his kin. Me own brother. I had to protect us. I hadta.*

Conall could never persuade his father to speak of his uncle Ronan while sober, and engaging Dáire while he was in his cups was dangerous, his drunken temper poisoned by bad memories and held only by a thin thread, liable to snap and strike at whoever was around him. But Conall and his brother, Duncan, had heard whispers from the townsfolk and had assembled the story themselves as best they could.

Ronan MacKerrick, brother to Dáire, had fallen in love with a woman from the Buchanan clan—sworn enemies of the MacKerricks. The greedy clan bordering bountiful Loch Lomond repeatedly encroached on MacKerrick lands, stealing their game and pushing their own northernmost boundary ever onward by sheer force. The Buchanan town dwarfed the MacKerrick and, although never a clan to take insult lightly, engaging Angus Buchanan's people in a full-on war would have been foolhardy.

But Ronan had pressed that if he married a Buchanan woman, the two towns could find peace. Conall's father staunchly disagreed, arguing that once Angus Buchanan had his claws in the MacKerrick town he would swallow it up whole, and the MacKerricks would cease to exist.

The rest of the details were spotty for Conall and Duncan, but there had been some sort of clandestine meeting between Ronan and the Buchanans, and Dáire MacKerrick's suspicions had been confirmed. Then, the battle had commenced—Ronan MacKerrick giving his own life to protect his poisoned love, Minerva Buchanan. The Buchanan's own wife was dead, and many of the Buchanan clan elders.

Ronan had been the only MacKerrick to die.

Neither Conall or Duncan had any memories of Ronan, having just come into the world when the two towns came to catastrophic blows. But their mother had told them that Ronan had been a good man, not so much the traitorous monster that Dáire described.

"Folk will do desperate things for love," she defended Ronan many times. "Some good, some nae so good. Your da is a good man. He loved his brother, and he loves his clan."

"Good day to you, Ronan," Conall said aloud, his voice muffled by the smothering cold. "'Tis your nephew, Conall. I'm the MacKerrick now—Da's passed on. Five years this spring." He paused, feeling both foolish and somewhat justified to be speaking to a pile of rocks around a tree.

"I've got me a Buchanan woman at the hut in the vale, brought back to Scotland by your own Minerva. I'm going to set it to rights. You can tell her to let us be now. She's already taken it all—my wife, my bairn, my pride. I'm doing what Da couldna—I'm payin' her quarter. Enough is enough."

A soft sound, like a woman weeping, floated on a gust of icy wind, and chills caressed Conall's neck like a warning. He listened for a breathless moment until he heard it again.

It sounded as if it was coming from the other side of the tree.

Conall's boots crunched the snow as he slowly, slowly stepped around the wide island of rocks in the sea of white. And he thought he was, in that moment, to meet his own death.

Lying on the rocky pyre was one of the evil grays—smaller than Alinor and sickly thin, its fur full of impossible age. Its teeth were bared in a nasty, yellow grin below a muzzle wrinkled away in a snarl.

Conall knew then that he faced the beast he once thought he'd killed at the hut. Steamy breath

hissed out at Conall as the growl grew into one of
recognition from the beast's emaciated belly. It
trembled, whether from disease or preparation to
spring.

Conall swallowed. If he ran, it would chase him
and, even as obviously ill as it was, Conall knew it
would be upon his back before he could take a
score of strides. It would kill him, for certain, and
then what would become of Eve?

He dared not try to nock an arrow—too much
time. His hand went slowly to the hilt of his sword
and he gripped it firmly, began to inch it upward.
If the wolf charged him, he could run it through
again, as he'd done in the clearing.

He will only come back, a quiet voice in the back of
his mind warned.

Conall stared at the wolf, and the wolf stared
back, still growling and shaking. Its eyes were so
black. Conall's own eyes were beginning to feel as
though they were freezing in their sockets. He had
to blink.

The wolf was gone.

Conall cried out hoarsely and spun around, his
sword drawn in a flash and ready to swing, but he
was alone in the still wood.

His bowels suddenly felt watery and hot.

He turned back to the tree and saw that in the
place where the wolf had lain was a limp pool of
black. Conall stepped toward it as if he could do
nothing else. Climbing the rocks, he bent and
picked up what revealed itself to be a long length
of cloth.

'Twas an old, patched cloak, smelling of smoke
and cold and bitter spice. Smallish, a woman's cloak.

Conall began to tremble, much as the old wolf had.

And then the chorus of howls broke through the frigid gray light, its singers invisible behind thousands of trees. Conall turned, the cloak in one hand, his sword in the other, and stumbled on the loose rock underfoot. The howls seemed to be coming from all around him, screaming out his name, sucking the weak light from before his eyes. He felt as though his heart was breaking.

Conall stumbled down the rocks and ran toward the hut. To sanity. And to Eve.

"The grays have returned," was the greeting Evelyn received from MacKerrick upon his return to the hut.

She looked up at the large highlander from her seat on the stool, where she sat with Whiskers in her lap. Alinor and Bonnie both trotted over to greet MacKerrick as he closed the door and dropped the bar in place. Evelyn thought the wolves must be quite near for MacKerrick to sentence the hut's occupants to a long evening of choking peat smoke. He leaned his quiver and bow against the wall.

"Did you see them?" she asked, returning Whiskers to his bowl near her feet and then rising.

"One of them," MacKerrick replied uneasily. When he turned, Evelyn noticed his ashen face and the long, black cloth in his hand. She would have demanded further explanation of his encounter with the animal, but she gasped when she recognized the patched fabric he held.

"Where did you get that?" Evelyn asked, walking to MacKerrick and taking the cloak, holding it in both hands with a pang of melancholy.

"It's yours, then—good." Conall nodded once

and then brushed past Evelyn to retrieve the mead jug from the shelf. He claimed Evelyn's vacated seat and removed the jug's cork. "I reckoned you had lost it on your way to the hut."

"Nay—my cloak has long since become rags. This is not mine," Evelyn said, stroking the worn wool and remembering the woman who'd worn it. "It belonged to Minerva. She—" Evelyn swallowed. "She was wearing it when she died. I can only assume there is naught left of her now but bones."

Her eyes flew to the highlander as he choked on the mead.

"Wearing it?" he gasped.

"Yea, she . . . Wasn't it with her?" Evelyn frowned. "But where did . . . how . . . ?"

"Ronan's tree. Where he's buried," MacKerrick was finally able to choke out, although his voice was still gravelly and strained. "It's surrounded by—"

"Rocks," Evelyn finished faintly. "'Tis where Minerva . . . She wasn't there?"

MacKerrick shook his head, his eyes a bit wild and fixed on the cloak held between her hands, as if he could not look away.

"She wasna there. The gray—" He broke off as if he'd forgotten what he was to say.

"The gray?" she prompted.

MacKerrick started. He looked at Evelyn at last. "The gray I saw . . . was lying on it. On top of the pyre."

It was now Evelyn's turn to be at a loss. She returned MacKerrick's stare. "I don't understand."

His eyes dropped to the cloak again and his brows lowered menacingly. He set the jug aside without a glance and rose slowly from the stool.

MacKerrick held out a long arm toward Evelyn, his palm open.

"Give it to me, Eve."

As if he'd commanded them, Alinor and Bonnie skittered away to the lower end of the hut and disappeared into the farthest pen.

"Why?" Evelyn asked warily, and her instincts prompted her to pull the cloak to her bosom.

MacKerrick was before her in two great strides. "It's cursed. I should've known, should have never brought it back. I must destroy it." He snagged a corner of the cloak and pulled.

Evelyn held tight, curling her fingers into the thin wool. "Don't be ridiculous, MacKerrick. 'Tis but a cloak. You sound like Minerva, with talk of curses and spells."

"It *is* cursed. How else do you explain that I found the cloak where she died, but no body? Not even a single bone! And the gray was lying *atop* it—*protecting* it!" He tugged again, drawing the cloak closer to him.

Evelyn pulled harder, worrying for the rotten material. "*I know not,*" she growled. "But if the gray was lying on it, how did you get it? Did you kill the wolf?"

MacKerrick looked into her eyes for an unsettling moment and Eve shivered at the chill in his gaze. It was as if he wanted to tell her something, but was too frightened of whatever it was to speak it aloud. She could feel the fever of him from where she stood.

"'Tis unsafe," he said at last. "Give it to me."

"I will not! I loved her, and this is all I have—"

"Eve, give it—"

"*Nay!*"

MacKerrick gave a mighty tug on the cloak and Evelyn was jerked against his chest. In a blink, MacKerrick had dropped his mouth to hers in a hard kiss, wrapping one long arm around her shoulders and pulling her to him.

Evelyn was so shocked that she froze, her very toes tingling from the sensation of MacKerrick's warm, dry lips against hers. The scruff on his upper lip chafed at hers with a delicious prickle. He eased his head back and softened his mouth, kissing first her upper lip and then her lower, then sliding his tongue along the seam. He kissed her mouth again gently, wetly, and Evelyn felt her knees go watery, her eyes close, her fingers uncurl.

MacKerrick's solid chest twisted for an instant, and then his other arm was around Evelyn, pulling her even closer. His skin smelled of fresh winter air and his own masculinity and Evelyn let her hands creep up over his chest, let her mouth soften and her head tilt. It was achingly brilliant, his kissing, his strength all around her and she felt protected from the harsh season, from the grays, from her haunting past . . .

She realized Minerva's cloak was no longer between them.

Evelyn shoved MacKerrick away with a cry and her eyes searched the floor around her frantically.

Minerva's cloak lay tossed across the fire pit, slender whips of smoke now curling around it. Evelyn darted to the pit and MacKerrick moved in the same moment, meeting her there. He grabbed Evelyn's arm as she reached for the cloak, but she twisted with a cry and grabbed a fold with her other hand.

"Let go!" she cried as MacKerrick snaked an arm about her waist.

"You'll set the house afire, Eve!" He tried to swing her away from the pit.

Evelyn raised a leg and swung her heel down hard into MacKerrick's shin, drove an elbow into his ribs, and twisted, all in the same moment, dragging the smoking cloak from the fire pit and whirling away from MacKerrick.

The highlander laid hand to a bucket of melt water in an instant and turned toward Eve, his arm in motion even as she raised a warding hand and whipped the cloak behind her.

"MacKerrick, nay! It's not—"

The cold water hit Evelyn full in the face and she would have shrieked if not for the flood that smacked into her open mouth and sluiced up both nostrils. She was instantly drenched in the icy wash and coughed and spat, trying to catch her breath.

MacKerrick stood near the fire pit, holding the now-empty bucket and looking like a great, angry lummox.

"It wasn't afire," Evelyn managed to gasp. She brought the cloak—bone dry and completely unsinged, as well—to her face to mop at the dripping rivulets.

"See?" MacKerrick said smugly. "What fabric willna burn? *Cursed fabric.*"

"You. Are. Mad!" Evelyn yelled. She held her arms akimbo. "Look what you've done! This is my only suit of clothes! I'll likely catch fever and die now, thank you very much, sir."

To her surprise, MacKerrick looked genuinely aghast at the idea. The bucket fell from his hand with a hollow conk as he stepped toward her.

Evelyn backed away. "Nay! You stay far, far, far away from me. You—you . . . *sneak*! You *kissed* me! To trick me!"

"Eve—"

"Get out!" Evelyn was now embarrassed to tears but would not allow them to fall in MacKerrick's presence. How could she have been so foolish, so gullible, as to have fallen, face first, as it was, into such a despicable trap? She had let him kiss her! She had kissed him back!

She'd had no idea she was of such loose morals.

"Get out!" she repeated with a stamp of her foot and flung an arm toward the door. Water droplets arced away from her and her face felt as though it was on fire. "I must get dry and I'll not have you about watching lecherously!"

MacKerrick sent her an exasperated look. "Eve—"

"*Out!*" she shrieked. "Get out! Get out! Get out! Get—"

"*All right!*" MacKerrick bellowed. He stomped to the door and paused, grabbing up his bow and arrows. "But if the grays—"

"I hope they eat you!" she screamed, beyond all reason now.

The highlander raised the bar and opened the door. He stopped to look over his shoulder. "Be sure to dry your hair, lass, else—"

Evelyn shrieked and snatched the mead jug from the floor. She hurled it at MacKerrick, who went wide-eyed before darting outside. He slammed the door just as the jug smashed into it, exploding mead and broken slivers onto the floor.

Evelyn threw the cloak after the jug and then crossed to the door to drop the bar in place. She stepped back, her chin quivering.

"And stay out!" she yelled.

MacKerrick made no response, and so Evelyn turned and stomped back across the floor.

She had barely thrown herself onto the bed before she began to sob.

Chapter Eight

Well, he'd done it now.

Conall threw his quiver and bow to the ground and slumped into a cold, wet seat, his back to the hut. He balled a fist and took a swing at the frigid air, a short bark of frustration released as a fluffy, ineffective cloud of steam.

His da had always criticized Conall as being too impulsive, too like his uncle Ronan, and Conall had to at last admit that Dáire had been right. It had always been Conall's manner when faced with a problem to heed his first, knee-jerk reaction, rather than step back and think. Thinking an issue to death wasted time, in Conall's opinion. 'Twas best to take action—any action.

He was no idiot, after all. His instincts were usually spot-on. If an animal attacked you, you killed it.

If an item—particularly an item once belonging to a now-deceased old witch who had condemned your people to the brink of extinction—was cursed, you destroyed it.

If something was afire, you put it out.

If a bullheaded lass would not heed your warning for her own bloody safety—

Well, you shouldna kiss her, obviously.

Conall groaned and dropped his head into his hands.

What had possessed him to heed such a foolish impulse? Had it been the sweet longing in her eyes as she'd clutched the witch's cloak to her breast? The rosy flush of her cheeks in her otherwise pale face as she'd argued with him? Or had it been but a remainder of Conall's jangling nerves from his encounter with the gray at Ronan's tree? He'd needed to distract Eve from the blasted cloak, aye, but surely he could have thought of a way to do it that didn't involve further stirring his own already strained libido. It was as if he'd been unable to stop himself.

He'd likely frightened her—she'd at one time been committed to a religious life, for Christ's sake—how much experience with a man could she have? And he knew he'd made her angry, as evidenced by the sound of the mead jug shattering against the door. Conall would likely have to start all over again to regain any semblance of Eve's trust.

If she ever let him back in the hut.

But hadn't Eve returned his kiss, there at the end? In fact, hadn't she been sliding her small, cool hands up the front of his léine, toward his neck?

Conall shook his head in disgust. She'd likely been readying to strangle him, was all.

A sharp crack, like the sound of a branch being stepped on, and the hollow snuffling of a large animal drew Conall's attention.

He looked at the sky. Evening was fast approaching

and the grays would likely win the deer before Conall could stalk it to a kill. 'Twas too late in the day to enter the wood. On the trail of big game, Conall knew how easy it was to lose track of time and distance, making himself a bit of a hunt for the crazed wolves. If he never returned to the hut, Eve would be damned.

Mayhap the deer would step from the tree line, giving Conall a clear shot with his bow. He sighed.

And mayhap Alinor would take up on her hind legs and dance a jig.

It seemed as though he was thwarted at every turn. Conall suspected the best thing to do would be to wait until the weather gentled a bit and deliver Eve to the Buchanans. Mayhap Angus Buchanan would be so pleased at having a member of his clan returned that he would forgive the debt he believed he was owed and the curse would be lifted. Conall could return to the MacKerrick town and never have to mention the days spent with Eve Buchanan. No one would starve, and the tension on all sides—between the clans and also between him and Eve—would at last come to an end.

Conall could forget Eve, her wolf, her ridiculous mouse, had ever existed. The lass had certainly been through enough of a trial, journeying from England to find her ancestral home.

She did not need Conall further mucking up her life.

A flash of gray on the fringe of the wood caught his eye and Conall felt his heart skip, fearing the wicked wolves.

But it *was* a deer, now frozen in place, its muzzle raised and sniffing the air. It took a hesitant step into the clearing.

Conall slid his hand to his quiver lying near his hip, never taking his eyes from the scrawny, leggy deer. His fingertips brushed the fletching of an arrow, and he slowly inched it from the quiver along the ground. He slid his bow up flat onto his lap.

The deer started and turned its head, its ears flicking, its tail up. Conall froze, not daring to even breathe.

Please, God . . . just a moment longer . . .

After what seemed an eternity, the deer dropped its nose to the snow.

Conall was trembling from deep inside his gut, nerves and excitement causing his heart to thrash in his chest. He nocked the arrow while the bow still lay flat in his lap.

He had but one shot. And whether he made the kill or nae would decide his course of action with Eve. Should he take the deer, they would both stay at the hut in the vale. Should he miss, he would relinquish her to the Buchanans.

He took a slow, slow, deep breath. Conall raised his bow in one fluid motion and let loose his arrow.

Evelyn raised her head from her arms after the short but intense crying jag to see two furry muzzles— one black and sleek, one brown and white and wooly—pointed at her over the edge of the ticking. Bonnie's thick, rough tongue was licking at the woolen blanket and Alinor's tail began to wag enthusiastically. Evelyn sniffed and pushed herself upright, not being able to help the watery smile that pulled at her mouth.

"Hallow, lovelies. 'Tis all right. Bonnie, naughty— don't eat the bedclothes, please." Evelyn swiped at her cheeks with the back of one hand and reached out with the other to pat the two animals in turn. "Move out of the way, then, so that I might get up." She pushed herself to the edge of the box bed, her legs dangling over the side, and sighed.

Well, she'd done it now.

Not only had she humiliated and debased herself by allowing MacKerrick to kiss her, she'd worsened the situation by behaving like a crazed harpy and throwing him out of his own home. Yea, he was despicable and underhanded and possessed of some strange fear of Minerva's cloak, but Evelyn had come to a sort of revelation after MacKerrick had left the hut—one she should have realized days ago.

Her life depended on his charity. Not only her health, which she had regained quickly thanks to MacKerrick's knowledge and swift action, but her very survival in Scotland. She'd lied to him upon their first encounter, claiming to be of Buchanan blood, and that had bought her refuge, true. But Evelyn realized that the situation could be viewed as temporary by MacKerrick. Her behavior toward him thus far had been appalling. The hut belonged to his clan and he owed her neither allegiance or charity. Should he tire of her tantrums and demands, he could easily return to his village and be quit of her, taking sweet Bonnie and his precious supplies with him. Evelyn and Alinor and Whiskers would be left to starve. The horsemeat and stew were consumed and there was no more to be had. She could not hunt, and the rivers were thick with ice.

Or, worse, MacKerrick could take her to the Buchanans and leave her to explain her lie to a town full of strangers.

"Oh, hallow," she said to the big black wolf. "I am Lady Evelyn Godewin from England. I accompanied your kin, Minerva Buchanan, to yonder forest where she died and I left her poor old body on a pile of rock. I've told the MacKerrick that I'm related to you, so could you do a lass a favor and play along?"

Alinor whined anxiously.

"Precisely," Evelyn sighed. She rose from the bed. She was no lady in this land.

She needed MacKerrick—needed him for her own survival. She realized that now, and the truth was devastating. But how could she keep him at the hut? What could she promise him, what could she say?

Evelyn picked up Minerva's cloak and held it before her, looking at the beggarly material and wishing for a bit of the old woman's wisdom and cunning. But even though she concentrated with all her might, strained to hear a whisper from the beyond, all she heard was the clatter of claw and hoof as Alinor chased Bonnie around the fire pit.

Eve sighed and crossed the room, dodging the racing animals underfoot to hang Minerva's cloak on a peg beneath the shelf. It just hung there, old and dirty and limp, but its very presence seemed to tease her.

Would that she were a Buchanan, with even a drop of Scots witchery in her veins! How much simpler it would be if she could babble a cryptic chant, cast bones for a spell, and have all her problems resolved.

But she didn't know any magic chants. And the only idea that came to her caused horrifying images to bloom in her mind like blood soaking through linen. She tried to push that dark possibility away. MacKerrick would likely laugh in her face or, at the least, be highly offended at the suggestion. 'Twas scandalous, really, even for a Scot.

Although, what other choice did she have, but to at least try? She could claim no wealth to tempt him with, no royal favor. She no longer had even humble horsemeat to barter with.

Evelyn had only one thing to offer.

I won't! her old self screamed in childish temper.

You must, Evelyn, the grown woman, answered.

Alinor suddenly charged the door and jumped, startling Evelyn from her thoughts. The wolf was rearing on her hind legs, tail swinging in a blur, Bonnie at her side.

Then she heard the highlander's long, ragged yell. A chill raced up her damp back, climbed her plait like a rope, and crept across her scalp.

She crossed to where the animals paraded and buffeted them aside. Evelyn gripped the bar grimly and hoisted it from its brackets while Alinor raised one paw and scratched impatiently at the door.

Beyond the hut lay Evelyn's future, likely to end in her own death by one of two bloody paths.

'Twas time to see which she would travel.

Conall could scarce believe his eyes when the deer fell like a stone to the ground. And so he sat like a ninny in the snow, staring at the spot in which it had fallen.

A part of him was afraid to go and look. Afraid that the deer was like the enchanted gray and would be vanished should he dare walk to the edge of the clearing to look upon it. But he heard

Alinor's muffled yelp from within the hut behind him and it stirred him from his superstitious hesitation.

Conall was on his feet and loping toward the wood, his heart beating in heavy rhythm with his footfalls. When he saw the small deer lying dead on its side—Conall's arrow landed as perfectly as if he had walked up to the animal and drove it in with his own fist—Conall gave a triumphant whoop.

The animal would feed the hut's occupants for weeks.

And he would not be returning Eve to the Buchanans.

In truth, Conall did not know which pleased him more.

He heard the hut door's echoey scrape and Alinor barked again as she bounded across the clearing in a low, black streak. Conall stepped in front of his kill protectively, his arms spread wide.

"Argh! Back!" he yelled. "Alinor, nae!"

The wolf skidded to a halt in the snow, but fell into an excited pace before Conall, her tongue lolling out of her grinning, slobbery mouth.

"You'll get yours," Conall promised her. "But you'll wait your turn, ken?"

Conall then raised his eyes to the hut and saw Eve framed by the low doorway, her fingers tangled in Bonnie's long wool. From his vantage point, Eve resembled a typical highland wife, at her home with her sheep, her long plait hanging over her shoulder and down to her hip. Conall wondered for a wild moment what she would look like with his plaid wrapped around her shoulders, as a wife would do. As Nonna had never done.

"Eve!" he called and raised an arm.

Alinor turned and raced back to the hut at his words.

"What is it?" Eve asked, hesitantly, but loudly enough to be heard through the thickening dusk, and raising up on her toes as if trying to see what he was about. She swatted at Alinor, who spun around and flew back toward Conall. "A gray?"

"Nae—come!"

She pulled the sheep back inside and closed the door, leaving Bonnie to the safety of the hut, and began to trudge through the snow.

Conall cast a wary eye to the sky. Evening was nigh upon them. Soon, the grays would be afoot, the scent of fresh blood drawing them to the clearing as surely as bees are drawn to a field of sweet clover.

"Food," Conall said proudly, just as Eve's eyes fell on the slain deer.

She gasped and her face went whiter than the snow she stood in. "Oh, nay," she whispered and dropped to her knees near the deer's head.

Conall's mouth fell open. "Oh, nae?" he repeated. "I was expecting more of a 'Huzzah, Conall, well done,' actually."

"Oh, I—" Eve turned her face up to look at him and he saw the big, silvery tears in her eyes, already suspiciously reddened. "Of course, this is . . . 'tis a miracle, of course. But . . ." She dropped her gaze back to the deer. "He's so beautiful. Young," she whispered and reached out a slender, pale hand to stroke the deer's still head.

Conall was more than a little perturbed with himself that he hadn't foreseen Eve's reaction. Of course the sight of a dead animal would affect her—had she not sworn to protect Bonnie from such an intended fate?

Bollocks.

Conall crouched down next to Eve. "I'm sorry, lass. If it will lessen your grief, the shot was perfect—it didna feel the slightest prick, I swear it."

Eve nodded but did not look at him.

"Eve, had I not taken it, it would have starved for certain—suffered greatly. This way was more merciful, you must believe me. And now"—he hesitated, but then reached out a palm to turn her face toward him, away from the deer's sightless brown eyes, mesmerizing her—"we can eat. You and I and Alinor." He gave her a smile.

To his amazement, her lips lifted in the most meager smile. "And Bonnie."

"Bonnie, as well."

"And Whiskers."

Conall could not help but roll his eyes. "And Whiskers, aye. But heed me, lass"—Conall glanced uneasily to the wood, sidling, it seemed, ever closer to them, as if it would reach out with long, tree-trunk arms and sweep them all into its rapidly darkening interior. "We must move quickly—I must drag the deer into the hut. I'll have need to butcher it inside for the light and safety. You ken?"

Eve nodded and stood, her manner swiftly changed from brokenhearted English maiden to fierce highland dame. "Shall I help you drag it?"

Conall rose too and shook his head as he moved to the animal's hindquarters. Alinor was once again running the span of the clearing, this time as if eager for all of them to be back inside the hut. She could sense the grays, Conall suspected, and knew they would soon be upon them.

"Nay, lass." Conall picked up the rear legs and swung the deer in the snow so that its head was now pointed at the wood. "Only collect Alinor and run ahead to open the door." He leaned back and pulled, his boots sinking deep in the snow as he dragged the deer.

Eve dashed away to the hut and Conall could hear Alinor's nervous whines bouncing off the door before Eve opened it. As if on cue, a chorus of howls erupted over the clearing and Conall tried to move quicker, nearly running backward in the snow. He backed into the hut and as soon as the deer's head cleared the portal, the door swung shut. Eve had been waiting behind it, bar at the ready.

Conall moved toward the pens and saw that Eve had incarcerated both Alinor and Bonnie together in the one enclosure that still boasted a working gate. The two unlikely roommates were curled up with one another on the pine boughs, Alinor panting nervously. Conall dragged the carcass to the other, open, pen and dropped its legs with a grunt. Indoors, the animal appeared larger than what it had seemed in the clearing.

Eve appeared at the pen's opening, a coil of hemp rope and Ronan's ancient wooden gambrel in her hands. She offered them to Conall, all the while trying not to look directly at the dead deer.

"My thanks, lass," Conall said, mildly surprised at her initiative.

She stepped around the deer as Conall bent to attach the gambrel by driving the pointed ends into the space between bone and tendon on the animal's rear legs. He paused, looked over his shoulder at Eve, who faced away from him and leaned over the rickety half wall separating the two pens. Conall couldn't help but note the swell of her buttocks under her worn gown, or the raised bones of her spine at her neckline as she bent to speak softly to the animals. Eve needed to eat, and eat she would. But the wet part of this necessary business would likely be more than her delicate sensibilities could tolerate.

"Eve," he called gently, "would that you take yourself to the other end of the cottage, lass. I must open—"

"I know what you must do, MacKerrick," she said sharply, cutting off his warning and straightening from the low wall. She turned and her eyes went to the beam across the ceiling. "I'll help you raise it and then start the water. Is your blade sharp or shall I take up the whetstone?"

Conall didn't know whether to be pleased or offended and so he just nodded dumbly. He picked up the end of the rope and tossed it over the beam. Eve stepped to his side and together they heaved the deer into the air in a series of short bursts.

Conall tied the rope to an anchor set deep into the thick wall and they both stepped away, the creaking rope slashing the air diagonally between them. They stared at each other.

"'Tis a fine animal, MacKerrick," Eve said solemnly. "Huzzah. Well done."

Conall felt a grin lighten his face. "I am sorry for . . . for kissin' you and all. Earlier." He could not believe a man of his age could still feel such heat in his cheeks like some stripling lad. "I'll nae—"

"Don't," Eve said suddenly, her eyes going nervous and shifty and her fingers strangling each other as she twisted her hands.

Conall raised his eyebrows. "Doona?"

Eve rolled her lips inward, chewed on them for a moment. Her eyes found Conall's for only an instant before flitting away again.

"MacKerrick, I—" She blew out a breath. "I have a question to ask you, but before you say nay out of hand, would that you give your answer a bit of thought."

Conall's stomach clenched. She was going to ask him to leave. Or ask him to take her to the Buchanan town. Either one had logical reasoning to it, from Eve Buchanan's point of view, certainly. But his answer to either would be—had to be—nae.

He could not let her go. Could not, and didn't want to.

"Go on, then," Conall said warily, nodding.

Eve took a deep breath and then met his gaze squarely.

"MacKerrick, will you marry me?"

"Will I—" MacKerrick stopped and shook his head as if to clear it. "Say again, lass?"

Evelyn's face felt as if it would melt from her skull and her stomach lurched sickly. Of course he would make her repeat it.

"'Tis most improper for us to carry on like this," she said stiffly, hoping the hasty reasoning she'd concocted in her head would still sound plausible when proposed aloud to the highlander. "You've already said that journeying to the Buchanan village—"

"Town," MacKerrick corrected vaguely.

"*Town*—I beg your pardon—is impossible because of the weather, correct?"

MacKerrick nodded. "A death sentence, for certain. And the grays . . ."

"Exactly," Evelyn said quickly, thankful for the suggestion. "So travel to the Buchanan village is impossible in the foreseeable future."

"Town," MacKerrick corrected again. "But impossible, aye."

"And . . ." Evelyn swallowed and tried to regain her train of thought. She'd little time to tidy her speech in her mind, but 'twas more sorely difficult to maintain her focus with MacKerrick's amber eyes pinned so intently to her, as if he could sense her desperation, was feeding off it.

She forged on. "And we've already been together, alone, for far too long. Your brother knows someone else is residing with you at the hut. What will he think when he discovers it is I, a woman? And both of us unmarried?"

"Well, ah . . ." MacKerrick stuttered. "He'd likely think the very worst, is what. Mayhap if you didna look as you do . . . although you canna help the way you look, of course," he rushed. "Naught you can do about it."

Evelyn blinked. Was MacKerrick saying she was attractive or homely?

The highlander grimaced. "I would be hard-pressed to convince him that naught improper had occurred betwixt us. And Duncan is prone to gossip, as it is."

"Is he?" Evelyn's eyes widened.

"A terrible habit o' his." MacKerrick frowned and shook his head regretfully. "And the Buchanans . . ."

Evelyn thought this was going much, much better than she had ever expected. 'Twas almost as if MacKerrick was helping her convince him. "My honor would be in tatters," she said.

"As would me own," the highlander insisted.

Evelyn hesitated, trying to ignore the fluttering of her stomach. She was unsure how to broach the next obstacle. "But you are recently widowed. Would your people accept—"

"They expect me to one day take another wife, Eve. And that I would find a fine Scots lass would please them."

Evelyn cringed inwardly. "'Twould be of no consequence if your wife was not . . . a full-blooded Scot?"

MacKerrick seemed to ponder this and Evelyn held her breath.

"I am the MacKerrick. They would accept whoever I took as a wife."

Tentative relief flooded her.

"But the Buchanans mayna be so accommodating," MacKerrick warned. "They may take offense that you would marry without your clan chief's permission."

"Oh, I don't think that will be a problem," Evelyn offered quickly and then cursed herself when MacKerrick's eyebrows rose. *Imbecile* . . .

"You've saved my life, after all," she scrambled, eager to make some excuse for her rash words. "And my virtue, by marrying me. I think 'twould be considered quite a coup, having married the MacKerrick and uniting both villages."

"Towns."

"Towns," Evelyn amended.

"A coup, indeed," MacKerrick agreed quietly, still staring at Evelyn with his glowing amber eyes. "But you'd be a MacKerrick then, lass. You'd nae live at the Buchanan town."

"I can accept that," Evelyn said, striving for the proper martyrish air.

"And there is one more thing." MacKerrick hesitated. "Because I am the clan chief, my wife . . ."

Evelyn leaned forward "Yea, MacKerrick?"

"I'm expected to have a family, Eve," he finished, a wicked gleam in his eyes.

So there it was, at last out in the open. The biggest hurdle between them.

"I would be willing to . . . discuss it," Eve said stiffly, returning to her upright posture as her ears tingled with heat.

"*Discuss* it? You doona get bairns by talkin'." MacKerrick grinned mischievously. "Or do you nae know—"

"Of course I do!" Evelyn snapped.

"Then you would withhold yourself from your husband?"

"Is that something that must be decided immediately?" Evelyn noticed her voice sounded high and panicked to her own ears.

"I'm nae different from any other man, Eve," MacKerrick said mildly. "I'd know if I'd have a wife true, or a woman who would not yield to her husband."

"I don't even *know* you, sir!"

"You've asked me to marry you."

"Yea, but—"

"*And* you kissed me!" MacKerrick taunted.

"*You* kissed *me!*"

He winked at her "You kissed me back."

Evelyn's chest heaved. "Never mind," she snapped. "Forget I suggested it. Obviously it was a poor idea." She turned and left the pen, stalking over shards of the broken mead jug toward the upper end of the hut and the strips of rags she'd made from her ruined kirtle and cloak dangling from the ceiling—her hair was still icy wet. "When the weather clears, I'll simply take my chances with a journey to the Buchanan village."

"Town."

"Oh, do shut up!" She snatched a cloth from the rafters. "They'll either accept me or nay."

"Now, Eve . . ." MacKerrick cajoled, beginning his grisly work on the deer. "There's nae shame in fearing your first time with a man."

"I am *not* discussing this with you." She'd rather starve. Or face the entire pack of grays. Suggesting that MacKerrick marry her had been a foolish, impetuous, naïve, *mad* idea, and the highlander wasn't taking her seriously, any matter—latching onto the most sordid detail of becoming man and wife. What of companionship? Trust? Safety?

She sat down on the stool, her back to the pens, and undid her clammy plait. She wanted to cry but would not humiliate herself further. She picked up the cloth and began rubbing at her wet, tangled hair, and her eyes fell onto Minerva's black cloak.

She stuck her tongue out at it petulantly.

Her hair as dry as she could hope to get it, Evelyn rose from the stool and retrieved the cloak, the black wool likely scratchy when worn on its own, but dry. She had no other choice save to remain in her own wet clothes and catch her death.

Besides, the sight of the garment would irritate MacKerrick.

Evelyn turned toward the far end of the hut, cloak in hand, where the highlander had opened the deer's torso into an empty cavity. He hadn't said another word to her, only kept on with his gruesome chore.

"I'd change my clothes," she announced. "And then I'm going to sleep."

MacKerrick's knife paused but he did not turn. "Very well, Eve."

"Be certain you keep your distance, sir," she warned, a bit loudly.

When he did not answer, Evelyn ignored the pinch in her heart and climbed into the box bed, drawing the ragged, moth-chewed curtain closed with as much force as she dared.

Savage Scots dwelling—at least in a proper keep she might have a door to slam.

Chapter Nine

Evelyn awoke to warm, glowing light beyond the bed's tattered curtain and a savory aroma that threatened to turn her stomach inside out. She lay still for some time, blinking in the gloom of the box bed and trying to determine if she was dreaming or nay. The hut had never felt so warm, even though she was clothed only in Minerva's old cloak, which was surprisingly soft against her skin.

Then she heard a voice—MacKerrick's—singing soft and low. Evelyn strained to hear the words, but they were in Gaelic and too quiet for her to make out. Goose bumps pushed beneath the wool at the sound of the highlander's smooth, masculine voice. She would have to ask him what the words meant when she was no longer angry at him.

Evelyn pushed herself aright and looked around for her kirtle and underdress, which she had spread out beside her to dry.

They were both gone.

Evelyn frowned at the thought of MacKerrick pulling back the curtain whilst she slept and absconding with her clothing. She looked down and

was somewhat placated by the fact that Minerva's
cloak completely enveloped her, although she would
have to be mindful of her modesty when she alighted
from the bed in search of her gowns.

She clutched at the front of the cloak with one
hand and pulled back the curtain slightly with the
other to see if MacKerrick was still moving about.
At first glimpse of what lay beyond the ragged
cloth, Evelyn gasped and pushed the curtain completely aside.

The upper living end of the hut had been trans-
formed. MacKerrick's brother must have brought
more than foodstuffs, for the area around the fire
pit glowed a golden yellow from the light of now
two small oil lamps, washing the room in a shim-
mery incandescence. And the fire itself was a
wonder, the usual peat fuel enhanced by the addi-
tion of several lengths of wood, creating merry,
high-dancing flames that crackled and hissed. The
broken pottery had been swept from the floor, and
the crock and urn sat on a flat rock within the fire
ring, their rustic lids cocked and whistling aro-
matic steam. Another wide wooden bowl Evelyn
had not seen before sat nearby, filled with water
and what looked like a wadded length of linen
from Evelyn's old kirtle. The flagstones near the
bowl and under the low stool were dark gray and
chalky with drying water.

Evelyn's eyes were drawn to the shelf on the wall,
where her gowns—and she recognized MacKerrick's long tunic and plaid, dark and dripping with
water, as well—were suspended by items placed
along their hems on the shelf.

"You're awake." MacKerrick's voice startled her
from the far end of the hut, where he stepped

from the shadows carrying a bucket. Evelyn knew she was staring, but could not help it.

The highlander was . . . magnificent, and Evelyn saw him as she never had before. MacKerrick wore a different long, creamy, shin-length shirt, but this one was sleeveless and boasted a deep V at the neckline, which revealed not only long, muscular arms from the shoulders down, but the high ridge of his chest and the cleft of his breastbone, his leather necklace resting above the golden hair. The tunic was caught low about his hips by his belt, although he wore no blade. The tops of his boots nearly met the hem of his shirt, but in the gap Evelyn glimpsed chiseled calves softened by the same gilded hair.

Her eyes traveled back up to his face, the stubble of beard gone from around his slight smile. His hair was damp and curling over one shoulder, leaving a dark patch of wet over one breast, and he had redone his long, skinny braid and added its twin on the other side of his head. He looked . . . well, clean. And strong and masculine and quite delicious, actually. Evelyn was startled by her awareness of this new MacKerrick.

"Did you sleep well?" MacKerrick asked and Evelyn's trance was interrupted by his voice and by Alinor, who also stepped from the shadows.

The wolf trotted to the box bed, Bonnie close at her tail, and as Evelyn reached out her free hand to pat them both, she noted their smooth fur and the wide, lopsided bows tied inexpertly around each of their necks. She couldn't help the smile that spread across her mouth at the lovely sight of them.

She looked up as the highlander approached the fire, realizing she had yet to speak to him. "Mac-

Kerrick . . . what—" She let her eyes flit about the room pointedly and then return to his. "What is all this?"

"I would have dressed wee Whiskers as well, but he wouldna keep still long enough for me to make the knot."

Evelyn laughed uneasily. "But the fire, the clothes—" She gestured vaguely toward his person as he bent to place the empty bucket near the stool. "What is all this?" she repeated, realizing she sounded like a dunce.

"A feast," he said, tossing her a grin that flashed white teeth in his freshly shaven skin and caused Evelyn's heart to lurch stupidly. He was beyond sensual. MacKerrick crossed to the shelf and retrieved a small jug and then faced her once more. "We are celebrating. Come." He beckoned to her with a wave of his hand, indicating the stool, and Evelyn had the distinct impression she was being tempted by sin made flesh.

She rose, but then hesitated. "What is it we are celebrating?"

"Our kill, for one," MacKerrick said, moving to the fire and uncorking the jug. He set aside the lid of the large crock and poured in a splash of liquid before taking a swig from the jug himself. He gave a satisfied sigh. "Come, Eve, sit. I'll nae bite you."

Evelyn wasn't so certain he would not—and even less certain that she did not wish for him to at least *try*—but she moved to the stool anyway, out of curiosity as to what MacKerrick was about. She sat carefully, quite aware of her nakedness beneath the cloak and taking pains to arrange it.

"You said 'for one'—is there aught else to celebrate?" she asked warily as he stepped closer to her, but still an arm's length away. The sight of him so . . . *exposed* was doing odd things to Evelyn's senses. She really ought to demand that he don more clothing.

She ought to.

He handed her the jug. "Mead?"

"Thank you." She took it and tipped it to her mouth awkwardly with one hand while he resumed puttering with this thing and that about the hut.

"I thought you might fancy a bath," he continued, his eyes flicking to the bowl and rag near her slippers. "The lot of us have already cleaned up a bit."

"I see that." By all that was holy, did she surely see it. She couldn't help but wonder if MacKerrick was naked beneath his long tunic, and if he had disrobed entirely whilst she napped, only steps away from her. Goose bumps prickled her skin again.

But under no circumstances was she about to wash while MacKerrick was in the hut with her. Absolutely not.

She glanced at the bowl, struggling to keep the longing from her face. "I don't think I shall," she said. "I've already been wet once today and I'd not risk a chill."

"The water's warm, and there's a scant drop of oil in it—lavender." MacKerrick grinned at her temptingly and Evelyn groaned to herself. He looked her up and down. "You should be able to retain your modesty in that blasted cloak if you but turn 'round."

Evelyn hesitated and hated herself for showing MacKerrick she was wavering. But he was right. If she faced the wall and kept the cloak around her . . . Dear God! She would love to feel clean again. She had never felt so gritty and smelly and dry.

"And I willna peek," MacKerrick said, his solemn words betrayed by his grin.

Everything she knew logically screamed at her that this was yet another terrible idea. She should just wash her hands and face and be done with it. The food smelled delicious and she was starving, as usual.

"Be sure you *don't* peek, sir." The warning was out of her mouth and she had turned away from him before she'd even realized she'd made the decision. Evelyn dragged the bowl to between her feet— carefully, so as not to spill one drop of the precious, oil-laced water—and slipped off her shoes. She bent to wring the water from the rag and began to wash.

Conall caught himself staring at Eve's back and forced himself to another task, any task that would take the images of her touching her bare skin with the water-laden rag. But his eyes still strayed to her with every seductive glug of water, every near-silent sigh of pleasure from her mouth. Once, when he happened to glance at her, the cloak had dropped behind the curve of her shoulder, glistening like the palest honey in the firelight. Conall turned his groan into a cough and looked quickly away before Eve caught him looking at her skin, her hair tangled wild down her back . . .

Conall turned completely away and looked down: his léine tented away from his hips, pushed out by his cock. He squatted down by the fire and tried to think of his bony, balding brother, Duncan; of a dung heap; of rotten fish.

It didn't help. His head turned back to her as if of its own accord, her shoulders hunched beneath the cloak, her head bent low, and Conall imagined her washing her most private, feminine parts, the cloth sliding up and down . . .

He stood abruptly, fists clenched. He could stand no more. Conall took a step toward her, stopped.

Eve's head came up, immediately on alert, and she showed him her profile. "Did you want something, MacKerrick?"

"Can I—" He cleared his throat, hoping she would not turn completely and see proof of his arousal. "Can I wash your hair for you, Eve?"

She froze, like the deer in the clearing, and Conall could not help but note the similarities: slender, long-legged, skittish beauty . . .

"My hair?" she asked, her alarm and confusion obvious in her tone.

But Conall ignored it, stepping within reach of her, somehow restraining himself from touching her.

"When you've finished," he offered, his eyes devouring the sight of her dewy skin where a sheen of perspiration glistened along her hairline. "I could rinse your hair with the wash water. I used to do so for Nonna when 'twas too cold to bathe outdoors."

Eve stiffened. "Nonna was your wife?"

"Aye." Conall wondered for a moment if it was a mistake to mention Nonna, but he wanted Eve to begin to understand what he was asking. He wanted to touch her, wanted her leave for him to do so.

"I don't think that's wise, MacKerrick," Eve said, and Conall took the way her voice had gone breathy as a favorable sign. Her face was still turned partially toward him, but now her gaze dropped to the flagstones.

"Why, lass?" he asked quietly, taking a slow step

toward her. If he but raised a hand, his fingertips would graze her back now, he was so near. "I willna hurt you." His hand twitched and he let it brush across the ends of her hair, just enough so that she could feel his touch. He saw her shoulders rise slightly with an intake of breath. "If you doona like it, I'll stop."

"MacKerrick, I—"

"Eve," he said, cutting her off as he bent to one knee behind her. His face was now near hers and she turned her head minutely toward him, although her eyes still would not meet his. Then Conall did let his hand go to her hair, grasping a handful of it gently and stroking it once to its end. "Let me," he said in a whisper, the tendrils around her ear fluttering beneath his breath.

He brought his hand up again and let his fingers comb jerkily, lightly through the length of snarls. "I'll be gentle," he said, his own breath coming heavier as he realized the double meaning behind his promise.

His hand came up again and Conall let his fingertips grasp Eve's scalp, massaging beneath her soft, silky hair. Her eyes fluttered closed.

"Slide the bowl to me," he directed softly and was surprised when he heard the scrape of the wooden vessel on the flagstones. Eve had pushed it to the side with one foot, the rag floating in it limply.

Conall reached down and pulled the bowl closer, then lifted the soaking rag. With his other hand he grasped her hair again and tugged. Eve's head dropped back slightly, exposing her neck. Conall raised the rag and squeezed it over her crown, repeated the movement until her hair was thick and dark with water. Then he began to rub her scalp, press the length of her tresses between his fingers, sluicing the water down and out.

She sighed and Conall looked down to see one pale knee peeking out of the cloak. He began to rub Eve's scalp again, letting his fingertips trail to her hairline at her nape, wrapping his fingers around her warm skin and massaging.

When Eve gave a little hum of pleasure, 'twas all Conall could do to keep from dragging her from the stool backward into his arms. His whole body shook with desire, the smell of the lavender oil warmed by her body making him drunk. 'Twas Conall who was supposed to be seducing Eve, but without any effort at all, the lass had bewitched him in his own game.

He dropped his mouth near her ear. "Eve," he whispered and felt her shiver.

"Hmmm?" Her eyes remained closed and Conall saw her hands fisted in the black wool of the cloak.

"Does it feel good?" He let go of her for an instant to retrieve the bowl and her head raised, her eyes opened.

"Yea, thank you, MacK—"

Conall grabbed the wet rope of her hair and pulled, more roughly this time, dropping Eve's head back once more. She gasped.

"I'm nae finished," he warned quietly.

Her throat convulsed as she swallowed, glancing up at him through her lashes. He might have seen a flash of fear. Her eyes flitted away.

Conall poured the scant bit of water over her hair, liking the primitive sound it made on the stones. Some of it ran down the sides of her face, her neck, inside the cloak. Conall set the bowl aside and ran his fists hand over hand down her hair, squeezing the water from it. Then slowly, deliberately, starting from the bottom, he wound Eve's hair around his palm, over and over until his fist rested against her exposed nape. Her head was now drawn back fully and she whimpered.

Her breasts rose and fell quietly, rapidly, and Conall brought his mouth to her ear once more.

"Eve," he whispered. "I want to marry you."

Her eyelids fluttered open and she looked at him from the corner of her eye.

"I want you"—Conall tugged her head back even farther, bringing the soft skin behind her ear to a hairsbreadth from his lips—"to be my wife. Do you understand, lass?"

She squeezed her eyes closed again and Conall could not resist pressing his lips to the curve of her jaw near her earlobe—so soft and warm there. His breath swirled in the hollow of her neck. He pulled her back gently but surely by her hair, until her shoulders rested against his chest, and skimmed his lips down her neck, damp with the fragrant oil. He flicked out his tongue for the tiniest taste.

"MacKerrick," she said, her voice low and choked.

"What, lass?" Conall kissed her neck again, nuzzled deeper with his face, pushing the cloak aside. His hand not holding her hair came up to stroke her arm through the thin wool. He could feel her trembling. He hoped 'twas with desire. "You only have to answer aye or nae," he whispered in her ear. "If 'tis nae, I'll stop, although I doona want to. I want to kiss you. I want to kiss the whole of you and make you my wife. Will you marry me, Eve?"

"Is it . . . is it legal?" she asked hesitantly.

"Aye." He pressed her to him tighter, pulling her arm back by the crook of her elbow so that her

back arched and her breasts pressed against the
cloak. She gave a little cry. More of her milky leg
was revealed, the slit of the cloak widening. He gritted his teeth before continuing.

"If you wish, we can have a priest's blessing when
he comes in the summer. But till then, we say it,
and 'tis done. Our words are our vows. So, heed
me, Eve"—he tugged on her hair to look into her
eyes, his want of her barely held in check—"if you
say aye, you are mine. You are bound to me."

"And you would be mine," she said, her tone low
but bold, as if challenging him even in her submis-
sive position. "No matter what should ever happen?"

Her innocent query fed the flames of Conall's
desire so that he could hardly reply. He took in a
long, deep breath through his nose and nodded. "I
would make my vow to you now, lass: I, Conall,
marry you, Eve."

He heard the wolfsong from beyond the hut,
eerie music to accompany the thunderous rhythm
of his heart, the blood rushing in his veins. He felt
a vibrating in his core like lightning, and the
rumble of thunder in his ears. She was staring at
him, her eyes searching his face, her lips slightly
parted for her fast, shallow breaths. He worried
that she would now refuse him. He shook her
once, curtly, and she gasped.

"If you want me, say it, Eve," he growled.

A single tear slipped from the corner of her eye
and slid down her cheek. She nodded jerkily, the
slight movement all her captivity would allow.

"I, Evelyn, marry you, Conall."

Conall felt a wave of dizziness spin around him
and the hut seemed to fade in and out of focus for
a moment.

"'Tis done," he whispered and then flicked away her tear with his tongue.

She glanced at his mouth. "We're married?"

"We are." Conall stood in one powerful movement, pulling Eve with him by her hair and arm. The bowl and stool went clattering underfoot and he kicked them away. He let go of her elbow to spin her to face him and wrapped his arm about her, still holding her head captive.

"We are indeed married. And now, you will become my wife."

Evelyn wanted to weep, to scream, to sing—she had never felt so earth-shatteringly alive as she did in the moment when MacKerrick released her hair and swung her to the box bed. Her skin tingled beneath the ancient cloak, clean and chilled and sensitized to every caress of fabric, every minute pressing of MacKerrick's touch. Her heart fluttered and snapped like a regal banner unfurled, bravely announcing her new allegiance on this foreign and daunting battlefield she now faced.

He pushed her backward and she would have stumbled except that he was holding on to her arms with bruising fingers.

Why wasn't he kissing her? Why was he just staring—

"Take off the cloak," he commanded gruffly. He released her but held his hands only slightly away from her body, as if ready to snatch her up again in the next second.

Evelyn hesitated, the first real shiver of fear rippling through her at the thought of what was about to take place.

She waited an instant too long. Minerva's old clasp gave way with little protest, the ancient threads shredding like cobwebs as MacKerrick seized the cloak and pulled it apart in one swift, short motion of his hands. The black wool fell away from Evelyn's naked body and she cried out, trying to drape her arms across her breasts and down her front. She'd never been nude with another person save a lady's maid the whole of her grown life, and she was now embarrassed of her body. She was so thin now, bony, her flesh still discolored from her fall weeks ago and her illness. Surely this man, so hardy, so strong, so physically perfect, would be repulsed by her.

But he brought his palms back to her arms again with a harsh hiss of breath. His skin felt as hot as one of the stones from the fire ring and Evelyn flinched at his touch. She had gone over the brink now, married to this savage highlander who thought she was someone else. She knew he was going to make love to her and there was no turning back. She was his wife and she would yield to him. She must. A bittersweet penance for her deception, a double-edged payment for her safety. She tried not to think about the possibility that she would get with child.

She tried.

"Ah, Eve," MacKerrick sighed and drew her close, rubbing his face in her hair at her crown, his fingertips pressing painlessly into the flesh of her upper arms. Evelyn stood stiffly, her arms still shielding her from full contact with his body. "Are you afraid?"

She nodded, her mind tripping over horrifying visions with every thought: her body swelling and then bursting in a wash of blood, screaming herself away to her own death.

"Doona be," MacKerrick whispered, sliding his palms around to splay over her cool back. He pulled her to him gently. "I'll go slowly. So slowly . . ." His brogue trilled in her ear and he pressed his lips there, squeezed her again. "Relax, lass."

"I can't. I—" She couldn't tell him that her fear did not spring from the idea of MacKerrick breaching her body with his own. She knew that any pain she felt would be fleeting and soon forgotten. 'Twas the result of their lovemaking that terrified her.

"I'm cold," she finally managed to choke out, the plea barely more than a whisper.

"Of course you are," he said ruefully and guided her backward until she felt the box bed on the backs of her thighs. He leaned to the side and threw back the blanket and then, in a rush of movement, swung her up into his arms. She gasped and clutched at his front, revealing herself fully to him.

MacKerrick's eyes roamed her body as he bent and carefully placed her on the thin ticking. Evelyn scrambled from her back to her side and snatched at the blanket to pull it over her, but MacKerrick stayed her with one long arm.

"Nae, lass, let me look at you for a moment. Please."

She kept the blanket wrinkled in her fist, but left the bulk of it draped over her hip. Her eyes studied the edge of the ticking where MacKerrick's tunic was illuminated against the dark shadow of his thigh by the firelight behind him.

After what seemed an eternity, neither of them moving, MacKerrick's hands went to his belt. Evelyn felt her stomach knot as he loosened the thick brown leather and let it fall away, his tunic sagging over his hips. She felt a hitch in her throat and swallowed it down. She wanted this finality, this consummation, but her fear paralyzed her. Was it only moments ago she had been wanting of MacKerrick, breathless with thoughts of his touch, his possession of her? Now 'twas only terror that held her tighter than any lover. She could not draw a full breath and her eyes ached with unshed tears.

Then MacKerrick's tunic rose up over hairy thighs and Evelyn heard the whisper of it as it, too, fell to the floor. Her gaze flicked to his manhood, fully erect and aimed at her as surely as an arrow. It was long and dusky and somehow ominous looking, its intent clear. A weapon. A nightmare waiting.

The breathy sob came out of nowhere, startling her, and she brought her hand to her mouth to stifle it.

She felt MacKerrick's sudden alarm as he climbed onto the bed and tried to gather her rigid body to his.

"Eve, Eve," he crooned. "Shh—doona fear me so, I canna stand it." He stroked her hair, still wet and fragrant with the oil.

She felt another jagged bubble lodge in her throat and fought it back down. Her arms were crossed in front of her breasts again, denying him full contact with her body, and yet she felt his warmth. Part of her wanted to wrap her arms around MacKerrick's lean waist and sob out her fear, wanted his arms about her as well, comforting her.

But that wasn't what MacKerrick wanted, and Evelyn knew she owed him this marriage rite. She wanted it over with.

"Are you ready to mount me now?" she asked into his chest, and she could hear the brittle tension in her own voice.

MacKerrick was still for a moment. "I am," he admitted quietly.

Evelyn pushed away from him to lie on her back, her eyes squeezed shut. "All right." She swallowed. "I'm ready."

He had the audacity to laugh at her. Evelyn's eyes snapped open and she turned her head to look at him. The highlander was smiling as he scooted closer to her side. She flinched when he brought a wide palm to her face.

"'Tis nae punishment to brace yourself against, Eve," he said, the corners of his eyes crinkling. "I'd have you enjoy it as much as I."

"Well, I'll not, sir, so do what you must." She turned her head away to stare at the box bed's wooden canopy once more. She swallowed again, gathering her courage into the center of her body. "Shall I . . . shall I spread my legs?"

MacKerrick chuckled again and Evelyn's face burned.

"Ah, lass, you are a wonder," he breathed, his smile louder than his words.

"You'll wonder where I went do you not get on with it," she snapped. "I'll not lie here forever, MacKerrick. I'm still cold, never mind hungry, and—"

His mouth cut off her shrill lecture, his lips hard on hers at first, pressing against her teeth painfully. After a moment, though, they softened and opened to caress her mouth. His lips pulled at hers once, twice, then he looked down into her eyes. He still appeared rather amused, but the amber fire in his gaze sparkled with obvious desire.

"Very well, Eve. I'd nae have you runnin' off on those fine legs of yours," he said solemnly and then the smile dropped from his face, replaced by an intensity that resuscitated Eve's fear. "Spread them for me."

Evelyn commanded her thighs to move away from each other and one knee at last twitched, bumping into MacKerrick's lean, hard thigh.

"Will that do?"

"For now," MacKerrick said.

His hand slid from her face to her collarbone and his fingers danced over the ridge of her shoulder, pushing her arms away. When his palm cupped her breast, Evelyn caught her breath against the prickling sensation of her nipple.

"Shh . . . relax," MacKerrick whispered as he lowered his head. He rubbed his lips against her other nipple and the stinging sensation struck her again. She released her held breath with a whoosh when his hot mouth opened over her breast, his other palm stroking gentle circles over her raised peak as he sucked.

Evelyn felt a spasming deep in her abdomen, persistent and terrifying and oddly pleasurable. She continued to stare at the box bed's ceiling as MacKerrick licked her with a flat tongue and she could see the crown of his head weaving in time to the sensations she felt. Her sigh betrayed her rigid throat, surprising her, embarrassing her.

"That's right," MacKerrick whispered against her wet skin, bringing gooseflesh over her body. "Enjoy it—naught to fear, Eve. My Eve . . ." His mouth claimed her nipple again and the hand over her breast slipped down over her ribs to flutter at her navel.

Evelyn swallowed, trying to ignore her body's traitorous response. Her mind was still terrified, but her flesh . . . oh, 'twas weak! She didn't want Mac-

Kerrick's touch to arouse her, to bring her pleasure. Not when it might mean her death. But she was steadily losing control of herself as MacKerrick's hand trailed even lower, massaging the hollow of her abdomen between her hips, soothing the throbbing there, and at the same time, stirring it.

"I don't want to do this, MacKerrick," she choked out.

He did not pull away, but continued suckling her leisurely, as if he pulled mead from the mouth of a jug. "Why?" he asked, then licked the curve of her breast, pushed his fingertips into the curly hair between her legs.

"I . . . I don't want a baby." He was cupping her sex with his palm now, kneading the flesh. Evelyn had the urge to push her hips into his touch.

"Mmm-hmm," MacKerrick murmured against her skin. "Perhaps you'll nae get one."

Evelyn frowned, wanted to moan. If he would but stop touching her . . . *there*. Mayhap her thoughts would come to order.

"But we're going to—"

"'Tis your first time, is it nae?" he asked easily, the kneading of her mound replaced by his palm now sliding up and down through her hair, the deliberate friction disturbing her flesh to nearly the point that Evelyn thought she could no longer keep a proper silence.

"It is," she managed to answer.

"'Tis unlikely, then," MacKerrick said, raising up slightly and flicking his tongue across her other nipple. "You doona get a bairn every time you make love, Eve." He latched on to her fully.

Evelyn could not help but writhe slightly, her mind a blur of logic and reason and base, physical lust. What MacKerrick had just told her, of course she knew it was true, but so many of the young girls who'd come to the priory had sworn they'd only allowed a man to use them one time . . .

"I'm frightened, MacKerrick. So frightened . . ."

He shook his head, not breaking contact with her nipple. Lower down, his fingers were scissoring, spreading and closing the folds of her sex. She gasped and her eyes rolled back.

MacKerrick released her breast with a loud slurp. "Doona be." His eyes bored into hers. "Eve, do you want me? If you say nae, I'll stop. I'll not force myself upon you."

His movements between her legs stilled, as if proving to her that, should she but say the word, MacKerrick would leave her untouched. Her body throbbed in ghostly echoes of the rhythm he'd created deep inside her and she wanted to whimper at the emptiness she felt.

"Eve, do you want me to stop?" MacKerrick repeated.

"Nay," she said quietly. God help her, she meant it.

Then she felt one long finger slide between the folds, where it was wet and hot and oh so very, very sensitive.

"Then trust me."

"I do . . ." Evelyn did arch then, and heard her own pitiful mew as if from outside her body. Her mind let go of her fear as another of MacKerrick's fingers joined in the play, smoothing over her firm nub and circling there. Then the pair of fingers slid further into her cleft, dipping briefly into the innermost recesses of her body. Evelyn cried out again, a gasp, a moan, and her legs spread wider, one thigh now captured between MacKerrick's. She felt his erection hot and hard against her skin.

MacKerrick began a slow, steady, firm rhythm the length of her sex, up and down and in and around, his hand sliding faster. He latched on to her breast when Evelyn began to move her hips in time with his hand. She felt frenzied and mad and dizzy, anticipating this unknown slowly revealed by MacKerrick's deliberate touch.

"You'll nae hold out much longer, Eve," he said gruffly, looking into her eyes with wild amber sparks lighting his own gaze. "Nor will I. I'd take you now— 'twill make it easier on you." He was sliding his erection along her thigh and it was slick and hot.

"Do it," she panted. She wanted it, whatever he had to give her. All of him. "Do it now."

MacKerrick swung over her in a swift motion, removing the hand between her legs for a moment to push her thighs wide and up.

"Hold on to your knees," he commanded.

Evelyn did, writhing on her back as the sight of him knelt between her legs like some stone god, his erection waving heavily over her shamefully exposed sex. It felt beyond sinful, and Evelyn was transported by the wicked sight of him.

MacKerrick ran his fingertips up her cleft and then grasped his manhood, stroking it. His other hand went back to her mound, his thumb testing her elastic flesh, circling her nub once more hypnotically.

Evelyn arched her hips, pulled at her legs. "MacKerrick," she begged, liking the pleading sound of her voice.

He leaned forward, sitting on his heels, and placed the head of his erection against her, his thumb still holding her enslaved. He let his other arm drop to dangle at his hip.

"Are you ready, Eve?" he asked in a low, dangerous voice and pushed at her slightly. His thumb quickened.

Evelyn bucked, feeling herself stretch around him. "Oh, help me," she cried. "MacKerrick, help me!"

He pushed in farther and sank in what felt like the whole of him. Evelyn felt her flesh yield in sweet agony and then her breath, her heart, her thoughts, the world itself, stopped as her climax took her.

And 'twas only then that MacKerrick pushed his length into her fully.

Her body resisted, and then accepted with pulsing, painful, shattering waves and Evelyn cried out with the hugeness of it all. MacKerrick pumped his hips into her fiercely as she throbbed, and in a moment he was stone still, his length jerking deep inside her.

Evelyn cried out again at the full sensation and felt tears on her own cheeks.

'Twas glorious. And holy.

And Evelyn Godewin was now Evelyn MacKerrick.

Chapter Ten

Conall felt as though he'd been tumbled over rapids as he collapsed at Eve's side, his skin clammy and damp, his muscles quaking, a full breath seeming to retreat ever beyond his next shudder, leaving him gasping still. He could hear his own heartbeat in the closeness of the box bed and he turned his head to look at Eve, now his wife.

She stared at the canopy above their heads, her lips parted slightly, her breasts bare and pointed and heaving with her own breaths. She turned her face to his, her cheeks flushed crimson. Perhaps 'twas only an aftereffect of their lovemaking, but Conall would have in that moment sworn on his life that never had he even *imagined* a woman could be of such beauty.

He gave her a smile and had to clear his throat before he could speak. "How fare thee, lass?" he asked quietly. "I didna hurt you?"

She shook her head against the ticking and her eyes searched his face, full of surprise and shyness. Conall wondered if she was satisfied with their lovemaking. He had tried to give her as much pleasure as he could before he'd taken her, but it had been so long since Conall had eased himself, and he was ashamed of his swiftness.

Eve continued to stare at him, but now her brows were furrowed slightly. Conall remembered their first meeting, when her face had appeared over Alinor's head with much the same expression. He'd thought she looked like an angel then, and he did now, as well.

An angel who would save your town.

The thought came as a leaden surprise in the light headiness he felt and smashed into Conall's conscience. He pushed the thought away—there would be time later to think upon his actions and their repercussions. For now, he simply wanted to enjoy the company of the woman in his bed.

Ronan's bed, the black voice whispered.

"Do you hunger?" he asked, searching for any task that would not remind him of the past, of his selfish motives—or that bloody curse.

Eve opened her mouth to answer, but closed it again with a grimace.

He trailed a finger along her cheek. "What? What troubles you, lass?"

Her flush deepened. "Are you certain . . . ?"

Conall smiled at her sweetness. Of course she would inquire of his pleasure, not knowing with her limited experience that Conall had indeed enjoyed himself of her body as much as any man was capable of enjoying a woman. She wished for reassurance, of course.

"Are you certain we . . . have not made a child?"

Conall felt as if Eve had slapped him. So much for tender confessions between lovers.

"Nae entirely, Eve," he said evenly, trying to curb his stung pride. "None can fortell that, save God."

In a blink she had scrambled from the bed and snatched the old black cloak from the floor, flashing Conall the small curves of her backside before gaining her feet and swirling the cloak about her. She stalked to the shelf where her clothes were still drying.

Conall raised up on an elbow in the changed atmosphere of the hut, wondering at her worry.

"Eve, why—?"

"Speak not to me, MacKerrick," she snapped, testing her clothes' dampness.

"Are you *angry* with me?"

Forsaking her gowns as too wet, she turned toward the fire pit, clutching the cloak together. Her eyes flicked to him and Conall could clearly see her fury.

"You took advantage of me—telling me what I wanted to hear so that you could gain what you desired."

"Now, just one bleedin' moment," Conall said, also climbing from the box bed and collecting his léine and belt from the floor. "I did nae such thing." He jerked his léine over his head. "You make as if I lied to you."

She sniffed and crouched awkwardly to the urn, mug in hand.

"Eve, I *didna* lie to you."

She shot to her feet and threw the mug to the flagstones where it exploded. "I told you I had no wish to bear children! I told you, MacKerrick!"

"And I told you the truth," he shot back. "'Tis unlikely you will conceive!" He jerked at his belt, fastening it. "'Twas your first time and—look at yourself, lass! Thin as a whip and just come away from illness." He ignored her flinch. "When did you last have your season?"

Eve's face blossomed red. "I don't know!" She seemed to think for a moment. "Shortly before gaining Scotland, I suppose."

Her answer troubled Conall, but he tried not to let his alarm show. He spread his arms. "Well, there you are, then. You're nae having a season—no bairn. Satisfied?"

Eve wrapped the cloak more securely and crouched once more to begin picking up the shards of the ruined mug. Alinor appeared from the far end of the hut, butting her elbow, but Eve pushed the wolf aside.

"Alinor, back—you'll have a sliver." Her mouth pressed into a stingy line before she addressed Conall once more, in a low voice, as if charging him with a despicable act. "You only wanted my body."

"I did want your body, aye. And you wanted mine, by your own confession. This wasna forced upon you, Eve, so doona play the victim with me."

She gaped at him, but said nothing, tossing pieces of the mug into a nearby bucket. "Disgusting," she mumbled, then rose to stand. "Like savages."

But Conall was not about to let her get away with further debasing what had occurred between them. He circled the fire pit and seized her elbow through the cloak.

"'Twas nae disgusting, and I'll thank you to keep your haughty English disdain out of our bed," he said through clenched teeth. "You are my wife now, Eve. I am your husband. What we did was sacred. 'Tis right that you enjoyed it."

"I forgot myself," Eve explained coolly. "'Twill not happen again." She tried to pull away.

Conall pulled her fully into his arms against her struggle. "It will. And soon, have I any say about it."

"Let go of me."

"Not until you tell me why," Conall demanded, not wanting to admit to himself how her demeanor hurt him. He'd tried so hard to make the evening a happy one for her, perhaps at first to ease his own conscience, but not entirely. "Why are you so against a bairn, Eve? Is it because of your mother? The maidens at the priory? Surely you know that not every birthing ends in tragedy." He leaned to the side to try to look at her face. "Lass, the way you are with Alinor, with Bonnie, with a *mouse*, for the love of Christ . . ."

He felt her surrender in his embrace as if he'd deflated her anger with his simple words.

"I grew up knowing I killed my own mother. *I ended her life*, MacKerrick. Her death was a terrible blow to my father, who loved her more than his own breath."

"Your da blamed you, did he?"

Eve sniffed and shook her head. "Of course not. He raised me himself and we did love each other true. Indeed, I held no love for any person greater than that for my father. It pained me that he never remarried. He simply had no wish for any woman save my mother, although I know that as I grew older, he became quite lonely."

Conall was touched by the tale of Eve's past more than he could tell her, but he felt he needed to reassure her somehow. It hurt him to see her so distressed. And 'twas the only way for her to be at ease with what Conall had planned for their future—and the future of the MacKerrick town.

"Your da loved you *both*, Eve. He wouldna have traded your life for your mother's." Conall noticed that he reached up to touch his necklace while he spoke, as if needing to validate his own words.

Eve shrugged. "'Twas why I joined the order—my mother made Papa promise it before she died. He said she'd wanted to protect me."

Conall's respect for Eve's dead sire increased. "It must have been difficult to send his only companion from him."

She grew still, her head pressing against his chest. "And for what? The priory was no haven. The monks were cruel, money-hungry. The maids we took in—most of them little more than girls, really—ill and poor and ignorant. The ones that did survive childbirth were then turned back out with a child to feed and nowhere to go. Oft times, I think 'twas more merciful for the ones who died. I found no comfort there, and could give none to those who sought it. So my father's sacrifice was for naught. I will never forgive myself for leaving him."

"But was not your home attacked and your father killed while you were away? Eve, your mother *did* protect you—your da, too. They saved your life by letting you go."

Conall was disturbed by Eve's shrug and twisted mouth. He grasped her shoulders so that she was forced to look at him.

"They sent you to me, Eve. For me. You doona see?" He looked around the hut pointedly. "You came to this place to find me, to find Alinor. To be my wife. Now, 'tis *my* duty to protect you."

Her chin dimpled an instant before she began to

weep. Conall pulled her head back to his chest and held her closely, letting her cry.

His eyes found the great black wolf sitting in the shadows near the door, eyes glistening, pinning Conall accusingly. Bonnie lay meekly near her feet.

Wasn't there an old fable of a sheep lying down with a wolf?

Conall tried not to think about what he promised Eve. He would protect her with his life, aye, but not against the one thing she most feared.

Conall prayed that his seed had taken.

Evelyn was at last able to stem her tears after several moments and reluctantly pull away from Mac-Kerrick. It had felt good to be held while she'd cried, a luxury she'd not been afforded in a long, long while.

"Thank you," she said, swiping at her face with Minerva's cloak whilst trying to remain covered. She looked about her, trying to locate her slippers—she needed them quickly to finish what she'd started before MacKerrick's touching speech.

"Not at all, lass," the highlander replied lightly. "Now, shall we eat?"

"In but a moment," Evelyn said while she crossed to the box bed and tossed the blanket about. Where were they? She had no desire to cut her feet if she could not find them, but one must do what one must do.

"MacKerrick, have you seen my slippers?"

"Aye. And 'tis sorry-looking they are."

Evelyn had dropped to her knees at the bedside and now gave him a wry look over her shoulder.

He grinned at her while ladling thick stew into

a wooden bowl. "You took them off by the stool. Do you have a need to go outdoors?"

"Yea, but—" She looked beneath the stool and found them. Eve slipped the thin—and admittedly sorry-looking—shoes on her feet, then stood.

"I'll accompany you." MacKerrick set the bowl aside, then snatched it back as Alinor rushed over to investigate its contents. "Och, this one's nae for you, Alinor. Back!" The wolf whined once and lay down immediately, her head between her paws and her ears flat.

Evelyn smiled at her girl's fine manners and crossed the floor to the animal pens. She reached down into the murky shadows and dug out a handful of hard, cold soil from the floor, then hurried back to the upper part of the hut. Ignoring MacKerrick's raised brow, Evelyn tossed the dirt into the bucket containing the bits of the broken mug.

She hoped she could remember the words.

Gathering up the folds of Minerva's cloak, and hoping more than a little that it would give the rhyme more significance, Evelyn looked down into the bucket as she stepped inside it carefully, swaying to regain her balance on cramped feet.

MacKerrick laughed. "Eve, I said I'd take you— you doona have to use the bucket."

"Shh!" she hissed at him and then muttered quietly aloud, *"Down and out, cleanse the spout, set me free for the next lout. Down and out, cleanse—"*

"Eve, what are you doing?" MacKerrick asked uneasily.

"—me free for the next lout." Evelyn paused and glanced over her shoulder. "I overheard the kitchen maids talking about this once. I never dreamed I would have need of it and, in truth, I don't know if

it works, but . . ." She shrugged, then turned her eyes back to her feet in the bucket. *"Down and out, cleanse the spout, set me free for the next lout. Down and—"*

MacKerrick had moved closer to her side, his head cocked, listening. He interrupted her again, his voice level and calm. "Explain to me, if you would, lass. Fully."

Evelyn sighed. She would be finished by now if he would only let her be.

"One of the kitchen maids at my father's home had a reputation for being rather . . . *generous* with her favors. When another maid inquired as to how she'd avoided . . . 'being caught,' is how I believe she put it, the loose maid said that you must take an empty bucket and fill it with pieces of broken pottery and soil. Then you stand in the bucket and say 'Down and out, cleanse the spout, set me free for the next lout' thirteen times." MacKerrick's mouth hung open, and she felt her cheeks pinkening. "I know, 'tis silly, but—"

Evelyn looked back to her feet and sighed again. "Now I've lost count and will have to start over. I hope saying it more than thirteen times doesn't mean it shan't work. *Down and out—*"

MacKerrick jerked her completely off her feet in the next instant, the bucket toppling and spilling its dubious contents across the flagstones.

"MacKerrick, stop! I wasn't finished!"

"Aye, you've finished," he growled, swinging her around behind him and setting her on her feet. He kicked the dirt and shards back into the overturned bucket and then snatched it from the floor. "And you'll nae be bustin' any more of me crockery for *this* superstitious nonsense." He shook the bucket at her as he crossed to the door. He lifted the bar, swung the door wide, and hurled the old wooden vessel into the night. Then he spat through the doorway for good measure.

MacKerrick turned to her, one long arm held toward the opening in polite, exaggerated invitation. "Do you have a need?"

Evelyn's cheeks warmed and she straightened her spine. She'd had no idea how superstitious about superstition her new husband was. He and Minerva Buchanan would have got on not at all.

She clutched the old witch's cloak about her protectively and, breezing past him, she said, "I'll want that bucket returned to me, sir."

"When Hell becomes an icy loch," she heard him mutter as he followed close on her heels.

After Evelyn—and Alinor and Bonnie and Mac-Kerrick, as well—had partaken of the outdoors quickly, they returned to the hut and sat around the fire pit, eating tender, delicious venison stew and sipping at the mead jug in turn. Alinor and Bonnie had devoured their meals of venison and barley, respectively, in a blink, and Whiskers the mouse's covering was released for a quick scattering of the dry grain in his bowl.

The hut was cozy and peaceful once more and Evelyn felt oddly gluttonous, her belly being warmed by the rich food and drink and her eyes feasting on the beautiful man across from her.

She was a married woman now. This was her home, her husband, all to herself. That was, until MacKerrick took her to his village.

Town, she corrected herself with a private smile.

"More?" The highlander gestured to her bowl with the ladle and Evelyn held it forth readily.

"Tell me about your home," she said, bringing the refilled bowl to rest on her chest and tucking into it with contented relish.

MacKerrick flashed his teeth at her as he topped off his own meal. "'Tis a small town," he said, replacing the lid of the crock and sitting back on his haunches. "Mayhap only a quarter of the size of your own kins'."

Evelyn knew the kin he spoke of was the Buchanans, and since she had not an inkling of knowledge about Minerva's clan, the comparison did little to enlighten her. She gave a hum of interest and kept a mild countenance.

The highlander chewed and swallowed. "The MacKerricks have lived in this part of Scotland since days unnumbered. Our town sits north of here, south of Ben Nevis."

"Ben Nevis?"

"What a poor Scot you are, lass," he tsked. "The mountain. You can see it in the distance if you journey across yonder bog and look to the east."

"Ah." Evelyn blew on the surface of the stew, stirred it lazily. Just the actions of eating and talking felt decadent, and she was enjoying the highlander's musical brogue. "Your parents? Do they reside with you?"

"Me mam lives with me, aye. And me brother, Dunc. You'll delight Mam, Eve. She's as meek as wee Whiskers, but loves a lively debate." He smiled as if calling the woman to mind. "And she makes the best bannock in Scotland."

"I'm looking forward to it." Evelyn draped an arm across Alinor's neck when the wolf lay down near her hip, throwing her wide, black head over Evelyn's thigh.

MacKerrick continued, casting an indulgent look at the pair. "Me da, he died five years past." He took another bite of his stew and offered no more.

"Was he ill?"

"Nae," Conall said around his venison.

"An accident, then?"

The highlander shook his head, shrugged. "He just . . . died."

Evelyn frowned. It was a terrible explanation—no explanation at all. "He just died."

"Aye." MacKerrick's expression seemed to tense a bit. "We'd had a . . . a pair of lean harvests—a drought. Several of the town's youngest children died. The MacKerrick took it hard."

"Hmm." Evelyn was certain there was more to that story than MacKerrick was telling, but she decided not to push him. Perhaps 'twas too painful. "Do you miss him?"

He was silent for several moments, examining the contents of his bowl. "Da took to drink in his last years." MacKerrick smiled, but it fell short of his eyes. "He was fond of our town's fine mead."

It was no explanation either, really, but the words Conall spoke hinted to Eve all that he had left painfully unsaid.

"What of Duncan? He's your younger brother, I assume."

"Only by moments, according to Mam."

Evelyn's eyebrows rose. "Twins?" How fortunate a town was the MacKerrick, to have two such fine-looking specimens as this man. "'Tis well that we are to spend some time together, then, so that I might be able to tell the two of you apart."

MacKerrick laughed. "I should hope you can." His grin remained this time, genuine and jocular. "Duncan is a wee fellow—made like a knobby stick. He's got more hair on his"—MacKerrick halted himself—"*arms*, than what graces his pate. And a temper!" He gave low whistle. "Dunc angry is a wet cat in a sack."

Evelyn laughed. "Obviously the two of you are twin in temperament then, if not in appearance."

MacKerrick gave her a mock frown. "I'm sure I doona know of what you speak, lass. I'm meek as Bonnie, I am."

They sat in smiling, companionable silence for several moments while they finished their meals and Evelyn mulled over the consequences of sating her curiosity to its fill.

She wanted to know about Nonna, the woman in Conall's life before her. But she didn't know if inviting the ghost of the MacKerrick's recently dead wife into the hut was wise. Would it prompt the highlander to draw comparisons between the two women? And if so, how would Evelyn measure?

She had to know.

Evelyn set her empty bowl on the flagstones near Alinor's head. The wolf immediately raised up and attended the remaining flecks of stew.

"Did Duncan and Nonna get on?" she asked casually.

MacKerrick tensed. "Nonna . . ." He paused, looked to the floor as if trying to order his words. "Nonna didna get on with many. She was . . . private. Wild as a girl, but she grew into a hard woman. I reckon she figured life had played her false." MacKerrick shrugged. "And Duncan, well— Duncan is mayhap a bit of a dreamer. He loves a good yarn, a fine tune. A bit superstitious, too, I'd dare to say, although he'd likely deny it if asked. He and Nonna had little tolerance for each other until the very end. They came to an understanding."

Evelyn was morbidly intrigued. "Before she died?" MacKerrick nodded. "Will you tell me about it?"

"Nonna was . . . ill. For several months before she died." The highlander's voice lowered and became gruff. "Duncan cared for her when I had to be about town business. He . . . tended her when she passed."

Evelyn was so shocked that the next question had left her mouth before she'd had time to think better of it.

"You weren't there when she died?" She shook herself. "I mean to say, you have cared so well for me, I would think—"

"Nonna didna want me," MacKerrick said. He raised his head and met Evelyn's eyes and she saw hurt in them, still fresh and raw. "At the end. In truth, she never wanted me. We were matched as bairns, but she never wanted to be the wife of the MacKerrick."

"But . . . why?" Evelyn could not understand.

"She had her reasons, I suppose," was all Mac-Kerrick would say. "Mayhap she told Dunc at the end. I doona know. I didna ask." Then he rose, signaling in no uncertain terms that the discussion of Nonna was over. And Evelyn was glad of it. "I tire, wife."

He held out a large palm to her and Evelyn took it, letting him pull her to her feet. Once she was standing, the highlander wrapped his arms about her. His demeanor had gone from maudlin reluctance to smoldering desire in an instant. He pressed his groin to Evelyn's stomach.

"MacKerrick," Evelyn began, the old worry springing into her mind. She did not wish to tempt fate by lying with him again.

But he dropped his mouth to her neck, kissed her there, and spoke softly into her ear. "Doona deny me, Eve. Please."

And she knew he was asking her to want him, as he had claimed his first wife never had. The sound of his request, so heartbreakingly vulnerable from a man so seemingly strong and able, melted Evelyn's resolve and her caution.

Besides, MacKerrick was right—she'd had no season for months. One more indulgence in his body could do no more damage.

"MacKerrick," she said again, raising her arms to circle his neck, the innocent action feeling wanton in itself. "Would you please take me to bed?"

Chapter Eleven

Three weeks passed what seemed like overnight to Conall, weeks full of peace and contentment that he had not known since he was a boy. Tucked away in the hut in the vale with Eve, buffered from the world by the mountains and rivers of thick, white snow, Conall felt he was living in a fantasy far removed from his previous existence of famine and hardship and death and curses. He drew a deep breath of the morning air, hitched his pack higher on his shoulder, and could not help but smile at the simple, cold, clean beauty of the forest around him.

He and Eve had not rowed a single time in three weeks, their days occupied instead with a deepening companionship, the hours buoyed by long discussions over the hearty venison and caring for the animals that resided with them. Conall now knew that Eve's favorite color was yellow, her favorite treat was boiled pudding. Her father's name was Handaar, and when she had been but four winters old, her sire had gifted her with her first horse—a buff pony Eve had dubbed Princess Dandelion.

The days were easy and joyous, aye, but the nights! God in Heaven, the nights! Gone were Conall's cold, hard hours alone on the icy floor, replaced with close, humid forays of Eve's silky-smooth skin, and waking with her warm, naked body draped over his. Dependable nourishment was transforming Eve, slowly bringing gentle cushion to her prominent hip and collarbones, softening the angle of her jaw, and bringing healthy color to creamy cheeks no longer hollowed by worry and illness and hunger.

Seven times they'd made love since promising themselves as man and wife. Seven glorious, mind-dizzying times, and Conall remembered each interlude distinctly. Each a separate miracle. Seven times.

'Twas more sex than he'd had with Nonna in the seven years they'd been married.

Conall tried to push thoughts of Nonna out of his mind as he hiked toward the morning sun, but it was difficult as he was headed to the MacKerrick town. When he'd left there weeks ago, it had been under the poisoned fog of grief and guilt, his thoughts centered on escape—escape from the loss of his family, the indigent state of his town, the burden of finding an end to the ancient witchery that was systematically destroying the MacKerrick clan. His burdens had been many and huge, his hopes few and emaciated.

He was returning to his town a new man, a newly married man, with a wife to care for and to care for him. And Evelyn Buchanan MacKerrick—God, even the name itself was nearly unbelievable—had cleaned out Conall's untapped wellspring of optimism and opened his heart to the possibility of a future full of . . . *life*.

For the MacKerrick town and for Conall. His fingers went to the precious knot of leather around his neck.

Had Eve been a pot-bellied, toothless harpy, Conall had to admit that he would have still gone ahead with his scheme to win her. She was a Buchanan, after all, and the only chance at destroying the old witch's curse on his people. But she was not some dowdy, haggard lass—she was kind and funny and had eyes the color of the gray winter sky. She was learned and mannered and passionate, generous with affection and curious about everything. She always wanted to know more, his Eve. More about—

Conall halted in the snow, the silence shot with the occasional birdsong pressing on his ears.

My Eve? Was that how he thought of her? He shook his head. She was his wife now—'twas natural he should use the possessive phrase. She belonged to him now.

He tried not to acknowledge that he'd never once thought of Nonna MacKerrick as "his Nonna."

Conall urged his feet forward once more. He wanted to return to the hut before nightfall and so must hurry in his chore. In his pack were six wild hares—small, aye, barely more than kittens—and a precious amount of venison. Conall would deliver the food to his town and be back to Eve posthaste. She'd wanted to come with him, but Conall had refused in no uncertain terms, telling her that the townsfolk would be sorely taken aback thinking that Conall had brought them another mouth to feed. A skewing of the truth, for certain, but for the good of all.

Bringing a Buchanan woman into town would

have indeed set his clan to furious rebellion and 'twould be only a matter of moments before Eve would discover Conall's original motive for marrying her.

He stopped again. *Original motive?*

Bugger it all, he thought. *See what a regular piece of arse does to you? You've got yourself half convinced you're in love with Eve Buchanan.*

He trundled on, at a faster pace now, his boots creating deep trenches in the blanket of white that hid the narrow path.

Conall prayed that Eve's cycle of womanly bleeding would commence again soon, and that he could then get a child on her by the spring thaw, still weeks away. Then they could return to the MacKerrick town together, in time to see the crops beginning to grow, to flourish, as Conall hoped his and Eve's marriage would also do.

But when will you tell her the truth? he asked himself.

When 'tis too late for her to deny me, he answered, with no little shame.

He hoped by the time he could tell Eve the truth, it would be of little importance to her. That, by then, her heart would have softened toward Conall as his already was toward her.

Majestic Ben Nevis appeared out of the morning mist as Conall broke through the dense wood, the snow spilled down its apron sparkling with shades of amber and red and deepest black with the sun rising behind it. His town would come into view in moments. Conall braced himself for the sorry sight of the deserted common areas snaking through the cluster of sod homes, stingy smoke from rotting rooftops breathing tomb silence as everyone huddled inside to conserve both heat and energy.

But when the first thatched roof poked up from over the rise, what Conall heard was music.

Evelyn's mood was jubilant, even as she crawled back into the box bed no sooner than Conall shut the hut door after himself. She already missed the highlander's company, but she was glad to have the day to herself, to nap and to revel in her good fortune.

This morn, when she'd gone into the woods to relieve her bladder, the snow beneath her had been tinged the very faintest pink, and Evelyn had wanted to shout with joy. She'd done an excited mental check of her body: her breasts were tender and full, her head ached dully, and she could sleep standing up. Evelyn had never been happier at feeling so poorly. It had been so long since her last season, she had almost not noticed the signs of her approaching monthly. In truth, she must have been more sickly from malnutrition than she'd ever realized, for her symptoms were mild and she had no abdominal discomfort save for one brief wave of nausea. She attributed the mild flow—spotty at very best—to her lingering physical weakness and looked forward to a leisurely day of rest and reflection on her new life, and her future as Conall Mac-Kerrick's wife.

She was both excited and nervous to her core to meet Lana MacKerrick and Conall's twin brother, Duncan. What an odd, wondrous concept it was to her—*family*. She hoped that they would be pleased with her as their kin.

Well, as pleased as they could be once they learned she was English.

Evelyn winced guiltily as Alinor laid her long, black muzzle on the edge of the mattress. "Hallow, lovely. All right, come up." She patted the ticking and the wolf sprang onto the bed in a graceful pounce. After circling in place twice, Alinor lay down, her head on Evelyn's stomach. The wolf gave a great sigh and closed her eyes, leaving Evelyn alone with her guilt.

She must tell MacKerrick the truth soon. They were man and wife now, and MacKerrick had assured her over and over that his clan would accept any bride he chose, so there really was no reason to keep up the ruse. 'Twas far better that she be the one to tell him, before they journeyed to his home, than for him to find out through other means. His gentle way with her and their deepening friendship was eating a black hole in her conscience so that the lie was all she could think of—now that her season had returned, of course.

Which brought up another troubling point: she'd have to tell him her cycle had started once more. Which meant they could no longer be as indulgent with their physical attraction as they had in the past twenty days and one morn. MacKerrick would balk at any mention of restraint, she was certain, and truth be told, Evelyn was not looking forward to withholding herself from her husband. The way he played her naked body was a pleasure she could have never imagined. He must have lain with many women, she reflected jealously, to know so intimately how to bring Evelyn to climax—in various, thrilling ways, no less.

But he was hers now. And the greatest challenge would be convincing MacKerrick that they could not freely make love, no matter how great of companions they had become.

She realized she needed to seek her relief out of doors again, and would have used the bucket in the far pen set there for that purpose—the broken mug bucket, Evelyn reminded herself with a wry grin—but Alinor had bounded from the bed and was now scratching at the door to be let out as well.

"Very well, Alinor," Evelyn groaned, dragging herself from the bed and giving a satisfying yawn. She spied the crock near the fire and her stomach growled. Perhaps a light meal was in order when they returned.

"Bonnie, to me," Evelyn called as she lifted the bar. Bonnie clattered over and the wolf whipped around with a low growl to jostle the smaller animal away from the door. "Be kind, Alinor."

Once the door was opened, the wolf bolted into the clearing, leaving Evelyn and Bonnie to trail after her. Alinor stopped at the fringe of the wood and ran along the tree line, her nose held high, sniffing, sniffing.

"He'll return soon," Evelyn assured the wolf as she approached the spot where the pink snow was still barely visible. She wanted to see the proof again.

But Alinor gave a sharp bark and disappeared into the wood before Evelyn could stop her. Evelyn frowned. 'Twas quite unlike Alinor to venture away. The wolf still lived in terror of the grays.

"Alinor!" Evelyn called into the quiet wood, striped gray and white with tree trunks and snow. "Alinor, to me!" She leaned this way and that, peering into the trees, and at last saw the black loping back toward her. "Come on, girl. What are you about? 'Tis too cold for sport."

Alinor neared and Evelyn caught her breath—the wolf grasped something, also black, but oddly angled and thrashing, in her mouth.

"Oh, God," she muttered and charged into the trees. "What have you done?" she demanded. "Alinor, drop it! Naughty!" She high-stepped through the snow and met the wolf halfway.

Alinor skidded to a stop and spat the black object at Evelyn's feet where it hitched in an awkward circle in the snow. The wolf barked once and wagged her tail happily.

For you.

'Twas a crow, its blue-black feathers matted with saliva, its yellow beak gaping and closing, its topmost wing mangled.

Evelyn gasped and fell to her knees before the wounded bird. The poor creature was nearly dead, and Evelyn's heart wrenched at the sight of its pitiful thrashing.

"Good girl, Alinor," Evelyn said with fierce pride as she pulled her kirtle over her head, shivering at the extra bite of the wind. Alinor pranced back and forth smugly.

"Shh, lovely," she called to the crow as she shook the overdress out to its full length. The poor thing would kill itself did it not be still. Its little mind was in a whirl of pain and fear so that Evelyn did not think it could even hear her.

She threw the gown over the bird and it immediately quieted. Moving gingerly, Evelyn scooped up the misshapen bundle and wrapped her kirtle around it loosely. She had no idea how she was going to help the bird, but she certainly was not going to leave it in the wood to suffer and die alone.

Evelyn rose and a wash of dizziness came upon her so suddenly it took her breath. She threw out the arm not clutching the bird for balance. A heated flush swept her so that Evelyn felt she stood under a blazing sun. In a moment, though, both the dizziness and heat had passed. She took a deep, steadying breath, tucked the bundle carefully under her arm, and turned back to the clearing.

She had yet to answer her body's call and she felt the urge now more insistently. She neared the spot she'd made use of earlier in the day and bent to set the cloth-wrapped bird on the ground.

It had poked its head from the kirtle and now regarded her with a swiveling profile and one bright, shiny eye. It gave a hoarse caw.

"But a moment," she promised the bird as she loosed it and stepped away to squat. She removed the length of linen she'd fashioned for her impending flow and was mildly surprised and a bit confused to find it clean. But she paid it no heed save for gratitude that she would not be pressed to wash it just yet and glanced at the bird while she relieved herself.

Alinor sat behind the crow, her faithful and unlikely companion, Bonnie, standing at her side. Evelyn chuckled as all the creatures seemed to be watching her with interest.

"Rude," she tossed at them.

Alinor sniffed the air in Evelyn's direction and Bonnie bleated.

The crow strangled then called again. "*Bay-bee*," it croaked.

Evelyn nearly fell on her bare bottom in the snow.

Then she shook herself with a self-deprecating laugh. She was naught but a clutch of silly nerves!

"Are you naming yourself, lovely?" she asked as she replaced the linen between her legs and stood. "Do you wish to be called—"

"*Ray-hee*," the crow squawked again.

The tree line to Evelyn's left seemed to tilt toward her. She tried to shake off the dizziness but then the heat crept upon her again. She had barely leaned over before the vomit came up, and she went to her knees, heaving in the snow.

After the wave had passed, leaving her sweaty and shaken, Evelyn raised her head to find her charges still regarding her. Alinor looked comically sympathetic and Bonnie flicked her long ears happily.

"Nay," Evelyn moaned, the sound like a sob.

"*Baby*," the crow called gleefully.

Conall walked warily through the main avenue of his town, following the lively tune, the hairs on the back of his neck prickling. 'Twas still early morning—a time when, normally, all should be quiet and still. Certainly there had been no cause for merrymaking in the MacKerrick town for . . . well, for years. But most assuredly, no one would have cause to play such an infectious melody this early in the day.

Even the cold air on which the honking music flew seemed to be changed, and although it wasn't at all ominous, Conall was wary. So wary, in fact, that he jumped when the door to his own long-house burst open, emitting a swell of music, raucous laughter, and his brother, Duncan, chuckling, cursing, and stumbling through the doorway into the street.

Duncan's shining, flushed face brightened around his already present grin and he gave a dramatic start of surprise, throwing his arms wide and crouching.

"Conall!" he shouted. "You're—oh, glory!" He broke off and turned back to the door, running into it in his haste and flopping like a moth before he managed to push it open. He ducked his head inside, causing his words to become only slightly muffled. "The MacKerrick has returned! The MacK—"

Duncan stopped again and turned mid-word to dance a bowlegged jig to where Conall stood, and Conall's dread increased tenfold.

His twin was obviously ill. The state of things must have deteriorated to an abysmal low, forcing the townsfolk to eat tainted food, and it had driven them all mad. Conall was too late to save them, Eve Buchanan or nay.

But when Duncan pranced right up to Conall, it wasn't madness in the merry green and bloodshot eyes he saw, it was joy and . . .

Conall gasped and jerked his head back. "Duncan, are you drunk?"

"As a monkfish!" Duncan laughed, emitting more noxious fumes into Conall's face. Duncan grasped his brother's upper arms and kissed each of his cheeks. Then his eyes widened and he looked to either side of Conall.

"But where is the lass? Surely you've nae left her—"

Conall brought his hands up in a blink, one gripping the back of Duncan's skull, the other pressing over his flapping lips.

"Shh!" Conall whispered. "I told you, no one is to—Christ, Dunc! You've nae told anyone—"

Duncan shook Conall's hands away and gave him a punching shove, his frown clearly conveying his offense. "O' course I havena, you big, braying ass! But your plan!" His happy grin returned. "It's worked, whatever it may be." Duncan seemed to be restraining himself from jumping up and down. "You must see! Come! Come inside!"

Duncan spun haphazardly and jigged back to the doorway of Conall's house and ducked inside, leaving Conall little choice but to follow. He took a deep breath and entered his home.

It was filled nearly to the bursting point with what seemed like half the town. People everywhere—in the beds, on low stools, cross-legged on the floor. Their faces turned to him as he stepped inside and they chorused a welcoming cry, vibrating the very rafters and Conall's eardrums.

The room smelt like a brewer's barrel and each of the townsfolk had a grasp on a mug or a jug or a bowl or a—

Hunk of meat?

'Twas then that Conall noticed not one, not a pair, but *five* deer carcasses hanging at the far end of his house, along with countless rabbit skins tacked on twig frames over a smoking trench.

Conall could not seem to form the words that would give voice to the tens of questions spinning in his head. He stuttered and looked to Duncan, who brayed like a drunken ass.

"*I know!*" Duncan hawed. Then he glanced around Conall, as looking over Conall's shoulder was impossible for him. "Someone wishes to speak to you, brother," he said, "and then you and I"—he wiggled his eyebrows—"will have our own chat, aye?"

Conall turned and saw his mother, Lana Mac-Kerrick, draped in Dáire's tired old plaid. Her arms were spread wide and her eyes glistened.

"Conall," she said with a melancholy smile. He embraced his mother, his mind still a whirl, and she spoke into his ear. "A miracle has occurred, my beloved son. One I never thought to see in my life."

Conall drew away and could at last voice a part of his confusion.

"What in the bloody hell is going on?"

His question was met by uproarious laughter. Then, one by one, the townsfolk, his mother and brother as well, bombarded Conall with their own questions.

"What is it, MacKerrick?"

"How did you do it?"

"—plague of hares!"

"Are the Buchanans all dead?"

"Fuck 'em's what I say!"

"—wood full of deer and—"

Conall raised his hands. "Quiet!" he shouted and the mob reluctantly settled. "Where did all of this meat come from?"

'Twas Duncan who answered. "Three days past," he said, his eyes dancing merrily, "'twas as if God himself sent them to us." He addressed the room now, and all leaned forward almost imperceptibly to hear the tale, although Conall suspected that those gathered in his home already knew the story by heart, by the way they contributed to the telling of it.

"I ventured out of doors, just before dawn," Duncan began.

"To have hisself a good piss," a little boy piped, earning him both a slap and a grin from his mother.

Duncan nodded. "Aye. And as I was making me way to the storehouse—"

"For the last bit of barley to be had, for certain," Lana said, and shook her head sadly.

Duncan paused, and it seemed as though the crowd held its breath.

"*There they were,*" Duncan whispered, and crouched down, as if back in that moment and afraid of spooking the animals. "Seven deer, standing in the middle of the street as if waitin' on me company!" Duncan whipped around with his elbows cocked. "I took aim, so careful, and—whoosh!—the first one fell clean."

Conall knew his mouth was hanging open, but he could not help it. "*Seven* deer?" he repeated, glancing at the five carcasses.

"Glory, Conall!" Duncan rolled his eyes. "Aye, I missed on two. You're never satisfied, are you?"

The crowd roared with laughter once again and Conall's face heated.

"And the hares?" he prompted.

Duncan wrinkled his nose and rocked back on his heels, puffing out his chest. "Bah," he scoffed. "Troublesome beasts. I canna go into the wood for a bit o' privacy without trippin' over a brace o' em."

The music started up again, a set of pipes played by an old codger in the corner, and several townsmen began to sing and stomp their feet in time.

"Her hair was long and her eyes were blu-uue! My highland lassie I loved so true!"

Conall's mother laid a gentle hand on his arm. "Have you come back to stay, Conall?" she asked, her eyes filled with concern.

"Nae, Mam, I—" He paused. "Ah, there is aught that I must tend to for a bit. I—"

"Of course, of course. Do what you must," she hurried to assure him, deepening Conall's confusion. She tugged him toward the fire. "Come and eat, though. *Eat!*" She laughed, the sound itself as sweet as the music filling his house. "Duncan's made a fine haggis!"

"'Tis a Buchanan woman, is it nae?" Duncan whispered near Conall's shoulder as they sat side by side on the perimeter of the room, eating.

Conall nearly fumbled his bowl of ground meat and grain. "Would you shut your bleedin' mouth? Christ, Dunc, did I nae know better, I'd think you'd have me mobbed."

Duncan chuckled and picked at his meal. "If it means the food we now have, the folk wouldna care were you entertaining the devil himself. Glory, I canna eat another morsel." He looked to Conall, then took a large bite of haggis. Duncan pointed at his brother with the spoon. "I'm right, though. I know it."

Conall was torn. He'd promised Eve he'd not tell anyone of her presence, and he meant to keep his word. But what did it matter now that they were married? And 'twas his brother. And Conall hadn't *told* Duncan anything, really—Duncan had guessed.

Conall cautioned himself to tread carefully. "Now why would you think that, brother?" He took a bite of his own haggis. Lana was right, Duncan had made a fine dish.

"The night before the deer came to us, I had a dream."

Conall waited. "Of . . . ?" he said around his food.

"A Buchanan woman, in a long, black cloak, at the hut in the vale." Duncan's gaze was without the haze of drink now, dark green and sparking. "She had a wolf at her side, and was round with child."

Conall could not swallow the mouthful of food that seemed to swell against his teeth. Dispensing with manners, he leaned to the side and spat it on the floor.

"What?" Conall whispered, glancing around to be sure no one else had overheard. "Are you certain?"

"As certain as I am your brother," Duncan replied. "Long hair, down to here." Duncan held a flat palm below his hip. "A wolf at her side, and she weepin', the poor lass."

Conall set his bowl aside, his appetite vanished. Could his brother's dream be a foretelling of events to come? The wolf by the woman's side—it had to be Alinor.

The words of the damning curse came flooding back to him, teasing him:

Only heartache and toil shall you reap until a Buchanan bairn is born to rule the MacKerrick clan.

Could Eve be with child . . . *now?*

Conall felt the blood leave his face and his stomach war with the heavy food. "How do you know the woman in your dreams was Buchanan?" he asked Duncan cautiously. "Did she speak to you? Tell you her name?"

"Nae," Duncan admitted. "She said nary a word, only looked toward our town and wept."

Conall felt as though he'd been struck by lightning. His nerves sang and his breath singed his lungs with each wheeze.

Of course the woman in his brother's vision had

been weeping—Eve would be terrified to be found with child. Hadn't she gone into hysterics at the mere mention of it? All the pieces fit together . . .

But it was only a dream. A dream—it meant naught. 'Twas Duncan's manner to believe in such nonsense, not Conall's. And he would not allow his brother's—likely drink-induced—vision to cloud his own logic.

Conall looked up and around the room slowly, his gaze landing on each member of his clan in turn. They were eating and singing and drinking and smiling and making plans.

Was what Conall was witnessing *now* logical, though, considering the years of hardship and loss? Was a *curse* logical?

He had to return to the hut immediately.

He stood, gestured toward his pack left forgotten by the door. "I've brought you venison and rabbit . . ." he said to Duncan questioningly.

Duncan waved a hand. "Take it, brother. You've greater need of it than us." A grin split his face. "I'll be paying you a visit soon, you ken?"

"Not yet, Duncan," Conall warned. "Give me some time to . . ." He didn't know how to explain. "Two months, mayhap."

"*Two months!*" Duncan screeched and then lowered his voice at Conall's wince. "Bite me pecker, two months!"

"I beg you, Dunc," Conall beseeched. "I need you here to look after Mam and the folk."

Duncan scowled. "You know I will, you great lummox! Fine. Go." He jumped up and leaned close to Conall's face. "But I'll come when I'm good and ready, brother. I'd see my vision in the flesh before the planting."

Conall picked up his pack and slipped into it quickly, catching Lana's eye as he did so. She gave him a sad smile and a wave before blowing him a kiss. She knew he was going, and she knew he was in a hurry.

Duncan followed Conall as he slipped out the door into the crisp noon air. Conall turned to look at his brother.

"Best you sober up if you're to rule in my stead," Conall teased.

"Bugger you," Duncan snorted. "Compared to last eve, I'm straight as an arrow."

Conall laughed and grasped his brother's arm. "You've done well, Dunc. I'll nae have a worry with you at the reins."

Duncan's thin lips quirked and Conall knew his brother was proud. "Hurry up with you. Go on."

"Take care when you come to the cottage," Conall called as he began walking backward away from Duncan. "A pack of wolves roams the vale from dusk to dawn—bloodthirsty, queer-acting. Come only in the light."

Duncan nodded and the smile never left his face.

"I'm nae afraid of wolves, Conall," he shot back. And then quietly, for his own ears, "Nae afraid of them at all."

Chapter Twelve

The meager hut was gloomy and dark—only the single flame of a solitary oil lamp lit—and it suited Evelyn's mood perfectly. She lay on her back on the box bed, staring up at the shadows. Alinor curled against her thigh and Bonnie had folded herself on the floor, while the crow perched on the framework of the bed, his broken wing bandaged close to his body. The bird appeared quite content in his new home, sidestepping the length of the beam from one end to the other, his good wing flapping awkwardly for balance.

Evelyn had barely left the lumpy comfort of the bed since venturing out that morning, stirring only to care for the animals and to vomit once more. Her appetite had completely vanished. Her time was spent waiting for the MacKerrick to return.

She didn't know if she would throw herself upon him and weep, or kill him on sight.

She was fairly certain she was pregnant. Her worst nightmare had become a reality while she wasn't looking and when she least expected it. She didn't know what to think, what to do.

Would this child kill her, leaving him or her with only a father? Would it be an agonizing and painful end for Evelyn, like the tens of tragic births she herself had witnessed?

Would MacKerrick be happy for a child? Would he now take Evelyn to his town for her care?

She didn't know the answers to any of the questions. She had thought perhaps to pray, but then dismissed the idea with a bitter laugh. God had forsaken her yet again, given her the one cross she had never thought to bear. Her penance for a selfish life.

Mayhap her punishment would at last be over upon her death. Or mayhap she would only be transferred to an eternity in a fiery hell. She took perverse pleasure in her maudlin musings.

Alinor growled, the sound a warm vibration through Evelyn's body. Then the wolf bounded from the bed, startling a squawk and a pair of black feathers from the bird above. Evelyn rose wearily and scooted from the ticking to her feet, her head pounding. She crossed the hut with dragging steps as MacKerrick rapped and called to her through the door.

"Eve? Eve?" His voice sounded alarmed and breathless, as if he'd been running. "'Tis only I— Conall MacKerrick. Your husband."

"As if I know a score other Conall MacKerricks," she mumbled crossly. She lifted the bar and stepped away from the door as it swung open.

The highlander rushed inside on a frigid breeze, already discarding his pack, which looked none lightened by his errand. He took abrupt hold of Eve's arms while she squawked indignantly and peered into her face, his eyes shadowed by the dim light of the hut.

He stared at her for several moments, as if waiting for her to speak.

"*What?*" Evelyn finally snapped and shrugged out of his hold. "Close the door, MacKerrick— you're losing all our warmth."

He turned and obeyed her command without rebuke for her sharp tone. Then he was fast on her heels once more, every inch of his large body seeming poised in anticipation.

"Eve." His eyes flicked over her from head to toe and back again. "Ah . . . how fare thee? Was your day good?"

Her eyes narrowed. What was he about, the cad, the defiler of innocence? 'Twas as if he already knew. She sought to escape him by climbing once more into bed.

"Oh, my day was grand, MacKerrick," she said, turning at once to face the wall. "Simply grand."

She heard him approach. "Ah, well . . . good. Good. Hallow, Alinor." He cleared his throat. "You're feeling well, then?"

"As well as I can feel for being pregnant."

Only silence followed her blunt proclamation and Evelyn lay still as a stone, staring at the rough wooden back of the box bed and waiting for a response. She heard a rustle of movement and the bed gave a small lurch as if something had run into it, but still the highlander said naught to breach the tense air.

She felt tears well in her eyes. She had yet to cry over her predicament, perhaps from the shock of it. But now that she had spoken the dreaded fact aloud and MacKerrick had not so much as gasped in sympathy, Evelyn felt her misery and fear seep up and threaten to drown her in a flood of tears. She swallowed.

He had naught to say, obviously. It didn't affect him in the least.

Of course it doesn't, a spiteful voice taunted her. He *doesn't have to carry the child.* He *doesn't have to endure the horror of birth.* He *can simply stand aside and observe,* his *body,* his *life,* his *sanity intact. Or he can leave, if he wishes.*

Evelyn felt she at last understood the plights of the poor young maidens at the priory. They had been so alone . . .

Her tears became tears of resentment as the hateful voice goaded her anger and Evelyn lay stewing in her growing ire as the long, quiet seconds ticked by.

He is probably smirking, she thought furiously. *Proud of himself.*

Evelyn could at last stand the highlander's silence no longer. She flung herself over to raise up on one arm, the motion spilling the tears over her cheeks, her mouth opening to curse him, to damn him for his unconcerned smugness at what he'd done to her.

But the vicious accusations never left her lips as she saw MacKerrick kneeling at the side of the bed. One forearm was braced upon the mattress and his other arm was wrapped around Alinor's neck, where his face also pressed, turned away from Evelyn. His shoulders shook, and Alinor was trying awkwardly to reach his ear with her tongue.

"MacKerrick?" Evelyn whispered through her frown.

And then he did look at her and when Evelyn saw

the streaks of wet on the highlander's chiseled face, her breath caught somewhere around her heart. But his eyes were flashing their highest amber fire and crinkled at the corners. His teeth gleamed in a wide smile.

"Ah, Eve," he said and released the wolf. He rose up only enough to join her on the bed. "Eve. Sweet Eve." He took her into his arms and squeezed her tightly against his chest, pressed his lips to the crown of her head.

His actions were so gentle, so caring, so . . . perfect, that Evelyn was sobbing into his tunic before she realized it.

"'Tis all right, Eve," he murmured into her hair. "Doona fear. I'm right here."

"It's n-not all . . . right!" she wailed and sniffed hard as her nose ran. "It's a n-night . . . m-mare!"

"Nae, nae," he soothed in a low, fierce voice and squeezed her tighter. "'Tis a wondrous thing, lass— a miracle. You doona know—oh, Eve, what you have given me!"

She struggled away from him, hiccoughing, and looked accusingly into his damnably hopeful, handsome face. She swung her arm and hit his chest with her fist. The blow was halfhearted at best.

"I gave you naught—you took it!"

MacKerrick grabbed her wrist and, just when Evelyn thought he would shake her, he brought the hand she'd struck him with to his mouth and kissed each knuckle.

"Nae, you gave it," he corrected and brought her hand to rest over his heart. He brought his other hand to the back of her head and pulled her mouth to his, gently but deliberately. His kiss was brief, sweet and warm, and he looked into her eyes after he released her lips. "You wanted to make love with me, each time."

"It matters naught," Evelyn said, not caring that her tone had turned petulant and juvenile. "I didn't think that—"

"Neither of us did," he interrupted quietly. "And that is the miracle of it—we have made the impossible possible." He rested his forehead against hers and smiled. "You willna die from our child, Eve— I'll nae allow it."

"You can't—"

"I'll nae allow it," he said solemnly. "Come the thaw, I will take you to the MacKerrick town and you will be well tended by my people. They will care for you as they would a queen, and see you healthy and fat and happy."

She shot him what she hoped was a deadly glare and he chuckled good-naturedly before continuing.

"When your time comes, you will have no better attendants at your side." He wiped a rogue tear from her cheek with the backs of his fingers. "And I will love this bairn with all my heart. In truth, I already do." He leaned forward and kissed her again, placing a hand low on her abdomen as he did so.

"I'm so frightened, Conall," she whispered against his mouth when he pulled away.

The highlander held her close. "I know you are, lass. I've got you, though. I'm here, and I will protect you—protect our family."

Evelyn let her eyes slide closed as Conall kissed her gently once more, and she felt now-familiar warmth in her middle at his sensual touch sliding over her hip. He turned her so that he leaned over her prone body, his hand smoothing up her flat stomach to her breast.

She hissed in pain when he kneaded one, and Conall immediately gentled his touch, whispering apologies and kissing the aching fullness.

He'd said "our family."

Evelyn's stomach tumbled at the very idea, as well as at Conall's lips traveling ever lower down her body.

God help her.

Conall wanted Eve's body more than he had on the night they'd wed, more than he ever had. He could hardly wait to take her, now as the mother of his child, and a passion for her burned in him like a spilled oil fire, crawling and consuming and out of control.

He turned his body so that his head was at her feet and removed each decrepit slipper, kissing her small, cold toes, one by one. Next he moved to her delicate ankle bones, pressing his lips there before sliding up to her calf. He felt the gooseflesh his touch raised. He looked up her body, the shadows painting her with a seductive veil full of sighs and heat.

She was carrying his child. *The Buchanan bairn that would rule the MacKerrick clan.* His town, his people, was saved. The curse would be lifted.

The scent of her skin, warmed slightly by the thin linen gown, made Conall dizzy. He pushed the skirt up high, bunching it around her hips. His erection throbbed painfully as he nuzzled the junction of her legs, flicked out his tongue. His wife moaned.

Oh, Eve . . .

A bairn. A wee life to mayhap help heal the broken

pieces of his heart that Conall thought had scattered to the very ends of the earth for the stillborn dark-haired little girl. His own flesh and blood who would love him as he had loved his own father. A seed that would grow in his place. A beautiful child from this beautiful, beautiful woman.

Conall at last drew his body atop Eve's, shoving down his breeches and pulling his léine aside. He poised at her opening, wanting to take a moment to look into her eyes, darkened by passion and the gloomy light.

He would tell her of the curse soon. When she had become used to the idea of the bairn. Mayhap then she would see what a miracle this child really was.

Or mayhap she will realize how badly you misled her.

Conall blocked the thought before it could grow longer arms of reason and strangle him. It had all worked out in the end. He cared for Eve, so much already. And his feelings grew each day. By the time he told her of the curse, it would not matter one whit. He was sure of it. He entered his wife.

Conall was just setting a steady rhythm, rocking the bed in a gentle motion, when a hellish, winged demon fell upon his head.

Conall roared and threw up an arm to shield his head while stretching out his full length to protect Eve. His erection shriveled like an icicle in a fire as he felt the evil minion tumble onto the mattress in a blur of black and dusky rose. But then it was upon him again, its demonic caws sending a chilling fear into Conall's core.

"Cover your face, Eve!" he yelled as Alinor began barking frantically and Conall made to seize the clawing beast. Bonnie's frantic bleats added to the chaos. "I'll have it!"

"Conall, nay!" Eve squirmed and twisted under him and managed to take hold of his wrist with one hand. "Stop!" Her other arm shot out to still the whirling, screeching mass of feathers. "You're frightening him!"

Conall oofed as Eve's knee found his groin and he rolled away, his hands covering his bashed manhood. He felt sick to his stomach from the pain.

Eve struggled to a seat, without inquiry of the injury she'd caused, and pulled the screaming, stinking thing onto her lap.

"Shh! Shh," she cooed, stroking and soothing it. Then she turned her frown upon Conall. "He was only protecting me!"

"What. In bloody *hell*," he hissed though clenched teeth, "is a bloody *crow* . . . bloody *doing* . . . in me bloody *bed?*"

Eve's frown deteriorated into a glare. "Alinor found him this morn in the wood. He is wounded."

At mention of her name, the wolf pounced gamely upon the bed—directly atop Conall's cupped hands.

He couldn't help but scream. At this rate, the bairn Eve now carried would be the last one Conall would be physically able to produce.

"*As am I,*" Conall wheezed. He could have sworn he tasted blood in his mouth.

Eve's frown lessened only slightly into a sliver of concern. "Oh. Are you all right, Conall?"

He gave her a glare of his own and shoved at Alinor with one hand against her deep chest. "Alinor, off!" he croaked and struggled to sit, gasping as his bits were jostled. "Eve, you canna keep—*damn!*— a crow . . . in the house."

"Why not?" she demanded. "I've bandaged his

wing so he won't fly about. It should heal soon, but if I turn him out now he'll surely die. What if one of the grays get him?"

"Then mayhap he'll be full of *crow* and not want to eat *us*," Conall grumbled. He scooted to the edge of the box bed and slowly, gingerly, released his manhood to pull up the waistband of his breeches to his knees.

"*Pay*," the crow cawed at him. "*Pay!*"

Conall froze, a ghostly voice whispering a memory of the curse in his ear: *Let it be only their song to fill your ears . . .*

"*Mee!*" the bird squawked. "*Pay! Me!*"

"Shh," Eve hushed the wild, wiry thing who ducked its head near Eve's breast. Its yellow eye stared at Conall warily. Eve looked back up to him. "'Tis what he was crying this morn, when I . . . when I suspected—" She broke off as if she could not bring herself to say it. Then she simply whispered, "Baby."

Baby?

Conall looked askance at the hideous creature.

"*Pay-me*," it croaked.

Conall looked back to Eve, a coil of dread winding tight in his stomach. That bird was a bad omen. The curse . . .

Not to mention its manner of introducing itself to Conall.

"*Pay*," the crow insisted again, this time more quietly, almost languorously, greedily.

Conall got up immediately from the bed and fastened his pants. "Nae. It canna stay here, Eve. Put it out."

"I will not."

"You *will*. It's filthy and noisy and . . ." He searched his mind for any other excuse. "Alinor doesn't like it."

"Alinor *rescued* him, sir."

So he was back to sir, now, was he? "I'll nae argue with you, Eve."

"Good," she said lightly. "Because he is staying."

Conall growled. "Eve. You have"—he ticked off his fingers—"a wolf, a sheep, a mouse, a husband, and a bairn. Isna that enough pets for you?"

She shrugged a delicate shoulder and rose from the bed, shaking her skirts back to her ankles and carrying the blasted bird under one arm. "Let us get you a nice drink, lovely," she said, ignoring Conall completely.

"He'll shit the house full!" Conall said threateningly. "Eve, I forbid it."

Eve poured melt water into a shallow bowl and the bird dipped his long, ugly, yellow beak into it. Then she looked up at Conall.

"You made me pregnant."

Conall cursed loudly.

He was defeated.

Chapter Thirteen

The snow was melting.

Evelyn sat upon the low stool midway between the fire pit and the open door, bent over her growing belly and the bucket between her feet. She scrubbed at her and Conall's meager excuses for extra clothing while Sebastian the crow perched on one of the pen walls, as if he, too, was enjoying the view of the outdoors.

The bird's wing was healed by the way he flapped about the hut, and Evelyn suspected 'twould be safe enough to turn the bird out of doors soon. Then Sebastian would be once again free to glide regally through the forest. In the meantime, the crow would continue to irritate Conall.

Evelyn grinned as her cold, stiff fingers wrung the last drops of water from MacKerrick's sleeveless léine. She would have to shut the door when her husband, Alinor, and Bonnie returned to the hut— Conall would be none too pleased that it stood open now. But each occupant of the small cottage was itching for the larger freedom of spring, mayhap Evelyn most of all. In the four months since discovering she was with child, the weather had improved incrementally so that, although 'twas still cold, some days the breeze no longer took your breath, and the snow outside was soft and loose and slick with melt water. The wood ran like a waterfall, the snow sliding from tree boughs like wet, heavy waves, spinning the rare sunlight into iridescent sheets of gold.

Yea, they were all anxious to be about in kinder weather, stretch their legs—whether two or four— and let the wind stir the stuffy lethargy from their heads. But Conall had taken the two "lassies" alone, ordering Evelyn to remain at the hut while he checked the traps, lest the grays be about.

She smiled gently. He was so protective of her and the babe.

Evelyn stood with the wet, heavy tangle of clothes and began shaking each piece out and tossing it over a rafter. She hoped Alinor was better behaved upon their return. For days now, the wolf had pestered them all nearly to insanity, herding poor Bonnie and nipping at her rump, taunting Sebastian on his perch to make him stumble, overturning Whiskers's bowl from the shelf, digging frantically in the earth of the pens. Alinor wanted to be let out, then she wanted back in immediately. She wanted to wrestle and roughhouse with Conall; she chased Evelyn's skirts and generally put herself underfoot.

When Alinor was outdoors, the wolf ran the clearing in a circuit, sniffing, sniffing the air madly, sometimes whining, before she was—oft times, physically— forced back inside the hut. Evelyn hoped that Conall would make good on his promise to give the wolf a good run this afternoon so that Alinor would return to her usual, calm self.

Her chore completed, Evelyn scooped Sebastian

from the pen wall and stood in the doorway of the hut, cradling and stroking the bird atop her over-turned bowl of a belly. They should be returning soon—dusk was perhaps only a pair of hours away.

"What is taking them so long, eh, boy?" Evelyn murmured to the bird. He turned his slick head to look at her in his sideways manner.

"Bay."

"Yea, yea—*baby*. I know." Evelyn shook her head and sighed. Sebastian was in sore need of an ex-pansion in his vocabulary. She paused as a mad idea seized her.

"Sebastian." Evelyn jostled the bird gently and then exaggerated her lips. "*Ma-ma.*"

The bird looked around wildly with it's glossy yellow eye.

"*Mama,*" she repeated. "Say *Mama.*"

"Be!"

"Nay—*Mama.*"

"Bay!"

"Ma—"

"Bay-bee!"

"Oh, never mind." Evelyn felt foolish for trying, but thoughts of the child growing inside her had stirred a curiosity about her future role as a mother. She wondered what it would be like when she and Conall moved to the MacKerrick town and became three. Her emotions rose and fell it seemed hourly, and Evelyn fluctuated between picturing a bloody nightmare of illness and hunger and death, to en-visioning a large, comfortable sod home where the three of them lived happily in the midst of a wel-coming people.

She sighed.

Who would have ever thought that Evelyn would

have fallen in love with Conall MacKerrick? Caring and capable and jocular—he and Evelyn could talk about nothing in particular for hours, which they frequently did. And he still desired her misshapen body, making love to her often and well.

If she could survive the birth of this child, Evelyn thought she would have everything she'd ever desired.

Just then, movement on the fringe of the wood caught her eye and Conall stepped from the trees, Bonnie's tether trailing after the sheep. The pair crossed the clearing and Evelyn leaned out the doorway slightly for sign of the big-boned black wolf. But Conall and Bonnie were nearly to the hut now and Alinor had still not emerged.

Conall's face was lined and weary, his breeches and léine wet to his hips. Bonnie cried out and ran toward Evelyn.

Evelyn felt a sick rippling in her stomach as she called out to her husband, her fear obvious in her tone.

"Where is Alinor?"

"What do you mean, 'she's run off'?"

Eve's face was pulled into a confused frown as she turned to follow Conall inside the house, that damned bird in her arms. Conall was worried, wet, and chilled to the very bone, and the sight of his extra léine hanging cold and dripping from the ceiling did little to improve his mood.

He sat upon the stool to undo his boots—at the very least, he had to get the soaked breeches away from his skin. He glanced up at Eve.

"We were nae farther into the wood than a score

of paces when she bolted," Conall said grimly, grunting as he jerked at the wet leather that clung to him like his own skin. "I thought mayhap she had picked up a scent, so I let her be while I checked the traps, thinking she would find her way back to us when she tired of her chase."

"You didn't see her again?" Eve demanded, her tone rising shrilly. She dropped Sebastian onto the pen wall while she spoke. "What of her tracks? Did you search for her?"

Conall stood and peeled the breeches from his legs, which felt like frozen hunks of venison. "The snow is melting, shifting—her tracks disappeared. But, aye, Bonnie and I looked for her—'tis why were so long away."

But Eve was out the cottage door already, and Conall could hear her calls, growing more faint as she ran through the clearing.

"Alinor! Alinor!"

"Damn!" Conall tried to step back into his boots, but they folded together wetly, denying him. He crossed to the doorway. "Eve!"

She stood at the edge of the wood, leaning this way and that, as if trying to discern the shape of the big black, and Conall's heart wrenched.

"Alinor, to me! *A-lin-or!*"

Conall had to fetch Eve back, boots or nae, lest she lose all good sense and go after the wolf. The grays were hunting again; their howls had stalked Conall and Bonnie through collapsing drifts of snow as they had searched fruitlessly for Alinor.

But he could not tell Eve that, nae. She would go mad with worry.

"Eve!" Conall stepped into the snow grimly, then

jogged to his wife's side. His feet felt afire when he grabbed for her arm. "Eve, the sun is setting."

She jerked away from him, her eyes bright with panic and full of tears. "She cannot be left out there all night alone!" She spun and shoved at Conall's chest with each word. "Find her! *You* took her—*you* go and *find her*, MacKerrick!"

"Eve, listen to me—"

"You find her, MacKerrick, *right now!*" She turned back to the wood and actually made to enter the tree line, her voice cracking with the intensity of her scream. "*Alinor!*"

Conall had no choice but to gather Eve in his arms and physically carry her back to the hut. She fought him the entire way, kicking and flailing and reaching over his shoulder, crying.

"Let me go! Alinor, t-to m-me!" Sobs racked her by the time Conall set her down inside the house, and he had to pull her away from the door and block the opening once she had her feet beneath her.

"Get out of m-my way!"

"Eve, you must listen to me. Stop. Stop!"

She sagged in his hands then, her energy weeping out of her, and her head dropped between her shoulders.

"H-how c-could you let her g-go?"

Conall's heart was breaking at her pain—he knew what Alinor meant to Eve. He knew they had saved each other in those first days and that Eve loved the beast more than anything or anyone.

Including Conall.

Which was why he had searched for so long— hours—in the danger of the stalking grays. The last thing in this world he'd wanted was to return to the hut without Eve's beloved animal.

Because Conall loved Alinor, as well. And he, too, worried for her safety, alone in the dark, cold night ahead.

He gathered Eve close and sat on the stool, holding her against him on his lap while she hiccoughed and gasped. Bonnie clattered over with a pitiful *baa* and butted Conall's arm.

"Listen to me, lass," he murmured into Eve's hair. "I know you fear for her, but Alinor is nae pet. She was a wild thing when you found her and she can care for herself better than you or I could in the wood. 'Twas her home once. She is well familiar with it."

"But it's not her home any longer," Eve argued with a sniff. "She is *mine*! And the grays—she's terrified of—"

"I know," Conall interrupted gently. "Mayhap her fear will make her all the more nimble. I vow she is better fed than those old devils. And she's survived them once already," he reminded her with a hopeful shake. "She's been hemmed in for far too long, a girl of her size—she may just need a night of good sport."

Eve moaned into his chest and clutched his léine with her fingers. "What if she doesn't return? I'll . . . I'll die without her, I love her so!"

Conall wanted to lie to Eve, to tell her anything that would take this pain from her, but he could not.

"You'll nae die," he whispered. "Alinor is a wild creature, Eve. If she chooses nae to return to us, we must let her go with love."

Eve had no reply to his reasoning, only lay limp in his arms for a long, long while, her sobs deteriorating into breathy gasps.

"I'll not give up," she whispered at last. "She would not abandon me. She shall return, I know it."

Conall smiled over the crown of her head. "She very well may."

Eve sniffed. "I washed your clothes today. But they're still wet."

"I know you did." He held her closer. "It's all right."

Evelyn did not sleep for an instant that night. She did try at Conall's repeated urging, but the wind beyond the hut teased her dreadful worry, every scrape of branch she heard was Alinor scratching at the door, every moaning gust was the evil grays' triumphant kill-howl, every creak of the rafters was Alinor's whimper.

So she'd paced the hut the whole of the dark hours, not daring to light a lamp lest its glow stir Conall, who only dozed, she knew. Twice she had tried to soundlessly raise the bar from the door, but Conall had awoken instantly, making her swear the final time that she would not go outdoors. She did so reluctantly, because she wanted to be alone in her vigil, and Conall would not let her be until she promised.

Well, as alone as Bonnie and Sebastian would leave her. The sheep dogged Evelyn's footfalls and Sebastian mimicked the pair's pacing on his own perch. Evelyn could feel their worry—especially Bonnie's misery at Alinor's absence. After hours and hours of pacing, Evelyn's lower back ached like it never had in her life and she finally gave in to the small comfort of the stool, dragging it to the door

so that she could rest there upright lest Alinor
come home.

Alinor, please come home . . .

Evelyn was in a semiconscious daze of exhaus-
tion when she heard the whisper of ferocious barking from beyond the hut door. Instantly alert, her
heart leaping, she shot to her feet and fumbled
clumsily at the bar.

"Conall! Conall, wake up!" she said in a loud,
shaky voice. "I hear her!" Evelyn threw the bar to
the floor and dragged open the door even as the
highlander sprang from the bed in naught but his
skin, his warning of "Wait, Eve" fading as she bolted
from the hut.

The sun had risen and was blindingly bright over
the sparkling snow, refrozen in the night. Evelyn ran
as fast as she dared toward the tree line, toward the
incessant barking, tears slipping from her eyes as the
frigid morning air rushed by her face and snatched
each frosty breath from her burning lungs.

"Alinor!" she cried, dashing into the wood without hesitation. "Alinor, where are you?"

She stopped to listen, and there, mayhap a hundred yards deeper into the forest, she saw a flash of
silky black. The barking picked up again, wild yelps
and snarls punctuating the otherwise still air.

"*Alinor!*" Evelyn whispered. She began running
toward the image flickering between the trees,
stumbling only once, and catching herself quickly
and continuing.

Then she heard a voice competing with Alinor's
barks.

"Help! Help! Oh, glory—he's goin' to eat me!"

Evelyn thought she might have seen a man
halfway up a tall, snow-laden pine, but she paid

him no heed, running even faster now toward the wolf who was bounding across the short span separating them.

The man in the tree cried shrilly, "Stay back, missus! Stay back. It'll slaughter ye!"

Evelyn stumbled again, but this time she let herself go to her knees as the wolf collided with her. Evelyn's arms went around the black neck like a trap, and both the woman and the animal tumbled sideways locked together.

"Oh, my God, Alinor!" Evelyn laughed and cried, her tears hot and heavy with relief and joy. A rough, pink tongue swiped them away as fast as they fell. "You naughty, naughty, *naughty* girl! I was so sick with—where have you been?"

She pulled herself up by the wiry ruff on either side of Alinor's head and then held the wolf there, pulling away to look at her properly. Alinor panted through an ecstatic lupine grin and Evelyn kissed the wolf's rough, wet nose.

"Look at yourself! You're a mess—oh, nay!"

'Twas then that Evelyn saw Alinor's bloody ear and felt the wet stickiness around her neck. "Did they get you, lovely? Did you get them back? I'll wager you did, my big, brave, *naughty* girl. I'll have you cleaned up in a thrice, not to worry. And this should learn you a—"

"Evelyn!" Conall's bellow fairly shook the mighty tree trunks surrounding them. Although the use of her full name did give her cause for a quirked eyebrow, Evelyn had no fear of Conall's anger.

"I'm here! *We're* here!" she called over her shoulder with a laugh as Alinor licked her neck frantically.

Conall was visible in an instant, stomping through the deep slush in only his tunic and boots. "Eve?

Where—?" Then he spied them and rushed to join the pair, going to his knees and throwing his long, strong arms about them both. He was laughing.

"Alinor, you ninny!" he barked in a joyous roar. Then he kissed the wolf's wide, matted forehead. "And *you*—" He pressed his lips to Evelyn's and she eagerly returned his smiling kiss. "You promised, Eve."

"I woke you!" Evelyn laughed and then paused as she heard Bonnie's panicked cries. "Bonnie, to us. Here, lovely!"

The sheep came skipping awkwardly through the trees, and Evelyn wanted to fall against Conall in hysterical laughter when she spied Sebastian balanced precariously on the sheep's shaggy shoulders. Alinor broke free from Evelyn and Conall to greet her friends with a playful snap of her jaws, Sebastian squawking and flapping madly for balance.

Conall turned his face to Evelyn's and gave her a mock frown. "Evelyn Buchanan Godewin MacKerrick—what were you thinking, lass, running in such a fashion? Have you nae care for the bairn you carry, wife?"

Evelyn rolled her eyes. "Conall, I—"

'Twas at that moment that the man Evelyn had completely forgotten about fell out of the tree with a strangled yelp and disappeared into a snowdrift.

"Christ!" Conall shouted and shot to his feet, jumping between the stranger and Evelyn.

"Nae Christ, I'm sorry to say." A wiry, balding, stick of a man scrambled from the snow and to his feet, still clutching at a bent twig trap containing a tiny, tumbling brown hare. His slim cheeks were high with color, and his clothing was askew and powdered white.

"Duncan?"

"Hallow, Conall," Duncan said breathlessly. "I didna know the wolf you warned me about was some sort of kin of our'n." His head turned to Evelyn and he smiled broadly, almost mischievously. "Hallow to *you*, missus." He thrust the trap toward her. "I've brung you a rabbit."

Evelyn's gaze flew from Duncan to Conall, back to Duncan, her mouth agape until Alinor tackled her again. She grabbed the wolf and dragged the animal half onto her lap when Duncan dropped into a crouch, his arms outstretched defensively.

"Hallow, Duncan," Evelyn laughed, so giddy with the feel of her beloved animal in her arms that good sense had fled her. "Alinor will not harm you, although she *is* a very naughty girl." She gave Duncan what she hoped was a sincere smile of welcome. "Thank you very much for the rabbit. I shall call him Robert."

Chapter Fourteen

Evelyn all but skipped back to the cottage, Sebastian under her arm, Robert in his trap in her other fist, and flanked by Bonnie and Alinor. Conall and Duncan followed some paces behind, talking in hushed tones and exchanging halfhearted shoves and punches, a particularly stiff blow from Conall nearly toppling the smaller Duncan.

What a mismatched pair they are, Evelyn thought as she led her menagerie through the open doorway. But Conall had warned her that he and his brother looked nothing alike. Conall had also told Eve that Lana MacKerrick doted on the more frail twin, but it did not seem to bother Conall in the least. He loved his brother and did not begrudge him their mother's attention. Conall had taken after their father, and Dáire MacKerrick had made Conall his own constant companion. Evelyn thought it quite lovely that each of the MacKerrick parents had a child to lavish their individual affection on.

Evelyn paused for an instant while cleaning out Whiskers's bowl and scattering a pinch of grain next to the mouse. Could she be carrying twins, as well? She could not discern the rush of emotion she felt as either fear or excitement and so tried to shut the possibility from her mind.

Conall ducked inside the hut for a moment to grab the mead jug with a boyish grin before returning to his brother outside.

Whiskers and then Sebastian tended to, Evelyn provided food and water for the skittish hare and then gathered some supplies in order to examine Alinor more thoroughly.

The wolf's ear was indeed torn, though not as badly as Evelyn had feared once the sticky blood was meticulously rinsed away. Searching gingerly through Alinor's thick fur to the skin revealed half a score of puncture marks, blossoming purple bruises on pale skin. Several of her long, black claws were torn and split. Alinor's sleek underbelly was crisscrossed with scratches and punctuated with small, crackling burrs, as if she had slid, spread-eagle, through brambles. And the stench of her!

The wolf appeared quite content to lie quietly under Evelyn's ministrations and to enjoy the loving attention being spilled over her. Her yellow eyes flickered closed and before Evelyn was half finished, Alinor was snoring softly.

"What a night you must have had," she murmured sympathetically as she swirled the rag in the water a final time—she didn't think Conall would mind that she'd used a drop or two of his precious oil. Alinor deserved a bit of pampering.

When Evelyn rose with her supplies, Bonnie clattered over out of a worried pace and settled on the floor nearly atop Alinor's rump. The wolf raised her wide head drowsily to look down her length at the sheep and then flopped back onto her side, instantly asleep once again.

Evelyn smiled and took a moment just to revel in the happiness she felt. She held her precious sense of well-being close as she stepped to the doorway to check on her husband and his brother.

They sat facing each other a short distance from the house, Conall making use of a rotted stump while Duncan perched upon an overturned bucket. They passed the jug between them while they talked and although Evelyn couldn't quite hear them, their gestures and volume hinted that their discussion was a lively one.

She could see a resemblance between them now—in their postures, the way they held out a palm to make a point, the identical angle of their arms when they raised the jug to drink.

Her husband and his brother. Evelyn's brother-in-law. Her child's uncle.

She laid a hand on her belly while she called out to the men.

"Duncan, will you stay?" she asked, noting happily the identical twists of the smaller and larger MacKerrick men as they turned to face her. "There is food aplenty, and I would that you feel welcome to linger."

Duncan's slender face split into a wide grin as he stood, sweeping his arm—and the mead jug—across his midsection as he fell into a deep bow.

"'Twould be me honor to enjoy your company, missus."

Conall shot out a leg and kicked his brother's backside, but Duncan was spry and came aright, swinging the jug backhanded at Conall's head.

Both men laughed and cursed at each other.

"I'll set about a meal," Evelyn called to them. "Conall, I'll have need of more water in a bit. Don't be in a hurry," she added when he made to rise. "And go lightly with the mead, husband—'tis still early in the day."

Evelyn turned back to the hut with a chuckle when Conall raised an acknowledging arm to her, and Duncan dealt him a stiff cuff on his ear.

"Dammit, Duncan!" Conall cried, bringing his hand to his ear with a hiss. He looked at his fingers. "Am I bleeding?"

"You're nae bleedin', you great, soft lass," Duncan scoffed before reclaiming his seat on the bucket. He took a swig of mead then passed the jug to Conall.

"Well," Duncan sighed while Conall drank. "This is a foine fuckin' mess you're in, me brother. A bloody fortunate one, to be certain," he added quickly. "But a mess, all the same."

Conall nodded, propped the jug on his knee. "Finish telling me what is about in town."

"Nae much else to tell. The folk are in high spirits that the stores have held with nae great losses; the deer remain plentiful, as do the hares; the seed is ready, and we've had three litters of swine born in one month, all the piglets hale and hardy."

Conall shook his head. In past years, they'd been lucky to have one or two piglets to survive as breeders. Half the stores would be lost to rot. 'Twas a miracle—a miracle brought on by his Buchanan wife.

How could he ever repay Eve for what she'd done?

"Any talk of the Buchanans amongst the folk?"
Conall ventured.

Duncan's face turned regretful and glanced
toward the hut. "Aye. O' course, I've told them
naught of the missus, so they feel we've overcome
the curse by sheer will. Thumbin' their noses south,
they are. Some have even spoken of a raid upon
your return."

Conall groaned. 'Twould not be a good atmosphere in which to introduce his new wife. His
Buchanan wife.

As if his brother had heard his thoughts, he
spoke. "Mayhap if you told Eve of the circumstances, prepared her beforehand . . . ?"

Conall shook his head and winced. "I doona
know, Dunc. I'd planned on telling her well before
now, but . . . I fear Eve would only be incensed by it.
She wasna pleased to find herself with child." At
Duncan's raised brow, Conall elaborated. "Her own
mother died giving birth to her. Eve worries . . ."

Duncan gave low whistle. "I can imagine her
dismay when she learned of Nonna's fate."

Conall winced.

"You didna tell Eve about your wife before her?"
Duncan ran a hand over his scalp. "You deceitful
sack o' sh—"

"She knows I was married, and that Nonna died,"
Conall interrupted. "Jesus, Dunc."

But his brother was unconvinced. "Oh, sure. But
you didna tell her how, though, did you? Or about
the wee lass." It was more of an accusation than a
question. "So doona 'Jesus, Dunc' me."

"I didna tell her of the bairn, nae," Conall admitted quietly.

"Do you nae care for your Eve at all?" Duncan

demanded. "Tell me true, Conall—I'd have nae secrets between us. Is she but a pawn for you to move about, then?"

"Of course not!" Conall frowned. "I—"

"How do you reckon Eve'll feel when she finds out? When she finds out you kept it from her? 'Tis playin' her false, brother, plain and simple."

Conall was not a little offended. "I know Eve. Telling her would only increase her fear."

Duncan shook his head emphatically. "It may at the present, aye," he conceded. "But I'd wager if she discovers it later—either by your own confession or, more likely, town gossip—she'll think that Nonna and the bairn meant naught to you."

Conall's brows lowered.

Duncan sighed and rolled his eyes. "Eve'll think she and her bairn mean just as little. Especially once she learns of the curse."

Conall could see his brother's point. "But what am I to tell her, Dunc? That I wasna in love with my first wife? That she died giving birth to my stillborn child, that she never wanted? How, pray tell, would that give her any comfort?"

"'Tis the truth of it, though," Duncan insisted. "She'll know eventually, any matter. Lance the boil, Conall."

Conall thought on his brother's advice for several moments while he and Duncan passed the jug between them again. Duncan was right, of course. 'Twas Conall's responsibility to see his clan cared for, and from what Duncan had told him, that task was well on its way to fruition. But now Eve was part of his clan, too—Eve *and* their bairn. He owed her the truth.

About everything.

"I'll tell her," Conall said at last. His gaze sought his brother's. "Once you have gone and we have our privacy, I'll tell her of Nonna and the bairn." Conall winced. "Eve has . . . a temper. I'd not have you caught in the crossfire."

"You'll tell her of the curse, as well?" Duncan prompted.

"I will, but not yet." Conall held up a palm to ward off his brother's imminent lecture. "From what you've told me of our townfolk, I need to put the past to rest for us all. Before I bring Eve home, I'd go to the Buchanan and make peace. I would have his blessing upon me and mine to carry back to our town."

Duncan's eyes rounded. "You'd have a stave in your ribs, is what you'd have."

"I think not," Conall said mildly. "Eve and the bairn she carries are direct descendants of Angus Buchanan—he'd nae harm his kin. Which, unfortunate for him, now includes me. I'll tell Eve of the curse there. Or better yet, the old goat can tell her himself."

"Yer mad," Duncan grumbled.

"I'm certain Eve'll wish to stay on a bit, visit with her kin before we set out for home," Conall said as though Duncan hadn't made the disparaging remark. "Once we return, I'll tell the town I've broken the curse and our land will at last know peace."

Duncan looked at his brother for a long, quiet moment. "A hero you're thinkin' to be, eh?"

The contemptive tone stung. Was that really Conall's ulterior motive? To arrive at the Mac-Kerrick town after single-handedly banishing an ancient demon? To prove he had accomplished what his father, Dáire MacKerrick, had been unable to do? Conall didn't want that to be so, and so he told himself that it wasn't. Surely he was more noble than that.

"'Twill be over," was his only reply to Duncan.

Duncan sighed and rose from the bucket, jerking the jug from Conall's hand. He took a healthy glug and then kicked the bucket to his brother. "You'd better go fetch your wife her water, you great, heroic ass."

Conall set off to the chore, not hearing his brother's parting whisper.

"I hope you're right, Conall. Glory, do I hope you're right." His eyes flicked to the wall of trees surrounding the clearing. They seemed to shiver with a malignant secret, one that Duncan could not begin to understand, and one he wanted no part of.

"The wolf in me dream wasna your black, brother. And the woman wasna Eve."

Conall watched Eve watching Duncan as they all sat around the peat fire, lingering over their meal. Duncan was regaling Conall's wife with tales from their shared childhood and Conall could tell from the enraptured look on Eve's face that she was thoroughly enchanted by his brother. Her eyes sparkled with entertainment as she listened to Duncan's animated—and exaggerated—retelling of how Conall had once gotten his arm stuck down a snake hole.

"He was a-screamin' an' flailin' an' kickin' his legs," Duncan said, throwing his own self about in a wild and unflattering manner. "'Mam! Mam! It's chewin' me arm off!'"

Eve brought her fingertips to her lips over a gasp and her head swiveled to Conall. "It *bit* you?"

Conall opened his mouth to answer, but Duncan beat him to it.

"That hole was as empty as the MacKerrick's fat head," Duncan scoffed. "Got his arm caught between a root and a rock, 'sall."

Eve's delighted laughter soothed some of the sting from Conall's heated face.

"We were but six, Duncan," Conall defended himself. "And I'd nae had to go into the hole at all had you nae tossed me sling down it."

Duncan whirled on him. "You wouldna let me have a go with it! Bad enough you bullied me with your great mass, but you wouldna share our single toy!"

"You kept aiming it at me!" Conall cried indignantly.

Duncan's face split with a wide, proud grin and he threw a rouguish wink at Eve.

Eve collapsed against Alinor's neck with laughter. Conall had never seen her so happy. Here in Ronan's hut, surrounded by a smiling Eve, his brother, too many animals, and plenty of food and warmth, Conall had to admit that he hadn't seen himself this happy, likely since he and Duncan were lads.

He wanted to stay at the cottage in the vale forever, just like this. It was perfect. He didn't want to return to his town, to once more don the mantle of responsibility the MacKerrick was forced to wear. Conall could recall in an instant the burden, the guilt, the turmoil that had plagued him since his father's death.

It will be different when you return, though, he told himself. *No more famine, no more illness, no more want.*

You will bring them Eve and the bairn, and they bring with them peace.

Eve's voice drew Conall out of his own head.

"How long do you stay, Duncan?"

"Ah, well." Duncan dropped his eyes to make a show of scraping his bowl, but he glanced surreptitiously at Conall. "I'll start out on the morn, missus. Someone has to keep watch over the town while me brother takes advantage of pretty lasses."

Conall stilled at Duncan's stinging remark, but to his great relief, Eve actually *giggled*.

She looked to Conall. "Is it time, too, Mac-Kerrick, for us to journey to your home? We could accompany Duncan in the morn."

Conall froze again. He'd not expected Eve to *want* to go to the MacKerrick town and was now at a loss for why they should not. Thankfully, Duncan rescued him.

"Oh, you doona want to come now, missus," he said solemnly, shaking his head.

"I don't?" Eve blinked. "Why not?"

"The place is a shambles," he said simply, taking the last bite of his supper. Duncan held up a finger while he chewed then swallowed. "From the winter. The whole of the town is shoddy-looking, littered with animal bones and great piles of dung, not to mention the drunks and ne'er-do-wells in the streets." Duncan gave an exaggerated shudder. "I doona want to go back, meself."

"What Duncan means," Conall said, "is that our people are proud. They would never forgive me if I was to bring my new wife to town without giving the folk time to prepare . . . to prepare you a proper welcome."

It was mostly true.

"Spot-on." Duncan clicked his tongue and winked at Eve.

"I see," she said and relaxed visibly. Conall suspected she had been more nervous than she let on about meeting his clan, and that only worked to his advantage. "Of course, I do not wish to offend them upon our first encounter."

"Oy! I've an idea!" Duncan said dramatically.

Conall made a mental note to chastise his brother for his over-the-top antics.

"Why do you nae bring the missus for the solstice feast? We'll be in foine form then, for certain."

"But that's . . ." Eve broke off and Conall could see that she was trying to calculate the time in her head. "Forgive me, I can't seem to recall what month it is—but surely the solstice is two months out?"

"'Tis nae that long, Eve," Conall assured her.

Duncan nodded. "Only a few weeks, missus." He snapped his fingers. "But a blink."

"Oh." Eve looked down at her belly and then turned worried eyes to Conall. "I won't be too . . . *ungainly* to make the journey then?"

Conall smiled at her, so innocent. "You'll be fine. The exercise and fresh air will do you good."

Her eyebrows rose haughtily, and 'twas then that Conall remembered that she was a titled lady. "Are you implying that I'll be plump, sir?"

"Why, ye right bastard," Duncan exclaimed, and then turned a humble countenance to Eve. "You'll be slim as a whip still, missus. But if you tire on the trail, just send for me and I'll carry you to town on me back. I'd nae have me sister so abused."

Eve's smile was so sweet it roused Conall's desire for her. He tried to stamp out the sizzle of jealousy he felt at his wife looking at his brother so gratefully.

"Thank you, Duncan. I will," she promised, and then stuck her pert tongue out at Conall.

Duncan rose and stretched, giving a great, obvious yawn. "'Tis to the pen I go. I'll likely set out at dawn," he said and then gave Eve an elaborate bow. "Sleep well, missus. I thank you for the hospitality you've shown me."

Eve started to roll to her feet and Duncan reached her before Conall could so much as stand, the spry little bastard. Duncan took Eve's elbow gently while Conall frowned.

"You are most welcome, Duncan," Eve said and squeezed his forearm as she leaned up to kiss his cheek. "The weeks will seem too long."

Conall's blood boiled.

Duncan flushed scarlet before moving a step away. He looked to each sleepy animal strewn about the hut in various positions of sloth.

"Miss Alinor, Miss Bonnie, good night. Robert, I would have fair enjoyed you in a nice pastry, but good night to you, you lucky bugger." Duncan saluted the shelf. "Whiskers, good night." Then he spun in a blur to put himself eye to eye with Eve's crow, and point a bony finger close to his beak.

"Sebastian, you shit on me head in the night, and I'll have your other wing, ken?"

The crow squawked as if offended and then flapped himself to the far end of the pen.

"Good night, Dunc," Conall laughed, all jealousy evaporated. How he loved his brother.

"Good night, good night." Duncan waved grumpily and moved into the shadows with a bony swagger.

Conall at last stepped to Eve's side and took her in his arms. She smiled up at him and Conall was glad 'twas not the same smile she'd given Duncan.

This one was sweet, aye, but full of private thoughts and feminine desire.

"You must be exhausted, lass," Conall said in a low voice before kissing her crown. After being up all night worrying over Alinor, then hosting Duncan all day, Conall was surprised Eve remained upright.

"I am rather weary," she admitted. "But not very sleepy." Her palms brushed down his back to clasp his buttocks. Conall was pleasantly shocked and greatly aroused.

"'Tis a shame we have company," she whispered on tiptoe.

Conall leaned down. "I'll throw him out in the snow." And he meant it, especially when Duncan's voice called from the blackness of the lower end of the hut.

"If yer nae sleepy, missus, have Conall tell you about the knot he wears 'round his neck!"

Eve turned inquisitive eyes to Conall's collarbone and then to his face. "There's a story behind this? I thought 'twas only . . . I don't know—adornment." She reached up, as if she would take the knot between her fingers.

Conall covered it with his fist before she could lay hand to it and tried to ignore the hurt look in her eyes. "'Tis a lengthy tale, Eve. Too long for this late hour. You need your rest."

Eve frowned as she stared at Conall's fist. He could not seem to release the knot for her gaze. 'Twas too painful, too private, still. For one final night, he wanted to hold the bittersweet memories greedily to himself.

"I'll tell you on the morrow," he promised her. And he meant that, too.

Chapter Fifteen

Evelyn could not help the pinch of sadness she felt when she woke the next morning to find that Duncan had indeed taken his leave at dawn. She had so enjoyed the company of her newly acquired brother-in-law. Something about the smaller Mac-Kerrick brother's personality comforted and delighted Evelyn thoroughly and she very much looked forward to seeing him again.

At her new home—the MacKerrick town. Where she and Conall would raise their child.

If she survived the birthing.

Evelyn raised her eyes from the cooking crock as Conall came through the door, wet from the rain falling in misty sheets outside. She could see the thick stew of fog swirling in the little bowl of their clearing before he shut the door.

He carried two buckets of water from a nearby stream—the snow had all but disappeared in the rain—and set them at Evelyn's side near the fire.

"We're in for a soaking," he said, leaving the buckets on the bumpy flagstones. "The stream is rising, and fast—more rain to our north and west."

Evelyn sighed, her melancholy settling on her even heavier than before. And Conall seemed as preoccupied and prickly this morn as she. If 'twas not deep snow trapping them all in the hut, 'twas rain, which would turn the little clearing around them into a bog. Evelyn dreaded the sticky mud that would be dragged into the cottage on the hooves, pads, and soles of many feet.

At least Alinor seemed recovered from her wanderlust. The wolf showed little interest in pestering the hut's occupants or of running wild to the wood again. But she was the only one, it seemed, without the desire to break free from the cramped dwelling. Evelyn longed for sunshine and green grass. For a long, leisurely stroll in which she could stretch her stiff muscles, free of smothering peat smoke.

The idea of such reckless freedom reminded her of the task she'd set herself to this day. She gave the stew one last stir before rapping the long-handled spoon on the edge of the crock and replacing the lid. She rose with a groan—she was growing bigger by the hour, it seemed—and moved to the pen to gather up the crow from his perch.

"I would test Sebastian's wing today," she announced to Conall, carefully stretching the bird's appendage to its full, inky length. "He seems strong enough now."

"Glory to God," Conall muttered, rolling his eyes. He'd grabbed the whetstone from the shelf and was sharpening the blade of his dagger. "That damned bird has given me nightmares, perched upon our bed all night, staring at me whilst I sleep." He threw a black frown at Sebastian. "Good riddance to you, you noisy bugger."

"Conall MacKerrick!" Evelyn pulled the bird close

to her bosom despite his squawk of protest. "For shame! Sebastian has been only well-behaved. He's a very smart creature—you'll hurt his feelings."

"Bah," Conall scoffed, hanging onto his sour countenance and addressing his chore once more. "Open the door and pitch him out, I say. Him *and* that damned rodent."

"*Someone* is in a foul mood today." Sebastian squirmed in her arms, as if he sensed his freedom was nigh, and Evelyn's conscience gave her a pinch. Perhaps she *should* set Whiskers loose, as well—the weather had improved at least to the point that Evelyn didn't think the small creature would freeze before he could find himself a nice, dry den.

Besides, she and Conall—and Alinor and Bonnie and Robert—would be leaving the hut soon. Far better for the animals that could be turned loose now to have done with it, lest they found need to return. It never crossed Evelyn's mind to liberate Robert—the rabbit had been a gift from Duncan, after all.

She sighed. "Very well, Conall." She moved Sebastian under her arm and crossed to the shelf to retrieve the shallow wooden bowl.

Conall was staring at her with a surprised expression when she turned, her hands full of animals.

"What?" she snapped crossly.

Conall's eyes dropped back to his blade. "Naught, Eve. Do what you would."

She had to juggle Whiskers's bowl while she struggled to open the door, her mood growing darker when Conall did not offer assistance. She stepped out into the misty rain and strode to the stump near the hut on which she sat the bowl.

Evelyn shifted Sebastian into both hands and

raised the bird to look into the yellow eye he showed her.

"Are you ready for this, my boy?" she asked in a low voice. She blinked as her eyelashes came over heavy with rain.

"Bay-bee," Sebastian cawed.

Evelyn nodded succinctly. She sat the crow on the wide, flat stump next to the bowl and slowly, reluctantly, removed her hands.

Sebastian gave a feather-ruffling shake and staggered sideways for an instant. Then he gave a tentative hop to the edge of the stump and swiveled his slick head, surveying the ground, the wood, the clearing, and the wide, low sky above them. He cawed again and Evelyn held her breath.

The crow dipped forward slightly, spread and stretched both wings, and then flapped from his perch. He flew only a short distance—perhaps ten feet—before landing awkwardly with an indignant squawk. He ran a bit, hopped, flapped his wings.

"Go on," Evelyn called to him through the lump in her throat. "You can do it, lovely. Try again."

The bird looked back at her a final time. Then he turned with a crouch and a mighty flap of his wings—

—and was away from the ground, rising higher and higher into the mist.

Evelyn rose onto her toes and clapped her hands in delight, despite the tears in her eyes. She watched with pride as Sebastian circled the clearing three times and then disappeared into the fog over the canopy of trees, his happy caws echoing back to her faintly in the gloom.

Evelyn took a deep breath and turned back to the stump. Undoing the twine twisted around the leather cover of the bowl, she peeled it away to reveal the small gray mouse hunkered down inside, watching her with tiny black eyes.

"There you are, my friend," she whispered. "The wood is yours for the taking."

The mouse remained frozen so that Evelyn had to force herself to tip the bowl to its side, tumbling Whiskers onto the stump. He sat up on his hind legs and sniffed the air daintily.

"Go on," she encouraged, with a soft tap on his bottom.

The mouse dropped to all fours and scurried across the stump, down the craggy side, and over the rutted mud, and in an instant, Evelyn had lost sight of him in the jumble of wet and rotting foliage.

She felt good. And sad.

She picked up the bowl, shook the waste from it, and turned once more to the hut. She stopped when she saw Conall standing in the doorway, a proud smile softening the rugged planes of his face.

"I did it," she croaked, the simple words catching in her throat.

"Well done, Eve," he said quietly and held his arms toward her. She stumbled into them, weeping like . . . well, like a maid who has lost her pets.

"Shh," he soothed and stroked her nape and back. "You have done a very good deed, lass."

She nodded but dared not speak lest she lose all control of her emotions. But she did let Conall tip up her chin and kiss her mouth.

And she did kiss him back.

And then she let him pull her inside the hut and close the door behind them.

* * *

Conall made love to Eve slowly, tenderly, both in deference to her blossoming shape as well as Conall's desire to savor this closeness with his wife. Their couplings were their most perfect time together; they did not row or argue when he was deep inside her, and kissing her mouth. There was no talk of towns or kin or journeys or the uncertain future they faced. Of secrets or fears or regrets. Just the heady give and take of lovers, when Conall could show Eve with his body what he could not express in words.

Every morning, he looked forward to waking with Eve at his side. Of seeing her body growing more round with his child. He found a deep contentment and a strange sense of strength in moving through the days at the hut with her in their simple, rugged chores and their care of the animals. Conall felt validated as a man, as a husband, as a leader. Eve let him indulge in his new role of helpmate as Nonna never had, and Conall's mind, heart, and body had flourished because of her.

The destruction of the curse was now secondary in his mind, for the other gifts she had given him overshadowed all the bad, spreading hope and light—

—and love.

And that was why, once they were both spent and dewed with sweat and lying tangled together in the box bed, Conall was ready to begin putting the past in its ready grave. He pulled a long strand of her auburn hair from across her throat and pushed it over her shoulder.

"Are you keen for a bit of a journey tomorrow, lass?"

She glanced up at him through spiky lashes, her

surprise obvious. "The MacKerrick town? But I thought—"

Conall shook his head and smoothed his forefinger over her soft lips. She was so beautiful, lush.

"There is a matter long in want of my attention; one that needs be settled before I—*we*—can go home."

Conall felt more than saw Eve relax. She was now smoothing a small, soft palm across his chest, ruffling the hair against her skin idly. "Oh? And where does this settling dictate we go?"

"I must meet with the Buchanan."

Eve froze, her gaze halted somewhere on Conall's throat. "Why?"

"'Tis customary that clans joined in marriage are aware of the fact prior to the intended couple wedding," he said in a teasing tone. "But since we have dispensed with that tradition, 'tis only respectful that we inform Angus of our union, and of his future"— Conall paused and looked at Eve curiously—"great-nephew? Grandchild?" He waited for her correction.

It never came. "I don't think that is such a good idea now, MacKerrick," she said grudgingly. She had removed her hand from his chest and pulled the blanket up over her as she rolled to her back.

"Why? I would think you eager to at last meet your kin and bring the news of the old witch's passing to her brother."

"Don't call her that," Eve snapped.

"I'm sorry, lass," he said, properly chastised. Conall snaked an arm over her belly to draw Eve closer to him but she held herself rigid. "Eve? What is it?"

"I simply don't want to go," she said.

"Why?"

"Because I *don't*, MacKerrick."

Conall frowned. Eve had been moody and contrary of late, true, but he could not fathom a reason for her reluctance to visit her kin.

"Is it the bairn, Eve? Or me?" he asked gently, needing to understand. "Do you fear the Buchanan will refuse you?"

"That is exactly what I fear." The words were spoken so softly that Conall had to lean forward to catch them. She turned her head and Conall could see the alarm in the gray-blue depths of her eyes. "I am a stranger to him. You do not understand."

He smiled at her self-conscious dread and cupped her cheek. "You'll be a right surprise, aye," he began.

Eve huffed a mirthless laugh. "You've no idea."

"But Angus will soon give over his shock," he continued, wanting Eve to find peace with the task. Needing her to. She must. "We are wed, after all. What choice will he have, hmm? It canna be undone. And the journey will be an easy one for you should we leave right away—two days, at most, following the valley west the whole of the way to Loch Lomond."

Eve shrugged again and shook her head.

"We must go," Conall insisted. "'Tis my duty as clan chief. To not inform the Buchanan that I have wed a member of his clan is a great affront. One my town canna afford the consequences of." He grimaced, but forged on. "Our towns have been . . . uneasy with each other for some time, as it is."

Her eyes flew to his. "How so?"

How much to tell her now? Conall had not thought the matter would be raised so soon, and he was unsure how Eve would take the tale of Minerva and Ronan's disastrous affair. Especially since she already feared the Buchanan's condemnation.

"An old feud," he finally said. "Of little consequence now, but I would not risk further insult."

Eve pressed her lips together, obviously in deep thought. "I understand," she said at last. "You must go. But you will go alone."

"Eve—"

"I'll not discuss it further, MacKerrick." She cut him off, her voice growing shrill.

He did not wish to upset her by telling her she had no choice, but he thought it to himself. He could not approach the Buchanan town alone with such news. If he was not killed immediately after revealing his identity, he would be shortly after telling of the curse's remedy. The clan heads would never believe him without Eve in the flesh, as proof.

Conall tried to quit his mind of the dark image of holding Eve before him as some sort of trophy— or, worse, a protective amulet, because she was so much more to him now. But to the bloodthirsty Buchanans, her existence was likely aught that would stay their vengeful pride.

Conall decided that there was still time to convince Eve. He would let her be for a few days to think upon it and come to the right decision on her own. But she would go.

She had no choice.

"Very well," Conall said, pulling her to him once more, even when she would have kept her distance. "We'll nae discuss it further this day. But as your husband, Eve, I bid you give it your thought. I'd have your support of my duties, wife."

She nodded stiffly, her hair rubbing against his chest. "I will think upon it."

Conall was placated, and content now to hold her for the better part of a quarter hour. He had almost dozed off into a comfortable slumber when Eve's low voice roused him.

"Tell me about your necklace."

Chapter Sixteen

Evelyn felt Conall stiffen and so she gave him a moment before she pressed. 'Twas obviously an item of great importance and of deep meaning for Conall, and she hungered to be let in on its secret. She felt he owed her as much after scaring the life out of her by suggesting that they visit the Buchanan town. She had avoided the journey without resorting to more lies—indeed, she had been completely honest. But she knew in her heart that neither Conall or his impending duty could be put off forever. The truth would be told, and soon.

"You promised," she reminded him.

"I know I did." It was his turn to roll away from her and onto his back. Evelyn tucked her arm under her head to watch him on her side.

"You'll nae find pleasure in this tale," he warned her, his eyes fixed on the box bed's slatted roof. "The telling of it, nor its end."

"I don't care," she said. "I want to know."

He gave a single nod. "Very well." Evelyn saw his throat working as he swallowed, as if he had to work up the courage to begin. "Me da, Dáire Mac-

Kerrick, arranged my marriage to Nonna when she was only days old. All were pleased with the match and spoke of the day when I would take Da's place as clan chief, with Nonna as my wife.

"We were playmates, the three of us—Nonna, Dunc, and meself—reared in the town side by side." A faint smile pulled at his mouth and Evelyn knew he was remembering. "She was a bonny, mischievous lass—long, dark hair, always a-tangle, her skirts pulled up and knotted. She never hesitated to join in a spot of trouble me an' Duncan had discovered and oft times, 'twas she who found us the merry to make."

The smile slipped from his face slowly, like silk sliding from a piece of rough-planed lumber.

"But as we grew older, and the day drew near to when we'd be expected to wed, Nonna changed. Times were nae easy then—crops were failing, we had to defend our lands from poachers—and I was oft away with Da, hunting or fighting. Each time I returned, she was more distant, cold. She made it clear she'd nae desire for my company when it wasna absolutely required of her.

"And then one day, out of the clear sky, it seemed, although I reckon I must've known, she says to me"—he pulled his face into a haughty, determined look—"'Conall, I doona fancy bein' yer wife.'"

The word "why" was nearly out of Evelyn's mouth before she caught herself. Thankfully, Conall either took pity on her or had planned on keeping his word to tell the tale to its end. Either way, he continued.

"She said the town was . . . damned, collapsing. A death trap, she called it. Said Da wasna doing anything about . . . anything to better it, and that she had little hope I would either." Evelyn was riveted by Conall's past and barely noticed she'd brought her hand to her mouth to cover her shock. But it was to get much, much worse.

"She didna want to be the chief's wife," he said. "Said she would accept any other man in the whole of Scotland, save me. She didna love me."

He paused for a moment. "She ran off the eve before we were to wed, but her da 'n mine fetched her back before the dawn."

Evelyn tried to imagine the humiliation Conall must have felt at his intended fleeing him and then felt her face heat. Hadn't she done nearly the same thing to the man she'd thought to marry in England? Only Evelyn had fled to the priory and no one had fetched her back until it was too late. She felt deep remorse for the heartache she now knew she'd caused what seemed to be years ago, and she was grateful to the bottom of her very soul that Nicholas FitzTodd had found his true happiness.

I'm so sorry, Nick—I didn't know. She sent the thought toward the heavens before concentrating once more on the man lying next to her.

"Nonna wept into the night. She was me first woman, but I was to find out the bitter truth that I wasna her first man. She had lain with another in hopes that it would make me refuse her." Conall swallowed. "'Twas how it was to be the whole of our marriage, until she died—she withheld herself from me, as a wife to a husband. Only when I would press her, shame her, guilt her into yielding would she relent to me. And 'twas always grudgingly, and with nae even the smallest kindness in her. I was . . . I was verra lonely. Especially after Da passed. Duncan had Mam. My town was sick, failing. I was failing. Me own wife didna want me."

Evelyn wanted to cry. Never had she thought to see or hear Conall MacKerrick so vulnerable, so needing. She had to struggle to maintain her quiet lest she break the spell of the highlander's dark memories. She wanted them all, greedily wanted every last, painful one of them.

"The last time Nonna and I were together as husband and wife, I was . . ." He paused, as if gathering his courage. "I was drunk. Loud and hateful. I demanded my due from her. She yielded to me, but when 'twas over, she vowed she would die by her own hand rather than let me touch her in that manner ever again. And I never did."

Now Evelyn could feel tears leaking from the corners of her eyes, slipping over the bridge of her nose and down her cheek to fall on the ticking below. Such sadness, for them both.

"And now, Eve," he said, startling her with his address, "I will tell you of my . . . my locket. Please . . ." He broke off as if he didn't know what he was going to ask of her, and then just let the plea dangle.

"I told you that Nonna died of illness, and that is true. She *was* ill. But I didna tell you that the illness that killed her was"—he swallowed—"it was my child."

Evelyn gasped and her stomach tried to turn itself inside out. A chill of fear swept over her and she felt herself curl instinctively around her belly.

"Nonna became pregnant on that drunken night. I was so"—he seemed to search for the right word—"*happy*. My bairn. Me own companion, to bestow my pride on. I cared not that it was a lad or a gel.

"Nonna, though—my God, she was inconsolable. She made it clear she didna want the child and, in

truth, I had to set Duncan upon her while I was
about town business to be certain she didna harm
herself or the bairn. She'd nae eat for days and by
the time she was half gone with child, she'd so little
strength left, so little flesh on her, she took to our
bed. And she never left it."

Evelyn turned her face into her arm so as not to
have to look at Conall and reveal her fear and pain.
His words stabbed at her mercilessly.

"She lasted longer than any of us dared hope. I
came immediately when her pains started. But she
wouldna have me at her side. Screamed that she
hated me, hated the bairn, hated the very earth on
which I stood. Duncan attended her in my stead,
God bless him."

Evelyn became very still while she waited for the
tale to find its vicious end.

"'Twas a wee, wee lass," Conall whispered. "So
tiny, like a mouse, but with thick, black hair like
her mother. She never had the strength to take her
first breath, never . . . never reached out a little
fist." Conall's voice grew choked and he paused as
he held up his own clenched hand, ignoring
Evelyn's silent sobs that shook the ticking. "Nonna
slipped away with the blood that ran out of her.
When I saw her—after—she looked . . . at peace.

"But my wee girl, she was gone!" His last words
were little more than a croak. Conall drew a long,
sniffling breath and blew it out harshly. "Although
her mother never wanted her, I could not bear . . . I
could not bear the thought of her little body laid to
rest all alone. So I washed her and wrapped her with
Nonna." He gave a harsh cry—anger, grief, deep,
deep pain. "But before I let her go, I took a lock of

her fine, black hair—like down. And I tied it into this love knot. And then—*and then*—I let her go."

He gasped and Evelyn looked up from her arm to see him cover his eyes with his hand, his mouth pulled wide in his grief.

Without hesitation, Evelyn wrapped herself around Conall's body, holding him more tightly than she had ever held another person while they both cried.

God, she was terrified. The tale of Nonna's childbed death haunted her and stirred up the creaky old fear of her own frailty, of her own bloody emergence into this world at the expense of her mother's life.

But now she was more frightened for Conall than for herself. Evelyn thought she now understood what the child growing inside her meant to Conall and it both thrilled and frightened her. If Evelyn was to die while birthing their baby—if the child was not strong and healthy—she knew it would kill him.

Conall's arms came around her at last, his hitching breaths finally controlled. "I have worsened your fear, have I not?" he asked, his voice heavy with regret.

Evelyn sniffed and shook her head. "Nay," she said and looked up at his face. She tried to give him a smile but feared it fell short. "'Tis no worse than it was before. But one thing has changed."

Conall stilled.

"I *want* to give you this child, Conall. I want you to have your bonny gel or wee lad for a companion, to mayhap one day lead your clan." She leaned up to frame his disbelieving face with her hands, very aware of her mounded belly pressing into him. "And I want him to have his father, the man who loves him with all his heart and would die for him."

"I do," he said. "And I would. Eve, I will keep you safe. Our family . . . I . . ."

Say it, she pleaded silently. *Tell me you love me, Conall.*

"What?" she whispered.

His lips pressed together tightly for a moment. "Thank you, Eve."

Evelyn returned his smile as best she could.

Chapter Seventeen

Six weeks passed, washing Conall and Eve along with great, cold showers that soaked the days and the clearing, dusting the trees and brambles in chilly, vivid, furry green.

Conall paused in his chore of mucking out the animal pens inside the hut, swiping at his brow with his forearm. The air was clammy yet humid, the warmest day of the season thus far. He leaned his shoulder against the stall beam and looked out the open door through the ever-present mist at Eve, poking along the edge of the clearing with a long, flat basket on her hip, plucking tender new greens for their evening meal. Alinor herded Bonnie in circles and Conall smiled at the sight of the great black beast—no longer the stringy, hollow-bellied animal he'd first met when the snow had been deep. Now her coat frizzed with new growth, her ribs and hips disappeared beneath lean muscle. She was more than a bit rounded, Conall realized and laughed to himself. The glutton.

Alinor was not the only female in the clearing more generous of frame. Conall guessed Eve at seven months gone, and her belly protruded from her switch-slender body like a kettle, causing the front hems of her kirtle and underdress to rise up from the ground several inches higher than the back hems.

For safety's sake, he could wait no longer. They must start for the Buchanan town on the morrow. And once they reached it, they could stay no more than a few days. Conall would take no chance of overexerting Eve, and he wanted her safely ensconced at his home well before her time was nigh.

He knew he was looking at a row with her, but it could not be avoided. He must have Angus Buchanan's acknowledgment and blessing, and Conall wanted it over and out of the way as soon as possible. 'Twas past time for him and Eve to start living their life from under this rotting pile of ancient sorcery. The memory of the curse had become little more than a nagging nuisance and Conall was eager to return to his clan—his mother, and Duncan—and simply be free.

Conall saw Eve coming back toward the hut, Alinor and Bonnie walking slowly on either side to match her swaying, leisurely pace. He leaned the old, splintered muckrake in a corner and moved through the doorway to wash the filth and sweat from his arms and face. Otherwise, Eve would wrinkle her pert nose at him when he went to kiss her. And he would likely need to kiss her several times to get her to acquiesce to the journey they'd be taking.

Conall didn't mind the kissing part in the least.

"The wood is alive with life," Eve said with a sparkling smile as she neared. Her cheeks were dewy and flushed, and her bosom rose and fell swiftly with the new effort walking now required. She stopped at his side while Conall rubbed at his wet hair with a linen.

"I can hear the little ones babbling and playing—squirrels, deer, birds, kits. 'Tis like a great, green nursery." She made to move past him into the hut.

Conall tossed the linen up to catch on the edge of the low-hanging roof and then wheeled around to snatch Eve back to him, his arms snaking beneath hers to encircle her ribs.

She laughed good-naturedly, placing one hand on his chest while trying to keep the basket aright on her hip.

He kissed her nose and she wrinkled it anyway. "You're wet, sir."

"Aye, but I'm clean." He snugged her body into his as best as her belly would allow. "Care to muss me up a bit?"

Eve smiled and kissed his rough jaw, her full lips like suede on his skin. "Not now, Conall. I would set these greens to cook before they wilt." She eased out of his arms, dragging her hand down his chest, and entered the hut. "Come, come, lovelies—ouch! Mind my foot if you would, Alinor."

Conall ducked through the doorway after her and was pleased that she took note of his efforts even as she tended to her own chores.

"The pens look quite smart," she said in an impressed tone and looked about the small hut as she kicked the stool closer to the fire pit and sat. "Indeed, the entire cottage is tidy." Her grin turned mischievous. "I'd not have taken you for a housemaid, Conall, but a fine one you'd make."

He laughed and bent to swat her bottom—nicely rounded, now—with the backside of his hand. As he crossed to the shelf to retrieve his léine from a peg, Conall decided 'twould be best to break the news to Eve when she was in a fair humor.

"Well, I'd nae leave Ronan's hut a shamble on the morrow," he said pointedly. He pulled the shirt over his head. When he turned to face Eve once more, she was looking at him with excitement.

"'Tis time, then? We leave for the MacKerrick town?"

Conall braced himself. "Nae, lass. 'Tis to the Buchanan town we hie."

A door slammed on Eve's open, easy expression and she immediately directed her gaze to the greens as she began trimming them and then dropping them into a crock. Her mouth was pinched into a frown.

"I've told you, MacKerrick, I'll not go. I've not changed my mind, and I won't."

"Eve," Conall sighed, and crouched at her side. He hated when she reverted to addressing him as MacKerrick. "We must. 'Tis my duty as clan chief. You'd nae have me insult your kin, would you?"

"I fail to see why it is of such grave concern, is all," she said tightly, her movements with the short, broken dagger becoming quick and jerky while she worked. "I am not acquainted with any of them and do not see the good of it. Am I not your wife now? Are you—and the rest of the MacKerrick clan—not my kin? How are the Buchanans to know I even exist unless we tell them?"

Conall could find little fault with her reasoning, save that he *needed* the Buchanans to be aware of Eve.

And her condition.

"'Twould be but a matter of time before word

reached them," Conall reasoned gently. "Peddlers, trade routes—the Buchanan would find out sooner or later, Eve, and how offended would he be to learn that his kin cared so little for her people that she had refused to pay them this small courtesy?" He held out his palms. "Do you wish to have such poor relations with your Scots blood at the start?"

"I care not," she said succinctly and brushed her hands together over the pot. Grabbing up her now-empty basket, she rose swiftly and moved to replace it on the shelf. "They are strangers to me. The MacKerricks are my only Scots kin." She whirled to face him. "And why is it so important to you that we go now, any matter? Why not later, after the babe has safely come, hmm?" Her eyes narrowed. "Are you shamed of me, MacKerrick? Do you hope to wheedle some sort of dowry from the Buchanan to increase my worth before you present me to your family? Am I so hideous and uncouth to your proud Scots sensibilities that—"

Eve continued her tirade and Conall rubbed at his eyes with a frustrated sigh. It could not be put off any longer. She must understand.

"—I've been schooled in Latin, and not a little cipher—"

"Eve, stop," Conall commanded.

"Just tell me if I humiliate you, MacKerrick. You—"

"Stop!" he shouted. He stood and took her elbow gently, leading her to the box bed before he helped her to sit on its edge. "Wait." He addressed her frown, then fetched the stool to sit before and slightly below her.

Conall plucked the blade from her fingers and

sat it aside on the ticking, then pulled her hands from their clench. He kissed each of her fists and then gave her fingers a squeeze.

"I am nae shamed of you, in the least," he said solemnly. "In truth, there is nae more prideful man in all of Scotland. And I will be fair to bursting with pride when I take you to my town."

He paused and Eve continued to frown at him. A knot had begun to form out of his guts.

"But I *am* shamed," he said. "Of meself. There is another reason why I must go to the Buchanan town, Eve, and why you must go with me. I am shamed of the fact that I have kept it from you these many months."

Evelyn's frown shifted into wary curiosity. "What is it, Conall?"

He took a deep breath. "Do you recall the night I first came to the hut?"

Eve's brow quirked. "How could I forget? You wanted to toss me and Alinor to the grays."

"I did," he admitted somberly. "And sorry I am for it. But once you made mention of Minerva Buchanan as your kin—"

"You changed your mind, quite abruptly," she supplied, her expression growing more worried. "What are you about, MacKerrick? Get on with it."

Conall nodded. "The MacKerrick town has been in dire straights indeed these some thirty years, Eve. And our relations with the Buchanans strained for as many."

"And?" Eve demanded. "What has this to do with me?"

"Everything," Conall whispered, and tightened his grip on her slender hands. "It has everything to do with you, Eve.

"Over thirty years ago, Ronan MacKerrick, my uncle, and Minerva Buchanan, your aunt, began an affair that neither family approved of. Minerva and Ronan sought to marry and, against my father's wishes, Ronan planned a secret meeting to beg favor from Angus Buchanan."

Conall began stroking the backs of Eve's hands with his thumbs. "My da found out about the meeting—an act of treachery against the MacKerricks on Ronan's part. Da organized a raid and surprised Ronan and the Buchanan clan heads here, at this hut."

Eve's eyes had slowly widened as the tale unfolded and her lips parted slightly. "What happened?" she whispered.

Conall swallowed. "A great battle. Many Buchanans died, including Angus's own wife." He paused. "Ronan died protecting Minerva."

"I still don't understand," Eve said. "Why—"

"When Ronan fell, the battle stopped," Conall forged on. "'Twas never my da's intent for his own brother to die. Indeed, I believe the guilt of it is what drove him to the drink, to his own death. But he was to pay an even greater price for his actions on that terrible day.

"Minerva Buchanan laid a curse on the MacKerricks, over Ronan's still-warm body. She tried to kill us all, Eve, and she was slowly succeeding, until you came along."

Conall took another deep breath. "But 'tis over now. You've put an end to the curse and, pray God, the entire feud. I would have Angus Buchanan's blessing on our union, to put this terrible past behind us, once and for all."

"The curse is ended because we married? But then why—?" Eve had paled to the color of the long-melted snow. Her lips barely moved when next she spoke, and her words were no more than a whisper. "What was the curse, Conall? Exactly—tell me the words."

Conall grimaced. "Eve—"

"Tell me." She did not raise her voice, but the intensity of the request frightened Conall more than any gray wolf ever had.

"Very well." He cleared his throat and recited each damning word, slowly, clearly, honestly. He only hesitated before the last few lines, the ones that had sealed Eve's fate. "'Only heartache and toil shall you reap until a Buchanan bairn is born to rule the MacKerrick clan. And then I will take what is due me. When you are on bended knee will I have my revenge.'"

'Twas Alinor's insistent scratching at the door that broke the heavy silence hanging in the cottage. Evelyn's eyes were blank, her expression stony and unreadable. Alinor scratched again and added an impatient, high-pitched whine to Bonnie's bleat.

"Not now, Alinor," Conall said over his shoulder.

Eve pulled her hands free from Conall's grasp. "Let them out," she ordered quietly. "Shut the door after them."

Conall frowned but rose to do her bidding, thinking Eve had no wish for the animals' distraction.

He had just turned from the chore when the three-legged stool glanced off his temple.

Eve flew at Conall even as he reeled from the stool bounding off his head with a surprised shout.

She wanted to kill him. Her fury, her pain was so great it choked her, stole her breath, the beating of her heart. Her body felt like a stone afire, and she wanted Conall MacKerrick to pay. To pay dearly for . . .

. . . for never loving her.

She reached him as he straightened and swung her right arm, her claws spread and a shriek on her tongue.

"You bastard!" Her nails just missed his face as he jerked out of her reach. She swung her left arm. "You *lied* to me! You *used* me!"

Conall caught her wrist and spun her away from him. "Eve, nae. Let me explain."

"'Tis why you wanted to—to marry me, seduce me! *To get me pregnant!*" she screamed. Her voice strained and hitched from the force of her shouts. She felt as though she had not enough breath to fuel her hungry, white-hot rage. Her ribs ached. "Even after—after I—*my greatest fear!*" She flew at him again.

"I didna think—" He caught her, held her away from him even as she twisted her wrists and clawed at his forearms. "Eve, I didna think you could get with child. I didna lie to you about that!"

"But that was your intent!" she wheezed, jerking away from him and finding that she was blinded by tears. She dashed a hand across her eyes. "Wasn't it, Conall? *Wasn't it?* From the start, that was your scheme—to use me to bear the child that would save your precious town full of backstabbing liars from their much-deserved fate!"

"Eve." Conall's face grew ruddy. "Doona say such things. And calm yourself—the bairn—"

"Oh, yea—*the bairn!*" she mocked. "Never mind *Evelyn's* heart, *her* pride, *her* soul—she is but the vessel!"

"That isna how I feel about you," Conall said.

"You. Lie!" She picked up an empty crock near her foot and hurled it at Conall. He batted it away and it smashed to the flagstones. "That's all you wanted me for, isn't it, MacKerrick? *Your brood mare!* Confess!"

Conall's lips whitened. "'Tis true, my first thoughts were to put an end to the wickedness that has been killing my people—my first wife, our first child—"

"Your first wife took her own life and that of your child, just as surely as if she'd used a blade!" Eve accused. "It was no curse! She likely saw through your selfishness as I never had chance to!"

Conall's nostrils flared. "Eve, I swear to you, my intentions changed. *You* changed me."

Evelyn felt she was bleeding from her heart. That she was slowly emptying out her life force, facing the dirty, evil truth. The man she loved, was willing to risk her life for, had betrayed her. Nothing he'd ever said to her meant anything. The truth had come out of its dark, fetid hole at last.

But not all of it. Oh, no. Not yet.

Evelyn began to chuckle madly, tears overflowing her eyes and washing down her face.

"Eve?" Conall took a step toward her, his face a fine imitation of concern.

Her sobs mated with her crazed laughter so that her words came out like the halting caws of a crow.

"Fooled . . . *you*, MacKerrick!" she gasped. It was becoming more difficult to draw breath. "Fooled . . . *you!*" She stumbled backward against the box bed, a wave of dizziness pummeling her so that she had to reach out and take hold of the curtain to steady herself.

"Eve, sit down," Conall warned, circling the pit and advancing on her, his hands out at his sides as if approaching a wild animal. "Sit down and we can talk."

"You . . . st-stay . . . away." She snatched the forgotten blade from the bed and held it before her, righting herself clumsily when the curtain began to rip. Their stances reminded her of their initial meeting. She flung her hair from her eyes with a wild toss of her head. Conall stopped midway in his approach.

"G-go," she stammered, gesturing toward the door with the blade. "Go back to your own evil town, MacKerrick, and you can tell them that you have failed! I have saved you from making a fool out of yourself before the Buchanan. Ha!"

"Eve, I'm worried for you."

Nonsensical laughter burst from her once more. "Don't be! No need! I shall relieve you of your ob-obligation p-posthaste, sir! 'Until a Buchanan bairn is born to rule the MacKerrick clan'?"

Evelyn thought for a moment that it might have been real concern on the highlander's face, and she relished this moment before she would erase it forever.

Erase *him* forever.

"*I am not Buchanan,*" she said in wretched triumph.

MacKerrick's head tilted as if he feared he had misheard her and for a moment he reminded Evelyn of Alinor, when she was listening intently.

"So you see," she continued, flinging her arms wide, "your scheming was for naught! Your town is as damned as it ever was, for the child I carry is *half* Scots and *half* English—I am of pure English blood."

"That canna be," Conall stammered. "Minerva—"

"I knew Minerva Buchanan for but a week before my escape from England, and I accompanied her to this hellish land in order to avoid a return to the priory I hated." Evelyn forced a laugh. "I knew just enough of her kin to save my own life when you would have abandoned me to die."

"You're not . . ." Conall shook his head as if he still did not comprehend what Evelyn was telling him. "You're not *at all* Buchanan, lass?"

"Not *at all* Buchanan, and *not your lass*," she hissed in satisfaction as the truth dawned on him.

MacKerrick's face seemed to transform before Evelyn's very eyes as he fit the pieces together—the bones shifted, the flesh melted and remolded into a mask of such utter hatred it thrilled her broken, bleeding heart.

"You lied to me," he whispered.

"That's right!" she laughed. "Smarts, does it not?"

She could see his body tremble from across the room and, in a blink, he was storming toward her. Evelyn let the blade fall from her hand to clatter to the flagstones and did not so much as raise an arm to defend herself.

She hoped he would kill her quickly. She closed her eyes on his angry, twisted face.

Surely just before he could lay hand to her, Evelyn heard the hut door burst inward. She opened her eyes to see the black blur that was Alinor launch at the highlander, white fangs bared, and pin him to the ground by his throat.

Evelyn stood shuddering violently, staring down at Conall MacKerrick, who lay absolutely still save for his shallowly rising chest. Evelyn could see his amber eyes aflame with hatred as they pierced her over Alinor's wrinkled muzzle. The wolf held him true, her long, pointed canines dimpling the skin to either side of the highlander's windpipe, the low growl coming from her making clear her intent:

Flinch and I will tear out your throat.

Gone was the amicable, four-legged companion, to be replaced by a wild, vicious, deadly beast. As Evelyn stood over the wolf, she couldn't help but note the commonality between herself and Alinor.

Gone was the happy, safe wife and mother with a bright future ahead. Conall had replaced her with this woman betrayed, and Evelyn realized at that moment her intentions were as potentially deadly as the wolf's.

"Alinor," Evelyn said, her voice aquiver. "To me."

The wolf did not twitch, only sent her growl into a higher range.

"To me, Alinor!" Evelyn shouted.

Alinor reluctantly released MacKerrick's neck, but kept her yellow eyes pinned to him as she backed awkwardly to Evelyn's side. Evelyn was morbidly pleased to see the four round puncture marks—two each on either side of MacKerrick's throat—bruises already blooming.

How many times had she kissed him there, in passion? Her stomach roiled.

Fool.

"Get up," she commanded.

MacKerrick heaved himself aright and backed away, glaring at Evelyn, his eyes flicking to Alinor as if he feared she might attack once again.

His fear fueled her, focused her.

"Now, get out," she said, eerily calm, glancing at the door. "If you ever think to return here, I will let Alinor kill you."

"Eve, you doona know what you've done," Mac-Kerrick said in a gravelly voice. "You have nae—"

"Get out," Evelyn repeated.

MacKerrick stood there for another moment. "I renounce you," he said at last, looking steadily into her eyes. "You are nae my wife any longer." He pointed—actually pointed—at her stomach, and shook his head. "Not my bairn. I renounce you both."

"I was never your wife," Evelyn said quietly, amazed that she could still speak. "You were married to a woman who never existed."

MacKerrick made to move toward the shelf where his plaid and pack hung innocently. Alinor growled and her hackles rose higher.

"Nay!" Evelyn said sharply, then lowered her voice when he stopped. "You'll take naught from this hut—you've taken enough already, sir."

MacKerrick stared at her for what seemed like an eternity.

Alinor took a menacing step forward, lowered her head, and bared her teeth once more.

Conall MacKerrick turned and departed through the open doorway into the misty fog of evening, and was gone.

Chapter Eighteen

Conall fought his way through the underbrush, having strayed from the trail that led to the MacKerrick town, but not caring. Old, brittle brambles slashed at his arms, chest, and thighs through his thin clothing, but he could not feel the scores of tears on his skin for the searing pain in his gut. Fiery and roiling, he knew 'twould paralyze him if he paused to catch his breath, and so he charged forward, recklessly grabbing great handfuls of spiny vines and ripping them out of his way.

Damned. They were . . . damned, now.

The curse would finish them and 'twould be the fault of none but Conall. But the danger was so much bigger now, so much more was at stake.

Mayhap if he moved faster . . .

His breath roared in and out of him as he spied a break in the choking brush and the stingy trail beyond it. Conall threw himself from the thickness of the tangle with a roar, stumbling onto the mired path. He began to run through the sucking mud. Night was swiftly falling, like the spreading wings of the midnight crow.

He needed Duncan. He needed—his mother, aye! Lana would know. She would understand and forgive him and . . .

And what?

Conall didn't know. But he was being called home, mayhap for the last time. He paid no heed to the tears on his face, save for running faster to dry their bitter wetness.

Evelyn did not bother barring the door. Mac-Kerrick would not return and even if he did, Evelyn felt she would keep her word and let Alinor tear him limb from long, lanky limb.

She backed up a step to again lower herself onto the edge of the box bed, Alinor nosing under her palm, once more the docile companion. From the far end of the hut, Bonnie bleated pitifully, her tether caught on a board.

He's left his sheep, Evelyn thought to herself in odd, quiet concern. *Poor Bonnie. She's sad.*

"Just a moment, Bonnie," Evelyn called faintly. "I only need to . . ."

What? Weep? Rest? Scream? Evelyn didn't know, save that she could not command her body to rise from the bed. The bed she and MacKerrick had shared for the past several months. Where she had taken his seed and given her heart.

God, how she'd loved him.

And he had done the very thing that could destroy her. She lost herself in the horrifying future left to her: black loneliness, death, blood . . .

Evelyn did not know how long she sat in the loud silence, but when she came aware with a start, the hut was gloomy pitch.

Something must be wrong. She must be ill. Perhaps the strain of her and MacKerrick's parting row had been too much, done unseen harm, for she felt an odd, deliberate plucking in her lower abdomen that she'd never felt before.

Still beneath her hand, Alinor turned her muzzle toward Evelyn, her ears pricking up. Evelyn brought her other palm to rest gingerly on her belly and held her breath, waited.

There it was again! A sort of punching of her insides; a tumbling, a lurch. Painless, but she felt it both inside and out and for a moment, icy-hot fear drenched her.

Then Alinor whined softly.

"It's moving," Evelyn whispered, realizing, looking down at her hand. Evelyn had felt the faint flutterings of the babe for several weeks now, but never like this. Not this strongly or insistently, as if he was adamantly stating his presence.

"It's really . . . *alive.*" She swallowed. "Hallow, babe."

And then she did weep, great wailing sobs of joy and pain and fear. This babe was a living being inside her, created in the deepest snows of the highland winter by a man and woman brought together by lies. And now he lay, turning innocently in Evelyn's body, blessedly unaware that his father had abandoned him, that his mother was completely alone and frightened.

Evelyn feared bringing this child into the world, yea. But the horror that now consumed her eclipsed her earlier worries completely. She had accepted that the ordeal might kill her, but if it did and she was alone at the remote hut, who would care for her child? Who would hold him and feed him and love him, as Evelyn's father had done for her? She had no one now. Should she die, so would her child.

Evelyn scrambled to close her mind to the memories of MacKerrick's stillborn daughter. She could not let her thoughts go to that possibility, nor to him, now. Not when the life of her own child depended on Evelyn's next decision.

'Twas then she realized she still wore Minerva Buchanan's patched, old cloak. And as if the old witch had whispered the solution in Evelyn's ear, she knew her path was decided.

She stood shakily from the bed, her palm cupping her belly as if to reassure her that the child was still within. She crossed the hut and lit an oil lamp with trembling fingers, dropping the little twig of flame twice. Once the golden glow bloomed on the rough walls, Evelyn moved to the shelf to retrieve the last bit of oats in the sack for Bonnie. On the morrow they would leave, and the less Evelyn had to carry, the faster they could travel.

A little gray bundle tumbled from the top of the sack, startling Evelyn for a moment.

"Whiskers?" she whispered, then huffed a weak laugh. Evelyn laid the back of her palm on the shelf and the little mouse clambered up without hesitation. "How did you—"

But before she could complete her question, a tap-tapping upon the door sent Alinor into a frenzy.

Evelyn closed her fingers securely around Whiskers and crossed the floor. She bumped Alinor aside with her hip and opened the door but a handsbreadth to peer out.

Sebastian popped through the narrow opening near Evelyn's feet with a squawk, and then quickly took wing to land on the pen wall, away from Alinor's playful but deadly snapping jaws. Evelyn closed the door, the evening's strange and terrible events pummeling her nerves. She turned to look at the disheveled room.

Alinor pranced and whined beneath Sebastian, who seemed quite pleased to be returned. Bonnie had become hopelessly tangled in her tether, pulling over the muckrake and finally laying down half atop it. Robert crouched contentedly in his trap-turned-hutch, still picking at the handful of greens Evelyn had dropped to him earlier. In her hand, Whiskers snuggled and nibbled at the folds of her palm.

In her belly, Evelyn's babe tumbled again.

"I am not alone," she said aloud, realization and hope—or mayhap mere determination—growing. Her eyes fell on each creature in the hut. "You are all my family. Perhaps I saved you once, but now it's you who will save me. And my babe."

Sebastian squawked. "Bay-bee!"

Evelyn took in the broader portrait of the hut, in complete disarray with toppled furniture and broken pottery, but also the precious surplus of supplies that had once belonged to MacKerrick. She calculated in her mind what they would require versus what she could carry.

Two days, MacKerrick had said. *Following the valley to the west the whole of the way to Loch Lomond.*

She thought she remembered the loch, having briefly spotted it on her fateful journey with Minerva Buchanan. As Evelyn crunched over broken shards to begin gathering their supplies in MacKerrick's pack, she hoped she could find it once again, for the babe's sake.

* * *

It was full-on dark and the moon was high when
Conall gasped his way into the MacKerrick town.
Only when he stood at the edge of the wood, but
a stone's throw from the main street, did he at last
pause to gather a score of burning, agonizing
breaths, bent double, his hands on his knees.

His whole body shook and sweat had conspired
with a light, misty rain to drench him to the skin.
His eyes burned, his ears rang. His heart screamed
like a wounded beast.

He shuddered and panted himself slowly aright.

Even though the hour was late, faint music trickled through the mist from inside one of the houses,
a lone flute, keening a soft tune slowly, as a lullaby.
Even in the wet shadows of night, the town was trans-
formed: the streets wide and recently smoothed; bas-
kets, traps, and bundles flanking neatly tended
dooryards adorned with windflowers and sleeping
primroses. Peat smoke drifted in orderly columns
from smoke holes and joined together in the dense
air to form a protective blanket over the MacKerrick
town. The air smelled sweet and musky with warm
sensual perfume. The scene was peaceful, prosper-
ous and welcoming.

Conall recognized somewhere deep inside him
that this façade of comfort should enrage him, en-
dangered as it now was by Eve's deception. But he
was not at all concerned for the welfare of the townsfolk, God forgive him. Not any longer—he was
done.

All that mattered was Eve. Eve and the bairn.

With great effort did he put one foot in front of
the other, moving him mechanically down the

dark, soft street to his longhouse. A bar of yellow light shone from beneath the door, as if it was in itself a threshold, and only then did Conall know a moment's hesitation. Once he had told all, it could not be untold. His father's wishes would be destroyed, Conall's own pride turned to dust. All the years of struggle, of perseverance, for naught.

Conall took a deep breath and pushed open the door.

His mother, Lana, sat near Duncan around the peat fire, and they were joined by a plump, copper-haired town lass Conall knew as Betsy. Had Conall been in a clearer state of mind, he might have given more notice to Betsy's hand upon his brother's knee, or the smile upon Duncan's face, or the way the couple's shoulders brushed together intimately. But the cozy scene gave him no pleasure and when the door scraped wide, Duncan turned to face Conall, and the easy smile fell at once from his mouth.

"Ah, glory," Duncan muttered on a sigh. Lana craned her neck to seek the visitor and, unlike his brother's melancholy welcome, Conall's mother immediately rose to greet him, her smile surprised and somewhat hesitant.

"Conall!" she gasped and stepped forward to embrace him. She pulled away to look him up and down. "Why, you're soaked! Come nearer the fire lest you catch your death." She tugged him away from the door, looking out into the street pointedly before closing it. "Where is this wonderful surprise Duncan has told us of? I vow, I—"

Conall let his mother lead him to her vacated stool and push him down onto the seat, chattering all the while. But his eyes never left Duncan's and after only a moment or two, his brother called order.

Duncan rose from his stool, pulling the pretty, voluptuous townswoman to her feet. "Forgive me, Bets, but I'd speak to the MacKerrick. He's been long away, has he nae?"

"Fer certain, Dunc." The woman smiled warmly and her eyes flicked to Conall's with a blush. "Good eve to you, MacKerrick. Glad to see you home at last."

Conall ignored the woman's overtures, turning his numb gaze to the fire pit. He deserved no kindness, no welcome.

Lana spun, a mug in her hand. "Och, now you doona need to go, Betsy! Why, we should—"

"Mam," Duncan said pointedly. "Conall and I must talk town business. Is that nae right, brother?"

Conall could only nod.

"So soon?" Lana frowned. "But he's only just returned and—"

"Good night, Bets," Duncan said softly and opened the door, leading the woman from the house. "I'll watch you get in safe. Hurry now, lass, 'tis wet."

Conall heard the faint snick of lips touching cheek and then a moment later the door scraped to.

Lana struggled to revive her faltering smile before bustling to Conall and pushing the mug she'd filled into his hands.

"Now then," she said breathlessly, perching upon a stool. "Tell me what you've been about this long winter, Conall MacKerrick, for Duncan has been as pinch-mouthed as an old tortoise."

"Go to bed, Mam," Duncan suggested gently,

pulling Lana to her feet. "I'm certain Conall will speak to you in the morn."

"I willna," Lana said and pulled her elbow free with a frown. "Havena I the right to visit with me own son?"

Duncan paused and both mother and brother looked to Conall questioningly.

"You may stay, Mam," Conall said. "'Tis now or later and, in truth, I'd only say what I must once."

"Are you certain, Conall?" Duncan asked pointedly as Lana sat with a smug look. When Conall nodded, Duncan, too, took his seat with a great, weary sigh. "'Tis bad, is it nae?"

Conall nodded. "The worst."

Lana's worried eyes flew between the two men. "What is it? Enough secrets—tell me."

"I'd start from the beginning, for Mam's sake," Duncan advised.

"Aye." Conall swallowed, trying to order his thoughts through the panic and fear that still chewed at him. "I took to the wood—to the hut in the vale—to hunt and to grieve." His fingertips automatically found the leather knot at his neck. "That is nae secret, I think."

"Of course it isna," Lana said gently. "And descrvcd of it you were, Conall. After Nonna . . ." Her words trailed away.

"When I arrived at the cottage, 'twas nae deserted," Conall continued, narrating aloud the portrait-like memories that flashed through his mind, no longer seeing his mother or brother or his own cozy house, but the snowy past in the recesses of his mind. "A woman was squatting there." Conall felt a hitch in his stomach. "Evelyn Godewin Buchanan."

"*Buchanan?*" Lana squawked and shot to her feet. "*Buchanan!*" She spun on Duncan. "You knew this? *You knew?*"

"Mam, please," Duncan commanded. "Sit and be still."

Lana looked to Conall, her eyes worried and furious at once. "But what was a lone Buchanan woman—"

"She came with Minerva Buchanan," Conall said bluntly.

Lana's face went as pale as the moon-washed windflowers outside the hut door, and she all but fell back onto her stool. "Min . . . Minerva Buchanan has returned to Scotland?" she croaked, her eyes flicking to the door as if expecting the woman to burst into the house at any moment.

"She did return," Conall said. "To die. She left Eve at Ronan's pyre."

"Oh, merciful God," Lana wheezed and squeezed her eyes shut for a long moment. They were glassy when she opened them again. "Go on, Conall."

"When she told me her name—Eve, that is—I thought—" Conall shook his head. "I thought I could—"

"You thought you could break the curse," Lana finished.

Conall nodded. He was ashamed of what he had to tell her next. "I seduced Eve. Persuaded her to marry me."

Lana bolted to stand again. "You *married* her?"

Duncan grabbed Lana's wrist and pulled her to sit without admonition, but prompting Lana to swing round and cuff him sharply on the head, all the same.

"Dammit, Mam!"

"Shame on you for keeping this from me, Duncan MacKerrick!" She turned back to Conall expectantly.

"I *did* marry her, with every mean intention of destroying this evilness unleashed upon our clan by that . . . that old witch," Conall growled.

He wasn't expecting his own cuff to the temple, precisely where Eve's stool had found its mark.

"Mam! Dammit!"

"You'll nae speak that way of"—Lana hesitated, stuttered—"of the dead."

Conall rubbed his head and glared at his mother. Then his indignation fell away as despair consumed him once more. "I thought—when Duncan first came to the hut after the storm, I thought 'twas working. The news from town was good, hopeful."

"Better days than we've seen in many a year," Lana agreed, her tone gentling. "But where is this woman now, Conall? Why have you nae brought your wife home to us?"

"I left her. At the hut." Conall's throat constricted as he thought of his sweet Eve alone in the vast darkness, as well as the fact that she was likely much safer there on her own with Alinor than anywhere near Conall. He struggled to clear the emotion from his throat. "And I hope she is nae longer my wife—I renounced her."

Lana gasped and the next instant Duncan had rammed into Conall, tackling him from the stool. Duncan raised up and drew back his fist. "You son of a bitch!"

"Stop! Stop!" Lana screamed, wrapping an arm about Duncan's neck and dragging him, flailing, from atop Conall, much as she had done when they were lads. "Stop it!" She turned Duncan away

and shoved him from her. She stood over Conall
and stared down, the rippling fire in her brown
eyes warning of her ire. "Conall MacKerrick, you
explain to me why you would do such a dreadful
thing."

Conall pulled himself up slowly, his cooling muscles singing agony now. He righted his stool and sat
upon it with a grunt, ran his hands through his
hair, and glanced up at his furious brother, having
already forgiven him.

"I love her, Mam. I do."

"Yer a fuckin' madder, you are," Duncan spat.
"There's nae good reason for you to have left Eve,
in her con—"

"She lied to me, Dunc," Conall interjected.

Duncan stopped abruptly and stood for a long,
quiet moment, digesting the blunt statement. Then
the blood seemed to drain from his face and a wiry
arm shot out to steady himself against a wall.

"Ah, glory. Nae. It canna be."

Lanna appeared immensely confused and frustrated. "You'd better explain fully to me, Conall,
for I doona ken why you would renounce your
wife, leave her to fend for herself if you love her as
you claim. Why not bring her back? Have you nae
looked about the town? Whatever has happened,
the curse is lifted."

Duncan had forsaken his mug for the whole jug
of spirits and turned its bottom toward the ceiling.

"It's nae lifted, Mam," Conall said.

"It *is*," Lana insisted. "Look—"

"She's nae Buchanan, Mam. She's English." But
Lana did not seem moved by this piece of informa-
tion.

Duncan at last lowered the jug. "And she's pregnant with Conall's child," he added bitterly.

That at last caused Lana to sit, stunned. "My . . . my grandchild?"

"I left her—renounced them both—hoping that . . ." Conall was unable to continue. Duncan crouched at his side and placed a bony palm on his shoulder, until Conall found the strength to finish. "I doona want them tainted by the curse, Mam. She is carrying"—he took a ragged breath—"*my bairn.* If anything would happen to them because of me . . . if I would have only told her . . ."

Duncan squeezed his shoulder.

In a moment, Conall continued. "I will set out for the Buchanan town at first light, to beg mercy from Angus Buchanan." He turned his head to look at Duncan. "You'll go with me, Dunc?"

"Damned right, I will."

Lana started. "Nae. Nae! Conall, your da would turn in his grave if you betrayed the clan as—"

"I care not about the clan!" Conall shouted. "This is Da's very doing! If he would have let go of a bit of his bloody pride long ago, if he would have nae been so hardhearted to his own flesh—*his brother*—none of this would have happened. None of it!"

"Conall, you doona ken." Lana's eyes flicked between the brothers, as if trying to convince them both. "Your da should have done different with Ronan, aye, and he could have begged peace with the Buchanan long ago. But there were other reasons, you must believe. For your own sake."

"For my own sake?" Conall asked in disbelief. "I doona care about anything or anyone save Eve and my child. This town has been poisoned by my father and his hateful, foolish grudge, and I mean to end it!" Conall was angry now, and glad of it—a relief from the smothering fear. "If Angus Buchanan should grant me pardon, I will run to Eve's side, for I'll know the curse willna touch her. If he doesna, if he refuses me"—he paused—"I will shake every home in this town on its side until I have its last farthing. And I will find someone to take Eve far, far from here and the MacKerrick taint. Someone that will care for her and our child."

Lana was on the verge of tears. "Ronan wasna the only one to lose his life that day, Conall. The Buchanan's own wife—!" She wrung her hands. "What if he kills you on sight, eh? How will you aid your Eve then?"

"Then I will do it." Duncan's voice was low and sure and Conall turned to him. "You're right, brother. 'Tis past time for this madness to cease. We shall do it together, you and me."

Conall grasped his brother's arm. "Thank you, Duncan."

Lana gave a long, long sigh and sat, a tear working loose from her eye. "Very well," she whispered. "Very well, my dear, dear lads. I knew 'twould one day come to this, I suppose." She was quiet for a moment, then raised her eyes to look at the two men before her. "I'm going with you."

Conall frowned. "Mam, nae."

"Oh, aye, I will," she said in a tone that warned against further argument. "I have a bigger responsibility in this muck that you both are too young to ken, and I'd nae let Angus Buchanan vent his wrath on you in my stead. I go," she said with finality.

Conall felt he had no choice but to relent. "Very well, Mam."

"But you should know, Conall," Lana began carefully, "after you return from the Buchanan town, the clan might nae fancy the choices you've made."

"I have thought of that," Conall answered. "And I am prepared."

Lana's eyes narrowed. "You are willing to give up your own town?"

Conall let a ghost of a smile touch his mouth. "I doona need to be the MacKerrick to love Eve."

Chapter Nineteen

The weather was kind to Evelyn and her company on their journey, and the showers of late held as if to give her dry passage through the long, narrow valley west. But fear dogged her every step, the long stretches of silence broken only by the squish and crackle of her careful footsteps and her own troubled thoughts to brood on.

She feared becoming lost in the wilderness. She feared the grays' appearance. She feared falling and injuring herself or the babe. She feared the Buchanan would turn her away. She feared Conall MacKerrick might come after her.

And she feared she might never see him again.

To add to her troubles, Evelyn was growing more concerned about Alinor. The wolf was unusually sluggish and disinterested in their travels, seeming to want to lag behind, leisurely inspecting hollow logs and abandoned badger dens and occasionally, but more frequently by the second morning, she stopped altogether to lie down in a soft patch of new, wet growth. Her previously hollowed belly was swollen and taut. She seemed fatigued and her keen yellow eyes were dull-looking and faraway.

Tired. Tired. Rest.

Evelyn could oft coax the wolf onward, but on a few instances Alinor would not be moved, forcing Evelyn to stop as well until the wolf deigned to rouse herself and continue. And each time, Evelyn's worry over the animal grew.

They traveled lightly. Evelyn carried MacKerrick's pack over Minerva's old cloak, and in it were only the most meager rations for the party's survival. Bonnie grazed at will, gamely carrying Robert's hutch secured over her side. Sebastian flitted in the bony canopy overhead, cawing encouragement, and Whiskers was content to tumble and ride tucked away in a pocket of Evelyn's kirtle.

There had been no sign—indeed, neither had there been sound—of the evil gray wolves, although Evelyn did not allow herself to be lulled into thinking they had abandoned the wood. The previous evening, Evelyn and her companions had huddled beneath the massive circumference of an ancient evergreen on deep, soft needles, but she had barely slept, each crack of twig or rustle of leaf causing her heart to pound, certain they would be attacked at any moment.

Now, the afternoon of the second day of travel quickly moved toward dusk and a lively stream slithered along the valley floor, its waters sweet and clear and musical. Ahead, the valley narrowed to a point between two falls of boulders and rose steeply, the stream disappearing beneath the rocky jumble. Evelyn looked up.

They would have to climb.

Evelyn did so slowly, calling encouragingly to

Alinor or sometimes retreating to the rear of the wolf to urge her onward with a hand upon her hip. Bonnie cleared the pass with spry leaps and clatters of hoof and awaited them at the summit, bleating happily. When at last Evelyn gained the peak, sweaty and panting at a stitch in her side, tears filled her eyes at the view spread out before her.

Loch Lomond lay long and wide and green under the mist, fringed by sporadic patches of evergreens, the surrounding hills cradling the body of the huge lake like a child. And on the far side of the waters, a wide break in the forest was dotted with what appeared to be, from Evelyn's vantage point, an army of smoking toadstools.

The Buchanan village.

"Town," she whispered aloud sadly.

She did not think she could make the settlement by nightfall. This side of the crag was not nearly as steep as the way they'd just come, but once she descended, she would have to skirt the near shore of the lake and make her way around the perimeter. A fair long distance, she estimated. Hours of walking at her lumbering pace and with coaxing Alinor. Her back and legs ached at the prospect and she sighed.

But there it was, at last. The one place she had sworn never to go, now her only haven. Evelyn felt so alone, so full of despair and heartbreak, she wanted only to sit down upon the ledge and cry. Then a wide ray of rare sunlight suddenly pierced the thick blanket of gray clouds and washed the rocky prominence where she stood in dazzling warmth. Evelyn closed her eyes and lifted her face, greedily relishing the luxurious glow through her eyelids.

When she opened her eyes, the sun had once

again hidden itself away, leaving only the cool gray mist and tears on her face, but she could now imagine what it was like to be warm again and it gave her hope. She sniffed and brushed at her cheeks with her fingertips.

From behind her, Evelyn heard Alinor's low growl and so she turned. "What is it, lovely?"

The wolf lay on her side, but her wide, black head was raised, muzzle rippling ominously. Upon the unyielding base of rock, Alinor's underbelly bulged.

But there was no time to run worried palms over the animal in search of wounds or fever, for Alinor struggled awkwardly to her feet with a clatter of rocky debris, her growl intensifying.

Stranger . . .

And then Evelyn heard what Alinor had: below the jagged shelf of rock where they rested, someone was whistling a cheery tune through their teeth.

Bonnie bleated and began to run in circles around Evelyn's legs, throwing Robert against the bent twigs of his hutch. Alinor's tone deepened.

The whistling stopped.

"Hallow?" called a surprised male voice in Gaelic. "Who's there?"

It was a man from the Buchanan town, it had to be. The moment of Evelyn's future was at hand, and her heart pounded.

Alinor looked up and whined, and Evelyn could clearly see the true condition of the animal: stiff, lackluster coat; dry, cracked nose; sad eyes. Evelyn thought morbidly of Alinor's distended abdomen, hanging between her legs.

Tired.

The wolf walked slowly to where Evelyn stood

and pushed her wide head between Evelyn's hip and wrist and leaned there heavily, telling Evelyn without the benefit of words that Alinor could not go on with her to the Buchanan town.

Evelyn fell awkwardly to her knees and threw her arms about the wolf's neck. "Oh, Alinor," she gasped into the prickly fur. "I know you are weary. Can you not press on just a bit farther? Please?"

But the wolf backed out of the embrace and shook awkwardly, looking down the rocky slope as the disembodied voice called again.

"I'm warnin' you! I am armed! Show yourself!"

Alinor looked back to Evelyn and gave her face a swipe with her long, dry, pink tongue, then turned to scrabble back up to the pinnacle. She turned her wide, black head to gaze down at Evelyn and Bonnie, crouched there together in the rubble.

Go.

Evelyn rose unsteadily to her feet and held out a hand to the wolf. "Alinor," she keened.

The great black beast disappeared over the far side of the peak.

"Holy mother of—" came the voice from directly behind her, and Evelyn spun on a sob.

Standing on a ledge just below was a stocky, handsome man, with long, wavy red locks tamed by a wide leather headband. His broad chest was draped in soft-looking suede and a red and gold plaid. An impossibly long sword gleamed at the ready in his hand.

His crisp blue eyes widened as he took in Evelyn and then a smile split his face, its brightness confusing her. "Well, I'll be." The Scot laughed. "Hallow, missus. We thought you'd never come." His eyes fell to Evelyn's rounded belly. "Brought along a companion, as well, I see."

Evelyn frowned and swiped at her face. "St-stay away, sir . . . I d-don't kn-know you!"

The man laughed again. "O' course nae! But we've been expecting you, all the same." He sheathed his sword and with one giant stride joined Evelyn and Bonnie on the ledge, prompting Evelyn to stumble back at his approach.

Once there, the Scot paused, glancing at the summit path over which Alinor had gone. "Do you wish for me to fetch back yer dog, missus?"

Evelyn was still for a moment, as pain sliced through her heart and she recalled the words Mac-Kerrick had spoken to her: *Alinor is a wild creature, Eve . . . we must let her go with love.*

"Nay," she was finally able to croak. "Not my dog. Just . . . just a wild creature of the wood."

"Ah," the man said, and then stepped forward unexpectedly and reached for MacKerrick's pack. Evelyn thought to resist too late and in a blink the Scot had slung the satchel over his own shoulder. "Lucky for you 'twas my turn at watch, then. There's been a pack o' rogue gray wolves roamin' the land this past winter. Queer beasts." He sniffed over his shoulder and frowned. "Pardon, missus, but this pack smells of piss."

Not able to help it, Evelyn gave a watery-sounding laugh. God, her heart was so broken, the pieces so small and splintered that she doubted it would ever be whole again.

"Well, then," the Scot said, reaching down to scratch Bonnie's head. "Shall we?" He swept an arm down the slope toward the loch.

"Who are you?" Evelyn demanded in exasperation.

"Och, forgive me, missus!" The man dipped into a low bow. "Andrew Buchanan—cousin of Angus, chief of the Buchanan clan—here to do yer bidding."

"I—" Evelyn's head was spinning so that she felt dizzy. "I don't understand."

"O' course nae!" Andrew Buchanan laughed again. "Let's be off, though, missus—the Buchanan is anxious to make your acquaintance." He paused. "You *were* coming to the town, were you nae? Upon Minerva Buchanan's request?"

"Ah . . . yea," Evelyn stammered. "I suppose I was, but—"

"Well, then I'm sure you're weary from your long journey." He took in her belly once more. "In fact"—he rushed forward and in an instant had scooped Evelyn into his thickly muscled arms as if she were no larger than Robert—"allow me to ease your burden a mite. 'Tis but a short distance to town."

Against all good sense, Evelyn laughed again. This man was . . . irresistible, with his eagerness, his sparkling eyes and quick mirth.

Sebastian chose just that moment to swoop low overhead with a concerned caw, causing Andrew Buchanan to duck and Evelyn to clutch at him with a shriek.

"Blasted sacavenger!" the Scot lamented.

Evelyn frowned. "He is a friend of mine, sir."

"Oh," Andrew said, nonplussed. "Oh. Well, then, my apologies, missus. Hold on, now."

And then Andrew Buchanan fairly leaped from the ledge and bounded down the mountain path, Evelyn and her babe in his arms. Bonnie bleated in panic before hurtling herself and Robert after them. They tripped toward the loch in time with the merry sound of Andrew Buchanan's carefree whistling.

It had done naught but rain since Conall, Duncan, and Lana had left the MacKerrick town, as if the cluster of black thunderheads followed the small party alone. But the weather suited Conall's mood—comforted his fear like a sick, swaddling wool and held it tight to his bosom.

Ronan's hut was deserted. The door ajar, the firepit cold as stone, the long room dark and hollow and damp. Not a trace of Eve remained save the rubble from her and Conall's parting row. At the discovery of her absence, Conall had nearly lost touch with reality.

'Twas Duncan who had saved Conall's sanity, remarking that the only obvious place for Eve to have gone was the Buchanan town. Conall knew a brief moment of relief when he realized he had indirectly told Eve of the Buchanan town's location. He knew she traveled out of desperation. Bonnie and Alinor, even Robert's hutch, were gone as well, and with her added charges, Conall thought he had a chance of keeping watch over Eve on the trail if they hurried. The thought of her alone in the wood after nightfall . . .

So they pushed on through the rain until 'twas too dark to safely continue for Conall's mother's sake. They made a primitive camp at the mouth of the westward valley, stretched a tarp between two trees for shelter. Duncan flitted about their flickering patch of forest in his usual brusque and efficient manner, gathering downed limbs and dry boughs. Lana set a crock of oats near the fire and laid out meat and bannock.

Conall sat and stared at the fire.

Eve, oh my Eve, that you are safe . . .

"Eat." Duncan shoved a piece of bannock-wrapped venison into Conall's hand, then sat down next to him. He took a large bite of meat and then spoke around his food. "Do we push on, we should make the Buchanan town by the morrow's dusk." He swallowed. "If Mam can hold out."

Lana threw Duncan a stinging glance. "I'm a mite sturdier than you believe me to be, Duncan MacKerrick."

Conall felt the food cooling in his hand, but had no appetite for it. He laid it on the ground in the shadows.

In a moment, Lana joined the two men, lowering herself to nest on the thick blanket of pine needles on Conall's other side. She picked up his discarded meal and began to eat it. The night was thick and clammy with mist and fog, the silence clung to the smoke from the fire, broken only by the sound of chewing and the cracking drips of water on the tarp stretched overhead.

"There's aught the pair of you should know before baring your souls to Angus Buchanan," Lana said after a long while. "Things of your da, of your uncle. Of Minerva Buchanan, and meself, as well."

Duncan stretched out his boots, his spindly arms cocked at the elbows, his hands behind his head. "Do tell, Mam. I've a fancy for a bedtime yarn."

"You know that Ronan had wish to marry the sister of the Buchanan, aye? That 'twas the reason for the battle that took Ronan's life? I've nae told

you—and neither would have Dáire, I'm certain—
but surely you've heard old gossip."

Conall nodded, although in truth, he was not in-
terested in his mother's tale of past tragedy. His
only concern was of Eve. Eve safe, Eve loved, Eve
where the taint of his own blood could not harm
her or the innocent babe in her womb. The past be
damned, the clan be damned.

Only Eve.

"Aye, we've heard," Duncan offered. "What of
it?"

Lana gave a heavy sigh before continuing. "The
troubles between the MacKerricks and the Buchanans
began long before that, although Minerva Buchanan
was still at its heart." She bent up her knees with a
quiet hiss, wrapped her arms about them. "She was a
beauty then. Strong woman. Powerful healer, even in
her youth. 'Twas said she could bewitch a man with
only a look, and I suppose 'twas true." Her voice
dropped to a whisper. "Dáire was mad for her."

This startled Conall from his stupor, even before
Duncan bolted upright with an outraged cry of
"Mam!"

"Oh, doona go on like that," Lana scoffed. "He
married me, did he nae? 'Twas said I was his second
choice, but I knew better." She looked at Conall.
"Your da loved me"—her gaze flicked to Duncan—
"loved both you lads. Never doubt that. We owned
his heart, true, and in time, he came to know that
Minerva Buchanan was a folly he could have never
made a life with. A family. She was fiery and impetuous and . . . a bit of a witch, aye. Much better suited
to Ronan's hotheadedness."

"Why tell us this, Mam?" Conall asked quietly,

even in his own pain marveling at the strength of his mother.

"Because 'twas nae your da's heart that got us all into this twist, 'twas his pride. His damned, stubborn pride." Lana nodded, almost to herself. "When Dáire was a young chief, he went to Angus Buchanan and asked for Minerva's hand. He had wish to unite our towns and claim the one who'd struck his fancy.

"Angus was nae disagreeable to the offer," Lana continued. "The MacKerrick hunting grounds were old, rich with food. Our men brave and true. Minerva ran wild and free and Angus hoped to settle her untamed ways by joining her with a man such as Dáire—careful, thoughtful, nae an impetuous bone in his body." The last she said with a smile in her voice, as if remembering the man with fondness.

"They didna marry, though," Conall said.

"Nae. They didna." Lana sighed. "Angus gave his sister the ultimate choice of taking Dáire as her husband. Although the woman oft acted with abandon, Angus always indulged her. Wanted her happiness.

"Me poor Dáire—Minerva laughed at him. Before the clan heads of both towns. Called him a 'young, old man,' with a small town too far from her home. Called him stingy and without humor. She had seen her soul mate, she'd said, in her dreams, and she would have no other."

Duncan hissed. "Poor Da, indeed."

Conall could all too well imagine the humiliation proud Dáire MacKerrick had endured. Even if Minerva Buchanan had not wanted him, there had been no need for such shaming and scorn. His father had never been one to easily yield or admit when he was wrong, choosing rather to stay his own course, regardless of calamity. *His* choices. *His* way. *His* laws.

A little shiver of recognition twisted around Conall's heart and he remembered the eve of his own wedding, when Nonna had run away. How Dáire had searched with relentless purpose and brought her back. And Conall had married her, against her will. Had his father been reliving a past slight?

But look how it had culminated—Nonna more bitter each day with Conall until the end, taking the one bright spot in his life with her when she went. Had Dáire died wondering if it would have been the same with him and Minerva Buchanan?

And, too, Conall thought of his own summary of his father's character—unyeilding, imperious. Was that not Conall's own behavior with Eve? If he had told her the truth, heard her own truth upon their first meeting, he knew he would have no reason to chase after her now.

But they would not have married. Would not have created the little miracle she carried with her through the dark wood to his enemies. His damned pride . . .

He needed the rest of the tale before making judgment. "Go on, Mam. Please."

Lana clucked her tongue. "Well, then. Ronan and Dáire, two brothers you've never seen the like. Day and night. Water and fire." She smiled at Conall and Duncan. "Or mayhap you have. But they were loyal to each other with a passion. When Ronan heard of the Buchanan woman's humiliation of his brother, reckless as he was, he set out at once for the Buchanan town to demand recompense for such a slight."

Conall noted he was holding his breath and he let it out slowly. "And Ronan saw her."

"He did." Lana nodded. "Minerva Buchanan herself told me that seeing Ronan for the first time was like a bolt of lightning striking a dead, dry forest, igniting a blaze that could never be banked."

Their own fire was dying out and, not wanting the tale to be interrupted, Conall scrambled to toss a thick, jagged chunk of dead wood on the embers, sending a red fountain of sparks dancing high into the night.

Lana smiled her thanks before continuing. "Ronan waited several months—Dáire and I were already wed—before telling his brother of his wish to marry Minerva. Dáire felt betrayed, as if his brother's request made a mockery of his humiliation, even though in truth, the flame he had once carried for Minerva Buchanan had long since burnt itself out."

Duncan snorted. "Humiliation might have aided his disenchantment."

"Perhaps," Lana conceded. "And if so, then glad I will be to my last breath that the woman scorned him. But Dáire's pride wouldna yield even to his beloved brother, and he banished Ronan to the old hut in the vale. Ronan wasna without his own temper, and so thought to join the Buchanans, hence the fateful ambush you already know a bit of."

Conall felt an added measure of sadness slide onto his already burdened shoulders. He had so many questions to ask . . .

But before he could voice the first one, a crackling of the underbrush beyond the fire caused the three gathered under the tarp to freeze. Conall slowly laid hand to his sword and saw from the corner of his eye Duncan doing the same.

The crackling sounded closer in the dark, then paused, a sick, whistling snarl taking its place.

Duncan's eyes flicked to Conall's. "Could it be your Alinor?" he whispered, and Conall could tell by the tremor in his voice that Duncan wanted it to be the great, black wolf.

But Conall knew it was not. He shook his head in answer, only the slightest twitch of movement.

The growl sounded again and, like fog made solid, the pointed, grizzled muzzle of the old gray oozed into the wide ring of firelight from the shadows beyond. The body slinked after the head, bony and crouched and trembling. A sharp, cold breeze smelling of silver snow blasted through the flimsy shelter.

"Oh dear Jesus," Duncan breathed. "It's him. The wolf in me dreams."

The gray paused, turned, paced the far perimeter, its teeth bared, tongue flicking madly over its grin. Patches of fur were now missing, its sides heaving beneath skeletal ribs.

Conall felt fear in his core.

"Ah," Lana sighed sadly. "I wondered . . ."

Before Conall could stop her, Lana rose to her feet and approached the fire to stand boldly before the menacing monster, now whining and snarling in crazed yips. Drool cascaded from pointed, yellowed teeth.

"Mam," Conall said evenly. "Doona so much as move."

"Doona the pair of *you* so much as move," Lana commanded, "if you doona wish to see your mother dead by this pitiful beast."

Duncan started to draw his legs beneath him. "Mam, please—"

"Nae!" Lana snapped over her shoulder, never taking her eyes from the gray.

Duncan stilled and Conall watched with his brother.

The wolf shortened his pace, doing little more now than swaying side to side on its spindly, cankered forelegs. Its eyes were milky with age.

"Come for your due, have you?" Lana asked softly. "You'll nae have it yet though, I vow. You remember me? Aye, you do. How could you forget?"

The gray crouched lower, its sparse, matted hackles raising in a prickly fan. Its snarl was little more than a primitive squeal.

"Mam," Conall said, begging through his rapidly closing throat.

"Please, Mam," Duncan added.

"Hush, now!" Lana gasped and Conall could see the rapid rise and fall of her bosom. She was frightened, but trying not to show it. "You'll have to wait," she said in a warning tone to the wolf. "Soon. But nae now. Nae here."

The wolf edged closer, staggering, and Conall knew it would spring at any moment.

Lana drew a deep breath, pointed her finger at the beast. "*Stay your ground.* Tell your mistress that I have kept my promise. Her son is safe."

Chapter Twenty

Young, bullish Andrew Buchanan had plucked Evelyn from the mountain like some Scots archangel and carried her the whole of the way into town. He never winded, whistling in time with each jarring step. Through streets lined with large, fine long-houses, and stores and stables and places of business, their thatched roofs home to a rainbow of wild summer blooms, Evelyn rode in Andrew's arms. Bonnie skipped along behind them with an affronted Robert; Sebastian swooped protectively overhead. Even wee Whiskers had poked his slim nose from the pocket of Evelyn's kirtle to take in the wondrous sight of the fair town.

And the sight of the entourage was being taken in by others, as well. Curious townsfolk ceased in their chores and emerged from dwellings as if summoned to follow the parade. Children ran alongside Andrew, calling to him and Evelyn in excited Gaelic, plucking at the hem of her gown, gesturing to each other and the animals.

As they neared the interior edge of the town, but a stone's throw from the loch itself, Evelyn could see the

the beginnings of a stone fortress being constructed, oddly enough, on a smallish, cleared island some distance from shore. An uneven base rose up mayhap three times the height of a man and was crisscrossed with a hive of scaffolding. Workers swarmed the project in the reddened afternoon light and the loch was alive with wide, shallow boats and rafts, ferrying supplies from shore.

"Our new keep," Andrew said with a broad, proud grin and inclined his head toward the loch. His blue eyes sparkled. "Do you fancy it, missus? Angus would have naught else since visiting his granddaughter in England."

"'Tis grand," Evelyn assured him faintly, glancing nervously at the smiling faces now crowding around them. She felt as though she was caught up in some strange dream, being carried through the vibrant town like royalty.

Andrew laughed—the man seemed to bracket everything he said with mirth. "O' course you have seen grander, but 'twill serve its purpose. A champion of Scotland will find shelter there one day, missus, 'tis foretold."

Evelyn could only smile weakly. She thought she might be ill if Andrew did not cease swinging her about so.

The Scot shouted to the crowd in Gaelic and a path opened for them. A score more jostling steps and Andrew was setting Evelyn on her feet before the open door of the largest longhouse, steadying her when she swayed on tingling legs.

"All right, then?" he asked her.

Evelyn nodded.

"Off you go." He swept a long arm toward the darkened interior of the cottage.

"You want me to go inside?" she asked in a creaky voice. "Alone?"

Andrew's eyes went wide. "Well, I hope you doona think me to accompany you, missus—the Buchanan, och, he's vicious!"

Evelyn thought she might faint. But Andrew took quick note of her distress and rushed with a laugh.

"I jest, missus! Ah, Jesus, forgive me for the fool I am." He laid a comforting arm across Evelyn's shoulders and turned her toward the doorway. "Go on," he said, gently this time. "He is anxious to meet you. Have nae fear."

Evelyn took a hesitant step toward the portal and then stopped and spun back to Andrew. "Bonnie! I need—where is my sheep, sir?"

Andrew turned this way and that, calling in his native tongue. A pair of young children—a boy and a girl—stepped forward, one holding Bonnie's tether and the other clutching a recently liberated Robert. They held forth their charges with spindly, outstretched arms and dazzling smiles.

"Me ladee," the girl piped.

Evelyn huffed a bemused laugh and took hold of Bonnie's tether and scooped Robert over her forearm.

"Thank you," she said.

"*Thank you*," the children mimicked in unison and then giggled.

With a squawk, Sebastian landed on the roof of the Buchanan's house, drawing delighted shrieks and gasps from the gathered townsfolk. Evelyn let her eyes flick over them once more before turning and ducking inside the doorway.

It took a moment for Evelyn's eyes to adjust to the interior gloom, so she paused a few steps into the home, blinking in time with her pounding heart. The sound of the door scraping shut with a final sounding thud caused Evelyn to start and look around with a gasp.

"You fear me, lass?" came the gravelly, melodious question from deeper in the room and Evelyn turned once more to seek the speaker.

He was seated in an armed, tall-backed wooden chair just beyond the wide fire pit full of glowing peat, and it struck Evelyn that Angus Buchanan was very, very old. 'Twas quite comfortable inside the longhouse, but the clan chief appeared to be dressed for a blizzard: long-sleeved, shin-length wool tunic with an undershirt peeking out at the neck, sheep's wool vest laced tightly to either end, a long plaid thrown over his knees and across one shoulder. Thick leather boots encased his legs. His hair was long, snowy white, and looked soft as dandelion fluff where it lay across his breast. His pate was bare, shiny, veined and spotted with age over sparse white eyebrows that overhung sunken blue eyes. He wore a long, full beard, more wiry looking than the rest of his hair, but the same glowing alabaster.

Evelyn had the strange notion that she looked upon an old Celtic nature god, or the mountains standing sentry over Loch Lomond in human form, or time itself. Ancient and strong and wise and . . . forever.

He was smiling at her, and Evelyn realized she had not answered the old chief's question.

"I do not fear you," she replied and was proud that her voice held no tremble. "But I do fear that you will deny me respite."

Angus's shoulders hitched as if he chuckled to himself. "What is your name, child?"

She swallowed. "Evelyn."

The chief's eyebrows rose only slightly, as if it was too much effort to move the blanket of wrinkles on his forehead higher. "Evelyn . . . ?" His question dangled.

She knew what he was asking of her, but had no immediate reply. Did she give him her maiden name, Godewin? Did the name MacKerrick still apply to her, or had it been revoked with Conall's promises? In truth, she wanted to give the old man all three names: Godewin Buchanan MacKerrick, for it was the moniker she'd lived under since coming to Scotland.

But she could truthfully give him none of them. Her chin tilted. "I know not, sir. Forgive me."

"Hmm." Angus nodded thoughtfully. "You are she, then. The prophesy fulfilled."

"I—I beg your pardon?"

"'A woman of no home will come, two of herself, in raiments of old,'" Angus said. "'Her heart revealed by the beasts she commands, and she brings with her a great and humbling peace.'"

The chief looked at her from head to toe. "Your cloak—I would know that rag amongst a hundred others. 'Tis me own sister's, is it nae? Minerva Buchanan. She is dead now, likely."

Evelyn nodded. "I'm sorry."

Angus's rheumy eyes glistened with sadness, yet he pushed on. "'Two of herself'—either you are with child, or a terrible glutton."

Evelyn found herself smiling.

"And these." He rose from his chair slowly, as if it pained him, and walked stiffly but regally to stand before her. He lifted Bonnie's face with a gentle hand under her bearded chin. "They've nae spell upon them? They follow you of their own free will?"

"Yea." Then Evelyn winced. "All but Robert, I should say." She lifted her arm to indicate the hare draped over it. "He rode in his hutch. I'm afraid I didn't think to turn him loose."

"Robert." Angus smiled, looked at the sheep. "And this is . . . ?"

"Bonnie," Evelyn answered. She reached into her pocket and withdrew the wriggling mouse. "Whiskers. And Sebastian is perched on yonder door frame."

"How do you do?" Angus said with mock formality. Then his wise old eyes met Evelyn's. "But where is the black one?"

Instantly the mental image of Alinor sprang into Evelyn's mind and her chest tightened. "We had come a long way together and . . . she was"—Evelyn had to pause—"ill. She could not continue. Mayhap she will yet come . . ."

The Buchanan smiled sadly, as if he knew but was too kind to say.

"My sister foretold of your coming, Eve." He paused. "*Eve*. Like the first woman. I knew your arrival would herald Minerva's death, but I anticipated it all the same. We are in dire need of the great and humbling peace you bring."

Evelyn wanted to believe the old man's words about this wondrous prophesy that made her arrival at the Buchanan town cause for celebration, but she was sick of lies and half-truths. Mayhap her coming had been foretold. Evelyn did not know what was

fantasy or reality anymore, but she would propagate
no illusions about her own purpose in coming.

"I bring you no peace," she said respectfully.
"Indeed, you may refuse me once I explain the
reason I have journeyed to your town. But I swear
to you, 'tis true that I . . . that I am of no home."

Angus Buchanan cupped her face in cool, wrinkled palms. "My child, I could nae refuse you,
never. Welcome." He kissed both her cheeks, then
brought her to his own chair. "Now, rest. And tell
me, where is your man? The father of your bairn?
Nae dead, I hope."

"Nay." Evelyn squirmed in the seat of honor in
which she'd been placed. "He returned to his
home. He doesn't want either of us."

"Och, now, what kind of man is that, I ask you?"
the old one said in furious outrage, dragging another chair to Evelyn's side. "A fool of a man!"

"A MacKerrick man," Evelyn said, bracing herself. "Conall MacKerrick."

Angus gave a wheezy gasp as he stared at her and
slowly his hand went to his chest, clutching and
splaying. "MacKerrick?" he gurgled. His eyes
bulged, and then he fell into the chair, unconscious.

The gray haunted them on the path through the
long valley, mirroring their journey like a ghost in
the underbrush. They saw no sight of him, but his
presence was constantly felt like a persistent icy drip
of water down the back of their necks, or an ache in
their teeth, dull and throbbing and maddening.

Conall in particular was consumed by thoughts
of the beast. Indeed, his brain swarmed with dangerous ideas. Eve under the shadowed evil of the

curse, and the demon who had unleashed it now traveling with the party to her side. As fast as Conall hiked, so with the same speed went the gray. A race with no winner, save death and destruction. Fear. Pain. Regret. Conall could taste each emotion on the air of the valley.

I have kept my promise. Your son is safe.

Lana's proclamation had stayed the beast from attack, true, but the words now strangled the three travelers like a noose. Lana MacKerrick would not explain her words to either Duncan or Conall, although Duncan still hounded the woman, stomping and cursing and demanding answer. Conall was silent.

He had already solved the riddle on his own. He was no imbecile, after all.

Conall and his brother looked nothing alike. Since Conall's earliest memories, Duncan had been doted on, protected by, Lana. Indeed, when Conall had left the MacKerrick town after the successful hunt, hadn't Lana seemed all too eager to see him go? Conall now knew why: so that Lana's son—her true son, Duncan—could rule in his proper place.

Conall was certain his father—or Dáire, he should think of him now—never knew the truth either, else Conall would never have been groomed to become the MacKerrick. Dáire had chosen the stronger son, the bigger, the swifter, as his successor. But he had chosen against his loins.

Of course the gray would haunt Conall. Minion of the woman he cursed, Minerva Buchanan, his real mother.

It explained the improved state of the Mac-Kerrick town. Although Eve was, in truth, not

Buchanan, Conall was. And as soon as his seed had taken root in her womb . . .

Until a Buchanan bairn is born to rule . . .

Conall still did not understand why Nonna and their girl babe had been lost, though. So many unanswered questions. He supposed he should be grateful Eve was not a Buchanan, for if she had been, their coupling would have been incestuous.

He huffed a dark laugh, drawing an anxious, guilty look from Lana. Conall did not meet her eyes. Could not. The lies, for so many years. The unnecessary guilt. Lana had promised to explain all once they reached their destination, and so Conall would wait.

He did not know where he belonged now. Not the MacKerrick town, but surely not with the Buchanans either. His very identity had been stripped.

He was now just a man. A man desperate to reach the two people who were undoubtedly his— Eve and their child.

A narrow pass now loomed high above them and, as if by unspoken agreement, the three stopped and stared at the steep, rocky path ahead. As if they knew that beyond it lay their unchangeable destinies; the past forever done, the future uncertain.

Conall met Duncan's eyes over Lana's head, and he saw anger and confusion there. Once through this pass, Conall knew they would no longer be brothers.

Would they then become enemies?

Duncan's eyes narrowed unexpectedly and his face hardened as if Conall's thoughts had been whispered on the wind. The smaller man nodded sharply once.

"Let's have it over with, then," Duncan said. "I'd know. Conall?"

Conall returned the gesture.

Lana led the way through the mountains without comment.

Echoing high above the valley, comprising the very sky it seemed, the gray's voice called mournfully, impatiently, jealously.

Evelyn thought for a moment that she had killed Angus Buchanan. The old man slumped in the chair, seemingly lifeless as Evelyn sprang awkwardly from hers and Bonnie ran in panicked circles, bleating her distress.

"Sir!" she whispered, clutching at the old man and leaning over him. "Er . . . Angus?" She didn't know how to address him. "Sir, answer me, please!"

He groaned and Evelyn's heart began beating once more.

"Oh, thank God," she whispered before speaking louder to the clan chief. "I'll get help—Andrew is just outside."

"Nae," Angus whispered and reached up to stay Evelyn with bony fingers around her forearm. "Raise nae alarm, lass. I beg you. Only help me . . . aright . . . if you would."

Evelyn was unconvinced that she should not call for the Buchanan's kin, but she gently pulled the old man up properly all the same. For all his bulky appearance, he could weigh no more than Bonnie, Evelyn guessed with a sad pang.

Once sitting, Angus Buchanan looked pale and

sweaty and still rested a hand over his chest. His breaths came fast and shallow, his lips the same color as his snowy beard.

"They'd have me abed again quicker than a frog's blink," he whispered, faded eyes flicking to the door. "They think keeping me an invalid would be a cure but, ah—we all know better than that." He ended his words on a wheeze and his eyes came back to Eve, still crouched over her belly before him.

"Sit down, lass." He waved to the chair. "It pains me to crane me neck so."

Evelyn sat reluctantly, her eyes finding the swiftest route to the door just in case. She noticed the sheep's continued fretting and called to the animal.

"Bonnie. Bonnie, to me."

The sheep clattered over and rested her bony chin on Evelyn's knee, startling Whiskers from her pocket. The mouse tumbled to the floor and raced to a seam between wall and flagstone. Robert was now happily nibbling on a woven mat near the fire pit, although Evelyn could not recall turning him loose.

"'Tis sorry I am for giving you a fright, Eve," Angus said, his voice a bit stronger but still breathy. "My heart . . . 'tis nae strong. Nearly spent, I'd wager. And the mention . . . that name."

"Forgive me." Evelyn leaned forward. "I know a little of the troubles between your clans. It must be a shock."

Angus huffed a weak laugh. "It shouldn't be, but it is, aye." Angus rubbed at his left breast with the heel of his hand. "Conall MacKerrick," he said thoughtfully, then looked to Evelyn. "Dáire's son, is he nae?"

Evelyn nodded.

"But you are nae Scots. You came with Minerva from England, I presume." The old man studied Evelyn. "Mayhap you should tell me the whole of it, lass."

And so she did. Starting with the icy-cold nightmare of Minerva's death, finding Alinor and Ronan's hut, Conall's arrival, the lie she'd told. The marriage, the arguments, her discovery about the curse and finally, her confession. Angus absorbed her tale in its entirety in silence, only nodding here or there, or raising his eyebrows. Evelyn cried through most of the telling, shame and regret coloring her words as she laid bare her broken heart and her fear to this old, old man, a stranger to her and yet her only hope.

"And so he renounced us both—the babe and me," she finished, feeling limp and spent. "I had destroyed the one hope of his town's redemption with my deceit." Evelyn looked at the old man, trying to retain a shred of dignity. "I truly have no home now. Would that you afford me shelter until my child has come, for bringing your sister her dying wish. When I am able, we will leave your town. Mayhap as early as next spring." She tilted her chin. "I am begging you, sir. Please. For my child."

Angus frowned. "I'd nae have you beg anything from me, Eve. There's nae need. Indeed, I do owe you a great deal for caring for Minerva—she wasna all alone at the end, and I know that was a fear of hers. I canna repay you for that, if you would stay at the Buchanan town for the whole of your life, and your bairn's life, and his bairns."

He leaned forward in his chair and held out a hand. Eve placed hers in it.

"Your coming was foretold, Eve. By Minerva herself, on the very day she left the Buchanan town with my only daughter for England many, many years ago." The old man's voice strained with the emotion of his words. "I doona know the why of your coming. How bringing the bairn of Dáire MacKerrick's only son into my clan is to bring us peace, or of this curse he has told you of. But I must have faith. I have borne the MacKerrick's a grudge since the day they took my happiness, but God forgive me, I will have faith."

Angus squeezed Evelyn's fingers. "You will stay. As long as your heart finds comfort here."

"Thank you," Evelyn whispered, blinking free the tears held captive by her lashes. "I do not know what peace I would bring you either, but thank you."

Angus nodded, squeezed her fingers a final time before releasing them.

But something the old man had said nagged at Evelyn. She was sure it was meaningless. But in her lessons learned of honesty and deceit by omission, Evelyn felt she must correct it.

"Dáire MacKerrick had two sons, sir," she said.

Angus frowned and shook his head. "I'd have heard that news, had his wife given birth again."

"Nay, you are correct," Evelyn hastened. "She had only one birthing, but two babes. Boys. Twins."

"That's nae possible," Angus insisted gently. "One son. You must be mistaken, lass."

"I'm not. I've met Conall's brother, Duncan."

Angus shook his head, "It canna be. Lana MacKerrick birthed one son. I know this, lass. *I know.*"

"I'd not lie to you, sir. Why would you think that?"

"Because Minerva attended the birth, Eve," Angus

said. "While Dáire MacKerrick was ambushing us, my sister was hidden away in his own home without his knowledge and gave his only son his first breath."

Evelyn knew her expression must betray her shock, and Angus Buchanan wore a similar expression of intense confusion.

"But," Evelyn stuttered, "why would they claim—?"

Her question was interrupted by a commotion beyond the door and in an instant, a group of Buchanan men burst through it, holding three captives in their midst—two men and a woman.

Andrew Buchanan shoved a man forward onto the dirt floor and spat on him. "Caught lurking north of town." His eyes found Evelyn. "Looking for our gel, they are." Andrew's voice was unmistakably possessive.

The man on the floor raised his face.

'Twas Conall.

Chapter Twenty-One

She was more beautiful than when he'd last seen her. Bedraggled and weary looking, undoubtedly from the journey, but safe and healthy and luminous and . . . *Eve*. God, how he had missed her face. How he loved her. Thank God, thank God she had made it. He was so proud of her.

But she was staring at him as if she had never seen him before, and Conall knew a shiver of cold fear.

"Why have you followed me here?" she asked quietly.

The stocky, dense-looking Buchanan who'd manhandled Conall gave his shoulder a shove with a booted foot, causing Conall to fall to his chest in the dirt. Behind him, he heard Lana cry out against this injury.

"Explain yourself, interloper. Who are you and what business have you trespassing on Buchanan lands?" the oaf demanded. Duncan let loose a string of vicious threats.

Conall raised himself slowly to his hands once more and then gained his feet carefully, not wishing to be attacked again. Eve's eyes never left him, wary, hurt.

"I am known," he began, "as the MacKerrick. I have come for my wife."

A collective, outraged roar erupted behind Conall at his statement, but he did not take his attention from Eve, even at the ring of sword against scabbard, at the hands once more seizing him.

Eve's eyes left his and went to the floor, and 'twas only then that Conall noticed the old man rising slowly from the chair on her left.

"Cease!" he commanded in a voice that belied his obvious age. The din quieted. "Andrew, release them and leave us."

"But, laird," the cocky one protested, "they are MacKerrick!"

"Go," the old man ordered and then looked at those gathered. "All of you. I have nae fear of this pup or his kin." When the fists gripping Conall did not relent, the old man boomed, *"Heed me!"*

The Scot released Conall with a shove. He bowed in Evelyn's direction and Conall felt a sickly rage in his stomach at the man's reverent "missus."

He heard Duncan thrashing behind him. "You'd better turn me loose if you know what's best for you, you stinkin' pig's arse!"

A moment later, the large house was filled with heavy silence. The old man's eyes went over Conall's shoulder.

"Lana MacKerrick," he said.

"Angus," she replied. "I never thought to see you again. Forgive us this intrusion." She stepped to Conall's side, her attention now on the woman still seated. "Is this her? Is this . . . Eve?"

Eve raised her eyes to look at Lana. "Yea. I am Evelyn."

"What business do you have at the Buchanan town, MacKerrick folk?" Angus interjected. "You are nae welcome here. State your intent and be gone, else I'll have you all bound and given over to the depths of yonder loch."

Conall stepped forward, away from Lana. "As I said, I have come for my wife, and to beg pardon from you, Angus Buchanan. I ask you to lift the curse placed upon the MacKerrick town by your own sister."

Angus scoffed. "If I am to believe Eve—and I do—she isna your wife any longer. You renounced her. She belongs to us now, part of the Buchanan clan and with our full protection." The old man studied Conall with obvious contempt. "Isna that what you always wanted, any matter, MacKerrick? For Eve to be Buchanan? Now you have your wish. I give you no pardon. Be gone."

Conall's jaw tightened and he saw Eve flush and turn her face away.

"Aye, 'tis what I wanted in the beginning, but it matters not to me now."

Eve shot to her feet, sending Bonnie clattering behind her chair in fright. "Then why did you leave me?" she shouted. "You disavowed me"—she placed her hands on her swollen belly—"this innocent child who asked not for such a life! You left us in the wood to die because we served you no further purpose!"

"Nae. Nae, Eve," Conall said and took a step toward her. "I know that's what you must think, but I swear to you that it's nae the reason I left."

"You lie!" Eve insisted with a stamp of her foot.

"You tricked me into carrying your child and then when you discovered it would not lift some imagined curse, you discarded us like rubbish."

"This curse, this curse," Angus cried. "You beg me for mercy, MacKerrick, but I have no knowledge of this curse, though deserved of one your da was!"

Lana held out a supplicating hand. "Angus, Eve—the curse isna imagined. Please, only listen."

Eve's eyes turned cold. "I know you not, woman, and naught you say to me holds any sway." She glanced at Conall, then Duncan, before pinning Lana with cold eyes once more. "The Buchanan has told me that you bore only one son—that Minerva is the one who attended you. So which is yours, hmm? Can you tell the truth? Or is it in the MacKerrick blood to deceive?"

Lana blanched, and had any other person dared to speak to the woman Conall had known as his mother in such a manner, he would have flown into a rage.

But 'twas Eve. And the question she'd raised was the very one tormenting Conall. He, too, wanted answers, and so he let Eve's condemning words hang in the room like dirty linen.

Duncan also came forward. "Aye, Mam. You vowed you would tell us, and it seems as though the Buchanan knows more about our lives than is proper." Duncan looked to the old man. "Would you indulge this explanation, Buchanan?"

Angus Buchanan sat once more. "Indeed, I demand it. Eve, please." He gestured to the chair beneath her. "You've had nae rest."

Conall wanted to go to her. To kneel at her feet, to take her hands in his and kiss them. To just sit at her side and soak up her presence. But the look she gave him forbade it, and so he chose instead to stand near Duncan, leaving Lana alone in the center of the room to tell her tale.

"There was—*is*—a curse," Lana began. "Cast by Minerva Buchanan. But 'twas nae the day that Ronan or your wife"—she looked sorrowfully to Angus— "fell. And 'tis nae to be blamed on Dáire." She swallowed. "'Twas me. The curse was meant for me."

"Mam!" Duncan exclaimed. "What on earth—?"

Lana held up a hand for silence. "Minerva and Ronan had been living at the hut in the vale for nearly a year—since Dáire and Ronan had their row." She looked to Angus once more. "I assume you and your sister had words, as well?"

Angus nodded, almost regretfully. "I would nae have her carry on in such a manner. She wasna a young girl any longer, having so far never married, denying each suit offered her. A spinster healer, the clan wise woman. Acting like a brazen wench with the brother of the man she had boldly refused."

Lana pressed her lips together briefly. "Aye, Minerva was nearly two score when I met her. Late in life indeed, to be entertaining a younger woman's thoughts of marriage."

She swallowed. "On the night Ronan was to meet you, Angus, he brought Minerva to me, against her will. To the one place he knew Dáire wouldna be and the last place his brother would think to look. He somehow knew that Dáire would try to stop him. So Ronan brought them to me for safekeeping—his woman. And their newborn son."

"Holy Christ," Angus whispered, and his hand moved to his chest.

Duncan sank to a seat near Conall's feet. Conall stood through the waves of warning washing over him. He would hear his truth like a man, before the woman he loved, and with what little pride he retained.

Lana wrung her hands together, glanced between the two men she claimed as her offspring. "Nae even a fortnight old, so wee and frail. Ronan and Minerva were struggling at the hut and the babe wouldna suckle—Minerva's milk wouldna come. But she was doing her best and although delicate, the babe was loved. Cherished.

"My own pains started that night, soon after a townsman had brought word of the battle. Minerva was terrified for Ronan but she didna take her babe and leave me. She stayed, until my own son was born." Tears now trickled down the worn, wrinkled face that Conall had loved the whole of his life.

"When my son had come at last, Minerva could keep herself from Ronan nae longer—her soul mate, she called him. But she knew she couldna take her babe into such danger. She made me swear to care for him, keep him safe, and I couldna refuse her. Not when she had cared for me and mine so well."

Conall felt a lurch in his stomach. "She never came back for . . . him?"

"Ohhh," Lana breathed, rocking back and forth. "Aye, she did. She did. But nae for days. Days and days, so that I thought she was dead, like Ronan. Perhaps took her own life."

The old man groaned and Conall saw that he had dropped his head into his hands. "Oh, forgive me, Minerva. I thought—I thought she would. I thought she was to waste away atop a useless grave. I—I kept her from leaving. I was crazed with grief myself, and I locked her away. Blamed her."

Lana let a pause settle between them before continuing. "Dáire returned from the battle a broken man. His . . . his mind was nae whole, knowing that his brother was gone. He cursed the Buchanans, Minerva. I was worried what he would do if he discovered I harbored her son, even though the babe was Ronan's, as well."

"What did you tell him, Lana?" Conall asked quietly. "Of the two babes?"

"I told him . . . I told him naught. He assumed the pair of you were twins." She gave a watery smile. "After Minerva had been gone for hours, her babe hungered and I was too weak to fetch more goat's milk. So I tried to nurse him and he took to me. And that's how Dáire found us—the three of us." Her eyes looked lovingly upon Conall and Duncan.

Then Duncan stirred. "But she came back, Mam. Did you then refuse her?"

"I did," Lana confessed in little more than a whisper. "Nae directly—I was too afraid of her to face her. I hid in my house like the coward I was when she came, but I refused her all the same.

"Dáire discovered her creeping about the wood with her wild wolf like a madwoman and went to her. I thought one of them might kill the other. I could have stopped it. I could have admitted the truth to Dáire and given Minerva her son. But the truth would have broken Dáire completely, knowing his pride had cost a little boy his father, and he already hurt so much!"

Lana squeezed her eyes shut for a moment. "And the bairn—he thrived! Each day he was stronger, sturdier—I had milk aplenty for the both of you and I had grown to love Minerva's child as fiercely as my own flesh. I feared for him with her, deep in her own grief, estranged from her kin and, by then, what little milk she had would have been gone. I told myself I was saving him." She averted her face. "But I admit my greed now. I wanted you both. I heard her screaming from the wood and yet I kept still. 'Twas *then* that she cursed the town—nae after the battle, nae over Ronan's body. She cursed us because of me. And I never, ever told."

Conall heard a sniffling and looked up to see tears streaming down Eve's face, a look of horrified sorrow in her eyes. She swallowed and spoke to Lana in a creaky voice.

"Which one?" she asked. "Minerva's son—which one?"

Conall took a step forward. "'Tis I, Eve. Could you nae fit the pieces together? When I left town . . . then our bairn." He stopped, looked to Lana. "Tell her 'tis I, Mam."

"Oh, Conall," Lana whispered. "Dear, sweet, brave, Conall. My love, forgive me." Her smile grew even sadder. "'Tis Duncan."

Evelyn did not know whose shock was greater—Conall's, Duncan's, or Angus Buchanan's. The longhouse was instantly flooded with silent but palpable, crashing emotion, and the sadness of Lana MacKerrick's tale combined with the discovery of a new reality to create a wave of feeling in Evelyn so intense it caused an uncomfortable twinge low in her belly. She gasped but her reaction was lost on those in the room with her. She, too, forgot about her discomfort in the face of the maelstrom.

"Nae," Duncan moaned, dropping onto his hands. "Oh, Mam, nae—tell me it isna so!"

Conall staggered back two paces to lean his shoulders against the wall, his face bloodless and drawn, staring at the man in agony on the floor. No longer his brother.

"Duncan," Conall rasped. "Dunc, it means naught. It changes naught."

Angus Buchanan, too, stared at the wiry man as if, in the instant Evelyn saw it, he also saw in Duncan an essence of the aged, gray old healer who had breathed her last on a rocky grave in Evelyn's arms.

"*It changes all*," Angus said. He rose slowly, slowly, and Evelyn kept a keen eye on the old chief for the telltale signs of his earlier spasms.

Lana stumbled across the room on a sob and fell to her knees at Duncan's side, throwing her arms about his shoulders and clinging there even when he struggled to free himself.

"Listen to Conall, Duncan," she pleaded. "He speaks true! Aye, I've done a terrible wrong, but 'twas only because I loved you so! You are still mine—still ours! Still MacKerrick! Your da was—"

Duncan shot to his feet, flinging Lana onto her backside. His slender face was twisted and reddened with pain, his eyes leaking angry, resentful tears.

"I doona know who me da was!" he shouted. "All those years when Da—*Dáire*—favored Conall"—he flung an arm toward the silent man against the wall—"I thought 'twas because of *my* failings! When I was looked over as the weaker, the lesser—"

"Dunc, you were never the lesser," Conall croaked.

"You know not, Conall!" Duncan gasped and

swiped at his eyes angrily with his forearm. "'Twas *you* Dáire depended on, *you* who he groomed to lead the clan, *you* who he fought to secure a bride for, a life, a future, while I had to be resigned to being tied to Mam's apron. And you pissed on it at every turn! You didn't love Nonna, but you took her anyways. Just like the town! You couldn't love *our people*"—he barked a mirthless laugh—"enough to let go of your pride to save them! The cost was too high for proud Conall MacKerrick!"

Duncan drew a gasping breath. "But I longed to help them—would have handed over me own bollocks to Angus Buchanan himself had I thought 'twould be of any relief. And I did help them, too! Once you had gone to the hut in the vale, I worked tirelessly for food, to bring cheer and hope to the people, and *I succeeded* where *you failed*! Each and every time!"

Conall's lips thinned and his head dropped. "I know it, Duncan. You are the better man,"

"You're fuckin' right, I am!" Duncan clenched his fists and shook them in the air with a growl of rage. "But what good does it do me now, eh, Conall? Tell me! I have nae place in me own home!"

Angus Buchanan took a step toward Duncan, a thin, trembling palm held open. "You have a place here, though," he said in a quavering voice. "My sister's son . . . My"—Angus wheezed—"my nephew."

Duncan spun on Angus. "I doona want yer fuckin' inheritance, old man—you are as much to blame as any!"

The twinge came to Evelyn's stomach again and she winced.

Still on the floor, Lana MacKerrick held a hand

to Duncan. "We'll go home straight away, Duncan. 'Twill be fine, you'll see."

"I'll go nowhere with you, you greedy, lying woman," Duncan spat, then glanced at Evelyn, his eyes hooded as if ashamed. "I'm sorry for you, missus, and for the babe you carry. Truly, I am."

Then he turned to Angus Buchanan. "If you have a mite of respect for your sister—for the woman who gave me life—you'll accompany me through this door and secure me safe passage from your town."

"Dunc, doona set out alone," Conall said quietly.

"*You*," Duncan said, disgust creeping around his words, "are nae me brother, nae me laird. You're naught to me. All of you!" He looked to Angus once more. "What say you, old man? Do you grant me leave or do I fall beyond your door?"

Angus nodded, his features heavy with resignation. "Come," he said and he shuffled to the door and passed through it, Duncan at his back.

Lana scrambled to her feet and made to follow, but Conall stayed her with a hand on her arm.

"Leave him, Mam," he advised, more gently than Evelyn thought the woman deserved. "Duncan needs time. 'Tis the least we can offer to him."

Lana turned into her only son's chest with a wail as Angus reentered the longhouse alone. The old man all but collapsed in his chair.

The cramping came again, more intense this time, and insistent, like a giant, thorny fist. Evelyn hissed in air through her teeth.

The babe could not be coming. 'Twas too soon.

Then Conall had turned Lana aside and stepped to face Evelyn, his arms hanging at his sides, his face full of regret.

"Now you know, Eve," he said and his amber eyes bored into hers.

"Now I know what?" she whispered as another strident wave gripped her.

Conall frowned. "Why I left the hut. I feared that because you werena Buchanan—the babe we'd created wasna Buchanan—that Minerva's curse would find you, harm you. I wanted to get away from you to keep you both safe, until I could come to Angus myself."

Evelyn felt a swelling of pain seize her heart more intense than the spasms in her belly. "You abandoned us to keep us safe?" she asked and then huffed a disbelieving laugh.

"I did." Conall rushed to his knees before her. "I went to get Dunc and Mam. To explain what terrible things I'd done and what I had to do to right it—all of it. Then I was coming back for you!"

She shook her head for several moments, staring into those deep, amber eyes while her entire abdomen clenched. Only when it relented could she speak.

"I don't believe you," she whispered, and felt a tear break loose from her eye. "You deceived me from the start. You never cared for me. You only . . . you only wanted what you thought I could give you."

"I love you, Eve," Conall ground out between his teeth. "I would die for you. I will do anything you ask of me. I want to spend the rest of my life with you."

Evelyn could not let Conall reach her. She refused to let him destroy her again.

And now she felt a wetness between her legs and a dull, throbbing ache.

"I don't believe you," she repeated. "And I want no part of you or your life. I do not love you. Leave me."

"Eve, please," Conall croaked, wincing and cocking his head so that his cheek lay nearly on her thigh. "Give me time to show you—"

"Leave me," Evelyn repeated, looking to the door—anywhere but at those hurt, golden eyes. "You do it so well. Be gone."

"Nae!" Conall gave a noisy sniff. "I willna! I'll fight for you! I'll—"

Evelyn hadn't noticed Angus returning to the door until a half dozen Buchanan men filled the house. When Angus interrupted Conall's declarations, his voice was cold.

"Take your leave, MacKerrick, as the lass bade you. I'd nae have you dragged out—Eve's been through enough at your hand."

Conall glanced over his shoulder only briefly before turning back to Evelyn, and when his hand went to the leather choker at his neck, she nearly let go of her resolve.

"Eve, please," he whispered and he glanced at her belly. "I love you both so, you'll never know . . ."

Her breath hitched and 'twas all she could do to speak over the screaming pain.

"Go, sir."

Angus waved at Conall and Lana. "Take them both and throw them out. Stand watch that they doona return."

Two sets of hands seized Conall and dragged him to his feet backward. And he roared.

"Nae! Eve, nae!" Through the door they dragged him as he shouted, "I'll come back for you! I swear it! Eve! I love you!"

Angus shut out the sounds of Conall's desperate cries and turned to Evelyn, looking a score of years aged from only an hour ago.

"They won't"—she caught her breath—"they won't harm him, will they?"

"Nae unless he strikes first." The old man sighed and sat in his chair, rubbing once more at his chest. His gaze was sorrowful. "'Tis what you want? You're certain, lass?"

"I can't—" She closed her eyes and tried to will the clenching, searing pain away. Her very teeth ached from the strain. Her heart and her belly fought to be the victor of who would kill her first. "I can't concern myself with the MacKerrick's motives. Not now."

She looked at the old man as the inevitable horror crashed around her.

"My babe is coming."

Chapter Twenty-Two

Evelyn was burning, freezing in an endless, icy hell. For two days she had fought the pains, the fever, the crushing, delusional fear. The only solace she found was in the brief moments of unconsciousness between surges, when her exhausted body and mind blinked out in desperation.

Buchanan women tended her, a stranger, carefully, lovingly, and well. They spoke quietly to each other in Gaelic, but as the hours dragged on, it didn't matter to Evelyn that she could not understand their words—the dire tone of their conversations and short, clipped instructions to each other were terrifyingly clear:

Things were not well.

The women had brewed potions, ground herbs, mixed salves; they had held Evelyn's hands and stroked her brow. But naught had eased the pains, the intense pressure of something determined to part with her body.

Her child. Her and Conall MacKerrick's child. Born two cycles of the moon too early, with little chance of survival.

Evelyn tried to concentrate on and mimic the actions of the Buchanan women as they pantomimed for her to take long, deep breaths and curl herself over her midsection. And all the while she hated Conall MacKerrick. Not for the physical trauma she was experiencing, but for not loving her or their child enough for the truth. Angus Buchanan's grand longhouse reeked of blood and sweat and agony and Evelyn knew 'twas unlikely that she or the babe would survive. But if she did and the child died, if she was left alone without Conall, without Alinor, left with no one, Evelyn had decided that she would simply take to the wood one day and never come out.

But it seemed as though she would not have to take that sin upon herself, as the wives' voices were steadily fading into gray nothing, and Evelyn was so thankful for the peace of it. The wrenching pain swelled into a blanket of humming numbness, and even as she heard the women calling panickedly to her as if from far, far away, Evelyn let her eyes close, let the slow thump of her own heartbeat lull her away into a world of gray lightening to soft white. Quiet, cool, peaceful—

—snow falling at dawn.

She was in the great Caledonian forest once more, but not. Evelyn could see with perfect clarity the rough skin of the trees and smell the fragrant detritus of the forest floor. She could breathe deeply at last, fill her lungs with fresh, clean green, and feel the cool, shivery breeze, but she could not find herself. 'Twas as if her soul had left her body behind to swoop weightless, formless, and free through the shadowy light of the wood.

And 'twas snowing. Millions of starburst snowflakes fell with gentle haste, only to melt at once on the bobbing heads of riotous wildflowers waving in an endless wash around the rocky pyre of the oak tree.

And on that pyre sat Minerva Buchanan, her wizened face peaceful and relaxed.

"Hallow, Eve," she called with a gentle smile, her sparkling black eyes searching the snow-sprinkled air above her head as if she sensed Evelyn's presence. "Almost at its end now, is it nae? I'm glad you've come."

Evelyn wanted to answer the old woman. Wanted to ask her so many questions in this peaceful, quiet place that housed no pain, no fear. But she could not seem to find a voice. The wind picked up a bit, driving the snow shower at a pretty angle against the swaying tree trunks.

"I want to thank you, Eve," Minerva continued. "Since my man and my son were taken from me, I have given to others. All my life, I gave, so that I wouldna feel the empty place in my own heart, so that I wouldna collapse in on myself. I promised Ronan that I would live our love, and I am satisfied that I have done so.

"I am home," Minerva said in a wondrous whisper. "My son knows me. And he is loved. Soon, I will be free." She looked about the snowflakes again. "Love him, Eve. Love them all. You and I, we traveled here together, each of us seemingly alone in the world. Nae so, though." She thumped her breast gently. *"For each hurt you feel, I give you threefold love to heal. For each loss, a new treasure, for each tear, two smiles."*

She paused. "Love them all," she repeated quietly, "in my stead. I gave them to you the night I left this earth—do you remember? The blood on your lip?" Minerva nodded. "It will pain you for a great while, but . . . love them. Each one is a gift."

Then Minerva suddenly turned her head and seemed to look right past where Evelyn imagined herself to be. The old witch's eyes were full of soft, ripe love and she smiled.

"Ah, there's my lad. Farewell, Eve. *Fare. Well.*"

Evelyn came into her body in the midst of a blood-boiling scream. Her body was wild with pain, afire with it, and Conall's face was clear in her mind. She heard herself scream his name.

She wanted him, needed him. Oh, God how she needed him. She was so frightened and hurt so badly, to the ends of her soul it seemed . . .

The pain wanted to recede but was then thrown back upon her in a crushing blow so that another throat-ripping scream burst from her.

Then a cool, thin palm stroked her forehead and for an instant, Evelyn thought Minerva's pointed face hovered over hers. But 'twas the son, not the mother.

"Hallow, missus," Duncan said gently. "I'm here to aid you. Now, heed me. Heed me—Eve, can you hear me?"

Evelyn managed to nod before twisting her head away for another scream. She wanted to die.

"You there, woman." Duncan's voice faded as he spoke over his shoulder. "Get up behind her, under her. Bend her up."

White-hot terror sizzled through Evelyn's brain. "Nay!" she shrieked. "Do not move me!"

But she could already feel her shoulders lifting,

heaving her over a cliff of unimaginable pain as Duncan appeared before her half-blind eyes once again.

"We must, missus—quickly." He knelt between Evelyn's legs, placed a hand upon her belly. "Come on, now, Eve, let us both bring forth your bairn. Help me!"

"Nay!" She squealed as the most violent spasm overtook her, yanking her breath from her. She wanted to arch her back, straighten her legs, but the woman behind her and Duncan at her heels pressed her together like a limber, green spring limb.

"For the love of God, Eve, bear down! Now!"

Evelyn pushed. And for one blinding, paralyzing instant, the universe paused as her body yielded. She felt tremendous pressure and then a void; a gush of her lifeblood leaving her in a rush, then shouting voices crashed through the concentrated silence.

The woman beneath her shoulders skittered backward to lay Eve down and Duncan was hoisting a small, limp, hairless mass of wet, red flesh by its ankles onto her sunken belly.

"Stop the blood, stop the blood," he commanded as he scrambled to Evelyn's side. He grabbed each of her limp arms in turn and brought them around the still-warm body of the baby lying on its side. "Hold him, missus. Hold yer son."

Oh, 'twas a boy. And he was not moving, his eyes closed, no rising of the little ribs bumping beneath thin, raw skin. Between her legs two women worked with huge wads of linen, water and herbs, but their ministrations were unfelt.

"Duncan?" Evelyn cried. *"Duncan!"*

"Hold on to him," Duncan repeated. Then he pushed a finger into the tiny, slack mouth and bent low to blow a harsh breath onto the baby's face, once, twice, three times. He jiggled the slender back, patted him firmly. "Come on, laddie!" he shouted.

Evelyn gave a wordless scream of fear as the reddened skin began to fade to lavender.

Then the little chest hitched, an impossibly small arm jerked, and a watery-sounding mew bubbled at plump, bluish lips.

Evelyn had no logical reason for her actions, but at the feeble cry, she pulled the baby from Duncan's reach, high on her chest to beneath her chin, and shook him.

"Baby!" she sobbed. "Hear your mama! Breathe for Mama!"

The mew came again, then a rattling, gasping cough, and finally a weak, high-pitched wail, reedy and knotted.

Duncan's laughter burst from him triumphantly and he scrambled higher to Evelyn's side, kissed her forehead and that of the crying babe.

"You did it, missus!" he rejoiced and wrapped his arms about them both. "You did it!"

Evelyn felt such peaceful, exhausted relief as one of the wives brought forth a soft length of wool and rubbed briskly at the little being on her chest. Her head spun and bobbed as if she was at sea and Evelyn could feel herself slipping away. Her vision blurred, doubled.

"Duncan," she whispered against the baby's smooth head. "Thank you. I—"

"Shh," Duncan hastened. "Save your strength, missus."

But she had to say it lest she never return from the quiet place that once more beckoned her.

"I love him, Duncan." She tried to focus on the baby's face, to memorize each tiny, perfect detail to take with her. "Tell him. Tell them both."

And then Evelyn slipped away. And this time, she was not afraid.

Conall sat before the cold fire in Ronan's hut, staring at the soft, dead ash. He felt as if he was looking at his own heart—empty, forgotten, forsaken.

He'd been alone at the hut in the vale for two days, having sent Lana on to the MacKerrick town after a week of her company. She was his mother and he loved her still, but the knowledge of her past, her mistakes, had prevented Conall from doing little more than acknowledging her existence. He'd had no answer for her when she'd asked what to tell the townsfolk. In truth, he did not care what she told them. Conall and his mother'd had no word from Duncan since he'd taken his leave from the Buchanan's house. If Conall could not return to his town with his brother—his cousin, rather—and his wife, he did not wish to ever return.

He needed time alone, to think.

He must find a way to reach Eve, to show her how much he truly loved her—for her, not for what he'd at one time thought she could gain him. Conall wanted her as his wife, his friend, forever. Wanted the two of them to bring their child up together, as a proper family. But he had hurt her so terribly, done to her the one thing she feared most, and then he, out of his own fear, had left her.

He would do anything, anything, just to see her,
speak to her, know that she was well. How he
missed her, here at the hut where he had fallen in
love with her. Each square inch of space, each
empty hour, sighed her name. Conall hadn't eaten,
had barely slept. His only task was staring at the fire
pit, and thinking, thinking, *What can I do? How can
I remedy this?*

He heard the scrape of the door as if from far
away but did not turn, hoping 'twas only the wind,
willing the universe to leave him with no distrac-
tions. He could not have cared less had it been the
vengeful gray wolf.

"You have a son."

The combination of Duncan's familiar voice and
the meaning behind his words stopped Conall's
heart. He turned his head slowly so that, if this was
some dream, he would not frighten it away.

Duncan came into the hut fully and sat a large
pack near the fire pit. "I thought I'd find you here,
you great coward," he said, his face shuttered,
hard, as he set about coaxing flame from the ashes.

Conall's mind was consumed by loud buzzing.
He shook his head but it did not clear the noise.
"What did you say?" he asked, his voice hoarse
from disuse.

Bitter green eyes flicked to Conall's for only an
instant. "I called you a coward, MacKerrick. Do you
wish to challenge me for it?"

"Like it or nae, you're MacKerrick, too, Duncan,"
Conall clipped. "Before that—a son?"

Duncan was silent until flames had crawled over
the fresh fuel in the pit. Then he reached into the
pack and pulled out a jug. After taking a deep

swallow, he capped it and tossed it over the smoky fire to Conall.

"Drink up—you're a father."

Conall felt the jug's heavy, smooth weight in his palms, smelled the tangy smoke creeping to the ceiling, but it was as if the world had stopped.

"Eve . . . Eve had the bairn?" he whispered.

Duncan nodded curtly. "Aye."

"But 'tis too soon," Conall argued, as if he could convince Duncan of this and undo the deed. "Not until September. August at the very—"

"He was early," Duncan interrupted. "'Twas bad, Conall. You must know."

His blood turned to ice, his throat closed. "Eve?" he choked out.

Duncan stared at the flames, his face haggard and gray. "She lost so much blood. Two days, she labored. The lad hadna turned—stuck tight."

"She's . . . she's dead, isn't she?" Conall whispered, but inside his head he screamed. Felt as though he would never stop screaming.

Duncan frowned slightly, then his mouth drew completely downward. "You're a right arsehole. D'ye think so little of me that I'd nae have sent for you? That I'd come here and nae tell you that straight away?"

Hope grew. A timid, spindly green shoot out of the black mire of Conall's heart. "She lives?"

Duncan shot to his feet and flung out his wiry arms. "O' course she lives, you shitmonger! Christ, Conall!" He grabbed up his pack. "You know—*fuck you*! I come all this way, when I swore I wouldna, for you—*for Eve*—and you treat me—" He broke off and stomped toward the door.

But Conall dove from his stool and tackled

Duncan at the knees, bringing the smaller man down with a yelp. He grabbed Duncan by the front of his rough léine and jerked him upright.

"You'll nae go anywhere until you tell me straight," he growled. "What of my wife and child? Are they both well? Tell me!" He shook Duncan like a branch of dried leaves.

"Your son," Duncan spat, "is small. Weak. The first three nights, we didna know if he would live. 'Tis the same with Evc. She caught a fever and still she canna leave her childbed for weakness. It takes all her strength to nurse."

"When?" Conall demanded, his stomach lurching. "When was he born?"

"He was five days old when I left. Now, turn me loose."

Conall's eyes narrowed. "Will you stay? Tell me what I need to know if I do?"

"Why do you think I came in the first place?"

Conall let his fingers uncurl from Duncan's léine and helped him to stand. He brushed at the bits of dirt clinging to Duncan's clothes until the smaller man slapped his hands away.

It was difficult for Conall to meet his cousin's eyes. He was so shamed. "'Tis good to see you again, Dunc."

But Duncan let the attempt at peace lay untouched, grabbing up the forgotten jug and returning to his spot near the fire. Conall righted his own stool and sat.

"I thought you left the Buchanan town," he began again, desperate to restart a dialogue with the man.

"I did." Duncan drank from the jug. "I took to the wood for a pair of days. But I returned."

"Why?"

"Something told me to go back, that I was needed. Eve needed someone." Duncan paused. "And because I promised you I would look after her if you couldna."

Conall felt his chest tighten, hot wetness well in his eyes. This man sitting across from him—Conall owed him all. He struggled to compose himself enough to speak.

"Did she send for me?" he asked hopefully, praying to himself that Duncan's presence was a sign of forgiveness.

"Nae." The short word crushed Conall, even before he saw the regret in Duncan's eyes. "She loves you—she told me as much—but she doesna want to see you."

"Because of what I did to her. One lie." 'Twas not a question.

"Aye. Because of what you did."

A flicker of anger sprang to life in his mind. "She lied to me as well!"

Duncan nodded. "She did. But she did it to save her own life. You lied to serve your pride, your selfishness."

Conall let the truth batter him and he surrendered to his defeat without further struggle. His head drooped, too heavy for him to hold upright.

"Then why did you come here?" he asked tiredly. "To punish me?"

"Nae, you dumb toad," Duncan scoffed. "I've come to help you get her back."

Conall slowly raised his eyes to stare at his cousin. "You think I can?"

"Nae if yer sittin' here like tits on a boar, that's for certain."

Despite his misery, Conall felt his lip curl. "How? I'll do anything, I swear."

"You must go to her. Court her. Wear down her resolve. Angus Buchanan has claimed her and her bairn—"

"*My son*," Conall clarified.

Duncan merely arched a slender brow. "He has claimed them *both* as his kin, and they are under his protection. As am I. You'll have to win the Buchanan, as well. Prove your worth."

Conall sat up straight. "Done. When do we leave?"

"Ah-ah. Nae so fast," Duncan tsked. "You're banned from the Buchanan town. There are orders to beat your guts to pulp if you're found inside its borders."

Conall sighed and threw up his hands. "Then how?"

"You go proper, and with respect," Duncan insisted. "As should have been done years ago. First through the Buchanan. Beg audience with him. Tell him of your love for Eve. Your intentions."

"Of course," Conall rushed to agree.

"But." Duncan raised a finger. "Eve has sworn to never return with you as the MacKerrick's wife. She is no pawn, no trophy, and would never again allow you to treat her or the babe thusly."

Conall frowned, then realized that Duncan still did not understand.

"I could never do that, Dunc," he said quietly. "Even if I had want to."

"Why is that, now?"

"Duncan," Conall swallowed. "*You are the MacKerrick.*"

Duncan pressed his lips into a tight line and his chin flinched, but only once.

"I was . . . I was hoping you'd say that."

Chapter Twenty-Three

Evelyn was going outdoors for the first time in eight weeks. She dressed slowly, carefully, then crossed her small, private sleeping area partitioned by woven screens—to peer down into the low cradle.

Gregory was awake, but lying happily quiet, his muddy blue eyes searching the ceiling, his slender, ruddy arms swinging wildly and then clasping on each other. His little pink mouth opened and closed with innocent sweetness, practicing faint sighs and coos. He was so small yet, fragile looking even after two months. But he had come leagues from his first, tremulous breaths. Each day his miniature fist showed more strength in its grasp as he clutched at Evelyn's finger. Each feeding seemed to reveal a growing appetite, a brave hunger to survive and even thrive, and Evelyn wanted to weep in gratitude from simply looking at him.

"Gregory," she called in a quiet singsong. He didn't start, but his wise little face turned toward the sound of Evelyn's voice. For an instant, his expression whispered a secret of his sire, and it caused a stinging in her heart.

"Hallow, lovely," she cooed, ignoring the pain of Conall's remembrance. "Do you fancy a bit of sunshine this day? Mayhap we'll catch a glimpse of Sebastian in the trees."

His arms waved aimlessly and the slender bumps of tiny knees pushed beneath his gown. Evelyn scooped him up carefully, drawing a soft square of Buchanan plaid about his shoulders, and held him up on her chest, pressing her cheek against his velvety skin.

A familiar shuffling of footsteps prompted her to turn just as Angus Buchanan scratched politely at the screen.

"Is my wee lad ready for his grand adventure?"

"Good morn, Angus." Evelyn smiled and looked down at Gregory. "I think he is. I know his mama is more than ready." Her eyes found the kind old man again. "Have you come to escort us?"

"Aye, if you've a wish for company. But I've also come to give you the warning I promised you I would—MacKerrick has returned. *Again*," he said pointedly.

Evelyn felt her lips thin. "Is he about now?" She didn't understand the Buchanan allowing Conall MacKerrick access to the town. For six weeks, Conall had made his presence known on a nearly daily basis, begging audience with Eve.

She had denied him every time. She could not see him—her hurt was still too great. And she would not give him the undeserved gift of even a glimpse of Gregory, although her conscience pained her from it.

Angus shook his head and sighed. "He's made such a nuisance of himself, Andrew's finally taken to putting him to work on the keep on the loch."

"Angus!" Evelyn gasped, feeling betrayed. "'Tis

bad enough that you torment me with granting the man leave to come and go as he pleases—must you gainfully employ him, as well? He'll never leave!"

The old man shrugged sheepishly. "Winter approaches on swift feet, Eve. We need every pair of hands." He stepped to her side and plucked gently at Gregory's gown with two frail fingers and cooed at him. "If you'd but speak to him, tell him yourself that there is nae hope of reconciliation, that you have nae wish to ever see him again, mayhap he would give you the peace you *claim* you desire."

The veiled rebuke stung. "He needs return to his beloved town. I have no wish to hear his lying voice. And I trust him not with Gregory."

Angus rolled his rheumy eyes. "Think you any member of this clan would allow Conall Mac-Kerrick to abscond with one of their own? Fie on thee, lass. MacKerrick has asked of the bairn's welfare, aye, but his every request is of you—to see you, speak with you."

Evelyn shrugged and knew that the gesture was petulant, but she didn't want the old man to see how difficult it was for her to hear those words. Conall had obviously been shirking his duties as the MacKerrick to haunt her here at the Buchanan town.

"If he is about, then Gregory and I will simply go out another day," she said firmly, turning to sit on her cot with the babe, feeling hugely disappointed. And furious that Conall MacKerrick was still ruling her days.

"As I said, Andrew has him enslaved at the loch," Angus offered. "Go out, Eve. Take some air and clear your thoughts. I've a feeling Conall Mac-

Kerrick will hound the both of us until you speak
with him directly. For all our sanity, think upon it."

Evelyn frowned. She did so long to be free of the
dark, stuffy longhouse. "I wish Duncan had stayed."

"As do I," Angus sighed. "But I'll go along with
you if you've nae wish to be alone."

"Nay, Angus, I'll take Bonnie. You rest," she said,
considering the old man's gray complexion. "You've
not been sleeping well with Gregory crying through
the night." Evelyn stood. "I'll just venture to the
edge of town near the stream. I shan't be long away."
She kissed the wrinkled cheek before moving to the
door. "Bonnie, to me."

Setting her jaw, Evelyn opened the door fully
and then drew in a deep breath as the warm sunlight hit her face—it was delicious. She set off in
the opposite direction of the loch, determined not
to think of the man laboring only a stone's throw
away.

As far as Evelyn was concerned, Conall Mac-
Kerrick had ceased to exist.

She strolled down the wide main thoroughfare,
and was nearing the edge of the town when a
child's frantic scream in Gaelic split the air. One
word only, but Evelyn understood it clearly.

Faol.

Wolf.

"Oy! MacKerrick!"

The warning was given in the very instant the
wet, heavy hunk of straw and mortar smacked into
Conall's temple.

"Catch it, now!"

Conall staggered sideways on his feet, the unwieldy load of long timber supports on his shoulder shifting and sliding. He strained to steady the load but gave a hoarse cry as the topmost board slid free and the whole lot fell to the ground with an echoing crash.

Conall's face burned as the amused guffaws of the Buchanan workers taunted him. He wanted to fight them all, one by one, if he had to. They goaded his temper mercilessly, constantly, as if daring him to lose control. But Conall gathered every shred of patience and humility he could scrounge and took their provocation. Took the jabs, the jests, the outright insults. He had been reduced little more than a slave, and yet he welcomed it.

Eve was so close, he could feel her with his waking breath each morning in the primitive tent he'd erected just beyond the Buchanan town. She was here, his wife, and Gregory, his son. Conall would be patient if it killed him. He would endure the Buchanan ridicule until the day he died if that was how long it took for Eve to come to him.

He would wait. And he would be here for her whenever and if ever she wanted him again.

Conall scraped the sticky mess from the side of his face with his fingertips, then bent to begin restacking the fallen beams. Andrew Buchanan's loathsome boots came into his line of sight.

"Leave it," the Scot said imperiously. "I'll take them from here. We're out of mortar."

Conall stopped, taking a slow, deep breath. Could the man not be bothered the courtesy of asking? Conall wanted to smash his knuckles into Andrew Buchanan's face, pound his flapping tongue down his throat.

"I'll go back to shore and ready another batch," he gritted between his teeth and straightened.

Andrew clapped a hand on Conall's shoulder with a booming "Good man!" before turning away. He didn't make the first move to collect the fallen beams, and Conall knew the pile would still be waiting on him once he made the laborious journey to shore and back.

At least he would be fatigued come nightfall. Mayhap he could find some small escape in sleep.

Conall made his way to the island's rocky beach where a line of primitive rafts were landed. Grabbing up a long, wide-tipped staff, he shoved one of the rafts into the quiet, lapping water and splashed aboard, pushing himself out into the deep.

It took him the better part of a half hour to reach the far shore, and as he drew near, he could both hear and see the commotion on the edge of town. Conall ran the raft aground and scrambled up the bank to the knot of women and children gathered together.

"What is it?" he demanded of the closest Buchanan wife. She was clutching her reluctant daughter to her side.

"'Tis the missus—she's gone mad," the woman said grudgingly, her eyes barely meeting Conall's.

Conall's heart began to pound. The missus was Eve.

"What do you mean, woman?" he barked.

The wife grew tight-lipped, as if she knew she'd already said too much, but her daughter was all too eager to reply.

"Wee Barney found a wolf pup in the weeds and was playing with it like a ninny when its mama came out of the wood after it," she said around a

breathless smile. "Missus was walking with her
bairn and flew to Barney's rescue, but then she
dashed off into the wood after the wolf. *Into the
wood!* Ran after it, a wailin' and weepin', babe and
all!" she finished, wide-eyed.

Conall swallowed. "Missus followed a wolf into
the wood?"

The little girl nodded. "The biggest, meanest-
looking black wolf I've ever seen! I fear the missus'll
be ate!"

Conall's feet could not move fast enough.

Evelyn could not run any longer. Already she
could feel the freshened bleeding and pulling pain
between her legs, the weak trembling of her limbs.
In her arms, Gregory wailed at being so rudely jostled. Evelyn stopped, gasping, tears streaming down
her face in the middle of the wood. She was already
lost, but she did not care in the least.

"Alinor!" she wailed into the dense, dark shadows of the trees. *"Alinor!"*

It had to be her. It *had* to be. Evelyn would know
her girl's big-boned shape anywhere, and her heart
was rejoicing, breaking.

Why had she run?

"Alinor, please!" Evelyn cried, turning in a circle.
"To me, Alinor!"

Evelyn hadn't realized that Bonnie had followed
her into the wood until she heard the sheep's anxious bleat.

She saw Bonnie running in frantic circles before
two large boulders, leaned together in a hillside like
lovers. And atop those boulders sat Alinor, peering
down at the manic sheep with mild interest.

"Alinor," Evelyn whispered the sob and Gregory fell silent. She took a step forward. "To me, my beautiful girl! To me!"

The black wolf stood and leisurely, carefully, picked her way down from her perch, buffeting a joyous Bonnie aside as she walked across the forest floor. Evelyn fell to her knees, one arm held away from her body in readiness of an embrace.

But Alinor was reserved, keeping two paces between them before sitting on her haunches once more. Bonnie collapsed happily, stubby tail twitching, at the wolf's rear. Alinor's long, slender muzzle reached forward, sniffing curiously at the plaid-wrapped bundle in Evelyn's other arm.

Evelyn could barely speak with the confusion, hurt and joy she felt. "'Tis all right, lovely,'tis only I. And Gregory." She lifted the baby slightly. "Won't you greet me, Alinor? I've missed you so—I thought you were ill. Dead!"

But Alinor withdrew even her curiosity of the babe, sitting upright regally and looking aloofly away. Then her ears perked, her shoulders tensed.

Alinor's thick tail thumped the ground wildly and Evelyn heard the crunching leaves behind her. She felt Conall's presence before he spoke.

"Ah, my three favorite lasses," he said hoarsely. "And my little lad."

Chapter Twenty-Four

"Never have I seen aught of such beauty," he managed to choke out.

Eve's back was stiff, frozen, and Conall could see the flutter of Buchanan plaid at her hip. Alinor's tail wagged, but she did not rise and come to him, as if remembering the last moments they'd shared at the hut in the vale. Only Bonnie bleated and scrambled awkwardly to her feet to run at Conall and butt repeatedly at his thigh. He scratched her head mindlessly, willing Eve to speak, to move, anything.

The moments dragged on into what seemed a silent hour.

"Eve, can I—" He had to stop, clear his throat. "Can I approach you?"

"I wish you wouldn't, MacKerrick," she said at last, and Conall's heart expanded at just hearing the melody of her voice.

"Why?" he pressed, begged. He took a single, slow, short step toward her. "My God, Eve, I've missed you so!"

"I don't want to see you, MacKerrick!" she snapped, turning her head a bit so that Conall could nearly make out her profile. "Go back to your town."

"Nae," Conall said. "Nae, I'll nae go back." Although he knew she couldn't see them, Conall held out his palms to her. "Won't you please just talk with me, Eve? Or at least listen to what I have to say to you?"

"Ha!" she barked. "More lies?"

"No more lies," he promised quietly. "Never again."

She made no reply, so Conall advanced another tentative step. It took every speck of restraint he'd ever thought of possessing not to run at her and throw his arms about her.

"For certain, you're wondering why I'm at the Buchanan town," he offered, hoping 'twould coax a response from her. But none came, so he continued doggedly.

"I've pleaded my case to the Buchanan and he's given his blessing for us to wed, if you'll have me."

"I've been married once," Eve said stiffly. "I did not care for it. So you may return to the Mac-Kerrick town with a clear conscience, sir. Nay is my answer."

"I'm nae going back," he repeated firmly. "If I must labor under that bastard, Andrew Buchanan, for the rest of my life while waiting for you, Eve, I will. *I love you.* With all my heart, I do. And as long as it takes to convince you, to make up for how I've hurt you, that's how long I'll remain and not one day less."

She said nothing and Conall let his eyes go to the wolf, lest he lose control of himself and run to Eve anyway, frightening her away.

"Hallow, Alinor. Where have you been, lass?"

Alinor's tail thumped the ground again and her eyes flicked between Conall and Eve.

"You just want my child," Eve accused suddenly. "That's all you've ever cared about."

"That isna true," Conall insisted and took another step forward. "Eve, how much more simple would it have been for me, after you confessed you werena Buchanan, to find another woman to bear me a child, were that my only desire? I'm nae toad, after all, and I was chief of my clan."

She shook her head and shrugged.

"If I had nae love for you, I wouldna have had to bring Duncan and my mother to the Buchanan town after you, scared out of me bloody mind. Reopened old wounds. Destroyed Duncan's life. I wouldna have given up my place at the MacKerrick town to await your slightest whisper amongst a people who detest the very sight of me." He took a deep breath. "I've given up everything I ever thought I wanted, Eve. Because I know that you're the only thing I need. You and our son."

Eve's voice was barely a whisper. "What do you mean you've given up your place at the MacKerrick town?"

"Duncan is chief now. He was always meant for it, in so many ways that I never was. I like to think that if Da had known he was Ronan's son, he would have felt the same."

Her head turned a bit more. "I don't understand. Why have you done this?"

"I've asked Angus Buchanan for his blessing upon us. If you will have me, we will live amongst the Buchanans, if it is your wish. I'll build us our own house, here, near the loch, if you wish. Wherever—whatever—you wish, Eve."

"I wish I could go back six months," she said, and Conall could hear the longing in her voice. "When we lived at the hut in the vale and I was happy."

Conall stepped closer. "I doona wish that."

Eve stiffened. "You don't?"

"Nae." He could now almost see over her shoulder when he looked down upon where Eve knelt. "There were still lies between us then. Secrets. I doona long for our past, Eve—I long for our future." He dropped to his knees behind her. "I will give you everything you want and need. I swear it on my very life." He was close to breaking down now, because he knew in his heart that if she refused him again, this time it would be final.

He swallowed. "If you will but *look* at me, Eve! *Please!* Do you nae love me even a little?"

Just then a small, perturbed mewing met Conall's ears and the sound of his son fussing enchanted him. Eve's shoulders shook as she jostled and comforted the bairn.

"Gregory is hungry," she said quietly.

And then Conall's heart slowed to a thump-thump-stop as she halfway turned on her knees and for the first time in months, he looked into her eyes.

"Would you hold him while I loosen my gown?"

He looked . . . beautiful, Evelyn thought as she took in the sight of the large highlander kneeling behind her. He had put on weight and his worn léine strained wonderfully across his chest. His hair was longer, burnished from the sun, his skin tanned and golden to match his fiery amber eyes. Eyes that glistened with unshed tears.

In Evelyn's heart lived hope, and a great fear.

At her query, his throat lurched and he nodded, a weak, boyish smile lifting his full lips.

"Mayhap you should introduce the pair of us first, lass," he said hoarsely and looked down at Gregory, rooting against her breast.

Evelyn crossed the short span separating her from Conall awkwardly on her knees. She paused, held Gregory tight to her for one sweet moment, before slowly extending her arms.

"Gregory Godewin MacKerrick," she said softly, proudly, "your father, Conall."

Conall held out his wide, trembling hands and took the squawking baby as if Evelyn handed him the most valuable, holy object on God's earth. His chiseled face stared down into Gregory's frowning features, and a look of rapturous, heartbreaking wonder washed over him. He pulled the baby close to his face, closed his eyes, and drew a deep, deep breath. Then he kissed the little boy on his forehead.

"Hallow, Gregory," he whispered in a hitching voice. "A fine name, Gregory. Strong."

Evelyn felt vulnerable and alone, having relinquished the one thing that belonged to her. She did not know what to say to Conall. So she began loosening her gown in preparation for the feeding.

She hadn't gotten very far when Conall dragged her to him with one long arm, holding her tightly to his chest, the baby between them. He pressed his lips to hers painfully and Evelyn could feel the wetness of his tears on her skin.

And she finally let go. Her love for Conall, for their son, her regrets of the past months, her fear and loneliness and sadness and anger came pour-

ing out of her in heaving sobs and she clung to
him, digging her fingers into his back and stomach, burying her face in the crook of his neck and
weeping.

"Don't ever l-leave m-me again!" she wailed, and
Conall squeezed her even tighter.

"Never," he vowed fiercely. "I swear it—I will
never leave you, Eve. Oh, I love you so!"

She looked up from his neck into his eyes. "I love
you, too," she said between sniffles.

"Nae more regrets, then, for either of us. 'Tis
over, ken?" He glanced down at Gregory. "Only the
future now, only good."

Evelyn nodded. "The future," she agreed. Then
she looked to Bonnie and Alinor, who had both
gained their feet and seemed as though they
wished to join them.

"Come, lovelies," Evelyn called. "You are our
family, as well."

As Bonnie trotted over, Evelyn looked up at
Conall. "But I don't wish to live at the Buchanan
town," she said. "Not now, any matter."

His eyebrows rose. "You want to join Duncan and
my mother?"

She shook her head. "I want *our* house—Ronan
and Minerva's house. I want to live at the hut in
the vale. For a little while, at least."

"Are you certain?"

"I am." She tried to give him a smile through her
tears. "I love the Buchanans, and I love Duncan, but
I don't believe we could make a home at either town
right away, with such rawness still between us all. I
want the five of us—you and I and Gregory and
Bonnie and Alinor—to live where we first found

each other. Where we are certain to find our family once more."

Conall's smile tendered and he kissed her mouth. "As you wish, Eve. But I doona think Alinor needs find our family." His eyes flicked beyond Evelyn's shoulder and she turned.

Alinor had not joined them, but stood before the leaning boulders once more. This time, 'twas not Bonnie who romped about her, but five roly-poly pups, some black, some dark gray, tumbling around and between her paws. A moment later, a large, robust-looking gray wolf slinked from a burrow hidden beneath the seam of the boulders to stand between Alinor and the humans on the ground. His hackles ruffled and he growled menacingly.

"Oh, Alinor," Evelyn whispered, at last realizing the truth. The night the wolf had been missing, her deteriorating condition, her long absence—

Alinor had made a family of her own.

Evelyn now knew that her beloved girl would never return to the little hut in the vale with them, and the pain of it took Evelyn's breath. The kinship she felt with this great black beast was unexplainable—they had saved each other's lives once. They had survived together against seemingly impossible odds.

And now they would forever part.

The gray wolf seemed hostile toward the trio of humans and the solitary sheep, but a sharp bark and nip from Alinor persuaded him to back away. Alinor stepped forward, looking at Evelyn expectantly.

"Go to her," Conall whispered in Evelyn's ear.

Evelyn nodded and moved away, crawling to a neutral location between their respective families, and waited for the wolf to come in her own time. Evelyn could sense a return of the wild animal in the Alinor she loved so deeply and so gave her the space to feel that all was safe.

"'Tis all right, lovely," Evelyn whispered as Alinor paced nervously and stared at her. "I'll not force you to come with me. You'll not have to make that decision."

The wolf whined once and Evelyn could feel her confusion.

"Alinor," she called with a smile. "To me."

The wolf broke pace and bounded to Evelyn, throwing her big, black body into Evelyn's arms and licking her face madly, and in that precious, priceless moment, Evelyn felt that Alinor was once more *her* Alinor.

The wolf whined and licked and nipped and jumped.

Happy.

Happy.

Sad.

"I know, my love," Evelyn crooned and squeezed Alinor's neck as tightly as she could. "Me, too." Behind Alinor, the gray herded the pups. Behind Evelyn, Conall held Gregory. "It's all right, though. It's wonderful. I swear, it is."

Alinor suddenly broke free of Evelyn's arms and loped back to the mouth of the den. Evelyn swiped at her eyes while the massive black mother roughly nosed the pups. Then Alinor seized one—the smallest, blackest pup—by its scruff and trotted past Evelyn to Conall. Evelyn turned to watch.

The pup yelped and squirmed, hanging from her mother's jaws while Alinor pawed gently at Conall's arm. When he opened his protective embrace around Gregory, Alinor delicately placed her pup in Conall's other crooked elbow and then gave her a rough nudge with her nose. She paid no heed to Gregory or to Conall, rather turned and walked back to Evelyn to put herself muzzle to nose.

Alinor's big, clear, yellow eyes bored into Evelyn's somberly.

Evelyn could barely choke out, "Thank you."

Alinor's long, rough tongue swiped Evelyn's face and Evelyn reached out for one final, fierce embrace. Alinor gave the softest, quietest whine.

"I love you, too, my girl," Evelyn whispered near the wolf's pointed ear. "And I always will. Forever and ever."

Then Alinor backed out of Evelyn's arms abruptly, and the animal who now stood there was wild and deadly. She growled at Evelyn, and her muzzle lifted away to show long, pearly fangs.

Go.

Evelyn gained her feet on shaky legs. Alinor, her friend, her girl, was no more than a beautiful memory, now replaced by this awesome wild creature before her.

Conall's voice, low with concern, called to her.

"Come back, Eve. Slowly."

The command seemed to hold deep, deep meaning.

Evelyn backed away until she felt Conall's strong arms bump against her back.

The black wolf was joined by her growling mate.

"Let's go, Conall," Evelyn whispered. She reached down and tangled a hand in Bonnie's long wool, to keep the ninny from running foolishly to her death. The black and her family were no friends of theirs now. "Just turn and walk away. I have Bonnie."

Conall handed the crying pup to Evelyn, then drew her close to his side, urging them through the trees quickly, as if he understood the danger.

Abrupt wolfsong sang the group from the wood, the howls and the pup's yips strong and wild and beautiful. And in the highest notes, Evelyn heard Alinor's good-bye.

Epilogue

They had been back at the hut in the vale for seven days. Seven days filled with love and wonder and tears and family and awkwardness, too. Evelyn and Conall were reintroducing themselves to each other slowly and becoming familiar with their new love. The deepness of it, the honesty of it. Seven days they had been back, but this night was their first alone.

Evelyn lay in the small box bed and watched as her husband bent over Gregory's crib near the bedside, the firelight playing over his broad shoulders as he tucked the sleeping baby inside the swaddling and whispered words of love and good dreams. The flickering light mirrored the sensations in Evelyn's body and she waited with secret, anxious anticipation for Conall to join her.

It had been so long . . .

He turned and sent Bonnie and the clumsy little pup, Alexandra, off to their pen with a swat on Bonnie's shaggy rump. He checked the bar on the door, banked the fire in the pit. Then at last Conall turned to her and gave her a smile that made her heart sing.

"You're nae asleep yet, are you, lass?"

She shook her head and wondered if he could see her smile in the shadows. "Nay. I was waiting for you." She scooted back until she felt the wall behind her and tossed the covers back in invitation.

It took him only seconds to undress and join her and in a moment she felt his fevered skin against hers. Evelyn heard Conall's sharp gasp as he realized her nudity.

"'Tis glad I am that our kin have departed," he murmured, pulling her close and nuzzling her neck.

"As am I," Evelyn replied, tangling her fingers in Conall's thick, wavy hair. "It was wonderful for them to come for the wedding, and to bring all the gifts and supplies."

Conall agreed wordlessly, running his mouth along her jaw. "My mother wouldna have missed it. Thank you for welcoming her as you did. We'll need visit soon, else she'll be heartsick for Gregory. And I'm sure 'twill be only a matter of weeks before Dunc and Betsy wed."

"I'm so thankful for Angus," she whispered thoughtfully. "For all the Buchanans—and the MacKerricks. To think that they were all gathered here together, in this place . . ."

"'Tis a miracle, for certain." Conall's hand slid languorously down Evelyn's hip to clasp her buttock. "Ronan and Minerva would be proud."

Evelyn pushed her hips into Conall's insistent erection. "I am proud of us."

He kissed her mouth then, slowly, deeply, tasting her fully. Evelyn groaned when he pulled away.

"Are you certain, Eve?" he asked somewhat timidly for Conall. "It's nae too soon? I doona wish to hurt you."

"It's nae too soon," she mimicked with a smile. "I need you, Conall."

That was all the encouragement he required. Rolling Evelyn onto her back, Conall knelt between her legs, laving her full breasts with his tongue, suckling her as Gregory did.

"Take me," she whispered at his ear, needing the feel of him inside her.

He slid into her slowly, gently, pausing to give her body time to accommodate him. And within moments, Eve was lost in pleasure, in the wonderful sensations of her husband loving her with his body, as deeply as he had shown her with his heart and with his words. She felt she was at last at home.

Evelyn climaxed first, the twinges pleasantly and erotically strong, and Conall soon after spilled himself into her. They lay in each other's arms for a long time, staring at the fire. The howling from the wood beyond their walls was no longer menacing, but like a comforting lullaby, and rain beat down upon the cottage in the vale like laughter.

The moonlight brightened the wood like noontime, turning the rocky pyre into a bright haven. A lanky figure leaned against the wide oak, outlined in shadow and silvery, sparkling moonlight.

The woman approached, slowly, tentatively, hopefully. Then she stopped in self-conscious fear, looked down at gnarled, spotted hands, her age-wrinkled skin. It had been so long, and she was so old . . . she could not face him now. Even after longing for him for so many, many years.

"Minnie," he called softly to her, and the sound of his voice—oh, like sweet music!—brought a sob bubbling at her lips.

"Ronan?" she whispered into the dark.

The figure straightened from the tree and when he stepped from the pyre, the moonlight fully revealed him. His hawkish features, his high forehead beneath auburn hair, his sparkling green eyes, his lanky gait—all of it so like their son's.

Minerva fell to her knees with a cry and buried her face in her hands. "Oh, Ronan! Look not upon me, I beg you! I am an old woman now, and doona wish for you to see me."

She felt his light upon her scalp as he came to stand before her and she wept into her palms when she realized he could see clearly her thin, gray hair, her wrinkled neck and bony back through her patched old healer's gown.

"Minnie," he said gently again. "You are a beauty—the most beautiful lass in all of Scotland. Have I nae always told you that?"

"I am old and worn and wretched," she sobbed. "Too old for you now. Used up and wasted!"

"Nae, never wasted, nae for a single instant," he said firmly and to her horror, he knelt and took her old, wrinkled hands in his. "Look at me, Minerva Buchanan. *Look at me.*"

She raised her face reluctantly, hating that he would now see the full truth of her words: her lined and ashen face; her dull, black eyes, glazed by hard years without him; her flat and bony bosom; wide, jutting hips, like an old mare.

But his face—his eyes—were rapturous and full of tears.

"You are," he said hoarsely, emphatically, "*still* the most beautiful lass in all of Scotland." He held her hands out to her sides as if they would take up a dance together. "Just look, Minnie—*look!*"

Then she *did* look, and saw that her gown was not the old, patched gray wool, but a vibrant green velvet, with a smart gold, braided belt. Her hands were smooth and pink, her thighs full beneath her skirt. Her chest jutted boldly over a curving waist and rich, red, curling locks spilled over her shoulder to her hip.

She gasped and looked into Ronan's beautiful eyes. There she saw her face reflected—strong jaw, smooth skin, slim nose. Her lips were full once more and parted in wonder, her eyes clear and bright and ringed with thick lashes.

"Ronan," she whispered. "Kiss me!"

Then he did and when their lips met, the bright moonlight was outdone by the blinding luminescence of a thousand bolts of lightning, a million sparkling stars, heavenly, bursting sunlight of an endless dawn.

When they finally parted, he spoke again. "You have done well in your life, Minnie. I have watched you, every day. You lived our love."

"But our Duncan—" she began.

"Duncan is well," Ronan said with an easy smile. "A fine man, with his father's good looks. He will lead the MacKerrick clan with honor. You did what you felt you must, and it was right. *You have done well,*" he repeated. "Young Corinne, Haith, Simone, Evelyn—you guided them all to love, *with* love. And now it is our turn, my woman. My beautiful, beautiful Minerva. How I have missed you."

Out of the shadows of the wood limped a sickly, piteous wolf, gray as ash and lurching like a skeleton. Its matted fur was missing in great patches, its teeth gone now, its eyes milky and blind. It snarled and whined and its tongue lolled out of its mouth sickly.

"Cain," Minerva called lovingly, and held out her arm. Ronan mirrored her stance. "Cain, my beloved."

The wolf stepped between the two figures and collapsed, at last at the end of his impossibly long journey. In a blink his corporeal form disintegrated into dust and was blown away on a gust of sweet night air.

And then a strong, massive beast sprang up in its place, jumping and yipping, his thick fur fragrant with freedom and youth.

Minerva and Ronan laughed as the wolf bounded away to bark and howl and circle around them, and their joy fell like rain on the endless Caledonian forest surrounding them.

Minerva and Ronan kissed for an eternity.

Discover the Romances of
Hannah Howell

Put a Little Romance in Your Life With
Georgina Gentry

Cheyenne Song
0-8217-5844-6 $5.99US/$7.99CAN

Apache Tears
0-8217-6435-7 $5.99US/$7.99CAN

Warrior's Heart
0-8217-7076-4 $5.99US/$7.99CAN

To Tame a Savage
0-8217-7077-2 $5.99US/$7.99CAN

To Tame a Texan
0-8217-7402-6 $5.99US/$7.99CAN

To Tame a Rebel
0-8217-7403-4 $5.99US/$7.99CAN

To Tempt a Texan
0-8217-7705-X $5.99US/$7.99CAN

Available Wherever Books Are Sold!

Visit our website at **www.kensingtonbooks.com.**